STANDALONES AND STEPPING STONES
LEMONS LOOM LIKE RAIN

STANDALONES AND STEPPING STONES
LEMONS LOOM LIKE RAIN

STEVEN SHINDER

Table of Contents

Part One
The Scent

Chapter 1
The Approaching Rain

ises him, said the voice in Randy Morales' mind as a passing presence approached him. Sitting on a bench facing a pond at a park, in the town of Copper Petal, he saw a short shadow on the sidewalk. When he looked up, Randy recoiled. A tall man with long hair, a ducktail beard, and a stoic expression loomed over him. This stranger was about 6'5", towering him by seven inches. At least that was his estimate; Randy kinda sucked at math and measuring at a glance. The stranger wore a royal blue pea coat, lime green suit pants, and black combat boots. There was something familiar about the stranger's face, but Randy was too much of a mess to figure out whether he had seen it anywhere before. He noticed a vertical scar on the upper left eyelid, but that did not tell him anything.

"Do I know you?" Randy asked, face still wet from tears.

"We have never met," the man replied.

"Well your face looks familiar."

"Why do you cry?"

It was a lot to explain. On this second Tuesday evening in September, Randy was stuffed with the gut feeling that his senior year at Copper Petal University, a 50-year-old school just a few miles away from here, would be the last year of his life. All of his friends, who had come from all over, would no longer be close to him in a convenient nexus that allowed distant travelers to become a community. He would have to get a job to pay off his debts, which had now amounted to $20,000. He had heard that it was not unusual for students to have that much debt, but he was sickened by the thought of doing something that he did not enjoy in order to make ends meet. And he did not know whether he would find a job in time for post-grad life. He would have to make payments that, for a while, would probably hinder him from having his own place to live. He was also uncertain how he would feel even if he did find a place. He wanted to live independently, but he knew that the loneliness from the loss of so many friends would weigh down on him every day. He had neither a car nor a driver's license. And he did not know whether he would even be able to afford a car and gas to travel to his friends' hometowns whenever he desired.

Randy realized that he must have felt so vulnerable if he was willing to spill his troubles upon a complete stranger. Then again, it was easier than telling the truth to people he saw regularly. People who, for all he knew, might judge him and deem him pathetic. If this stranger found him to be pathetic, at least there was a chance he would probably never see him again. Randy looked at the pond again, keeping his eyes fixed upon the water as he spoke.

"This year. It will be my last chance to spend a lot of time with friends."

"How so?"

"I'm graduating in June, I live six hours away, and I'll have to work to pay off loans. I love to draw, but I don't know how I'm gonna find steady pay with that. I don't wanna have some boring job. It's not who I am."

"And who are you?"

"I don't know. Maybe I'm just a waste of space. My friends seem like they know their purpose, and then there's just me. The only reason I applied to college was to get out of my old town and make *real* and *authentic* friends."

"That's a strange-ass dream."

"You don't think much about deep stuff like that?"

"I don't reflect. But I suppose you've lived and are gonna wake up soon, so to speak. Time passes quickly."

Randy nodded. The years had been too quick for his comfort.

"Some summer vacation. I miss my friends."

"When was the last time you saw them?"

"Three months ago. We drove a half hour to get to this really good taco truck. We had a fun time, had some great food. But knowing that the friendships are probably temporary, I get this pain. I get hit by the taco truck. I don't feel capable of facing the real world."

The stranger stared at him for a cold moment.

"You can't stare into the eyes of the flesh-faced crystal."

Randy's eyebrows got closer together, and he turned his head toward the stranger.

"What?"

"The earth is yours. Humanity is just a fraction on top of it. Once you've seen your own eyes, *their* eyes betray you."

"Huh?"

The stranger crossed his arms.

"In truth, you have nobody. Just people wishing to shape everyone to be like them. Nobody wants you for all that you are. Just the commonalities."

"Oh god!" Randy broke into tears again.

"Oh cry me a river!" The stranger rolled his eyes and uncrossed his arms. "Tell you what? Why don't I help you pay off your debts quicker? You'd owe me, but it'd be half the amount you've taken. I'll get the paperwork ready."

Randy wiped his face with his sleeves.

"Are you serious?"

"Yes. Have something to write the address?"

"I have my phone."

Randy typed up a note as the stranger recited his address.

"Whenever you feel comfortable coming on by, call me in advance and we can schedule an appointment. No surprise visits. Might already have someone over."

It sounded like this stranger had more luck with relationships than Randy, who had never been on a date.

"Understood. What's your name, by the way?"

"You can call me...Mathis Dillard."

Something about the first name sounded familiar to Randy, but he could not put his finger on why.

"My name's Randy."

A name for a name; the bare minimum. As Mathis walked away, Randy walked over to the pond and saw his own reflection. Just him, with nobody beside him. Clearer than crystal. Likely to stand alone in the end.

He looked up at the sky and its scattered clouds, knowing that his friend August Wilhelm was somewhere up there. August, now gone in September. A good friend of three years who had departed from this earth in the darkness of the early hours. Randy was not sure how he would manage his last school year without the support of this friend in person. August had said Randy could talk to him about anything, and there were definitely some things he wanted to talk about. His anxiety over the debts looming over him. The romantic feelings he had for their friend Naomi Clutcher, who had broken up with another mutual friend, Reginald Webber, at the end of sophomore year. Randy needed someone in this confusing time. Sure he had other friends, but August was somehow the easiest to talk to about his troubles. But without August being physically present, it felt different. Perhaps they could communicate a different way, but it felt more distant and removed, awkward and impersonal to an extent. Still, Randy wanted to maintain the friendship somehow, whenever he felt ready.

Chapter 2
Disorientation

August Wilhelm, definitely alive, awoke from his bumpy slumber within the left side of an airplane. He could not remember a single dream he had during this flight. Through the window, he could see the dark Atlantic below, and a bit of light on the horizon, where England was. His destination was near.

Though there were other people on the plane, he felt very much alone, unable to use his cell phone to contact his parents or his friends while the flight was in progress. He knew that he would have access later, but even then the phone would feel less personal. He preferred to be in close proximity to those whose company he appreciated. At this moment, on this artificial bird, he was a stray feather floating alone in the night. His mind drifted into random observations.

The feather of a red-tailed hawk sports the symmetry of a tiger. Black stripes against a burning shade of orange.

August missed walking through Petal Lock Park in the middle of campus where he observed the magical ducks and geese. Redhead ducks and Egyptian geese, from the looks of them. They had sparked his interest in birds and surrounded two supernatural inhabitants. The elementals known as Stagmantel and Unicoren. He thought of them as friends, but they probably just viewed him as an acquaintance, despite the conversations he had shared with them. Back when they told him about Miunis Grund, the first planet from which all other planets had broken off. But those days in the park were behind him.

He had spent nine months preparing to study abroad in England. His friends at Copper Petal University on the West Coast of the US were far away. He missed them, and part of him felt terrible about having to spend his final year as an undergrad without them. But he knew that he had to push forward. He knew that he had to let go of normality. Or, at least, as normal as things could be at CPU.

Hopefully, his cousin Grady, an incoming CPU freshman, would fill the void, if there was one at all. And August hoped to make some new friends who would fill the void while he was abroad. He took comfort in knowing that his online pen pal, Cassie Julura, got accepted into the same university where he would now be studying. They were both in an online group that discussed types of birds. Together, they could tackle this adventure abroad together.

August wondered how different he would be beyond the blue division that was the ocean. From above, it seemed still and harmless. But he knew that it was not so simple.

Meeting strangers is like dealing with the ocean. At first, there is no telling whether a lot of time spent in the water would result in leisure with a trusted friend, or whether it would result in drowning as the association got deeper. His overly cautious parents had told him to be careful, and he promised that he would.

The flight seemed to take forever. Through the glass of the window, he could see the present, both inwardly and outwardly. As he got closer to the island, the sunlight grew stronger, and the vibrant green below became more present. The clouds were like sea foam afloat in the air, the sky being a phantom stranger through which travelers passed. Yes, strangers often pass by one another with little regard about each other's well-being.

This was the case at the airport. Each traveler seemed to only care about whether they or their close friends and family would be permitted to enter the country. Those who worked at customs cared about who entered, but only to a certain extent. They had to make sure that each person seemed safe. And when August was allowed through, after they checked his passport and such, he finally felt safe. All the anxiety from double-checking the paperwork he needed for this moment just melted away. Even with the overstuffed luggage case he had to lug around on wheels, August felt like a weight had been lifted.

He took a train through the countryside, passing by houses settled in the green unification. The sunlight seemed different to him here. But perhaps he was just super-imposing his feeling of being in a new, faraway place. It felt unreal to be here at last.

When he got to the streets of London, he had a bit of trouble finding the hotel. It did not help that the towering buildings distracted him with their shining glass. London looked pretty much how one would expect after doing an image search on Google. Thankfully, August was only lost for half an hour. A few hours before orientation, he arrived at Tree Culler Hotel, its outward appearance consisting of red bricks. He entered the lobby and checked in at the front desk. The walls on the inside were yellowish-white. Red and black plaid carpeting covered the floors. Dropping off his luggage, he decided to kill time at an art gallery down the street, in a tower filled with white-walled rooms that looked very identical to each other. He was not quite sure whether he had gone through every room. He overheard a tour guide mention a hat with peacock feathers that was once stolen from this place, but he was too tired to dwell too much on the thought. Every blink that he made was weighted with drowsiness. He felt so jet lagged that he could not even describe any of the paintings, or even the building itself, once he was back for orientation.

First, there was the dinner in the dining room, where students slumped in their seats and seldom made eye contact. Some were from the States, and some were from other countries. August's eyes were mainly set on his Yorkshire pudding, a first for him. A baked pudding bowl containing sausages, peas, mashed potatoes, and gravy. He knew that some people had qualms about peas touching mashed potatoes, but he liked the combination. He also had a block of Swiss cheese on the side.

He looked up and noticed another male student walking toward his table at a slug's pace, carrying a bowl of soup, filled to the brim. August was so jet lagged that he was not quite certain whether this student was moving that slowly or whether he was simply imagining that time was slower. After a minute had passed, the student reached the edge of the table and set down the bowl slowly. But once the bottom of it reached the surface, some soup spilled onto the table.

"Damn it!" the student said. "I was so close."

"No worries," August said. "I have a lot of...napkins."

August stared into space for a moment, and his eyes began to water.

"Napkins get you very emotional?"

"Sorry." August wiped his eyes with a napkin. "I was just reminded of some friends back home. We are part of a napping club called the Nap Kin."

"Clever name."

"Speaking of which, what's yours?"

"Verner Werner," he answered as he seated himself. "You?"

"August Wilhelm."

"August?" Verner arched an eyebrow. "Not Augustus?"

"Nope. My parents named me after the month."

"Your birth month?"

"Nah. More like when I was conceived." August chuckled. "They wanted a May baby so that my birthday would be almost halfway between the winter holidays."

"Ah." Verner took a sip of his hot chocolate. "So not in the middle of summer."

"Right. They wanted my classmates to wish me a happy birthday."

"Sounds like your parents had your best interests in mind. Mine just mind my interests."

"What interests?"

"Chemistry."

"Ah. I'm into history."

"History. Quite a subject."

"You a history buff?"

"I'd be better off as a history *bluff* if I could make shit up."

There was a laugh from a young woman sitting further down the table. August and Verner turned their heads in her direction.

"How long have you been there?" August asked.

"She was there when I got to this table," Verner said.

"True," the woman replied. She sounded American. "I'm just tired. But I guess we all are."

"What's your name?" August asked.

"Jade Teal." She waved. "Pleased to meet you, I guess. I'm from the east coast."

"I'm from the west."

"No wonder we've never met before."

"Y'all think the three of us will remain friends throughout this school year?"

"Maybe if we keep sitting at the same table," Jade replied with a shrug.

"Sounds like a plan," Verner said before taking another sip.

"Do they cook food here for us every day?" August asked, looking around the dining room.

"I think it's just for orientation," Jade answered. "After that, we use the kitchen ourselves. Apparently there's a stairway in there to a basement with some fridges for us."

"That small kitchen for all *eighty* of us?"

"Yeah." She yawned and then proceeded. "I don't imagine I'll be using it that often."

"Not much patience for people?" Verner asked.

"Not really. I just want this day to end already." She crossed her arms on the table, and then set her chin on top. "After this, we've got some seminar about culture shock. Sounds more like a snoozefest than a boozefest."

She was correct. Though the seminar was brief, many people nodded off.

After the seminar, Jade walked with August to the lift. Her room was 307, and his was 314. When the doors to the lift opened, though, its space looked compact, as though it could only fit one person at a time.

"I'll just take the stairs," Jade said. "No biggie."

"You sure? You can take the lift if you'd like."

"Next time, maybe. Right now, it looks pretty sketch. Good luck."

She walked up the stairs, and August entered the lift. The tightness of the space made August anxious, especially when the doors shut. But once he looked up at the stained glass ceiling of red triangles, and blue rectangles, he felt a sense of tranquility as the lift rose up to the third floor. The doors opened, and he felt like he was in paradise again.

But this was jarred by the right turn to a carpeted staircase consisting of only three steps. He got to the top of it, looked to the right where another connecting staircase continued to the fourth floor, and then stepped down the other side of the smaller staircase. The design made him feel uneasy. He had to go through two fire exit doors in the hallway before reaching room 314. Pulling the hotel key out of his pocket, he inserted it into the keyhole and opened the door, in that order.

The room was small, but not as small as the lift. There was just enough space for him to walk between the bed and the lavatory. By the end of his bed was a desk with a TV beside a window with orange drapes tied to the sides, displaying a sunny view of an ancient-looking London building across the street. The view seemed too perfect, like a play between the drapes. He imagined that if he were to close the drapes, the play would be over and he would be on a different, more plain and boring plane of reality.

He heard the rolling wheels of a luggage case out in a hallway. The sound got closer, and then it stopped.

"August?"

He turned around to see a familiar young woman out in the hallway.

"Cassie?" He had seen her profile picture, but it had been difficult to extrapolate a three-dimensional impression from a two-dimensional image.

"Wow," she said, approaching him. "It's great to finally meet you in person."

"Same! How are you? I didn't see you at dinner."

"I was exhausted. I already ate on the plane. I saw you at the seminar, but you were sound asleep."

"Guilty." August tried to laugh, but a yawn interrupted it.

"Is this your room?" Cassie asked before yawning.

"Sure is."

"So it's just you here?"

"Yeah. Got a single. Lucky me, huh? You have a roommate?"

"No, actually. I have a single as well. It's right here."

She pointed at room 315, right across from 314.

"Nice!" August said. "Guess we're hallmates!"

"Yeah. Haven't checked it out yet. That lift is pretty terrifying, and the first floor's so convenient if you're taking stairs. Crashed in my new friend Bessie's room."

"Oh yeah. I've been feeling jet lag all day. I was early for orientation, so I tried killing some time by going to this art gallery. I felt like I was sleepwalking through a dream. There were so many rooms that looked the same, and I lost track of which artworks I'd seen. I really couldn't tell whether I'd already been in each room. It's like a labyrinth."

"Well you got out!"

"Yes! And there was much cheese to be had. I looked at the Swiss cheese, holes and all, and thought, 'Same.' My head's a mess right now."

"I'm sure you'll feel better after you rest. Oh! I got you something."

Cassie zipped open her luggage case and took out two bracelets. Each one had a zigzag labyrinthine pattern, purple outlining pink. She took one out and gave it to August, whose entire face lit up.

"Are these friendship bracelets?"

"Yep! Tada! I made them myself."

"Oh wow! That's so nice of you."

August put the bracelet around his left wrist.

"Glad you like it!"

"I really do." August ran his fingers over the threads that comprised the accessory. "And we really need to hang out."

"Definitely. Later, though. I feel a bit rested, but you look like you're about to collapse. No offense."

"Nah, it's true."

"How about we meet up in the morning for breakfast downstairs?"

"For sure!"

Cassie smiled, put her hand on the handle of her luggage case, inserted her room key into the lock to her door, and got sucked into the key-hole, in that order.

August was shocked to see Cassie and her luggage vanish. And then he was shocked again when a bolt of electricity shot out of the same doorknob and hit his friendship bracelet. The pain subsided after a second. Wanting to examine the door to 315, he stepped out of his room. But once he was in the hall, the desire disappeared. He blinked and then laughed.

"Jet lagged," he said to himself before returning to his room and collapsing onto his bed. After so much exhaustion, he felt as if he was in for one of his best naps thus far.

Chapter 3
Come to Mansion It

Randy paced in circles within his room, in the apartment he shared with three flatmates. At the moment, Ted was the only other person who was home. They each had their own room, so it seemed likely to Randy that they would not be talking much. Randy would have preferred living with his close friends, but they had already made arrangements and filled up spaces. So he had to resort to finding other fellow students online and getting clumped together with them at random.

He had considered reaching out to Frederick Filler, with whom he shared a room during freshman year. They had considered being roommates again for sophomore year, but Frederick had said Randy's next living space was not in his budget. These days, Randy had no idea how to get in touch with Frederick, who now appeared to be absent from social media. His old phone number did not work anymore either. He was not sure what had become of Frederick Filler, philosophy major.

With every step on the carpet in his socks, Randy feared the possibility of being struck by a static shock. Holding up his phone with Mathis' number ready for dialing, his hand was shaking. For two weeks, Randy had been considering whether to go through with this. It all seemed too good to be true. For all Randy knew, this man was just trying to lure him so he could kill him, or worse.

Don't chicken out, he told himself.

Impulsively, he dialed the number and held the phone to his ear with a motion so quick it nearly hit his face. It rang a few times. Part of him hoped that nobody would pick up. But if leaving a voicemail became an option, he would be anxious even then, searching for words to speak in the right tone after the tone.

He heard a voice that was very much present.

"Hello?" a woman answered.

"Um..." Randy scratched the back of his head. "Is Mathis Dillard there?"

"Oh yeah. He's just taking a leak real quick. Who is this?"

"Can you have him call back? This is really important. Is he gonna be busy?"

"Well, we're gonna be watching a movie. But I'm sure he could make time. No worries. Oh, here he is."

There was a quiet conversation at the other end of the line, but he could not make it out.

"Hello. Mathis speaking."

"Uh, hi." Randy felt his blood freeze. "So, this is Randy. The college student. We talked a couple weeks ago."

"You're the one who was crying on the bench."

"Uh...yeah."

"Good. So would you like to make an appointment then?"

Just get it over with, Randy thought to himself.

"I'm free tonight."

"Oh, tonight's no good. I have company, you know?"

"Oh, right right right. Uh..." Randy tapped his forehead repeatedly. "How about Saturday night?"

"Saturday night works. Shall we say...seven?"

"Yeah. Sure! Sounds good. Okay. Talk to you later."

He hung up before he could hear another word, and then a fluttering fan that had been on fire left his chest. There was a temptation to scope out Mathis' home now that he had company over. To view the enemy through a magnifying glass. But the thought passed over him like a train on an overpass, full of fleeting steam. He felt too frightened to spy on Mathis. Randy did not want to be mistaken for a stalker. Unable to scope, he hoped that it would be a safe visit.

"Damn it!" he heard Ted say. Randy left his room.

"What's wrong?"

"We've got ants in the kitchen." Ted pointed toward a line of ants crawling on the wall beside the window. "Do you have any bug spray?"

"No." Randy walked closer, getting a better look at the line. "But I have lemons."

"Lemons?"

"An old trick my mom taught me. Just put lemon juice by the windows and under the door."

"That shit works?"

"Time and time again."

"Huh."

"I'll take care of it."

"All right." Ted started walking back to his room. "We'll use the old Randy remedy."

Randy faked a chuckle. He took his lemons out of the cabinet and used his knife to cut some in half. He squirted some juice onto the windowsill and under the door. Once he had those areas covered, he cut up pieces of peels and left them in front of the door. If he were a kid again, he would have been walking around the entire perimeter of the building, squeezing lemons dry. They were his stress balls. They were his ritual. His tactic to keep any unwanted pests away from his place of rest.

When Saturday arrived, Randy did not feel quite ready. As a precaution, Randy grabbed three knives from his apartment kitchen and put them in the pockets of his trench coat. He walked up to Ted's room door. He almost knocked, intending to tell Ted the address of his destination so he could call for help if he was not back by a certain time. But Randy stopped himself, deciding that he would rather risk making the meeting a private matter to avoid any unwanted questions. On one hand, Ted was busy doing schoolwork, and college students did not ask too many questions when they had questions of their own to answer. Regardless, Randy found himself willing to accept having to confront potential danger without any help.

Part of him was ready to just give up and accept defeat.

Randy took the city bus to a stop that was two blocks away from the address. He felt heavier with each step closer to the place, which turned out to be a daunting building surrounded mainly by a black bar fence with barbed wire and sharp spires at the top. Garlic bulbs were wrapped around the bars. The building itself looked as if a Gothic mansion and a stone castle tried having a baby. In terms of the vibe, it felt as if a kidney stone, rather than a baby, was the result, and then it laid countless eggs around itself. For the mansion grounds consisted of round stones that one would find on a pebbly shore, and there was no pathway leading to the porch. Baby or kidney stone, Randy could picture the screams. This was beyond the type of sketchiness he had expected. He wanted to sketch it but doubted that he could truly capture the terror it evoked.

He dialed Mathis' number again. It only took one ring to get an answer.

"Hello."

"This is Randy Morales. I called earlier."

"Come on in," he whispered before the gates opened.

Very alert, Randy walked upon the pebbly yard, trying not to trip. As he got closer to the mansion, he noticed the car parked beside it to the right. He got to the steps of the stairs to the porch. He made it alive to the front door, which opened before he could even knock. There was the tower of a man. Behind him, there was no light. Randy was worried that he would die sooner than he expected.

Clapping startled him. The white light bulbs of the golden chandelier up above shone upon the white marble floor. Mathis stood at the top of the stairs, its steps velvet red and its rails violet against black walls. His ensemble looked the same as what he had worn on day that Randy had first met him. There was a stairlift against the wall to the left of the stairs, white with beige cushioning. But Mathis did not seem like he needed it. He spread out his arms as if they were wings being stretched outward.

"Welcome to my abode."

This doesn't bode well, Randy thought.

"Uh, hi," he said with a weak wave of the hand. "Do you wear the same outfit all the time?"

"I have multiple changes of these. I care little about varying the colors. Though sometimes they do get messy getting one more color on them."

"Messy from what?"

"Just some hobbies. Anyway, my office is up here."

Randy stood still for an awkward moment before deciding to walk up the steps, trying to avoid eye contact with Mathis. Once he got to the top, they were standing right in front of each other. Mathis stared into Randy's eyes for a moment, fueling his fear with an unsettling intensity, like speeding cars upsetting the monotony of a quiet city. Mathis then turned around casually and walked toward his office. Randy followed him, slightly relieved, but heart still pounding on the doors of desperation.

The office seemed very ordinary. There was an oak desk with a stack of paperwork on top. Randy and Mathis sat down in creaky rocking chairs on opposite sides. If the chairs were different, this could have been just about what anyone would expect from a generic office. That is, if one were to ignore the intimidating blowtorch sitting beside the paperwork. And the two scythes hanging on the wall to the right. While Mathis had his eyes on the papers, Randy glanced at one of the scythe blades, where a speck of blood remained.

"So, Randy Morales." Randy turned his head quickly to face Mathis again. "That's an interesting first name. I'm sure you got picked on for it, right?"

"Like a scab."

Mathis hit the shape of a nail on the forehead. Randy had felt dead all throughout high school, an institution full of immature students who constantly repeated the phrase "Randy's feeling Randy!" He was so fed up with this behavior that it was a relief when he arrived at CPU and met people whom he felt treated him as an equal, even though he felt like the odd one in the group. The toothpick in the sandwich. Despite the weirdness of the campus, these new bonds sparked life within him. A life he knew would be temporary.

"Typical people behavior," Mathis said, his chair rocking forward slightly. "People can be trouble."

Randy could still see the speck of blood in his mind's eye.

"How did you get so rich, if you don't mind me asking?"

"It's a boring story, really. Mother went to a convenience store and finally won the lottery."

"How convenient."

Randy did not quite buy it. Not that there was much he could buy.

"So I'm willing to give you however much you owe in loans, and then you'd only be paying me back half of that amount. With that in mind, how much did you wanna borrow?"

"Twenty thousand."

Mathis picked up a pen and started filling in the blanks.

"Okay. And when do you graduate?"

"Next June."

"All right. Now the procedure is that you need to start repaying me three months after your graduation. Do you know the exact date you graduate?"

"Not off the top of my head."

"All right. Well, how about this? You make your first payment by a year from today. What's today?"

"The...twenty-seventh?"

"Yeah. So on September twenty-seventh next year, I better have the first payment of one thousand. You've got plenty of time, so I expect to be paid. Otherwise, I'll have to come after you that night, if you catch my drift."

Something about this threat was appealing to Randy. A threat from someone who looked capable of murder should have been frightening. And it partially was. But Randy was surprised to find a bit of relief in the prospect of being killed and not having to deal with financial issues. As selfish as he was sure it made him seem, he saw it as a viable way to escape from all the pressures.

"Got it. You wouldn't want to beat me over the head with reminders that night, right?"

Mathis smiled.

"Seems like we understand each other perfectly."

Randy thought back to the woman who had been here days earlier when he called. He wanted to be sure he understood.

"Who—?" Randy stopped himself, regretting that he had let the start of a question escape his mouth.

"Go on," Mathis said. "Don't be shy. I can answer any questions you have about this process."

Randy had no choice but to finish his thought, despite the possible risk.

"Who was on the phone the other day?"

Mathis maintained the smile, accompanied by unblinking eye contact.

"Don't worry about her. She's gone from my life. Frankly, she was a bit of a trainwreck, going on about the pointlessness of life. She came to me for advice, and I did her a favor."

"Is there a point to life?"

"Not for you. Now, here's the form." Mathis blinked at last and turned a paper around to face Randy. "Be sure to write down your current address *and* your emergency contact info. You wouldn't want an emergency to worry anyone, but, you know, just in case."

This part worried Randy. In his hometown, he had his parents and a ten-year-old sister. Getting them involved was out of the question. Randy wanted to maintain their safety.

"So, would we meet here when I give you the first payment?"

"I'd prefer to take care of it at your residence, just to make sure that you're there. Would you be at your current address, or your permanent address?"

"They're the same," Randy answered quickly, committed to making his current address his future permanent address.

"Really?" The smile faded, the face laced with skepticism.

"Y-yes. Once the one-year lease ends, I'm gonna renew it."

Randy wrote down the apartment address, as well as Ted's contact info.

"Who's that?"

"A flatmate."

"Will he still be living with you next year?"

"I believe so. He said he'd stay in the area." That part was true, though Randy was uncertain whether Ted would remain at the same apartment itself after graduation. If anything, his flatmates could move out, and Randy could act like he would be well off enough to remain in the apartment. If it were just Randy there, Mathis would only go after him.

It's not assisted suicide if I don't ask him to kill me, he tried reasoning with himself, looking for loopholes in whatever laws of a possible afterlife there might have been.

After filling out the form, Randy made eye contact with Mathis and tried not to stare at the scar on his left eyelid. Debt-filled Randy thought he could sense a doubtful vibe coming from Mathis, so he was surprised by the subsequent smile and response.

"Perfect." Mathis grabbed the papers. "Looks like we have a deal. Now, I'm gonna need a photo." Mathis took out his phone and snapped a photo before Randy could react. Then Mathis pulled a suitcase out from under his side of the desk. He gave it to Randy, who opened it. There were stacks of hundred-dollar bills. Randy counted them, and they added up to twenty grand.

"We all good, then?" Randy asked, putting the bills in the coat pocket that did not contain the knives.

"Oh, Randy, Randy, Randy." Mathis shook his head. "We are not 'all good.' An ancient evil resides within each of us. Anyone can have the urge to hurt others, *and* themselves. If we were completely bereft of this ancient evil, would we really be ourselves?"

Mathis paused, and Randy could see that he was awaiting an answer. He tried to come up with something clever to seem unfazed.

"Perhaps...how we keep the darkness contained is what shapes us. One must shape oneself against their shadow rather than be shaped *by* the shadow. It sticks to you, but you can control where it goes."

"Shadows can loom larger than the progenitor."

"They're not solid, though."

"But they are invincible. When the person becomes a body, the shadow remains. And even when the remains decompose, the shadows linger as stealthy particles in the air. Are you a shadow in your group of friends?"

"I am part of them."

"Soon, you'll have to part *from* them."

Mathis opened his drawer and took out a knife. Then he took out a whole lemon.

"What are you doing?" Randy asked, ready to reach for the knives in his trench coat pocket with one hand and gripping the suitcase handle with the other.

"Showing you." Mathis used the knife to cut the lemon into slices. "One world gets fractured. Friendships get fractured. *All* friendships *die*. The *eye* is selfish, trying to see what it hopes is there. So bring on the pain. Lemons loom like rain."

"Is this the part where you make some cheeky Fruit of the Loom joke?"

With his left hand, Mathis raised the slice above his left eye, squeezing the juice onto the scar on his eyelid and into his unblinking eye. He did this with a gleeful smile.

"Holy shit!" Randy jumped out of his chair and backed away, still gripping the suitcase handle.

When Mathis was done, he threw what remained of the slice to the floor.

"When life gives you lemons, squeeze them over your tacos, which are *wounds*. The lemons sting the cuts. Pain is inevitable. Embrace it. Better to cry now rather than later. You *eat* the wounds, and they sicken your stomach. So sharp is the sorrow in your guts. But people get it out of their system, despite how painful it may be, flushing it away. Memories of the pain remain, and you may feel a bit empty. But at least a weight has been lifted."

"If it stings your eyes and your wounds, why would you put it in your body?"

"Just some food for thought."

Randy could not help but be a bit impressed by this walking monolith's monologues.

"Did you rehearse all that or was it improvised?"

"I'm very prepared. But, in the moment, I can surprise."

"So can I."

32

"Well, then I'll see you in a year, Randy Morales."

"Sounds like a plan."

Randy exited the office and casually closed the door behind him. Then he began to speedwalk, almost falling down the stairs. When he got to the bottom floor, he ran to the door and swung it open. Then he jumped off of the porch and tried running across the yard.

He tripped on a stone and bruised his knees. Trying to brush off the bruises, he got up, kept the suitcase in hand, and continued to the gate, which was still closed. He did not want to turn back and ask Mathis to open it.

Randy flinched when the gate opened. He looked back at the lit up window on the second floor of the mansion, where Mathis Dillard held a remote in one hand and waved goodbye with the other. Randy felt certain that Mathis was smiling, but he did not want to look for too long. So he walked out the gate and headed toward the bus stop.

When the bus arrived, he got aboard and reflected.

For the first three years of his college career, Randy had accepted loans from the office of financial aid since he was not academically significant enough to win scholarships. He had been given grants, but they were not enough to pay for all the expenses. He could have asked his mom and dad to take on parent loans for him, but he refused to burden them. Asking them for money made him feel uncomfortable, so he acted as if he was managing everything very well. He had submitted his resume to a few different places and done a few interviews, but no dice. In any case, he firmly believed that having a job would make his grades suffer and decrease the amount of quality time spent with friends. Summer was the loneliest season each year, and even then he had been unable to obtain work.

Near the end of summer before his senior year, he was offered the same loans again. He knew that they were piling up, and yet he had never gotten a single paycheck over the years. Now, he felt it was best to get loans elsewhere so that he could get beaten to a pulp.

He was certain that Mathis Dillard killed the woman who was on the phone. If this were true, then he wanted to take action. But he was weak at the moment, and he needed Mathis to go after him in a year.

Could we die together?

He would have to build up his strength. At the moment, he was in no good shape to fight. If Mathis could kill him, he wanted to take that murderer down with him. He was not sure how, but he wanted to eliminate Mathis from this world as a way of making an exit as Righteous Randy. They could part ways, Mathis descending and Randy ascending.

Self-defense, not murder, he tried reasoning.

He wanted a clean slate at his moment of death. No crimes, no debts. Only death. A scheduled one.

Deep in thought, Randy missed his stop. When he returned to reality, he tugged on the pull cord, requesting the next stop. The walk was slightly longer, but he returned to his apartment. It was dark.

Someone was in the kitchen.

An uncomfortable heat filled Randy. It fueled him with paranoia. He looked for the light switch and knew that he would regret the sight once he recognized the disgusting sound of smacking lips.

"Oh!" his flatmate Vic said with a raw pork chop hanging out of his mouth. "H-hey Randy! Uh..."

It was *Randy's* pork chop. The package sat on the counter, and half of its contents were gone. Randy sighed in frustration. But with his time limited and the deadline sealed, it all seemed irrelevant.

"I don't care."

"You're not mad?" Vic responded with meat still hanging from his mouth.

"No. I don't give a shit. Just make sure you pay the rent."

Vic chewed and swallowed before answering.

"Uh, yeah. No worries. I've got the automatic payment thing set up online."

Randy nodded and then walked toward the lavatory between his room and Vic's. Behind him, he heard Vic open the cabinet, the creaking of which brought Randy back to Mathis' office momentarily. He shivered and then shook the thought away. Judging from the next sound, Vic tore crumbs out of the communal cookies with his teeth.

In the lavatory, Randy flicked the switch, turning on the ceiling light. He locked eyes with his reflection as he prepared to brush his teeth. He took a huge step backward, away from the reflection, his back against the white wall. Raising the paste-filled brush to his orifice, he began the cleansing. This was a safe distance; no paste would splatter onto the mirror. He also found that he could examine himself better by taking a step back.

There he saw the face of a man who would never be happy working to pay off a loan and closing himself off from people who had brought him joy. It seemed best for the loaner to just end him when his life was at its peak. He had to make his senior year the best of his college career.

When he flossed, his gums bled a little bit, and he imagined blood splattering onto the mirror. A bit of the string got stuck between his teeth, and he pulled it out, nail to the floss.

The light bulb flashed a dying light, transforming the room into a dark space.

No matter how many times he tried, the switch did not ignite the light. Randy would have to file a work order to get the light bulb replaced. He walked out of the lavatory and into his bedroom. Pushing aside the mirror door of the closet, he dug around his mess of possessions until he found the red lamp. Its head was a red bowl with its inner walls white around an equally white bulb.

During his childhood, it was a cafe lamp in a fictional establishment where he served and ate light meals. Until a glass cup he had used fell to the tile floor and broke into shards. Playtime had been broken. Frustrated, his father facepalmed. From then on, Randy associated the cafe lamp with the facepalm, and fear of judgment was etched into his mind. He no longer visited the cafe. It had been rearranged and renovated into a studio. Sometimes, he visited that inverse.

He took the lamp to the lavatory, set it beside the sink, and plugged it in. Once the surface received the blessing of his index finger's touch, the bulb lit up.

And there, behind his reflection, he saw a shadow on the wall, a couple of inches taller than he was. At least, that was how it appeared when his back was against the wall. When he walked closer to the light, the shadow grew longer, towering over him. Spreading out his arms, he could see the shadow moving in synchronicity. But he did not feel as if he was in control. The shadow was like a puppeteer in black, moving him in front of the silent audience of a theater. Nobody could stop them from moving so that the shadow could use him to move the spectators: his friends.

He hoped that they would miss him.

Chapter 4
Aboard the Grave Train

Miles away, out in a desert, there was a train, motionless on the rails. It looked abandoned, but it was hard to tell for sure under the shroud of night. The sky was wide awake with stars, eyes ever open out in the wilderness. Candid Du Clips was far enough from town to be on edge. By now, she should have been used to going to sketchy places like this. But her benefactor always surprised her, sending her on scavenger hunts in all sorts of places. Not exactly what she had in mind when she told her parents she would like to travel someday.

She let the light of her lantern guide her. By the wheel of the front cart was a body. A woman, judging from her business attire which one could find in the women's section of a retail store. Candid hovered the light over the woman's bare hands, the skin having been scorched. Whatever fire had lit this woman seemed to have not extended beyond the wrists. She felt sure that this had been done on purpose by the attacker.

She moved the light to where the head should have been. The wheel of the train was the only thing above the shoulders. Candid had to search for the rest.

With latex gloved hands, she struggled to slide the car door open. Slowly, moonlight crept into the inner space, revealing a cool shade of green. The same shade of green used to print dollar bills. She shone her lantern around, looking for anything that seemed out of place. Surely, red would make a stark contrast against the surface.

There, in the corner, she saw the head of the woman. To Candid, she looked like she was in her mid-thirties. But Candid was not quite sure; she kinda sucked at guessing people's ages at a glance. The victim's eyes and mouth were wide open. It troubled Candid that the money was not where the mouth was. Carefully, yet shakily, she lifted the head.

A plastic bag plopped out of the throat, down onto the floor. Candid put the head back down and then pulled a brown paper bag out of her pocket. She placed the plastic bag above the brown paper bag, opened it, and let the cash rain down, unsoiled by blood. She then took out her camera and photographed the woman's head. Leaving the head behind, she almost forgot to close the door.

She paused. It still amazed her that she took the time to freeze during high-stress situations such as this. She found herself wondering whether she ought to leave the door open or make the effort to close it. The body was out in the open, so if someone were to spot it, then they would look for the head in one of these carts. But with the body unguarded out in the wilderness, coyotes or some other wild ilk were bound to come by.

There has to be something left intact, Candid thought.

Watching the moonlight shine in the woman's eyes, a glow that seemed to bring the victim to life, Candid pulled the cart door closed, leaving the moonlight uninvited.

All this time spent trying to desensitize herself given the nature of her job, and she still let herself be human. She looked up at the stars, but only for a moment, knowing that time was a limited resource preventing her from dwelling for too long.

Coyotes howled.

Candid ran back to her car with her reward and drove off. She did not feel like she was in control of her car. It seemed as if the car remained in place like the sun, the road orbiting underneath it.

When she first started her association with her benefactor four years earlier, she got an email with a pic of a card that read, "Ben F., Actor."

She rolled her eyes back then and still did from time to time. The moniker seemed fitting, given that she was only ever paid in one hundred-dollar bills.

She had been eager about the prospect of that first payment. It seemed suspicious when this Ben F. person said to meet at a boat at the dock to take a picture of what was there and then email it back. When she found the boat back then, she nearly fell in the water when she found the head of a sailor. She got *really* seasick back then. Desperate, though, she took the picture.

When she got home to her apartment, she did debate calling the police about her findings. But her heart was already set on her own financial needs, so she emailed the picture to Ben F. And then she wondered just how private email services really were, resulting in paranoia that made her heart run a marathon.

But she heard no sirens. Nobody questioned her within the last four years. She always deleted the emails after sending them, but she was sure that her benefactor kept them for his own private collection. She assumed that Ben had tech expertise that would come in handy, preventing one from getting caught. Just one, not both. She always feared that Ben might expose her, and exposure was not always good for a photographer like her. So she went along with the requests, hoping to keep Ben silent as the cash kept flowing.

Getting paid for her craft should have been the life, but the cost was unsettling. When she graduated, all she wanted was to pay off her debts. And now she was in too deep. Her benefactor seemed to get shits and giggles out of having her go out to strange places looking for cash placed on the dead. It was even more nerve-wracking during the day, when she felt more likely to be seen and caught. Nighttime was only slightly better, still sending chills through her core. The heat of the desert was definitely asleep.

Her life used to be normalish. She used to be a student at Copper Petal University. Before then, she was Candice Cornelia Cobb. Her

LEMONS LOOM LIKE RAIN

father was full of dad jokes, and her mother had an obsession with alliteration. Thus, this led to a life laced with inelegant insults rather than luck or luxury.

But during college, she reinvented herself, using the name Candid Du Clip as she showcased her knack for photography and cinematography. Seeing as how students at CPU were fond of the ducks in the park, she figured that such a name was good for getting attention. But the popular plural form "duck lips" influenced word of mouth, and so she was forced to rebrand as Candid Du Clips, on paper and online. She rarely spoke the full moniker aloud, preferring to pronounce the last name in a singular form.

In time, she also became known as "The Duplicator." And so her business cards read, "Candid Du Clips: Duplicatoring to your needs." It was the type of punny schtick that was guaranteed to attract the students. Eventually, she legally changed her name to this moniker. She did get some photography gigs throughout college, and still got some in the years since then. But actor mugshots, birthday parties, and grad photos were not enough. Hence her need to sneak around for some easy money.

Her parents did not care for photography, and she was tired of being lectured about her lack of direction in life. To be fair, it did sometimes feel like she was wandering aimlessly whenever she fulfilled each request from her benefactor. It was probably best to cut ties with her parents. Since they were all the way on the opposite coast, they were safe. She could only imagine what her benefactor would do to them. And sometimes she *did* imagine what could be done to them, and it unsettled her that she spent time dwelling on such scenarios. But without a face to factor in, the fantasies never felt quite so close to reality. Even so, she thought it best to keep her distance from both directions.

It was late at night when Candid arrived at the parking lot of her apartment complex. Two of her roommates had their own parking spaces, and she did not see anymore available spaces in the lot. So she drove a couple of blocks away until she found an open spot by the sidewalk. Once her car was secured, she walked to her apartment in the cold of the night.

When she got inside, she went straight to the living room couch. Her four roommates each had their own rooms. Candid held her cell phone to her face and considered checking her email. Then she placed it on the coffee table, opting to lie down and close her eyes. But after an hour of tossing and turning, she could still feel curiosity gnawing at her like a rat's teeth in watermelon. She grabbed her phone and checked it.

Ben F. had indeed sent her another email. Candid was assigned a new person to find. A living one this time. And for once, she was given the name: Randy Morales. For whatever reason, it was now her job to follow his routine.

Is he gonna make me watch this guy get killed? she wondered. *What's so special about him?*

Attached to the email was a picture of Randy's face. The additional info on him included his address, and a little bit of a surprise: Randy just so happened to be attending Candid's Alma Mater. She had not set foot on that campus in years. Now, it seemed that this would be a homecoming of sorts.

Chapter 5
Sitting Ducks

The following Monday, Peyton Sheer awoke on the bottom bunk within her dorm at Copper Petal University. The alarm on her phone was going off.

"Pam?"

Her younger sister did not answer.

"Pam!"

Peyton got out of bed and looked up at the top bunk. Nobody was there. Peyton picked up her phone and ended the alarm, deeming it obsolete at half past eight.

Do I sleep that heavily? she wondered. *Guess this is a wake-up call.*

To save money, Peyton had been attending community college for the past three years. When she got enough credits to transfer, she had a few options to consider. But knowing that CPU was the only university that accepted her sister Pamela, she suggested that they try living together again. Pamela did not seem fond of the idea at the time, but she relented. After listing each other as preferred roommates, they eventually got an answer back saying they could share a dorm. There was not much space within it, but it had to do.

Peyton tried calling Pamela on her phone, but it went straight to voicemail. She hung up before she could hear the beep.

So much for communication.

Once Peyton was changed and ready to head out, she left the dorm, locking the door behind her. If there was anywhere she expected Pamela to be, it was Sitting Ducks, an annual Welcome Week fair during fall quarter, at Petal Lock Park, in the middle of the egg-shaped campus. This was where various clubs boothed to attract new members, mainly the incoming freshmen.

When Peyton arrived, she saw that there were two sections of the park. The surrounding path was in the shape of the infinity symbol. The eastern section had redwoods while the western section had silver birches. The former was where the booths were. She found it odd that the western side was virtually bereft of people. On top of that, neither breed of trees were native to this county, and yet here they were. The east side had ducks while the west side had geese. Needless to say, there was a reason that the fair was named the Sitting Ducks Fair.

Various campus organizations were advertising, their booths and canopies decorated with posters and flyers. Some of them had academic foci. Others involved hobbies such as archery or bowling. One in particular seemed so mundane that it felt weirder than the others: Nap Kin at CPU. According to the banner, it was a napping club. A female student stood in front of a table, behind which another female student and a male student sat.

"Hi!" the standing student said, waving to Peyton. "Do you like our banner?"

"Yeah," Peyton answered with a nod. "All that gold glitter? Nice touch."

"I'm Gertrude Yose, by the way."

Gertrude held out her hand, and Peyton shook it.

"I'm Peyton. Nice to meet you. Are you one of the officers for this club?"

"Yep! Naomi and Reginald are the other board members. Not *bored* members, mind you. We don't bore you to sleep. But we do nap together without having to bore each other."

Peyton looked at the others behind the table. Naomi waved, but the man next to her seemed to be in his own world, staring off into space.

"I take it that's you two?" Peyton guessed. "Naomi and Reginald?"

"Huh?" the man said, blinking and then making eye contact. "Oh. Sorry. Name's Randy, not Reginald."

"He's out passing flyers with the Seashells," Naomi explained.

"Y'all pass out seashells?" Peyton asked.

"Oh, sorry," Naomi said. "That's what I call Chelsea and Shelley. Fellow club members. Volunteered to help out."

Gertrude pulled her phone out of her pocket, looked at the screen, and put it back. She groaned.

"Yo-Gert," Naomi said. "Something wrong?"

"Mitch says he'll be here in half an hour. Surprise surprise."

Naomi rolled her eyes.

"What's holding him up?"

"He just woke up."

Naomi shook her head.

"Classic Ditcher."

Wow, Gertrude thought. *Guess I'm not as bad when it comes to waking up.*

"So," Gertrude said, "you interested in joining the Nap Kin?"

"Sounds weird, but maybe. I mean, everyone needs a nap, so why not make a club out of it?"

"Exactly! We plan on meeting every Wednesday at five starting next week. Each time, it might be a different place on or off campus, based on member feedback at the end of each meeting. Would you like to sign up for our email list?"

"Sure."

Peyton walked over to the table and looked down at the paper, which already had a dozen names listed. Taking the pen beside it, she tried writing down her name and contact info. But it ran out of ink. She tried etching the pen into the paper in hopes that ink would return, but it only formed transparent chicken scratch.

"Hang on," Gertrude said, lifting a heavy backpack onto the table. She rummaged through it and took out three pens. She uncapped each one and tried them on the corner of the email list. Still no ink. "Nothing, nothing, and nothing. So glad my brother's not here to see this. Tim likes to tease me. Hold up."

She dug through her backpack again and took out four pencils. Three were dull and unsharpened, so Peyton grabbed the sharp one. But when she tried using it, the graphite broke off, leaving a tiny ash-like stain against the white surface. Gertrude kept digging until she found her pencil sharpener, which she then used on one of the dull pencils until it was sharp enough. This one was not so fragile, so Peyton was could finally write her info.

"So are you a freshman?" Gertrude asked.

"No. I'm actually a transfer."

"Oh, okay."

Once she was done, Peyton handed the pen back to Gertrude.

"Yeah. I was at my old school for three years. Came to this one for my sister. *She* is the freshman. When she found out about this school, she said she felt weirdly drawn to it. Isn't that strange?"

"For this school?" Gertrude shook her head, smiling. "Not strange at all."

"So why is Sitting Ducks only on this side of the park?"

"It's a tradition."

"A secret tradition?"

"Not at all! Sitting Ducks is on this side, and later in spring we have Goose Chase on the other side."

Gertrude pointed westward, and Peyton turned her head to look at the silver birch-filled portion of the park. From where she was standing, Peyton did not see any people. But she spotted a goose sitting on the grass. Peyton faced Gertrude again.

"Any specific reason for this tradition other than the ducks and the geese?"

45

"They figure into it a lot. I've heard there are thirty-two of each. The ducks and geese walk around on their own sides. They never cross over." Gertrude lowered her voice to a whisper. "A curse could happen that way."

"What?" Peyton sincerely did not hear.

"A curse could happen that way," Gertrude whispered again.

"What?" Peyton repeated, at the risk of sounding stupid. "Sorry, I didn't hear."

"I said," Gertrude continued at a normal volume, "that a curse could happen if the wrong bird crosses into the wrong side of the park."

"You're messing with me, right? A curse?"

"That's what I hear," Gertrude whispered.

Peyton did not hear this statement, but she gave no indication.

"I mean, they've gotta step on each other's grass sometimes, right? Are they that territorial?"

"I'm not so sure if it's a territorial thing," Gertrude replied at a reasonable volume. "All I know is that if one ends up on the wrong side, something bad could nappin' around here. Oh wow. I just said the wrong word again, didn't I? It's been a long day and I've got naps on the brain."

"Wait, so, says who? How do you know this?"

"Word gets around. People learn from Unicoren and Stagmantel."

Peyton was somewhat familiar with these names. Over the summer, she had seen the memes containing photos of what appeared to be a unicorn and a stag, though they were both bipedal, and instead of fur they had brown dirt faces and limbs, the rest of their bodies clothes in dark gray rocks. She had just written them off as bad Photoshop. Especially since their eyes glowed white. Skeptical, she could not quite believe what Gertrude was telling her.

"Do you mess with *all* of your potential club members this way?"

"Oh no! You know what? Forget all that." Gertrude's hands parted imaginary smoke. "Just come to the first meeting next week. It'll here in the redwoods. Easy to remember."

"Sure. I'll see you then."

Peyton walked away from the booth, wondering why she had agreed to go to the first meeting even after all that sketchiness.

My life must be boring as hell, she guessed.

* * *

Randy was deep in thought. Sitting next to Naomi, his thoughts remained firmly on her. He wanted to be alone with her so that he could set a new foundation via private conversation. With Reginald passing out flyers elsewhere, this seemed like an opportune moment to invite her to hang out with him sometime. She and Reginald had dated for a while. During freshman year, all of their friends speculated on whether they would get together. Their relationship lasted all of sophomore year, and then they broke up and had to get over the heartbreak during junior year, despite them insisting to everyone that the breakup was pretty mutual.

Now, Naomi and Reginald seemed like good friends, but Randy could not help wondering whether there might still be something there. He felt guilty having romantic feelings for a friend who had been with another friend, and he was not sure whether she would feel ready to move on. But it had been a year, and he was dying to find out. Especially now that it seemed this next year would be his last. If she were to turn him down, then it would not change the outcome he was expecting from his impending confrontation with Mathis. If she were to show interest, though, then perhaps they could make the most of his final year. But if it were to grow to the point where they both wanted the relationship to last forever...

What then? Randy wondered. *Can I commit?*

He knew that he was full of so many issues, truly a mess of a person. As such, he did not feel confident that Naomi would stay with him even beyond this school year. But he was ever curious. He wanted to act soon and let his future self worry about the rest.

As Gertrude stepped further from the table to attract attention from other students passing by, Randy turned his head toward Naomi and tried breaking the ice.

"I heard there's a movie screening at Loch Crystal Auditorium on Wednesday."

"Oh yeah?" Naomi looked at him. "Which one?"

"The original *The Texas Chain Saw Massacre*. It's the fortieth anniversary screening."

"Yikes."

Her grimace told him everything. And yet he gave into the impulse of pressing further.

"So... I take it you wouldn't be interested in seeing it?"

"I just don't do scary movies. Especially if they're bloody."

He could have left it at that. And he felt stupid when he continued to push the issue.

"It's actually not as bloody as people remember it. Very economical. That's a testament to how great of a horror movie it is. But it's totally cool if you don't wanna see it." It seemed that he could not make a date out of this. But then he got the idea to make it a group outing among friends. A way to hide the scent from Naomi to make things appear normal between them. "Yo-Gert!"

"Yeah?" she answered, turning around.

"Do you like horror movies?"

"Not really."

"Oh. Never mind."

The possibility of asking the other Nap Kin members about whether they would be interested came to mind, but he was afraid of hearing them pass on the invitation. Despite how much he hung out with them, he worried about being judged for his tastes.

Soon afterward, a woman with a cap covering her eyes walked up to the table, jotting down a name and an email address. As she walked away, Randy glanced at the name: Cate Cameron.

"Must be kinda shy," Naomi said with a shrug. "I'm sure we can get her out of her shell, though."

"I mean, you kinda have to," Randy said. "Wouldn't wanna give someone else *another* shell-related nickname."

Naomi laughed, making Randy feel joyous. Any instance in which a smile of hers was his doing made him feel on top of the world and invincible, even if he were to fall off the peak of the moment.

"I'll be sure not to recycle anything from my repertoire, Brandy."

Randy never minded this nickname. Way back when their friendship began, the Nap Kin had a conversation about alcoholic beverages they would like to try someday. Reginald was dubbed Gin from then on, and he referred to Naomi as Tonic, hoping she would fall for him. Randy believed himself to be the type of guy who would enjoy wine. So Naomi suggested Randywine, a Tolkien reference. But when he said it made him sound like a whiner, she thought of a short, cleaner sobriquet for him: Brandy. Admittedly, Randy believed he whined too often in his head, though that felt better than whining aloud. He thought it would be off-putting to express his problems to his friends.

He wondered how they would feel if they knew the truth about how he intended to end his final year.

* * *

Peyton was not sure where to walk to next, so she just passed through the fair, glancing at the other booths. At some book club booth, she saw someone dressed as the school mascot, Mandy the Mantleope. Wearing denim overalls, she resembled a brown horse with the horns of an antelope, though her snout was not as long, and these horns were flame-colored. The mascot was high-fiving students and dancing around.

Peyton made eye contact with the artificial eyes, and then the mascot stood still for a moment. Creeped out, Peyton continued walking.

But as she kept passing by more booths, she had the nagging feeling that she was being followed. She turned around and, sure enough, saw Mandy the Mantleope, walking on all fours.

"All right!" Peyton yelled. "What's your problem?"

Mandy stood up and waved.

"What?" Peyton crossed her arms. "Can I help you?"

A shake of the head.

"Why are you following me? What's your deal?"

"Don't you recognize me?" the voice within replied.

"Wait." Peyton uncrossed her arms, recognizing the familiar voice. "Pam?"

"Yeah!"

Peyton reached for the mascot head, but Pamela jumped back.

"Don't!" Pamela wagged the index fingers. "Nobody can know who I am. The mascot identity has to be kept secret."

"Oh. Right. Well, when were you gonna tell me about this?"

"I wanted to be sure I got the gig. I auditioned with a few other people last week. The chancellor seemed impressed, and I was so stoked when I got the email saying I won!"

"And you waited until now to tell me?"

"I thought it'd be funny."

"More like rude and creepy. You could've at least told me where you were going this morning."

"I couldn't sleep last night." She twirled twice. "I was just so darn excited to come out here and wear this outside for the first time."

"I bet you're sweating a lot under there, huh?"

"Strangely, no. It feels like normal room temperature in here. Anyway, I gotta go greet more people. See ya!"

With that, Pamela skipped away, leaving Peyton bewildered.

Pam is something else.

* * *

All throughout the fair, Pamela, dressed as Mandy the Mantleope, shook hands with students old and new. She knew that it was her duty to raise people's spirits during the depressing times of the school year, which intensified around testing time. She knew what it was like to feel glum. She was used to walking around school all alone during recess and lunchtime. But now she felt like a new person as she wore this iconic costume. She was expected to be more energetic, and she obliged to the requirements of this identity.

Some students were enthusiastic enough to take selfies with the mascot. It did not matter to Pamela that nobody knew who she was. She donned the mantle and got into character. She had no qualms galloping on the grass as a quadruped would, using all four limbs. It made her feel closer to the earth and one with the campus.

She halted when she saw a stoic woman with glowing white eyes. The horn adorning the woman's forehead offered a clue. From what Pamela could recall of CPU lore, this was Unicoren, normally seen in the eastern side of the park. She certainly had the aesthetic: a head and limbs that seemed to be made of dirt and somehow moved like flesh, with the rest of her covered in rocks. Up close, Pamela could see that Unicoren had digits on her hands, as well as hooves on her feet. Pamela wondered what she was doing here, away from her geese and the silver birches on the west side of the park.

"Do you normally come here?" Pamela asked.

"I am just here to visit."

"I thought you couldn't leave your side."

"I'm able to come and go as I please within the bounds of the park, though I rarely do. I choose occasions such as these. It's my geese who are not allowed over here."

"How come?"

"It would upset the balance."

Pamela had heard that it was bad luck for geese to walk to the ducks' side of the park, and vice versa. But nobody online seemed to know the reasoning. Only that it would start some sort of curse.

"What happens when things get unbalanced?" Pamela asked.

"We have been fortunate enough to never find out."

Pamela wanted to press further about this, but the woman turned away. Then another question popped into Pamela's head.

"Um, Unicoren?"

She halted and looked back at Pamela.

"Yes?"

"I was wondering..." Pamela almost kept herself from asking the question, but it was too difficult to think of a new one. "I was wondering if it'd be all right for me to hang around in your side of the park every now and then."

"In that costume?"

"If it's okay with you. I really enjoy playing around in it. It makes me feel more alive. Sorry. You probably think that's weird."

It was difficult to tell, but Pamela could have sworn that she saw the slight curl of a smile.

"As a matter of fact, it does not sound weird at all. You really know how to animate Mandy. Even better than anyone else who has taken on the role."

Pamela was pleasantly surprised by such flattery.

"Wow. Uh, thank you."

"Feel free to stop by whenever you wish. Perhaps you will even feel at home."

"YES!" Pamela said, fist bumping the sky.

She glimpsed Unicoren's face once more before the mysterious being turned around to walk away, and Pamela was certain that there was a smile. Pamela felt as though she had just made a new friend. One who was impressed with her performance as Mandy the Mantleope.

She felt confident and certain that many students also appreciated her performance even if they could not necessarily appreciate the person within. She wished that she could tell people, and she hoped that Peyton could keep her secret. It would certainly be a test of how strong their sisterhood could be, now that they might have a chance to reignite it after all these years. And if Peyton were to fail the test and tell other people, Pamela hoped that word would not reach the judge who had instructed her to keep her identity as Mandy a secret. The judge who had been impressed by her dancing and prancing around despite his intimidating 6'5" stature, long hair, ducktail beard, and shades.

The judge being Chancellor Mathias Moseley.

Chapter 6
Over the Moon

On Wednesday, October 1, Randy watched the 40th anniversary screening of *The Texas Chain Saw Massacre* in Loch Crystal Auditorium. He thought it was an odd choice since the name of the place brought *Friday the 13th* to mind, but perhaps they would play one of those films when it actually was Friday the 13th. But he was not complaining about the selection.

He sat alone in the first row, his mind taking in the bright Texas heat despite the darkness that surrounded his reality. When night fell on the screen, he saw the whole of the moon. But this was historically inaccurate; the full moon was on the night of August 13, 1973, not August 18, the date on which this film was set. He hated seeing so many full moons in films and wondered why media seldom depicted anything less than a full moon. Whether it be from a finger or a toe, the shape of a nail clipping in the sky might have been appropriate for a film such as this.

When the disturbing dinner scene arrived, he cried. Not because of the torture endured by the poor young woman in the movie, and not because of the drama that had been going on during the filming of this scene, but because he was watching this film by himself and, thus, could not savor it as much as he would have liked. He knew how taboo it was to talk about enjoying violent films, so he had nobody with whom to share this experience. Nobody to understand him. He wanted to be understood. To not be alone in feeling his curiosity at the prospect of wearing a mask and being feared. To talk about what it was like to grasp the heat of the sun in one hand.

One might think some of the upcoming films would be enough to encourage Randy to keep on living for years to come. But he actually felt discouraged. If movies could just be remade and rebooted, then he saw no point in getting invested in any future releases. He doubted that he would miss out on anything worth watching if he were to die. Even if he chose to continue living beyond senior year, he was not sure he would even try to see anything new.

Randy's apartment was two miles away from campus. Since the school's buses stopped running at night, walking home alone was an exercise in isolation. Between the campus and the apartment complex was a field of dead-looking grass, with patches of dirt here and there.

Randy looked up at the half moon, first quarter from the looks of it. Now *this* was real. People could see the moon for what it was. Not the full, fulfilled-looking face, but the half-full visage in a form akin to a skinless potato wedge. No make-up hiding the imperfections. Up between the stars, one smooth cheek and one scarred cheek, a crack drawing the line down between them to separate the light from the dark. Some people probably preferred not to look at the dark side.

As real life moved around him, he superimposed a familiar fantasy...

A studio containing an audience and a pink stage upon which a host sat behind a desk. The walls behind him were made of bricks, their shade an emerald green. From a distance, the white lines between each brick seemed like they could either be protruding outward or just be normal snow trenches between the rectangles.

The details of this setting were compiled from various talk shows that Randy had watched with his dad when he was very little. A ritual he eventually had to carry on by himself once his dad felt more tired when he got home from work. As a child, Randy believed that the talk show hosts were talking directly to him, not just to the audience in the studio.

In this fantasy, he knew the host very well. The program was The Tardy Party Show with Artie Docent. *The host was a clown, complete* with white makeup on his face and a round red nose. Artie's hands were like those of a white mannequin, though the fingers were batons, as seen in the hands of music conductors. His attire was a formal suit: black dress shoes, black slacks, white dress shirt, black blazer, and red tie.

"Welcome back everybody!" Artie, moving his hands actively, said to the live studio audience that applauded his presence. Once they were silent, he continued. "Our first guest for tonight, you know him. He's the set designer around here. He just finished summer vacation and is about to start his final year at Copper Petal University." A cheer and a whistle. "I know, right? It's crazy! Please welcome, my good friend Randy Morales!"

As the audience went wild with applause, Randy, wearing the same formal outfit as Artie, walked onto the stage and over to the clown, giving him a hug before sitting in the guest chair. With an air of confidence, Artie sat behind the pine desk, resting his feet on top. Behind Artie and Randy was a window with blue blinds. Through the spaces between the blinds was a black city, skyscraper silhouettes with yellow lights, against a purple sky. Those in the studio could see the outside world, but nobody could look inside.

"It's great to be back, Artie."

"Back here, or back at school?"

"Uh, both, I guess."

Laughter from the audience.

"So tell us! What can we expect from your final school year? You don't have to provide any spoilers, but just give us an idea."

"Well, it's gonna be bittersweet, I think. When you all watch it, you'll feel very aware that the end is coming. But hopefully it's executed well and there won't be too many problems."

"Now, some people from previous years won't be there, correct?"

"Right. My friend August is studying abroad for this whole school year."

"Do you guys still keep in touch?"

56

"Well, he hasn't messaged me yet, but I'm sure he's busy and has his own thing going on."

"What about you? Have you tried messaging him?"

"Well, I don't wanna be a bother."

"I think it'd be good for you to talk to him. I mean, when are you ever gonna see him in person again?"

"You have a point there. But, who knows? Maybe he'll pop up for a cameo at some point. I hope he does."

"That'd be great. You know that we here love guest appearances." *Artie faced the audience. "Isn't that right, everyone?!"*

Lots of claps. Randy smiled and nodded awkwardly in agreement.

"Right, right," he responded.

"All right," Artie said. "Well then, I guess if anyone comes back for a bit, it'll be a surprise for everyone. I have to say, it's been a while since last season's finale. So long without seeing these characters, and I really do miss—"

The fantasy was cut short when a flash of light ten yards ahead caught Randy's attention. In the distance, he could see a figure standing outside of his apartment building. The stranger stood for a long moment, and so did he. They were both aware of each other.

* * *

Shit! Candid thought. She had been certain that Randy, with his eyes to the sky, had not been paying attention. His lack of movement in this moment made her hope he really was not paying attention, and just staring into space.

And then he continued walking, though his face did not seem to be pointed at her.

Did he not see me after all?

Casually, she walked away, toward the street. She walked more quickly as she got closer to her car on the street outside of the apartment complex. She could see Randy taking out his key to open the door to his apartment. He did not look in her direction. Once he was inside, she drove away.

Her benefactor would probably be mad if Randy knew that he was being followed. If Randy suspected that he was being watched, he would probably be paranoid and scanning the area cautiously. But Candid could still track him to other places since she had put her alternate email on the Nap Kin email list. She just had to be more careful from here on out.

She really wondered just how much her benefactor knew. Sometimes she thought Ben F. was somehow omniscient. She had to keep reminding herself about how silly that sounded.

Since the night at the train, she had been keeping up with local news online. The remains by the train had been discovered by hikers, and the police had been alerted. For now, Candid knew the name of the woman: Darby Morineau. But she expected that, like the others, the name would fade from her mind, given enough time. She had skimmed the article on her phone, which included a video of her heartbroken parents. She could not imagine what it felt like for them, and she dared not listen to their reaction.

And then Candid felt selfish wondering how her own parents would feel and react if she were to die. As far as they knew, she was not in danger. But they knew nothing, so any possibilities in their minds were open season. And there was no telling what someone as resourceful as her benefactor could do. Sometimes she wondered whether it was just one person, or whether it was a group of people, perhaps some cult that subscribed to some creepy mantra like, "We are all Ben F., Actor."

She hoped that it was just one person. At least then it would be easier to eliminate Ben F. if necessary. If it was just one person, then it was a crafty one, seemingly careful enough to not leave DNA anywhere near the train, or at any of the other crime scenes, for that matter. She wanted him to get caught, but she knew that she would also be at risk for her association.

For the time being, it seemed best for her to keep her distance, to stay out of frame and focus.

Randy wondered whether the photographer was some agent of Mathis Dillard. He hoped they did not think he knew he was being followed. As scary of a thought as it was, he did not care too much about being watched. His fate may have been sealed, anyway. He just needed to be sure not to tip off where his family lived. So much for weekend visits.

He would just have to use school work as an excuse. Surely, his parents would buy that senior year was the toughest school year. He was lucky that his parents had once made a point to get themselves removed from websites that had personal info publicly available. Randy had done the same, feeling uncomfortable about people being able to look up his hometown, address, email address, and phone number. He also kept that information off of social media, which, thankfully, his parents never used.

When he was in his room, he considered messaging August. But he was too shaken by the fact that he was being followed. Randy would not be fully present in the conversation. It was also early morning in London, which meant that August was probably asleep.

Randy grabbed his backpack and took out his sketchbook. He used it for assignments from art classes, but he also let his mind wander out of bounds in his free time. He opened it up to the page where he had drawn and colored Artie Docent's studio in its full glory. He had once shown this to Naomi Clutcher. He could remember the conversation, word for word. A memory so potent that the past became present...

"Who's that?" Naomi asks, sitting next to Randy in front of a redwood tree.

"This was my imaginary friend, growing up," Randy answers.

"A clown? That's cute. Does he talk?"

The question catches him off guard. He believes that Naomi would label him as a looney if he were still communicating with his childhood imaginary friend.

"Pfft. What? You think he speaks to me?"

"No," Naomi says. "I mean, did you imagine him talking? Or was he a silent one?"

"Oh." Randy scratches the back of his head. "He talked. You know. Just...jokey things."

"Any dad jokes?"

He does not know what this means, but he feels compelled to move on, not wanting to repeat too much.

"Yeah. Dad jokes."

Randy wondered whether Naomi—or any other Nap Kin—would still accept him if they knew about his undying habit of visiting this mental manifestation. Artie was a substitute for the friend he used to have. There was a time when he had a stuffed animal. A gray rabbit with a voice, saying that her name was Aster. She and Randy played for a while, but then she went away when he wanted to get what he wanted, which was control over the scenarios that they were pretending. He tried to manage without her. Hence the cafe lamp, and then the creation of Artie Docent.

Lying in bed, he entertained a different type of fantasy. Another one he had visited often...

Randy and his friends walk into a dark alley. From out of the shadows appears a menacing assailant. His friends cower in fear, desperate for the helping hand of a hero. But Randy is ready. He takes out a handy knife and sticks it into the stomach of the assailant. This time, he can also stick it into the face, now shaped into something recognizable. The face of Mathis.

Giving in to the pleasure of imagining the act, Randy did not mind that he could not sleep right away. He would tire eventually. In the meantime, he could unwind, rewind, and relive the fantasy all over again.

I'll make sure we remain friends for life, he thought. *And then my remains will leave me.*

Chapter 7
Billiards and Dominoes

August Wilhelm had been in London for three weeks now, and he was having the time of his life with his new friends at the hotel. Fritz Fischer had some culinary flair in the kitchen (whenever the flares of the stove flames did not get out of control because of his divided attention). Fritz formed a friendship with Anton Becker, who baked very often. Bessie Hu organized gatherings in the common area, suggesting movies and video games. These often devolved into drinking games. Verner Werner often suggested getting drinks. This being a Friday night, a bunch of the students were free to go out. Jade, uninterested initially, decided to go when she realized that the only remaining activity was to do her homework.

Verner led them to a pub called Unsoberquet. The first floor was lit green, and the second floor was lit purple. Some remained downstairs, but August, Jade, and Verner accompanied a few who went upstairs to the billiards table. One student got competitive when it came to billiards. His name was Tate Melvin, and he was an American with a buzz cut. After defeating a couple of people, he bragged about his skills. Then August gave the game a try even though it had been months since the last time he played.

"You familiar with this game?" Tate asked, holding a cue like a wizard staff.

"I've played a bit with my friends back home," August replied.

"Nice to finally meet an equal." Tate rubbed the blue chalk over the tip of his cue. "These chumps got nothing on me."

"Jerk," Verner said.

"Watch your mouth. I beat you carnival and square."

"Carnival? What carnival?"

"Instead of fair. I'm saying I beat you fair and square."

"Whatever you say, Melvin."

"You got a problem?"

"Nothing. It's just... It is my understanding that a Melvin is another name for a wedgie, no?"

"Nobody uses it like that anymore."

"Whatever you say, Tate Wedgie."

Jade, sitting at the bar, snickered. Then Tate shot her a scowl. The smile faded from Jade's face, though slight facial movements revealed that it was trying to escape the weight of the disguise.

"Ru-hude!" she said, with a hint of laughter.

"Fellas!" August said, raising his hands. "Come on! There's no need for toxic rivalries here. We may have come from different places, but we're all just trying to have a good time traveling and making friends."

"He's right," Verner said. "Sorry."

"You know," August began, "if my friend Naomi were here, she'd be giving all of you some neat nicknames."

"Sobriquets," Verner said, raising his glass from the table and then putting it back down. "What's mine?"

"Not sure yet. I'm not as adept as she is. She called me Eight-ball."

"Makes sense," Jade said. "August is the eighth month."

August picked up the cue leaning against the pool table.

"Actually, a game of pool is how we met, and I sucked so much that I got the eight-ball in the pocket right away."

"Tate-ball!" Verner suggested, pointing at Tate. "We can call him Tate-ball."

"Too similar," August said. "Naomi probably would've figured something out by now. She's superb with her nomenclature. And that word, come to think of it, sounds similar to her name, Naomi Clutcher. Funny how life works sometimes."

"No nickname for me, thanks," Tate said unenthusiastically.

"If I can come up with a good one," August said, "I'll run it by you."

Tate scoffed.

"You're just a friendly guy, aren't you?"

"People have *got* to be friendly." August looked at the triangular formation of balls and aimed his cue. "I know a couple of people back home who told me a tale about a world where everyone was on the same page. But then there was chaos, disagreement." August pushed the cue forward, breaking the triangle and sending two balls into corner pockets. "And then they all went in separate directions. One world divided into many. Some of them may have fallen into black holes. People died *instantly*. Other worlds floated, lost, wayward, until they stopped and settled in their places. Habitable worlds are very far apart from each other now. We're lucky that we have starlight to fill the space so that we don't feel so darn alone."

"You actually believe all that?" Jade asked.

"What? Do none of you believe in life on other planets?"

"I mean," Tate began, "it wouldn't be terrible for humankind to be the only intelligent life in the universe. But since it's so big, and there are all these stories about sightings, how can one not believe? I just have trouble grasping this whole thing about a giant planet splitting into many smaller planets and then moving around like marbles. You sure *you* haven't lost *your* marbles? How could life survive an event like that?"

"If you ever meet the couple who told me this stuff, you might change your tune. One has antlers, and the other has a horn."

"Like the instrument?" Verner asked, miming some horn-playing.

"No. Like a unicorn."

"Aliens?" Jade asked.

"I mean, if it was all one planet before, *are* they aliens?"

"Well, maybe we'll find some intelligent life on the trip to Stonehenge. You know what they say about that place."

"Wait, is that *this* coming Sunday?"

"Yep."

"Okay. I *knew* I was forgetting something." August rubbed his chin. "Weird. I still kinda have that feeling."

"You need to dial back on the beer," Verner said, lifting his own glass from the table and then accidentally spilling a bit on the floor.

"You buzzed already?" Tate asked.

"I haven't even had a sip yet," Verner said, taking one and then wincing. "Ugh, that's awful."

"What'd you get?"

"I ordered the special. I thought it'd be a good idea. I was wrong."

"That bad, huh?" August said.

"Yeah. Sucks that I paid for this. Oh well. Might as well kill it."

He chugged the beer as quickly as he could and then set the glass on the table.

"You all right there, buddy?" August said.

"Yeah. Now if you'll excuse me, I'm off to the toilet. I'm gonna leave a special."

* * *

Sunday came, and they took the bus to Stonehenge. Each student received a device containing an audio tour complete with known facts about the site. The cold October winds blew across the lush green grass that surrounded the ring of standing stones. As the students walked around it, August kept his gaze fixed upon the stones, wondering whether he would notice anything. August wondered whether they could fall like dominoes. Jade was mostly silent as she walked beside him, but she did speak from time to time.

"Are you listening to the energy?" she asked with fake enthusiasm.

"Oh yeah," August said, lifting the device to his ear and pressing a button to listen to the audio tour.

"Smart-hass," Jade said with a laugh. "So is there some interesting story about how Stonehenge came to be that you haven't told us?"

"Not that I'm aware of."

"No alien stories?"

"What do I look like, the History Channel? I only know what my friends told me, and even *they* don't know everything."

"What proof do they have about the way one world broke into many?"

"They were there when it happened."

"And you believe them?" Jade raised an eyebrow. "That they actually survived something like that?"

"It's hard *not* to when they seem so out of this world. It's not every day you meet people with glowing white eyes."

"I feel like you're messing with me," Jade said, shaking her head.

"What would I have to gain from that? I don't lie to my friends."

"I mean, we haven't known each other long. Doesn't seem too out there for you to do this in the early stages of a friendship."

"I swear I'm not lying," August promised, raising his hand in a pledge position.

"Well," Jade sighed, "I won't hold this against you. Not sure if I believe any of this. But weird, unexplained stuff *does* happen. Sometimes."

"You sound surprisingly sure about that."

"It's personal. And we barely know each other."

"Fair enough. You're not obligated to tell me, obviously. But if you ever *do* want to tell me, I'll be here. Well, not *here*. Back at the hotel."

"You don't think we'll come all the way back here to talk about crazy stuff?"

"Nah. This place looks pretty plain to me."

And so, they continued on with this mundane visit to Stonehenge, during which absolutely nothing unusual happened. In fact, the majority of that day was pretty normal.

But in the middle of the night, August awoke in room 314 when he heard a toilet flush. It did not sound as near to him as the toilet in his lavatory, but it also sounded too close to be from another hotel room. The walls seemed thin at times, but he still found this sound to be suspicious. Getting up, he turned on the light switch outside the lavatory, next to the door. He walked inside and saw no sign of his toilet having gone off. He turned around and did a double take.

In the mirror, he saw a room that was not identical to the one in which he was standing. It took him a moment to grasp what it showed. He could see that there was a glass sliding door a yard away from a sink that was not his own. He felt his heart sink in horror as he screamed.

"AAHHHH! AAAAHHHHH!"

It was all too jarring for him to fathom. And he just continued to scream in confusion when a door on the side of the reflection creaked open, and a man who looked familiar came out. August screamed, but the man did not even flinch.

"What's going on?!" August demanded to know.

Recovering his memories of CPU, August realized why this man looked familiar. Though the man was not wearing the iconic shades—thus leaving a scar visible on an eyelid—there was no doubt that this was the spitting image of Chancellor Moseley. (What August did not know was that the image was reversed.) He could hear the steps that the reflection was making on the tiles of a floor, outside the door of the room that, apparently, contained a toilet. He could hear the creak of water rushing out of the sink faucet. August almost wanted the man to acknowledge him. But August went unheard.

LEMONS LOOM LIKE RAIN

Once the man stepped out of view, the normal reflection of August and his own lavatory reappeared in the mirror. He feared the glass, so he stepped out of the lavatory. Desperately, he wanted to tell the receptionist about this problem.

Don't be stupid! he thought to himself, fearing that the man in the mirror would hear him. *They'll never believe you... And they could be in on it.*

For all he knew, there was nobody in the hotel whom he could trust. What he knew for sure was that he no longer wished to be within this room. Every step on the carpeted floor beneath him sounded so fragile that he could fall. Still in his pajamas, he grabbed the key and swung his room door open. A hallway lamp lit up. He shut the self-locking door behind him.

Running back toward the lift, he could feel the skeleton of the structure supporting the floor. He tripped over the small staircase, stubbing his left big toe and scratching his face against the carpet. Getting up, he pressed the lift button frantically. After ten seconds, it reached his level. He got inside and expected a drop. Luckily, it took him to his destination at a steady pace.

Reaching the ground floor, he walked calmly to the receptionist desk. The receptionist was playing what sounded like elevator music. August wondered why the lift itself did not have anything installed that could play music. The receptionist turned to him with a smile.

"Can I help you?" he asked.

"I..." August uttered, searching through his memory. "I came down here for a *reason*. I was running from my room for some *reason*, because there was *something* I needed to say. But before that... I have no clue."

"That's...odd."

"Isn't it?"

"Did you need something for your room? Any extra bedding?"

"No. I have everything. Hm. I guess it's kinda like when you pull out your phone to look something up, and then you forget what it was.

Huh. Look up. That's a weird phrase, right? We look *straight ahead* at computers or *down* at our phones." He reached for a pocket, but then realized that his pajamas had no pockets. "Did I forget my phone somewhere? I know I don't have my key with me."

"Would you like for me to send someone up to help you look for it?"

"Yeah. That'd be great."

The receptionist sent one of the cleaners up with him. Once at the door, she unlocked it and took out her phone.

"What's your phone number?" she asked.

"I... I don't know. I mean, who knows their number when you can just program it?"

"You don't even know your own?"

He reached down into his laundry hamper and dug through the pocket of a pair of jeans he had worn earlier in the day. There, he found the phone. He had often forgotten to empty his pockets of receipts and coins before throwing his pants into the hamper, but it seemed odd for him to have forgotten his phone.

"Here it is. Sorry about all the trouble."

Chapter 8
Show and Stagmantel

On Wednesday, during the first full week of classes at CPU, Peyton met up with the Nap Kin in Petal Lock Park, just as the sun was setting. Her sister had seemed disinterested when she invited her. Pamela provided no explanation. But Peyton really wanted to try making friends, especially if her sister would not be hanging around her that often. If Peyton could ever get Pamela to hang out with the Nap Kin in the future, then perhaps Pamela could inherit Peyton's new friends. And then they could share. But first, Peyton wanted to be sure they were decent.

Present at the meeting spot—which was filled with sleeping bags and pillows, surrounded by redwoods—were the familiar faces of Gertrude, Naomi, and Randy. The latter, with a pencil in hand, was pretty occupied with his sketchbook. Peyton was finally introduced to the others about whom she had heard: Reginald, Chelsea, and Shelley.

"Hi," Reginald said, politely shaking hands with Peyton. "Reginald Webber."

"Peyton Sheer. So, what, are you a computer science major?"

"Just 'cause of my name? Psh. No. I'm a bio-sci major."

"I was close. It was one of the sci's."

"Sigh..." Reginald shook his head. "Everyone just clumps 'em all together like different ice cream flavors."

The two young women who were new to Peyton spoke up.

"Nice to meet you! I'm Chelsea Keltie."

"And I'm Shelley Bogdal."

"Hi," Peyton replied. "Are you two also club officers?"

"We might as well be," Shelley answered. "We do a lot of volunteer work boothing for the club and shit. Sometimes we do better while the others slack a little sometimes."

"We started out in the background," Chelsea continued, "just sitting in the back at club meetings and only talking to each other. But then we got close with the officers. You know, scooting up a few desks. And now we hang out with them pretty much all the time."

"We didn't want the titles, though," Shelley explained. "Thought it'd be kinda sad if almost all the members were officers."

"Are these *all* the members?" Peyton asked, looking around at the few in attendance.

"Seems like it," Shelley said. "Pretty average. Take it from me. I'm a math minor."

"What's your major?"

"That's generic. Don't ask that. If people can't make conversation, then they should ask something better, or fuck off."

"Oh!" Chelsea said. "There's also Mitch. He should be here... sometime. Who knows? Maybe at the end of the meeting."

Peyton heard a twig snap. She turned to look, and noticed a young man in the distance, coming out from behind a redwood.

"Is that him over there?"

"Actually," Reginald said squinting, "no. Huh. How about that?"

"This is so exciting!" Gertrude said before approaching the newcomer. "Hi! Are you here for the Nap Kin?"

"Yeah," the newcomer answered, approaching slowly with his hands tucked into his pants pockets.

"How'd you hear about us? Sitting Ducks?"

"I'm actually August's cousin."

"Wait, Grady?"

"Yeah, Grady Stuart."

"Oh! He's told us so much about you!" Gertrude turned to the other Nap Kin. "Remember?"

"Oh yeah!" almost all the members said, pointing at one another with smiles and nods.

"I don't," Shelley said, prompting Chelsea to elbow her in the ribs. "Ow."

"Hush," Chelsea said.

"I was at Sitting Ducks, though," Grady said. "I was the first one to put my name down. Didn't stay because I was shy, to be honest."

"Shy?" Gertrude repeated. "Hey, buddy, anyone connected to August is family here. You don't have to worry about people not liking you. It's nice to have fresh young faces in the club."

"We're not very popular," Shelley added.

Chelsea elbowed Shelley again.

"I've got the perfect nickname for you," Naomi said. "Gravy Stew."

"Wow!" Grady said with an overly enthusiastic smile. "I like it!"

Naomi turned to Peyton.

"Still wracking my brain trying to think of one for you."

"It's fine," Peyton responded. "No pressure."

"I wasn't sure I'd be accepted right away," Grady said. "You know, with August not being here and all. Still, I'm sure there will be some breaking in to win the crowd." He looked around at everyone. "Wow. August told me all about y'all and here you are, just as he described you. This guy with the sketchbook must be Randy!"

"Huh?" Randy stopped drawing and looked up from his sketchbook.

"Sorry. Didn't mean to break your flow. August told me you and Naomi are art majors. You're not gonna draw me—or draw *on* me— while I nap, are you?"

"No. I know boundaries, and I suck at drawing people. Naomi is wonderful at drawing people though."

72

"Bruh," Naomi said. "Give yourself some credit, Brandy. Show Gravy Stew your stuff! Peyton, check this out!"

Peyton, Naomi, and Grady gathered around Randy as he flipped through his sketchbook. One picture depicted the redwood trees, colored in. Another had the silver birches colored purple. The next page showed a red lamp with white surrounding a white bulb. Peyton was impressed, though Randy did not seem to feel completely satisfied by his craft.

"I like to think I have a knack, but I feel like I'm lacking."

"Don't be so tough on yourself," Grady said. "I think this all looks really neat!"

When Randy flipped to a picture of a stony figure with antlers, Peyton set a finger on the page, stopping him there.

"That one looks...interesting. You said you can't draw people?"

"Oh yeah. People are tough to figure out, but otherworldly beings I can handle."

"You thought of this?"

"Huh? No. This is Stagmantel."

"From the memes?"

"He's more than just a meme."

Peyton rolled her eyes.

"Yeah, yeah. He means a lot to people around this school. I get it."

"Why do you hate us?" Shelley asked.

This question caught Peyton off guard. She certainly did not hate these people whom she had just met. She was simply irritated by how they seemed to go along with what she firmly believed to be a charade.

"I-I don't."

"Prove it," Shelley said, stepping forward. "I fuckin' dare you."

"Calm down, edge lady," Chelsea said, grabbing her by the wrist.

"Sorry. You know how bored I get."

"See? This is why it's time for a nap!"

"Sheep..."

73

"Excuse me?"

"Uh, I meant it's time to *count* sheep."

"Oh."

"Calm down, Chels."

Everyone got in their sleeping bags and rested their heads on their pillows. Peyton waited until everyone else closed their eyes before rolling her own eyes and unrolling her sleeping bag. As everyone else fell asleep, Peyton remained alert, convinced that someone would try to prank her somehow.

In the distance, she could see a hill with rocks on its side. A miniature mountain. There, she spotted a silhouette with antlers. At first, she thought the figure might have been a pile of rocks, or perhaps a statue. But she saw it moving its hand over its mouth, presumably to cover a yawn. Peyton got up, determined to prevent whatever elaborate prank could have been in store for her.

Quietly, she got up from her sleeping bag, not wanting to alert anyone that she was walking away. Everyone else's heads remained still on their pillows. She walked around the back of the hill, where she discovered a hedge with a tunnel. Crouching down, she walked through the short tunnel until she reached the clearing, from where one could overlook the park. There, she saw someone sitting in a metal foldable chair, its back to her. This could only be Stagmantel.

"Not napping, then?" he said without turning his head around.

There was something about his voice that unnerved her. She could not quite place what it was. It sounded human, but also earthly. Not in a personal sense, but in the sense that one might expect from a talking boulder.

"Why don't you turn around?" Peyton asked. "Or are you afraid that those antlers will fall off?"

"They have never fallen off of me within all these years I have inhabited. I ask that you do not threaten me. Otherwise, I might start *caring* about the actions of your kind."

74

"My kind?" Peyton repeated, tilting her head.

"You normies, as I believe you are called now."

"What's a normie?"

"That's something a normie would say."

"Then what the hell are you?"

"A bridge between flesh and stone."

"Are you trolling me?"

"Trolls can dwell under bridges, but there are no trolls here. They dwell elsewhere. Far from here, thankfully."

"How long have you been sitting there?"

"I do not care enough to count. Indifference is key around these parts."

Peyton heard a quack and turned around. Four ducks came out of the tunnel and approached the chair. Still not turning his head, the man reached out with his right hand as a duck examined his fingers, made of dirt that somehow seemed like flesh. Peyton could not help but make the connection in her head.

"Are you a sitting duck?"

Stagmantel turned his head around, revealing his stoic stone-like face. It looked like dirt, and his demeanor seemed very cold. The antlers still stuck to his head. The glowing eyes were unnerving.

This has gotta be a mask, Peyton reasoned to herself.

But the muscle movements in the face made her second-guess.

"Sitting is a hobby of mine, but I do not mind moving around these parts whenever I feel like it."

"Does the school know that a weirdo like you hangs out here?"

"The Landlord and I have an understanding. I don't interfere with the school's affairs, and the school does not interfere with mine."

"What are your affairs?"

"It is just the one, really. We are a bit private about it though. You and I have only just met, and it may not yet time for you to be in the know. A newcomer such as yourself needs time to adjust. Take all the naps that you can. You may find that they will help you catch up to the logic of this place."

Peyton thought she saw a slight smile, but then she reasoned that it must have been some confirmation bias. She still had so many questions.

"Where are you from?" she pressed on.

"From the top."

"What?"

"We will take it from the top once you are ready to know."

"What's your aesthetic?"

"That is enough questions for now. Run along and rest."

Perplexed, Peyton stepped backward toward the tunnel, partially expecting Stagmantel to rise out of the chair quickly and give her a jump scare. But he just remained on his minimalist throne, overlooking the park and its redwoods as ducks waddled around him.

Going back through the hedge tunnel, and trying not to step on any incoming ducks, Peyton still had many questions. But she knew that Stagmantel was reluctant to give her answers. Going back down the hill, she could see the club members still lying on their bedding. A few were napping. Others were simply staring up at the sky. Gertrude was among the latter group. She turned her head to Peyton as she got closer.

"Where'd you go?" Gertrude asked.

Peyton pointed up at the hill.

"Notice anything unusual up there?"

Gertrude sat up and looked in the direction to which Peyton pointed. After a few seconds, she shook her head.

"No. I don't see anything."

Peyton, with her eyes now widened, turned to look at the hill. She could still see Stagmantel, antlers and all, sitting on the chair.

"You don't see him?!"

"Oh! Sorry. I forget this is all new to you. Yeah, I see Stagmantel over there. He likes sitting there. No big deal."

"Doesn't it freak you out?"

"Not really."

"Okay. This has got to be some joke. If he's really what he looks like, then why isn't everyone here more freaked out?"

"You just get used to strangeness around here. And it's not like he does anything wrong. He just walks around as he pleases. Sometimes he walks on the path around the park. I waved at him once, but he didn't wave back. Maybe he didn't see me."

"Or maybe he just didn't care."

"You think?"

"He made a huge deal about indifference."

"Huh. Funny. We kinda like him around here. Apparently he can bring you luck, but I've never really felt the need to get some from him."

"How does he give you luck?"

"Through the ducks."

"The ducks? What the fuck are you talking about?"

"I don't know all the details." Gertrude shrugged. "He could explain it better, probably."

Looking back at the hill, Peyton wanted to ask Stagmantel about the matter of luck. But it seemed like such a long distance away at the moment, and she was feeling tired. So she decided to lay herself down on her bedding, close her eyes, and drift into the undecipherable…

For a little while, she rested soundly, drifting between abstract images of oceans and canyons. And then she saw her sleeping bag. But it was a caterpillar. It rose and became a monolith cocoon. And then it transformed into a butterfly made of dog ears. It flew closer and closer to her face, until it turned into a bat, with lemon slices as wings. A fruit bat, so to speak. Blood dripped out of the citrus slices. And for a moment she could see three silhouetted creatures, with the ocean and a fiery sky behind them. And then something with blue fur emerged from a tunnel below.

A howl woke her up.

"Did you all hear that?" Peyton asked.

"It's a full moon," Randy observed. "Fuck the full moon."

"Does something happen during the full moon?"

"Not that I know of. I'm just tired of it."

"Hey!"

A new young man was running toward them.

"Mitch?" Reginald said.

"I just saw something furry running on all fours between the silver trees." He stopped to take a breath, and then he continued. "It howled. It *howled.* Holy shit, what the hell's going on?"

"You don't think...?" Reginald trailed off.

"Oh, come on, guys," Peyton said. "This isn't funny!"

"I'll say," Grady agreed. "It's downright terrifying. A werewolf at CPU? August never told me about this!"

"A werewolf?" Peyton repeated. "Come on! Y'all expect me to believe this? I bet it was Mitch who howled before coming over here!"

"Hey, I'm just telling you what I heard, whoever you two are."

"I'm Grady."

"Wait, Grady Stuart?"

"Heck yeah!"

"August's cousin? Ah, gimme a hug, bro!"

Grady and Mitch ran up to each other and hugged as friends acting like there was nothing threatening at all in the world.

"Mitch," Reginald said. "You saw this thing lurking among the silver birches?"

"Yeah."

"Okay. I think it's ridiculous to say it's a werewolf."

"Thank you!" Peyton said. "See? Werewolves aren't real."

"Oh, I'm not saying they're not real. I'm just saying that they can't be around silver."

"What?"

"The silver birches. Werewolves can't be around silver. They're allergic. Trust me. I'm a bio-sci major."

"Hang on," Randy said. "Are they allergic to silver the metal, or silver the color?"

"Huh," Reginald said, scratching his head. "I actually hadn't considered that."

Peyton facepalmed. She noticed that Randy looked down at the ground when she did this. Brushing aside the observation, she decided that she wanted to end this far-fetched speculation.

"Fine. I'll bite."

"You *will* if you become one," Mitch said.

"Hush! I'm gonna head over there and see what it is. Don't you *dare* follow me. I mean it."

"This is how people die in movies," Randy said. "And in real life."

"Nothing's gonna happen!"

"Nice knowing you," Shelley said. Chelsea tried elbowing her again, but then Shelley did a back flip and avoided the attack.

"Where'd you learn to do that?" Chelsea asked.

"I dream big," Shelley said with a shrug.

"Peyton," Gertrude said. "Are you sure you wanna go alone?"

"If I scream, then y'all can come to my rescue. Trust me. There's nothing threatening out here."

Peyton walked away from them as quickly as possible. When she got to the other section of the park, she noticed how much darker the night sky was getting, and she regretted her decision.

A honk startled her. Looking around, she noticed geese walking about.

Twigs snapped.

A four-legged shadow jumped between trees in the distance. A bush rustled. And then out leaped an animal that she recognized right away: Mandy the Mantleope.

"Pam? Is that you?"

Mandy's head then got removed, revealing Pamela within the costume.

"Hi!"

"Damn it, Pam! I thought my friends were playing a prank on me."

"Oh. I'm sorry." Her voice got quieter, and she looked down, her foot sweeping the ground. "I know that must be tough. Didn't mean for you to feel that way."

"What are you doing out here at night? If you could be here, then you could've come with me to hang out with the Nap Kin!"

"Well, I wanted to hang out here in costume, and I can't let your friends know who I am. Plus, I already have a friend here."

"Who?"

Peyton looked around and saw a woman with glowing white eyes and a horn on her forehead descending from the hill.

"Welcome to my side of Petal Lock Park."

"Your side? Oh, I get it. You're the ever legendary Unicoren." Peyton bowed insincerely. "Pleased to meet you, I'm not worthy, et cetera."

"Peyton!" Pamela said. "Stop being rude!"

"So this is your sister," Unicoren said.

"What have you told her about me?" Peyton asked Pamela.

"Nothing! I just mentioned we're living together. You know, normal sister stuff."

Peyton turned back to Unicoren.

"You know him, don't you? Stagmantel?"

"You have met him," Unicoren replied with a nod.

"Yeah. I'm trying to figure out what his deal is, but he says some napping might help me understand." She tried to recall the dream, but barely any of it was retained in her memory. "Any idea what a dream about a butterfly made of dog ears means?"

"Dreams can just be dreams. They do not have to mean anything. Stagmantel was just feeling reluctant to tell you a lot."

"Because it's too much for me to handle?"

"Too much for *him*, rather. When he sits upon the chair, he prefers not to speak too much. But if you catch him walking about, he is more open."

"And I guess you're not gonna give me answers either."

"I do not feel the need to, but I also see no harm in answering whatever questions you may ask. It makes no difference to me."

"Okay then..." Peyton dug through her mind, trying to figure out where to begin. "So, what's the deal with there being two sides the park, one with ducks and one with geese?"

"My side is the right brain. You will find such schools bordering the eastern side of of the pathway. Stagmantel's side is the left brain. You will find the other schools near there."

"Huh. I guess I haven't paid too much attention to the campus map. And you two just, what, live here? How does that work? They just let you?"

"We have an understanding with Chancellor Moseley."

"Why did he let you live here?"

"He allowed us to live here as long as we were okay with Mandy being the mascot."

"You came up with Mandy the Mantleope?"

"With Stagmantel, yes. But the chancellor provided her name, as well as mine and Stagmantel's. I cannot recall what our original names were. The chancellor leased this land to us in exchange for Mandy, our greatest contribution to this school. Whenever people see Mandy jumping around and being peppy at games and events, their spirits are lifted. That is, as long as they are *open* to having their spirits lifted."

"That sounds very ominous and weird and I'm not sure how I feel about that."

"I just meant that people can be happy if they allow themselves to be happy."

"Do you allow yourself to be happy?"

"I allow myself to be in between." She lifted her hands up toward the sky. "Up here is what it feels like to be full of happiness." She then reached downward as if to touch her toes. "Down here is what it feels like to be full of sorrow."

"Honestly," Pamela chimed in, "I'd rather just be happy all the time."

"For me," Unicoren continued, "to be very happy most of the time just makes the sad moments stand out more. And I do not want to be sad, with or without happiness. So I stay in between."

"Right here?" Peyton said. "In the park between all the different schools?"

"Yes."

Peyton noticed some geese walking by. She paid attention to the patterns on their feathers.

"Are these Egyptian geese?"

"They are of no particular breed. But when they saw the form of the Egyptian goose, they took on its colors. They had visions of all the different breeds, and this is the form they chose."

"Why are they all the same? Couldn't each of them have been a different type of goose? Or even a different type of bird?"

"They are unified. When you think about it, we may all as well be the same person going in circles..."

"You're gonna bring the word 'infinite' into this spiel, aren't you?"

"You are so quick to interject when you are in the process of obtaining answers."

"Yep," Pamela said. "That's my sister, all right."

"I'm sorry," Peyton said. "This is all just so...unusual to me. And people tell me I'll get used to it, but I feel out of place." Peyton focused on Unicoren's glowing eyes. "Don't *you* and Stagmantel feel out of place?"

"Not as long as we are *both* here."

"Right. How crazy is a school with a tornado if there are *two* tornadoes? Am I right?"

"Right brain."

"Heh. Guess you have a bit of a sense of humor."

"It happens unintentionally. But I have been told that the best humor is sometimes unintentional."

"Well, guess I better head back to the Nap Kin. They might be worried about me. Or not. I don't know."

"I'll see you later," Pamela said.

"How late are you gonna be out here?"

"I don't know. As long as I want."

"You can't be out here too long. Please come back to the dorm as soon as you can. If you're not there before midnight, I'm gonna do something about it."

"Relax. I won't be here long. Just another hour. I'll meet you at the dorm."

"Fine."

They parted ways for the moment. When Peyton returned to the Nap Kin, she wanted to tell them about Pamela, but she said she saw nothing, and that the park was probably safe. Once the Nap Kin meeting was over, the members went to their respective homes, leaving the park bathed in the full moonlight.

* * *

Stagmantel watched the students depart. Once they were gone, a familiar presence came through the hedge tunnel: Mathias. It was dark, but through his glowing eyes, Stagmantel could see the colors of the peacock feathers on the front of Chancellor Moseley's bowler hat. The patterns of the feathers resembled an extra pair of eyes. To mirror the pattern, the shades he wore over his eyes had dark blue glass and lime green frames. The chancellor also wore a black grad robe, which was unzipped to reveal an outfit with colors that conformed to the peacock pattern: dark blue formal slacks, a green dress shirt, and necktie with both of those colors forming many peacock feather eyes. And he also wore black dress shoes.

"Same question as always, I expect," Stagmantel anticipated. "Yes, I *have* seen the new mascot. And given your routine, I suppose you have disposed of the *others* who auditioned."

"Some were chicken, and some were mine. I had some company with which to dine. Though one candidate joined that company. Just one, so that there are not too many."

He removed his shades, revealing milky white eyes mirroring the moon and its light.

"Discarding your disguise," Stagmantel acknowledged.

"Too much color in this world alone. I am in need of my *Twilight Zone.*"

Stagmantel noticed something different about him.

"Did you use makeup to cover up that scar?"

"I wanted to see how it would feel," he answered with a nod. "Tell me, does the skin look real?"

"I suppose. Putting on makeup, then. One would think you would have to see yourself for that. How do you *do* it?"

Mathias gave him a scowl, not appreciating his wordplay. He hissed and then took an amulet out of his pants pocket. It was made of a clear cassette tape, though no reel was within it. He held it up toward the sky so that the moon could shine into it, turning the tape into a solid, glowing white.

"These worlds used to be one. But then you decided to run. Oh, the moon separated, a high cost. Oh, to have a part of yourself out of reach and lost. I ferried you out of a stagnant hell. And now, here you remain, Stagmantel."

"You changed that last syllable to conform to your rhyme. Sounds like you are getting rusty."

"Maybe I should just see you as a fool, and refer to you as Staman-*tool.*"

Stagmantel remained undeterred despite these words. He avoided further eye contact with the chancellor, who stood for a minute until the amulet was fully lit. He put it back in his pocket.

"Well, I have my pack to feed. They sure do wish to be freed."

Chapter 9
Still Water, Still Matter

The second full week of October was August's reading week, during which he had time to catch up on class readings. Of course, many students used their reading weeks to travel somewhere for a vacation. And so he decided to book a solo trip through the Scotland highlands.

The day before his scheduled departure, he had lunch at Paul A. Table Cafe. Not too many tables were full, so it was not too busy. He ordered bagels with cream cheese and seared salmon, with beans smothered in tomato sauce on the side. He also had a cup of hot chocolate with whipped cream on top. Once he was finished with his meal, the waitress returned. He wiped his mouth with a napkin before speaking.

"Thanks for recommending the seared salmon, Ella," August said to her. "I never would've thought to try it with cream cheese."

"I always tell people about the good stuff. It's a shame, really, that it's taken you this long."

"Better late than never." He set the napkin on the plate, which still had some beans covered in tomato sauce.

"Not too keen on the beans, I see."

"Well, I mean..." August smiled nervously and scratched his chin.

"It's okay. You can be honest. It's a bit shit, isn't it?"

August chuckled, and then he found a way out of this particular corner of the conversation.

"That's another thing I love about this country. 'It's a bit shit, isn't it?' has alliteration and is so fun to say!"

"Alliteration is a bit shit."

"And 'a bit shit' is alliteration."

"Fair enough," Ella said with a smile. "You ever think of becoming a food critic?"

"I probably wouldn't be nuanced enough. It does sound like a fun job. My friend Fritz is the food snob. The other day, he went on a rant about eggs after a carton of them went missing from his fridge."

"Sounds like you've made some interesting friends. You see some sights with them?"

"Some. We checked out the London Eye and some smaller things. I'm actually heading to Scotland tomorrow. I asked people when their reading weeks would be and whether they'd be free. And I didn't mean for that to rhyme."

"I won't hold that against you, then."

"Oh good. I thought for sure I just ruined a conversation. Heh. But yeah, they didn't get back to me. So I just assumed everyone was busy, and I needed to book this trip as soon as possible, while spots were available."

"Should be fun. Scotland's amazing."

"Yeah. I'm really looking forward to it."

* * *

When the day of the trip arrived, August took a plane to Edinburgh, the city from where the tour bus was set to depart. During his travels through the Scotland highlands, he was surrounded by company on the bus, but they were all strangers. He was normally sociable, but something within him kept telling him to keep to himself.

They could all be in on it, he kept hearing in a mental voice that did not sound like his own. But he was not sure what the people could be in on; he was stumped.

They stopped at various destinations throughout the week, hiking through green mountainsides. Even when it rained. August was thankful that he had his waterproof hiking boots to keep him from slipping. The rain did not bother him much. Somehow, it made him feel one with the elements of nature. Like he was an amphibian who could rise to the challenge of climbing the rocks that the earth offered him. He wondered what it would be like for the rocks to rise, with rain greeting the fire far beneath.

Now he was just thinking of what it might have been like to be on Miunis Grund— the original, unbroken planet—when the cataclysmic event occurred. The story fascinated him because of how fantastical and cinematic it sounded. In a seemingly commonplace planet such as Earth, it was difficult to imagine the sight and feel of the event.

The rain stopped falling by the time the bus reached Loch Ness one day. Once there, August looked into the waters that were fodder for legends. He saw no monster, but he had his eyes fixed on his own reflection in the still water. He felt like he was supposed remember something.

"What if our reflection in the water *is* the Loch Ness Monster?" he mused aloud. "Nessie... Bessie..." Amused, he wondered whether Bessie from the hotel would be okay with having the monster's name as a sobriquet. But the more he thought about the two names, the more the second syllable of each one stuck out. In his reflection, he noticed the bracelet on his wrist. And then the thought hit him like lightning on a key. "Cassie!"

His pen pal. They were supposed to meet at the hotel during orientation, but he did not remember seeing her there. And yet he had the strong feeling that this bracelet had something to do with her. There may not have been a monster in the loch, but in this moment, he was engulfed by fear, far-flung and far away from both his temporary home at the hotel and his permanent home in the States. Lost in a state of helplessness.

* * *

Cassie wondered whether there was a monster in the doorknob's lock, and whether she was in fact in the doorknob or within the room on the other side.

She was not sure how long it had been since she last saw August. It had definitely been long enough for her to work up an appetite. She had a raw egg now and then, in this cold, cold place. She felt like she was in a fridge, but there was more space around her. Maybe it *was* the room that she had been assigned. But she could not tell. She was not even sure how eggs were entering this place.

It was like she was floating in darkness, with no clue where she was. Whenever she tried to move her hands around, it felt like there was nothing around her and barely any movement at all. She could not feel her own face even when she knew that her hands were on it. Her whole body felt numb.

The only time she physically felt something was when she put her right hand on her left wrist where the friendship bracelet was. She could feel its material, giving her hope that she was still matter and that she still mattered. Though time was immeasurable, she hoped that it had not been too long since she saw August. He had seen her disappear.

He's probably working on finding me, she thought.

Cassie did not speak aloud. She was not sure whether she was simply incapable of speaking, or whether she was too afraid to say anything at all. Doing so could have alerted some unknown presence about where she was. Somehow, she felt alone and not alone at the same time. Even in the dark, she suspected that something was watching her. Something cruel. Something evil. Something unnatural. She was afraid to find out what it was. Part of her wanted it to say something just to confirm her fears, but another part of her wanted it to remain a mystery so that she could at least pretend that there was nothing else near her.

But if there's nothing, how will I be found?

* * *

August spent the tail end of his trip trying to get ahold of Cassie. He messaged her, asking how she was and explaining that he was in Scotland at the moment. But nothing indicated that the messages had been received and read. He felt guilty being out on an adventure, knowing he had not managed to get in touch with Cassie. Surely they should have encountered one another at the hotel this far into the term. He did not understand how she could have slipped his mind, and he questioned why she would not have tried contacting him to meet up in the hotel.

Once he returned to Tree Culler, he noticed Bessie just as she was about to walk up the stairwell from the lobby.

"Bessie," August said.

She turned around, standing on two stairs.

"Oh. Hey August."

"I just remembered something." He walked closer to her. "My friend Cassie mentioned that she'd hung out with you."

"Cassie?" she repeated, her face scrunched up, looking confused.

"I think I may have talked to her when we first got here. I vaguely remember her saying she crashed in your room."

Bessie looked up diagonally as if the answers were on the ceiling.

"I remember crashing..." Bessie faced him again. "But I don't remember any Cassie."

"You're sure?"

"Yeah. I'm sorry. The name doesn't ring a bell."

"Hang on."

August took out his cell phone and pulled up Cassie's profile pic. Her face as he remembered it. He held the screen up for Bessie to see.

"Uh..." Bessie uttered.

"You recognize her?"

"I don't see her."

"What?" August looked at the screen. Cassie's face was gone, and in its place was just a frame filled with all white. He tried refreshing her profile page, but it did not take him anywhere. "I don't understand. I could see her before..." He clicked repeatedly. "Now it's not letting me click her profile."

"Maybe she blocked you?"

August looked up from his phone, his mouth open in worry.

"Why would she do that?"

"I don't know. But you definitely need to charge your battery."

She was right. The battery icon showed only 10% remaining, when just a few minutes prior it had been at 50%.

"Would you excuse me?" August said, squeezing past her to run up the stairwell.

August left his phone in his room to charge, and then he went back downstairs, to sit in the dining room all day. He was there for a while, hoping to see Cassie walk in at some point. He thought about asking the receptionist which room was Cassie's, but he was afraid of looking like a stalker. He wanted nothing to cut his study abroad experience short. Paranoid and confused, he sat at the table for hours. As time passed, people came in and out, even sitting at other tables for a while, working on school assignments and eating snacks.

At one point, Anton and Fritz ended up sitting with him, so he could not help but listen to their conversation.

"So you don't like black pudding?" Anton asked.

"No," Fritz answered. "All that blood? I've always found it *off-putting*."

"I hate you," Anton said with a smile restraining a laugh. "You know, I had a revelation while dipping strawberries in chocolate fondue. The prints were on the plate. The proof was in the pudding. Strawberries and octopi are the same. The Beatles were onto something."

"Is it octopuses or octopi?" Fritz asked.

"Not sure. Either way, I could go for some strawberry pie."

"You ever try chocolate covered carrots?"

"Cool carrots! That could be a new thing, like cool beans."

"What about cool veggies?"

"Eh. That wouldn't quite cut it. Not like, say, 'Cut the cheese.'"

"You know," August chimed in, "I never understood the expression 'cool beans' until I tried the sweet ones covered in tomato sauce here. Well, *most* have been good here."

"Oh yeah," Fritz said. "The best beans I've ever had have probably been from around here."

Jade came down from her room. August was surprised; he hardly ever saw her in the dining area. It seemed that she preferred to be somewhat recluse in her room. She walked over to the shelves by the kitchen doorway and grabbed a cup of raw ramen from her shelf. August got up from the table and walked over to her.

"Jade," August said. "Have you seen anyone here named Cassie?"

"Cassie?" Jade said. "Cassie... No. I don't think I have. I'm probably the worst person to ask. Why?"

"Cassie Julura is a pen pal of mine."

"Oh. That's cute."

"Well, no physical writing. We message each other online about birds."

"Birds?"

"Yeah. Pigeons, peacocks, pelicans, nightjars, you name it."

"Uh-huh. Almost had an alliteration streak there."

"Alliteration's a bit shit."

"Carnival enough."

"Anyway, we found out we'd be going to the same school here. We even got allocated into the same hotel. It's hard to tell whether I dreamed this, but I may have seen her here during the first week. I can't remember where, and I haven't seen her around here since."

"That's weird."

"And she hasn't been responding to my messages. Doesn't say she's read them."

"Well, if I meet a Cassie around here, I'll let you know."

"All right. Cool carrots."

Bessie swung the kitchen doors open and walked into the dining area.

"All right, everyone!" Students at different tables turned to look at her. "Someone took my pan, and I wanna know who did it!" She looked at Anton and Fritz and pointed fingers at them. "Was it either of you? Were two pans not enough for your shenanigans?"

"We haven't been here all week," Fritz said.

"How convenient! Where were you?"

"We took a trip to Scotland," Anton said.

"No way!" August said. "I took a trip to Scotland, too! I went solo because I wasn't sure if anyone else was interested."

"Oh yeah," Verner said, walking into the room. "I meant to tell you I was interested in going, but I forgot and thought it was too late to tell you. So I went by myself."

"I went by myself on purpose," Jade said with a shrug.

"Wait a minute," Bessie said. "So you all went to Scotland separately?" Those who had spoken nodded. "Great planning. You're all *very* good at coordinating with each other."

"I didn't go to Scotland," Tate said as he came out of the kitchen.

"Aha!" Bessie pointed an accusatory finger at him.

"I went to Paris with my girlfriend and proposed to her."

"Oh." Bessie disarmed herself. "Well, what did she say?"

"I don't wanna talk about it."

Tate started to walk out of the dining room and toward the lift.

"Oh, Tate, wait up," August said.

"Piss off! Go drink a special!"

He pressed the lift button repeatedly until he got into the lift and left.

"Anyway," Bessie continued, "I'd very much appreciate it if the thief returned it. Because stealing stuff is messed up!"

With that, Bessie stormed off to the stairwell.

"Wow," August said. "Can't find Cassie, then Bessie can't find her pan..."

"You think there's some correlation?" Jade asked.

"That's ridiculous. Why would they have anything to do with each other?"

"Maybe Cassie took the pan and is hiding out."

"No. You don't know her like I do."

"Look, I know you two were pen pals, but even friends who see each other in person keep secrets from each other."

"But it seems so unlike her."

"I'm sorry to drop this on you, August, but do you know what's up with your friends back home? Do they let you in on everything that's going on with them?"

August was taken aback. But now that he thought about it, he realized that he had not heard from anyone back home. Not even his cousin Grady, other than that time that August had told him about that first trip to Unsoberquet.

"Well," August began, "I just have to initiate."

August reached into his pocket, but his phone was not there.

"Oh. I left my phone upstairs."

August left the dining room and pressed the button by the lift. As it was coming down, he remembered that Randy's birthday was coming up. He wanted to ask his friends whether they had anything planned for him. The previous year, August was the one who reminded them about when Randy's birthday was.

When the lift doors opened, he went inside. After the doors closed, it went up to the third floor.

But the doors did not open. And the lights went out, making the space pitch black. August reached for his pocket, but then remembered that he did not have his phone.

"Shit!" He knocked on the door. "Help! Get me out of here!"

The lights turned back on. And there, in the three mirrors that surrounded him, he saw the face he had seen before in the lavatory.

"AH!"

Three was just too much. The doors opened, and he ran to his room. He did not question why he was entering his room. He just wanted to be safely away from the lift. He got inside and grabbed his phone from his desk, wanting to dial a number immediately. But then he heard a sound. Cell in hand, he checked the mirror in his bathroom. The face was absent, but then it appeared. He screamed again, running out of his room and into the hallway, trying not to trip going down three flights of stairs.

When he got to the lobby, he forgot why he was there. Looking at his phone, he could not recall why he wanted to use it. He remembered not having it on him previously, so it seemed possible for him to have grabbed it to not feel naked without it.

He saw Verner walk out of the dining area. August had something to say. Something he felt was very important.

"I'm hungry."

"I agree," Verner said. "You wanna go to Unsoberquet?"

"Sure!"

They crossed the street and entered the pub. The purple room upstairs was out of seats, so they had no choice but to remain on the noisier floor. After much eating and drinking beneath the green lights, their conversations devolved into nonsense.

"I have an idea for a show," Verner said, his voice raised just enough for August to hear. "So you know how you hear about people who drink, black out, and end up somewhere else entirely?"

"Yeah yeah yeah!"

"Well, what if their drink actually took them to an alternate universe? A world that looks the same but has something different about it. It would be called *Ciders*. Good, yeah?"

"Greenlit!" August said, pointing up at the green lights and laughing. "It actually sounds vaguely familiar, but I'm too buzzed to comparehend!"

They continued to laugh, sip, and sit as people around them danced to music in the green room. People moved around, and so did time. August could not keep track of the time. As he stared into space, he felt his heart leap now and then. Part of him wondered whether it had to do with the drinking, but he knew, deep down, that he was scared. And not knowing what it was that scared him was very terrifying. Hardly able to speak audibly to Verner amidst all the noise, his mind wandered backward in time...

School has just ended. August is in fourth grade, and Grady is in first grade. They meet up with each other by the parking lot as they normally do. It is August's responsibility to walk Grady home on the way to his own home. A recent development, but a routine. In front of the school, they walk through a crowd of students and parents. And when August makes it to the other side, he turns around and sees that Grady is gone.

Frantically, he searches for his cousin. But he cannot see his face within the crowd. He asks around whether anyone has seen him, but his description does not help. August does not know what to do. He is scared of disappointing his parents, who have called him perfect time and time again.

So he runs down the street, the usual route he and Grady use. To a first grader like Grady, this path probably looks big and daunting.

August turns the usual corner and is startled by a barking dog behind a fence. It must be new, seeing as how he and Grady have never encountered it while walking this way. Though the hound is not visible behind the wood, the barking bores into his mind, and he worries about how Grady might feel walking this way all alone. August imagines what Grady would do: run.

August runs, and then he finally catches up to Grady's house, where he sees his cousin standing in front of the lawn.

"Grady!" August says, running toward him.

Grady turns around.

"I did it," he says. "I got home all by myself!"

"Don't scare me like that again! What happened?"

"I tried following you, but then I didn't see you. I thought you left without me."

"Why would I leave without you?"

"I don't know. I was scared. I couldn't find you, and I didn't know where to go. So I came home. I thought maybe if I got here, my mom and dad could help me find you."

"Have you talked to them yet?"

"No. I just got here."

August looks at the young boy. So innocent. And it makes him feel guilty about what he is going to ask of him.

"Grady, I don't wanna make you do this, but..." August trails off, trying to find the words.

"Don't," Grady says. "I won't tell them. I don't want you to get in trouble."

August sighs. A secret, and it seems a bit wrong. It is then that August knows himself to not be perfect. But he is sure that his parents will continue to perceive him this way.

"I'm sorry," August says.

"Don't worry. It's both our fault. Anyway, you're not always gonna be around to watch me, right? I've gotta grow up sometime."

August laughs.

"Just don't be in too much of a rush. And don't keep on lying. Not too much. My mom and dad say it's important to be honest about who you are. You understand?"

"Yeah."

They continue on toward the house.

"Did you see a dog on your way here?" August asks.

"I didn't see it. But I could hear it. And that was spooky enough."

These words stuck to August, who could not see the memories of what scared him about the hotel. But he could hear the screaming echoing far away in his head.

Chapter 10
Open Up, Open Down

Randy wanted to confide in August about his feelings for Naomi. But anytime he thought about doing so, he remembered that August had not taken the time to contact him and see how he was doing.

Randy did, however, receive contact from his parents on this Sunday night. They wanted him to come home for the upcoming weekend, but he did not want to risk being followed by some minion of Mathis, who could then attack his family. Naturally, he used school work as an excuse. It seemed pretty commonplace to have a heavy workload at universities, so his parents bought it. But he could tell that they were a bit disappointed. He felt sorry, knowing that there was the possibility that this could be his last birthday if things proceeded as planned. He was still somewhat on the fence, not having progressed in figuring out the Naomi aspect. But in either case, he had to be strong enough to face Mathis Dillard.

Randy stood in the darkness of his room, doing isometric exercises. He had seen videos of various exercises, and these seemed simple enough. He wanted to build muscle before facing Mathis, and this seemed like the easiest way to start. He was not comfortable being seen exercising at the gym. And he especially did not want to tip off the photographer, whom he was certain worked for Mathis and would probably spy on him in the gym if he went there.

His arms horizontal, he pressed his hands against each other for ten seconds, his chest vibrating. Then he changed the configuration, rotating one hand clockwise and the other counter. Ten more seconds. Then he crossed his arms against his chest, pressing an elbow against a hand. Ten more seconds. Hand and elbow switched. Ten more seconds. Then he raised a leg so that he could cradle his knee. Ten more seconds. Leg switch. Ten more seconds. He sat on the floor. Criss-cross applesauce. Like that game of Duck, Duck, Goose in Kindergarten, when nobody picked him to be the goose. When nobody threw a bone to the dog who wanted to be walked.

Feet pressed against each other. Ten more seconds. Isometrics and measurements of ten in a metric system.

He examined his results, clenching his fists and wanting so badly for the skin on his arms to be more muscular.

Stronger, he assessed.

He wanted to be the chosen goose, and chase Mathis as if he were a duck for him to prey upon.

Magnify, he aimed.

To be the attack dog on guard, protecting people from evil. To be strengthened by this new ritual. *This* was his ritual.

STRONGER.

* * *

Meanwhile, in the night-filled Petal Lock Park, Pamela, dressed as Mandy, met with Unicoren once again. This time, she was not as active. Her thoughts would not stop dwelling on her sister, and she wanted to vent everything out.

"I feel like Peyton looks at me with contempt when she sees me in this costume. Even though she can't see my eyes with this on, I can feel her gaze stabbing them with judgment. I don't know. Sometimes I wonder if I'm being too dramatic."

"Peyton has yet to understand how important Mandy is to people."

"I don't think she even *tries* to understand. Whenever I bring it up, she rolls her eyes. We weren't always like this, you know. We were closer when we were younger. I remember we were on a train with our dad. I was two and she was five. And we were just playing around, having the time of our lives."

Pamela let her mind drift through time as she explained the memory...

Pamela and Peyton sit across from their father, beside the window of the train, green scenery passing by. Their dad has his newspaper rolled up tightly. He uses it to stir the air and swing it a little as if to hit an invisible piñata.

"I am the warlock, and you two are about to be cursed! Zap!"

"Look out!" Peyton says, sidestepping to dodge the imaginary zap.

Pamela gets out of her seat and stands in front of her sister.

"I'll protect you, Peyton!"

Another zap, and Pamela catches it in her hand, throwing it to the window.

"We all used to pretend, in a fun way. Now we all just pretend like everything's all right."

"Then something changed," Unicoren said.

"You've got that right. A couple of years later, Mom and Dad got me this stuffed animal. A purple monkey. And then I was eight when things changed. I don't even wanna think about it."

"You don't have to."

"It's hard to stop it. So much change. There comes a point when you can't carry all the coins."

The coins went into the slot, activating another memory...

Pamela wears her purple unicorn onesie. She also has two unicorn slippers, each with a horn. The left one is white and the right one is blue. She carries her purple monkey, making her fly in the air of the living room. Her sister enters the room. Pamela is excited, perceiving Peyton as a potential playmate.

"The backyard is sunny!" Pamela says with a smile. "Do you wanna play with us?"

"Not really."

The smile fades.

"But...Peyton. We always play."

"I just don't feel like it."

"Well, later, then?" She holds up the monkey. "Aster and I can wait."

"Pam, it's a stuffed animal. It can wait forever."

"Don't talk about her like that, meanie!"

"That's what it is."

"You're a stuffed animal!"

"Ugh. Grow up."

"Grow up."

"Huh?"

"Huh?"

"Real mature."

"Real mature!"

"Shut up, copycat!"

"Open down!"

"What?"

"Not copying you! See? Open down Sesame Street. Open down!"

"The heck is that supposed to mean?"

"Like 'Open Sesame' and the opposite of 'shut up.'"

"Wow. So dumb."

Pamela gasps.

"That's a bad word! Don't call me that!"

"Too late! It's already happened. I win."

Peyton turns away and walks up the stairs to their room. Pamela waits until she knows for sure that her sister is out of sight before she cries softly.

"Peyton thinks she wins..." Pamela wipes her face. "We weren't even playing..."

"Let's go to the park," Aster says.

"I don't know if I wanna anymore."

"It'll be fun. I promise."

Pamela nods. She has no playmate other than Aster. So she leaves her house without giving a word to her family.

She runs for four blocks. There is a bit of fear, but also a bit of a thrill, going down the street without the guidance of her family.

Pamela and Aster make it to the park. There are people there, but Pamela does not know them. She is shy, keeping to herself and Aster. She looks down at her unicorn slippers.

"What's the matter?" Aster asks.

"I wish that we had more friends."

"I have plenty. Would you like me to introduce you?"

"But they're strangers."

"All right. Familiar friends then."

To Pamela's eyes, her slippers come off and turn into boys her age wearing unicorn onesies, the same colors as the slippers.

"I'm Junior!" says the boy in blue.

"And I'm Cory!" says the boy in white.

"Wow!"

"What do you want to do?" Aster asks.

"Let's race to the end!"

Pamela takes off, the boys managing to keep up with her, running parallel. The air is exhilarating. They run up a hill. This is the tough part, but then running down the other side is a breeze. And then they make it to the sidewalk, beside which a familiar car has parked. Her mom exits the car.

"Pamela!" she calls. "You had us worried! You can't just go to the park all by yourself!"

"But Aster was watching me, and we were playing with friends!"

"Aster is not a responsible adult!"

"Yes she is! She says she's so old that she's lost count of her age!"

"What friends were you playing with?"

"Junior and Cory," she answers, pointing down at her slippers.

Her mom does not say a word about the slippers. Instead, she points to the backseat, and Pamela gets inside. Though the drive is not long, there is an uncomfortable silence. Pamela knows that her mom is deep in thought about the situation, and it frightens her.

They return to the house. Her mom takes the monkey from her.

"You cannot play with Aster anymore."

"That's not fair!"

"You've taken this too far. This monkey didn't tell you to leave the house."

"Yes she did!"

"No. You thought of doing it and pretended it was Aster who said it. But she doesn't talk to you."

"She talks to me all the time! Give her back!"

"Pamela, this isn't funny!"

"I never said it was funny! Aster is my friend, and she's nicer than you, meanie!"

"This is just a stuffed animal!"

"She's not a stuffed animal!" Pamela reaches for the tail and successfully grasps it, beginning a tug of war. "You and Peyton are the same! All you want is for me to be sad! Aster talks to me! Let her go!"

"I have to keep you from running away!"

"If you take her away, I'll run away anyway!"

The tug of war intensifies, and then a rip happens. The monkey is torn in half. To Pamela, it feels like a rip in time and space. It horrifies her to see the white cotton guts spilling out of the monkey's torso.

"See?" her mom says. "It's stuffing."

"You ruined her! Aster! Can you hear me?" Not a sound. "You killed my best friend! I hate you! I wish you were never my mom!"

"Pamela, grow the fuck up!"

Pamela falls silent. Her mom covers her mouth with both hands. But it is too late to take back the words. Both of them let what remain of

Aster fall to the floor. Pamela starts to tear up, and her mom tries to speak up.

"Pam, I'm sorry."

"You cursed... You cursed me, Mom!"

Pamela runs upstairs to her room. Peyton is in there, much to Pamela's displeasure.

"Get out!"

"Pam?"

Pamela pulls on Peyton's arm, bringing her to the doorway.

"Get out of here!"

"This is my room, too! You can't just kick me out!"

"You ruined everything!"

Pamela pushes Peyton out of the room, so hard that Peyton falls down the stairs. When Peyton reaches the floor, Pamela is worried for the brief moment when there is no movement.

"Ow!" *Peyton groans.*

Her parents rush over to Peyton.

"Peyton?" *their dad says.*

"My arm! My arm hurts!"

"Honey," *their mom says their dad,* "take her to the hospital."

Not knowing what to do, Pamela runs back into the room and locks the door. With her back against the door, she slides down into a sitting position, and cradles her crying head into her arms.

A knock on the door, and then the unwelcome voice of her mom.

"Pamela?"

"Go away!"

"Pamela, you really hurt your sister."

"She started it! She stopped being my sister!"

"That's not true. We're all family. I was out of line saying what I said to you, and I'm sorry. I can't give Aster back to you, but I want you to know I'm sorry. You need to let go, but it was still no excuse for what I said. A parent should never have to say that to their child. I know you're *mad at me now, but I know you'll forgive me. It's part of becoming a big kid."*

"I eventually acted like everything was fine," Pamela explained to Unicoren. "But, if I'm being honest with myself, I think she was a terrible mother in that moment. And it's hard for me to separate that from how I see her now. Dad didn't really help. He took her side, saying that what she'd done was terrible but that I'd have to forgive her."

She looked at Unicoren, who now seemed deep in thought about something else. But what she said next still seemed relevant.

"It can be difficult to keep a family together after such a traumatic event."

"Do you have a family?"

"I am not sure. Am I forgiven?"

Pamela was overcome with a feeling, like she knew something that needed to be said.

"Something tells me you are."

Chapter 11
Off His Hours

The next day, the Nap Kin had their lunch together in the food court. Peyton was despondent, barely biting into her bean and cheese burrito, which was falling apart.

"Where's Mitch?" Grady asked.

"He just messaged me," Reginald said. "Says he's logging out."

"Using the library computers to study?"

"No. It means he's taking a shit."

"Oh."

Peyton looked over at Shelley, who was eating a sandwich. The crust pieces remained on her plate. She wrapped them in a paper towel. Chelsea spoke up.

"Why are you hiding the fact that you didn't eat the crust?"

"I'm not hiding it! This is preliminary crumpling up of a paper towel full of trash!"

"The core matters most."

"Huh?"

"Something Unicoren always says."

"Ugh," Peyton uttered.

"Something wrong?" Chelsea asked.

"What makes you think something's wrong?"

"Your burrito is shitting," Shelley said. "It's spilling the beans."

Peyton looked at her mess of a burrito and then set it down. She figured that there was no harm in fighting the desire to spill her feelings.

"Just some sister stuff."

"Wanna talk about it?"

"I mean, do any of *you* have sisters?"

"I do," Randy answered. "She's ten."

"Well, mine *acts* like she's ten, even though she's eighteen. She's a freshman here, but all she does is play around in the park. Sometimes I think she'd be more normal if it weren't for that Mantle—"

She paused and felt a nervous heat wash over her.

"Hold the cell," Chelsea said. "Your sister is Mandy the Mantleope?"

"Shit," Peyton said, facepalming. "Please don't tell anyone."

"Our lips are sealed," Gertrude said. "Right everyone?"

The others nodded.

"She'd probably be mad about this. Damn it! I don't know what to do about her."

Gertrude put a hand on Peyton's shoulder. It was Naomi's hand, since Naomi was sitting right next to Peyton.

"You could've just gotten up, Yo-Gert," Naomi said.

"Peyton," Gertrude began, "it's times like these when you need to turn to some open ears who can give you some advice."

"Thanks. I really appreci—"

"Let's go to office hours."

"Huh?"

"To see Professor Mortimer."

"Who?"

"We had him freshman year," Reginald explained, wiping his mouth with a napkin before continuing. "We got clumped into a study group for his class. We wouldn't have started this Nap Kin club without him."

"Is he your club's adviser?"

"No. We all fell asleep studying the textbook for his class and then came up with the idea."

Once they were finished with their food, they walked over to the building containing offices of history teachers. They knocked on the door of Professor Martin Mortimer. He opened it enthusiastically.

"Finally! Welcome to office hours! How may I...hell?" He paused, removed his glasses, wiped them with his sleeve, and then put them back on. "Damn. Of course it's you. It's *always* you kids. Haven't you graduated yet?"

"We don't graduate 'til next year, Old Timer," Naomi reminded him.

"I keep telling you I'm not old; I'm in my forties!"

"Still?"

"Yes! I turn forty-six tomorrow."

"Oh, that's right! Your birthday's on the twenty-first. Anyway, Fortimer, you're in luck! We have a couple new faces in our group, so they might need to come to you after we leave."

"Oh goodie. Look, whatever it is, I don't have time for it. There could be other students who want help with their course work."

Four new students walked up to the door.

"Professor," one of them said. "We have questions about the group project."

"No problem! Step into my office and I'll give you all the help you need."

"Come on, Fortimer," Naomi said.

"I'm sorry, but help needs to be a two-way street, and I don't get a whole lot out of helping you Crap Kin. You haven't had my class in three years, and I'm putting my foot down!"

"What about that time we convinced Moseley not to fire you for getting stuck in traffic?"

"Oh no. That was a long time ago. You can't hang that over my head anymore."

"If you want," Shelley began, "we could go to him and change his mind back."

"You wouldn't. There's no way you'd get me out of the job."

"She would," Chelsea said.

"Damn it. Fine." Mortimer looked at the freshmen. "Sorry kids. Email me your questions. I'll get back to you later. The rest of you, get the hell in my office before I change my mind."

Shelley smiled at the rest of the Nap Kin and led them in. Grady closed the door behind them.

"Thanks again," Reginald said.

Mortimer sat behind his desk, ready to wag his finger.

"You know, that was a low blow using that excuse again."

"Maybe," Naomi said. "Guess we could've mentioned that time Gin and I helped you impress your date."

"Wouldn't have done a thing. That relationship lasted no more than a week."

"What happened?" Peyton asked.

"She thought I had an unhealthy obsession with models."

Mortimer pointed to his shelves, filled with models he had constructed. Included among the collection were a castle, a plane, a ship, and a train. That last one was in a wine bottle. Chelsea walked over to the bottle, giving it a closer look.

"Is that ship new?" she asked.

"It's my most recent treasure. I've had the bottle since the date."

"Ah," Reginald said. "A memento. Really miss her, huh?"

"Please! Not even. Who even remembers her name?"

"I wanna say Dory," Randy said. "But that doesn't sound quite right."

"Anyway, we opened a bottle of wine on the date, and then I went on about how it'd be an interesting challenge to build a train in a bottle. Needless to say, that relationship went off the rails. She emptied the whole bottle on my head and told me she never wanted to see me again. And I wish you would all say the same!"

STEVEN SHINDER

"Look," Gertrude said. "Our friend Peyton needs help with her sister."

"All right." Mortimer removed his glasses to rub his eyelids. "I've heard it all. So what is it this time? She drive your car and now you're trying to get her to admit it?"

"No. She's the new school mascot, and she's not talking to me."

Peyton figured that it would make things simpler to reveal Pamela's job to Mortimer. Judging by his association with the Nap Kin—albeit a reluctant one—he seemed like he could keep the information confidential. Either that or he would just not care enough to remember it long-term.

"Oh, wow." He put his glasses back on. "The new Mandy? That's quite a responsibility for your sister."

"But I think it's going to her head. She'd rather wear that thing and greet other people than hang out with me just as herself."

Mortimer interlocked his hands together and set them on the desk.

"What I think is going on here is a clash of perspectives."

"Oh!" Shelley said. "Like the time one of your students gave you a black eye?"

"Must've been hard for you to see things," Randy said.

"It sure was hard for *us* to see *him*, am I right?" Reginald joked.

Some of them laughed.

"Shut it!" Mortimer said, slamming a fist on the desk. "We're past that. Yes, it was a clash of perspectives. I told him to pay attention, and he later revealed that he had a death in the family. We had a heart to heart, and he said he was sorry. I accepted his apology. Still pressed charges, but I accepted. The point is that you need to see things from your sister's point of view."

"So, I should wear the costume and see what it feels like to be in her shoes?" Peyton asked. "Just wear it around campus?"

"Yes! Wait what? Actually that's not... You know what? That's not a half bad idea. In fact, you should *all* try to hang out with her around campus. *Far* from here. Forever. Now, we good?"

"Yes," Peyton said. "Thanks for your time."

"No problem at all." Peyton detected the sarcasm. "If you can't use *my* time, then whose time can you use?"

* * *

As the group exited the office, Randy thought about Naomi.

"I'll catch up with y'all in a bit."

"Uh, ditto for me," Grady said.

"Okay," the rest said, walking off.

Grady staying behind was really not what Randy wanted for this private moment.

"What are you doing?" Randy asked.

"What are *you* doing?"

"I wanted to talk to Mortimer about something."

"So did I."

"My thing is personal."

"So is mine."

Copycat, Randy thought.

"Fine. Go in. I'll go after you're done."

"Thanks. I'll make it quick."

"Knowing Mortimer, *he'll* make it quick."

* * *

Mortimer noticed a student entering his office. Since it was one whom he did not recognize, he breathed a sigh of relief.

"Hello! Welcome to my office hours!"

"Um, it's me."

"You'll have to forgive me. I don't learn my students' names as quickly as I used to. I'm in my forties."

"I'm actually not in your class."

The hell? he thought.

"Oh. So you're thinking of dropping the course?" He stood up. "I see. Look, if you haven't dropped yet, I encourage you to stick with it at least for the next seminar. I assure you it'll be the most engaging one yet. But if you've already dropped the class, then good riddance. Have a Green Day. You're dead to me."

"Professor, I was never in your class."

"Waitlist? Feels kinda late for you, I'm afraid."

"I came in with the Nap Kin. I'm a new member."

Damn it, Mortimer thought, pinching the space between his eyebrows.

"Ah. Another one. Sorry, but, in my defense, how the hell am I supposed to remember the new guy? You'll have to stop being in the background. You hardly made an impression. So again, who the hell are you?"

"Grady Stuart. Cousin of August."

"Oh, yes." Mortimer sat back down. "I remember him. Last I saw him, he was getting ready to study abroad. We had some sort of heart to heart about how I'm kinda like a dad on campus to him or something. So you've got connections, I see. No wonder they let you into their little, cliquey group."

"See, about that. You've known them a while. They seem to like me, but I was wondering if there's anything I should keep in mind in order to maintain that."

"Don't be desperate. Desperation is for losers. Just be yourself and be more in the foreground. But I swear, if you're in the foreground, don't be annoying. Now, what do desperate people do?"

"Beg for help?"

"And what should you do right now to not seem desperate?"

"Leave?"

"Yes. *Now* you're branching out. All right. Get out."

"Right."

* * *

Grady exited the office and gave Randy a thumbs up. Randy heard a vibration. Grady took out his phone and read the screen.

"Mitch says, 'I'm in the food court. Where the fuck are y'all at?'"

"Typical Mitch," Randy said.

"Right? It's like he doesn't read the group chat."

"Wait. Hold the cell. There's a group chat?"

"Are you not in it?"

"N-no."

"But I am?" Grady looked confused. "Wow." He breathed out what sounded like a sigh of relief. "Guess they like me more than I realized. Oh, but, um, that's weird that you're not in the group chat."

You bet your stupidass face, it's weird, Randy thought.

All those years of loyalty, and there was a group chat in which he was not included. And apparently the new guy had more of a right to take part in the private conversations and inside jokes.

That should be me...

As Grady walked away, Randy shook these thoughts away and went back into the office.

"Professor?"

"Oh, holy copter cheese! Did I not tell you to make like an egg and scram?"

"Well, it's just that I have this huge problem, if you don't mind talking about it."

"Yeesh. Why does this always happen to me?" He looked up at the ceiling and groaned. Then he closed his eyes and crossed his arms. "You know, it's my own fault, really. I used to be bullied in high school. But in the middle of a beating, Mikey Briggs stopped and cried, told me

114

about his clique that encouraged him to hurt others, and asked me what he should do. And so I told him to stand up to them, and it was a success. From then on, everyone just assumed they could come up to me with their life problems, and everything would be okay. I should've just taken the beating. It was almost graduation anyway! He opened his eyes and pinched the air with a thumb and an index finger. "It was *that* close. And that one day has been haunting me ever since."

Seeing how frustrated Mortimer was, Randy realized that it would probably be futile trying to get helpful advice.

"You know what? It's cool. I'm sorry, Professor. I won't bother you anymore."

His head now sunken, he turned around, ready to leave.

"Ugh... Why do you all *do* this to me? Wait wait wait, come back. Fine. I give." He got up, stood in front of the window, and placed his hands on his own hips in a superhero pose. "I'll listen. After all, I suppose it's my calling as an educator to help students in their times of need. So I might as well accept it, and embrace it." He closed his eyes. "I'm fine with this. I've come to terms with this. It's time for me to make like a tree and believe..." He opened his eyes again and faced Randy. "Now, what do you need help with?"

"I have these romantic feelings—"

"Get the hell outta my office."

"Yes sir."

Randy headed home after this meeting. He spent a couple of hours lying on the couch of his apartment. He had trouble fathoming how he was not part of the group chat. He tried to replace the negative thoughts with positive ones. The only possibility he could come up with was that they were planning a birthday surprise for him. Surely they would remember that his birthday was on this coming Saturday. Apparently, they were planning on bringing a cake to Mortimer the next day, so it seemed natural for them to do something special for him as well.

Vic walked out of his room and saw Randy on the couch.

"How are you feeling, Randy?"

"Please don't ask like that."

"Is something wrong?"

Randy did not expect this. He and Vic had not really talked much.

"I got hit by the taco truck."

"Huh?"

"It's just too much to say."

"I know what it is, and I'm sorry."

"For what?" Randy asked, puzzled.

"All right. You want me to come out and say it. That's fair. I've been taking nibbles at your food, and it's wrong. I lose control, but that's no excuse. I guess it's my way of coping."

"Coping?"

"Haven't you noticed? Life is kinda shitty. Especially at this gloomy ass school. You can barely afford anything in this town. I want to make it up to you though. You're turning twenty-one this Saturday, right?"

"How'd you know?"

"Social media."

"Oh. Right."

"Are you gonna be here Saturday night?"

"Yeah."

"Do you have any plans?"

"Not that I know of. Some friends might surprise me, but I'm not sure."

"Well, if you're over here, I can bring us some drinks. The good stuff. And we can unwind and watch whatever you want."

Randy felt touched by this proposition.

"You really mean that?"

"Absolutely."

"Thanks, Vic. I appreciate that."

"I know it's not much, but..."

"It's a good step."

Randy smiled. Maybe his birthday would be fine after all. Even if the Nap Kin had nothing planned for him, he could still have a leisurely time with Vic. A contingency plan. Turning something negative into something positive. Like using feces as fertilizer. Fecal fecundity in a life so shitty.

* * *

The next day, Martin Mortimer sat behind his desk during office hours, hoping for any of his students to show up. A knock greeted the door, and he opened it quickly. But his excitement sank when he saw that it was not a student.

"Chancellor Moseley. Surprise to see you here."

"I hear that it is your day of birth. Would you like a bottle of mirth?"

Moseley presented a bottle of what appeared to be some sort of wine. It had a cork in it.

"Is this allowed here?"

"I allow it here. It is much better than beer."

Anything is better than beer, Mortimer thought.

"Well, I suppose there's no harm. It'll have to be a quick sip, though. I'm having office hours, and someone could show up any moment."

Chancellor Moseley locked the door behind him.

"Just a good old lock. People will be forced to knock."

The instructors often wondered why the chancellor spoke in couplets. A few years earlier, during a gathering of instructors, a new professor asked the chancellor about his habit. The room went silent for a moment, with no answer provided. And then she was never seen again. The general assumption was that Moseley fired her. So nobody else tried asking again.

"You got a corkscrew?" Mortimer asked.

The chancellor opened his mouth wide, revealing fangs, one of which he sank into the cork to pull it out of the bottle.

"Holy copter cheese! Do you go to the CPU Blood Donation Center?"

Moseley licked the cork off of the fang, his lips holding it like a cigar for a second before he spit it out.

"More often than you know. Down the hatch this will go!"

He rushed over to Mortimer and shoved the bottle into his mouth. The liquid tasted like wine, but there was something electric about it. He almost choked on the drink, but he managed to gulp some down the correct pipe. Once Moseley seemed satisfied with the amount that had left the bottle, he removed it from Mortimer's mouth. The professor shivered with intoxication.

"This doesn't taste like wine." He was feeling dizzy. "Bolt of lightning in a bottle! A martini for Martin, am I right?"

He laughed until Moseley slapped him in the face. He managed to make out what the chancellor was saying.

"It is not looking like a full glass. There are few students in your class."

"You're not saying what I think you're saying, are you, Chance?"

"It will be canceled, professor. Sorry to be your oppressor."

"Bu-but, what am I supposed to do now?"

"I heard you turned down students during office hours. Now you will have to answer to higher powers."

"How'd you know?"

"Professor Olson down the hall. She said she saw it all."

"Chance-lore, you have very sharp teeth. Are you a vampire? And are you turning me into one?"

"I am past trusting fellow blood-sucking cohorts. I got stabbed in the back, so I stabbed back in their hearts. This drink will turn you into my pet, a slave to the moon after sunset. Your day is a disaster, and you will call me master."

Mortimer laughed.

"This is a terrible birthday. And I've been to college, so that's saying something!"

The chancellor smiled.

"It is about to get worse. Come with me and join the curse."

"Whatever you say, Chance!"

Getting up, Mortimer stumbled, nearly falling. But Moseley grabbed him by the wrist and led the way.

* * *

When the Nap Kin arrived at Mortimer's office a half hour later, carrying an ice cream cake, they knocked on the door. But there was no answer. They turned the knob, but it was locked.

"Old Timer?" Naomi said. "Are you in there?"

"Maybe he's running late," Mitch suggested.

"It's not like him," Gertrude said. "He's always here during office hours."

"Was it something we did?" Reginald wondered aloud.

They waited until the end of his office hours. The ice cream cake was melting.

"We can't let it go to waste," Mitch said.

"Please, don't," Gertrude said.

"I'm sorry! But I'm tired of waiting, and I'm starving."

Mitch opened his mouth wide open and dug his face into the cake. How he moved his tongue through the frosting and the ice cream was truly a disgusting sight that made his friends wince.

"What even is this?" Grady asked.

Mitch looked up, his face marked up with frosting.

"This is what happens when you skip breakfast."

Part Two
The Sips

Chapter 12
Time Consuming

Unable to understand each other, Cackle Bucket, Harriet Harvester, and Mortimer Mutterer—all in their mid-forties—sat silently in chairs, within a room with a clock hanging above a locked door, a flickering light bulb hanging from the ceiling, steam pipes running along the wall, and a big generator whirring in the corner.

They sat for a minute.

Then an hour.

Then a day.

When it was nearly four full days since the beginning of his captivity, Mortimer Mutterer spoke to the other two.

"Water," he said. "We need water to live."

Delirious, Cackle Bucket laughed like a hyena.

"Silly little shit. We can go ninety-six hours without water!"

"It's been ninety-five."

Cackle Bucket's eyes and smile widened until the smile was gone.

"Don't *play* with me like that! I haven't heard the clock!"

"Funny thing," Harriet Harvester chimed in. "You don't hear the clock tick until you take a look at it."

Fatigued, she struggled to lift her finger and point at the clock with 24 numbers. It read 16:30.

"Wasn't it seventeen-thirty when we sat down?" Cackle Bucket asked.

"Precisely," Harriet Harvester replied. "We're almost dead."

"What about Daylight Savings Time?" Cackle Bucket asked. "Fall back and all that?"

Drained of strength, Mortimer fell backward in his chair, falling to the floor with it.

"Nobody moved the hands," he explained. "The hours have passed as I have professed. Daylight Savings hasn't come yet."

"Why do I understand you two?" Harriet Harvester asked. "We didn't all speak the same language four days ago."

Mortimer Mutterer wondered where they were from. And where *he* was from.

"More time..." Mortimer Mutterer said.

"Some names are given," Harriet Harvester said. "Henriette. Home ruler. The Landlord."

Cackle Bucket laughed as if he had an amusing realization. But then he stopped as if he forgot it. His grin morphed into a scowl.

"I can forge et cetera to live forever!"

Mortimer Mutterer's mind became occupied with thoughts of tin, sand, and glass.

"Oil is good for tin but bad for the heart. Fire forges liquid time. It rises above the heartless. The hour transparent surrounds the hour that blinds."

The door opened, a silhouette standing in the bright light beyond.

"I remember now!" Harriet Harvester said. "Tick, tick, lick the light! Liquid light! We all live above liquid light but below the light we feed upon!"

"Chancellor," Mortimer Mutterer uttered. "Where are we?"

"We are just below my office. By a tunnel, far from its orifice."

"Welcome to the pack," Harriet Harvester said to Mortimer Mutterer. "You missed some fresh meat."

"What meat?"

"Some wannabe Moscato additions." She looked at Chancellor Moseley's stern expression, then turned back to Mortimer Mutterer with a sly smile. "We tried hogging it all... Oink."

"Will you and Cackle Bucket behave?" Moseley asked. "Are you two worth a save?"

"We'll behave if you feed us!" Cackle Bucket snapped, both with his voice and with his fingers.

"Feeding you is a delight. Have some moonlight!"

Moseley smiled and pulled out the cassette tape amulet, which emanated moonlight. Cackle Bucket, Harriet Harvester, and Mortimer Mutterer's eyes turned white. They crawled up to the amulet and licked the air around it, absorbing the glow to quench their thirsts. A substitute for solid food, the light fueled the beasts within these beings. It kept them from starving as he deprived them of actual food, but it also pained their insides, much to Mathias' delight.

"Captive eyes glowing white, captivated by moonlight!"

* * *

Vic was not getting coffee from the shop this time; he had already gone on a resource run during his last visit to the supermarket over the previous weekend. Here at the off-campus the school-owned shop Copper Stop, he knew that the camera was peeking from its black dome in the ceiling's corner. So he turned his backpack toward it as he reached into the cup of plastic spoons, set there for anyone who wanted to stir their coffee.

Coffee cost money.

With a nonchalant disposition, Vic slid the spoon into his pants pocket and turned counter-clockwise toward the door so he could flee slowly through his only exit, trying not to catch the cashier's attention.

Once outside, he ran with tunnel vision, staying alert as he maneuvered himself to and through the parking lot. It was safer on the other side, at the tables beside the vegetarian restaurant.

A copper-colored truck backed out toward him. He backed an inch away from the license plate just in time, the numbers and letters slightly out of focus in his vision. A few flashes from the back window infected his eyes with sunspots. He turned away and kept running to the safe zone. Losing his sense of balance, he tried to move out of the way of the SUV up ahead.

It was not stopping.

He skipped to the right, his waist slightly slamming against a black beetle's buttocks as it pulled out of its parking space. He felt a sting across his jean-covered thigh and rubbed it momentarily before continuing onward.

The table under an umbrella of shade. Vic wanted it to be his haven, but he felt dizzy when he sat down. Feeling light-headed, he closed his eyes. But the flashes were disrupting the orange veil that usually soothed him under normal circumstances. It was as if a tumor was hovering over him, commencing an unwelcome invasion.

"Shit!" he defecated figuratively. "Make it stop! Make it stop!"

He did not want to reverse-consume the contents for which he had already paid; nothing should escape the orifice. He wondered whether scooping cold spaghetti into his burning eyes could cure him. Too many lights in the light-headed mind, like an aurora hurricane that never tired. He wanted to tire himself so he would not have to see too much. Dropping his heavy head onto the table, he forced himself to nap, which was mostly impossible due to the people passing by and conversing with each other. There were no wingless flights for him.

After half an hour had passed, Vic could finally open his eyes with ease, the sunspots having vanished from his vision. There was a resurgence of hunger. He could finally unzip his backpack and bust out the Tupperware pregnant with spaghetti and meatballs. With easy access to a utensil, his hands could remain clean. He reached into his right pocket...

Two fragments, the result of a diagonal cut through the oval. It had been broken by the buttocks slam. Not as sturdy as the metal one that he had back at the apartment, but he would make it work.

A plane replete with tomatoes was shoveled into the maw by a force whetting his appetite. Fruit or vegetables, they were edible, and that was all that mattered. He nearly suffocated on the beef boulders, but he managed to stuff them down into the depths of the correct tunnel. The entire meal was gone within a couple of minutes, a scarf of noodles scarfed down by a starving student.

The Sawton Bridge was a nexus between the stores and the campus. Vic walked across it, knowing he would have to consume time until Randy arrived home. Evan and Ted were out of town. Vic looked down at the belt loop where the phantom key chain had its muted jingle. He rarely left the thing on this desk at home, and this was one of those days.

At the end of the bridge hung a poster advertising a gathering complete with chicken wings and pizza. The logo of the club that was billed on the poster read "Feathers," a smile stretching from each "e," both of which resembled eyes. There was no description for the club. He hoped that the lack of specificity meant that he could blend in for a meal if he wanted to do so. The event was at seven, and he knew that he would need dinner if he was to last through the night. Especially if he was planning on drinking a lot with Randy.

Later, the stars above his head did not taint his eyes with queasiness; his body was ready, craving the feast. He entered the social science building, almost getting lost searching for the listed room number in the floor beneath the school. The walls did not seem to have been updated in two decades. Their only decorations were the webs crafted by spiders. If this were his home, he would have killed them. But for all he knew, they were invited and, therefore, welcome, like vampires given permission to enter.

He found the room door and knocked. Someone opened it.

"Hi!" a thirty-something said, wearing a shirt with two connected "e's." "My name is Lexa. Or, was. You can call me Host L. What's *your* name for now?"

"Vic," he answered reflexively, wondering whether he should have used a fake name.

"Vic! Nice to meet you! Grab some food! Have a seat!"

He looked over at a circular glass table surrounded by eleven other people. There were pizza boxes stacked on top of it. Behind the stack were dishes containing chicken legs and wings. The former were lemon-flavored and the latter were spicy. Chicken wings were the only spicy food that he tolerated. Of course, there was no reason that he could not try both types, as well as the cheese, pepperoni, and mushroom pizzas. There was also a tin bucket. He and Host L sat down.

"Do you like our timetable?" Mortimer Mutterer asked, rubbing the glass with his hands. "It is a line, but it looks circular from above and below. Like a clock. As above, so below."

Vic did not know how to respond, so he just began the feast. As he devoured the meat, he tossed the bones into the trash.

"Bones in a bucket!" shouted Cackle Bucket.

"Sand is the worst part of the potato salad," Mortimer Mutterer muttered.

"Huh?" Vic responded, not seeing potato salad anywhere on the table.

"Time makes potato salad go bad."

"Oh. I see."

"Time is rough, annoying, and all over the place. But here, time seems to stand still, softening the blow of time."

With each bite he took while sitting down, Vic was bombarded with questions from people whose names he was struggling to learn. Names he wanted to forget after the event. Normally, this was the case whenever he went to events on campus that had free food. But this time was different. Their names were names that he wished he had never known: Host L, ever smiling, with a grin that was somehow unwelcoming. Mortimer Mutterer, feeling the table, saying things that were barely audible. (Vic wondered whether he ought to hear the things that could not reach his ears.) Cackle Bucket, smiling with a permanent scowl in his brows. Harriet Harvester, slowly clawing at the table with her nails. Low Knife, a man who seemed to be around thirty, on his knees, resting his head on the table, his eyes facing Vic's direction. Stitch Tyke, a man who looked like he was in his early twenties, tapping the table energetically. Juggle Mint, a young-looking woman who moved her hands up and down in circular motions, juggling spheres that were not there. Shed Cheese, a man who looked to be in his fifties, his head sunken, looking to be asleep, his eyes too sunken to be unseen beyond the ridges of his brows from where Vic was sitting. Doggerel Grill, a woman who looked to be in her thirties, making unpleasant rhymes. Fork Feed, a woman who looked to be in her late twenties, hunched over the table. Tomb Scone, a wrinkly old man, licking his lips constantly. Spoon Drop, an elderly woman, resting her head upon her arms, on top of each other horizontally on the table. Vic partially regretted telling them his real name, along with other truthful facts that he tried to keep brief.

"What's your major?" Tomb Scone asked, taking a break from licking his lips.

"Psychology."

"How old are you?" Spoon Drop asked.

"Twenty-one."

"Where are you from?" Juggle Mint asked.

The names were blending together.

"Not important."

"Is that close to the border?"

"What?"

The spice of the chicken was getting to him. He tried balancing it with the lemon, but he needed milk, or anything to drink at all.

"I'm thirsty," he said.

"I'm thirty," Low Knife replied.

"No..."

"Who are you?"

"What's your name?"

"How old are you?"

"Where are you from?"

Why am I here? Vic wondered, biting into his thirtieth slice of pizza, and then his sixtieth piece of chicken, this one a drumstick.

"An edible fool's edible tool!" Doggerel Grill exclaimed, clapping.

"Edible tool for edible instrument," Low Knife said.

Vic started to believe he was becoming as lumpy as he felt. He even swallowed the bones that were left on his plate.

"Why am I swallowing bones?"

"Swallows!" Doggerel Grill said. "Birds of a feather flock together. But you're not part of our flock, bock bock bock."

"Why aren't any of you eating?" he asked.

"Cooking ruinsssss the food," Shed Cheese said. "And itch already been ruined."

"What do you mean?"

"This is what it means," Fork Feed said. "This is what it means. This is what it means."

The rest grinned in unison. The faces were beginning to blur, and eventually they swirled so much that they blended into each other. All one face, supported by multiple bodies that moved on their own as the head remained in place. The body of Fork Feed walked over to Vic, sticking another chicken wing into his mouth.

"This is what it means. This is what it means. This is what it means."

Vic bit the meat off of the bone, trying not to choke.

What does this all mean?

The fuel was not in his stomach anymore, but he was not reverse-consuming. He could feel a flaming heat all over himself, and he thought he could hear the banshee-like screeching of a fire alarm impaling his ears.

He could feel bones rising out of his back, like a creature was clawing its way out of him. He feared what was about to happen. He let out his cry unstifled.

"STOP!"

Crispy, meaty wings of both flavors burst out of his back, and they were glazed with blood. His spine was now exposed as the skin on his back peeled off. He tried to flap the wings so he could escape, but they did not move. So he remained seated as the other people gathered around the table drew themselves closer to him with exposed teeth and ravenous eyes turning white like the moon. Blue wolfish fur began to sprout from their skin.

"A big bird!" Stitch Tyke said.

Fork Feed then gave Vic the complete opposite of comfort.

"This is not a dream. This is not a dream. This is not a dream."

* * *

Randy had not heard from any of his friends. In the afternoon, he had gone to the on-campus pub Pitchers & Forks to get his free birthday drink, pear cider. He sat there for a while, hoping to hear from anyone. But he received no message.

He was hoping to be surprised when he returned to the apartment, but it was empty when he got there. Evan and Ted usually went home for the weekend. Vic was nowhere to be seen. Randy messaged him, but there was no response. He waited for a little while, and still no response.

He had received a call from his parents as expected. Earlier in the week, they had sent him a card in the mail, which came with a check and a gift card for wine he could order online. He never knew what to say when asked what he wanted for his birthday, so money was normally the default gift. But they wanted to throw in something special for his 21st.

That night, he went to the supermarket by himself to get a drink. He returned to the apartment with a bottle of vodka. The brand: Silver Silencer. He poured himself a glass when he returned to the apartment. He did not think of it as home. He had no idea what his home was, or if it even existed.

"Vic, are you here?" he checked again.

Nobody around.

"Fine. More ales for Morales."

Randy did not particularly care for Vic as much as his friends from the Nap Kin. But with the rest of them apparently busy and having forgotten his birthday, Vic seemed like the next best thing for company. And now Randy believed that it had been wrong to hope for that.

He sat alone at the kitchen table and took a sip. Not having much experience with vodka, it was a bit strong for him, causing him to cough. So he ended up mixing the Silencer with lemon-flavored soda. A chaser to chase away the sounds of stress that might reach the ears of one's tongue. He took sips now and then, staring at the night through the window. All alone.

This is what post-grad life would be like.

The more sips he took, the more he resented his friends for not coming over on his 21st birthday of all birthdays. And possibly his final birthday of all birthdays. He knew that they were all chummy with each other, and he felt like the outsider. Even when they were all together, he felt like the outsider. These days, it seemed to him that they even preferred Grady over him.

"Talk about a *Toy Story* situation," he said to himself bitterly. "Always the duck, never the goose. They've meant more to me than I have to them."

Not even August had messaged him to wish him a happy birthday. Drinking straight from the bottle, he could feel his time slipping away as he drowned submissively in a sea of sorrows. A silver sea. The silver division.

With each sip, he allowed his mind to slip back in time to his birthday the previous year...

Randy and Naomi finish attending their art class. They walk outside where there are empty tables and chairs next to a coffee shop.

"Do you wanna hang out at my place?" Naomi asks.

"You mean your place where some of our other friends live?" Randy smiles. "Gee. I wonder what's gonna happen."

"What do you mean?"

Naomi manages to keep a straight face, but Randy is privy to the surprise party. It is a guess, but he has a good feeling about it.

"Don't worry, Tonic. I'll play along."

"Oh gosh," Naomi says, breaking into tears, pressing her hands against her face.

"Oh, no no no," Randy says, his smile fading. "It's okay! It's not your fault. I'll enjoy and act surprised. You're fine. You're fine."

"No. I'm not. I'm a mess."

"It's just a party. You haven't ruined anything."

"It's not that. You called me Tonic."

"I mean, that's your—"

"Nobody's called me that since last school year. And it reminded me of the whole Gin and Tonic thing. How it seemed to everyone that Reginald and I were meant for each other."

Randy feels guilty about having believed her to be upset over spoiling a gathering meant for him. He views himself as selfish, not having considered another reason for Naomi to cry. He regrets uttering the nickname that is the reason for her tears in this moment. Her eyes are wet and red. He has never seen Naomi this sad, and he does not want her to keep being sad. He sees that she is hurting, and he wants her to be healed.

"I'm sorry," he says. "I shouldn't have said anything."

133

"Don't beat yourself up," she says. "I know you didn't mean to hurt me." She wipes her eyes with her knuckles. "Oh, gosh. I can't let anyone see me like this."

"It's okay. We can wait here until you finish crying."

"No, Brandy. This is your day. I don't wanna cry over your candles."

"Just cry here and they won't get over the candles."

Naomi laughs, a sunny smile juxtaposed with rainy eyes.

"I must look ridiculous," she says.

"Naomi, you need to cry. You owe it to yourself. Everyone needs to cry."

"It's just... I've been crying enough all summer. I had all that time to get over him. Didn't talk to him at all, and then when I saw him and everyone again... I just broke, Brandy. Could you tell?"

Randy feels bad about not realizing before that she might have been sad.

"You seemed fine to me."

"Oh, I bet. I was smiling on the surface, but I was holding in everything else. A whole year with him. It's hard to take away."

"I can't imagine."

They sit for a little longer. Naomi lets it all out as Randy stares forward into space, tapping his feet quietly. After a long moment during which he is silent, a possible course of action occurs to Randy.

"Would you like a hug?" he offers.

Naomi keeps her eyesight fixed on the ground.

"Don't do it out of pity."

"I swear I'm not. It's just...it's my birthday, and I really want a hug from you. You've been such a cool person to me all this time, and I appreciate the heck out of that. It hurts seeing you hurt. I've never been hurt the same way you have, but I know pain. And I want both of us to feel better."

Naomi looks at him for a moment, then opens her arms. Randy feels her face resting in his shoulder, still letting out the sorrow. They loosen up after a few seconds, and Naomi wipes her face again.

"Thanks," she says. "What's your pain, if you don't mind me asking?"

He wants to talk about Aster, but he is afraid.

"Maybe I'll tell you another time. You gonna be all right?"

"I'll try." She wipes her face. "How do I look?"

She still looks like she has been crying, but Randy knows that all evidence will fade once they arrive at the party. But rather than point this out, he says something else, though it is still truthful.

"You look strong. You've endured endearment, and you're strong."

She smiles, and Randy knows that she will be fine for the time being.

Once they arrive at the party, the rest of the Nap Kin jump out in surprise. Randy acts surprised, and they seem to buy it.

"Did you have any idea?" August asks.

"None at all!" Randy says with a stupid grin.

"Sweet! Mission accomplished! Nice going, Naomi!"

August holds up his hand for a high-five, and Naomi's hand meets his. Randy notices her glance at Reginald. It's very brief, but they both smile at each other before breaking eye contact. Randy wonders how this brief moment makes her feel. Throughout the duration of the party, he tries to avoid talking to Reginald, since he's unhappy about how his presence may affect Naomi. He knows that Reginald is not a bad guy, but Randy has lingering feelings of bitterness he wishes to direct at a familiar figure in the private thoughts between words.

All bridges that could possibly lead to violent thoughts are cut short when the cake that needs to be cut is brought out, adorned with two candles proclaiming that he is now two decades into his life.

"It's a good thing you arrived a little later than we expected," Mitch says. "Gave me time to get here for the cake."

"Wait for the rest of us," August says. "We were here first, so you go last."

"Aw, come on!"

"You need to learn, bud. And, of course, our good friend Randy gets the first piece. Go ahead and make a wish."

Surrounded by friends, Randy closes his eyes to think. Blowing out the candles, he wishes for Naomi to be happy.

After all, the thought of Naomi being happy makes him feel happy.

A year later, and Naomi seemed happier than she was back then. This time, there were no candles for Randy to blow out. But it barely mattered to him now. He could not imagine that he would have wished for anything at all this time around.

Chapter 13
Midterms and Conditions

The next week, Peyton was stressing. She kept thinking about wearing the Mandy costume, but she never had the chance since Pamela wore it often and never left it at the dorm by itself. Peyton did not think Pamela would give her permission to wear it. But she had to put the issue to the side for a bit as she studied for three in-class midterms. They were all scheduled for Friday morning—Halloween, as it happened. Peyton had kept herself in the dorm all week to force herself to study, but very little stuck. And when Thursday came, she was even more nervous.

She and Gertrude walked on the pathway around the park. Peyton looked through her stack of index cards. She was uncertain about the material. What should have already felt familiar to her seemed to fade very quickly after every glance.

"I don't get why we even get tested so much," Peyton complained. "We just vomit our knowledge onto the test, and then it's gone forever."

"Sounds like the random shit I throw on waffles at diners," Gertrude said.

"Like what?"

"Tapioca balls, fruit-flavored cereal, marshmallows..."

"You bring all that from home?"

"Yep. You know, if you go to that yogurt place across the street, you can save money by only getting the toppings."

"So, no yogurt?"

"Yeah." Gertrude stopped walking. "Wait, what's going on?"

Peyton paused as well. She looked up from her cards and noticed half a dozen students holding up their cell phones.

"Huh?" she uttered.

"Shh," one of them said. "Look behind you."

Peyton and Gertrude looked back, and there was Stagmantel walking their way. The students took pictures of him. He passed by all of them as if they were not even there. Looking at her cards again, Peyton got an idea.

"So this luck thing," Peyton said to Gertrude. "Is it *really* legit?"

"Definitely."

"How do I know you're telling the truth?"

Gertrude giggled.

"You don't. We fear the unknown. The yogurt passes the expiration date. Still smells normal but also looks questionable. Won't know anything until you take a chance. See you later!"

Gertrude walked to her next class, leaving Peyton in a state of confusion. She looked at her index cards again, then back at Stagmantel.

"Ah, what the hell," she said, running after Stagmantel. "Hey! Wait up!"

"You again," Stagmantel stated, stopping for her. "Had enough dreams?"

"Yeah, enough of that bullshit. Look, I've heard that you give students blessings or something so they can do well on midterms. Is that true?"

"A bit exaggerated."

"Then enlighten me."

"You are quite to the point."

"You should follow suit."

"Careful. You would not want to upset someone who has the power to potentially help you."

Peyton crossed her arms.

"Isn't it hard to upset someone who's indifferent?"

"Hm. You are good. Follow me to my home and I will show you how it all works."

Luckily, Peyton did not have to follow him all the way to the top of the hill. He approached a group of ducks who were sitting below by the trees.

"Here are the lucky ducks. Each duck is filled with luck. The catch is that I have no idea which ones have good luck and which ones have bad luck. You have a fifty-fifty chance. It is a gamble, but you are free to make it. Just select a duck."

Peyton thought over the risk. At worst, she could end up with a C in the class if she failed the midterm. She decided that it was a shot worth taking. She spent a good minute looking through all the ducks who were seated. They all looked the same to her, not one giving her a vibe different from any other. She closed her eyes, pointed outward, spun herself in a circle, and opened her eyes.

"That one," she picked.

"All right then," Stagmantel said, making eye contact with the duck she had chosen. He pointed at it. "You there! Stand a loan!"

The duck obeyed, standing up and turning to stone.

"Oh my damn!" Peyton said.

"There you go. Your luck is now in motion while the duck is not."

"How long does it stay like that? It's not dead, is it?"

"It still lives. And it will remain a statue until someone else wanting a luck loan comes along and chooses a different duck."

"How long does that normally take?"

"It varies. I tell students the odds, so they know what they are getting into. Understandably, a lot of them 'chicken out,' as they say. Bad luck could be dangerous."

"How dangerous?"

"Well, the last person who took out a loan died a few hours later. I could tell because the duck became flesh and feathers once again. So death is another way to end the loan."

Peyton started to have a mini heart attack.

"I really wish you'd told me that before!"

"Listen. Luck does not determine your fate. It just increases the likelihood of your fate leaning one way more than the other. So, just be cautious. But not too cautious."

"Gee. Thanks."

After this, Peyton walked to the other side of the park and see whether Pamela was there. Surely enough, there she was, speaking with Unicoren. Peyton stood behind a tree, trying to stay out of sight so that she could listen in.

"So you never go out for Halloween?" Pamela asked.

"No," Unicoren answered. "I am not allowed to leave."

"Why not?"

"Mathias is The Landlord. He lets me and Stagmantel live here, and only here. We have to honor the agreement."

What agreement? Peyton thought, continuing to listen to her sister.

"Don't you wish you could go out in the streets, though? I'm sure some people would think you're in costume. You'd blend in."

"I do wish that I could accompany you. But if it's you and Mandy, then at least there's a chance for some fun. Knowing this would make me feel...free."

Free? Peyton thought. *What the hell is up around here?*

"I'll be sure to bring Mandy out and go door to door," Pamela said. "It should be fun."

Peyton accidentally stepped on a twig.

Pamela turned around.

"Is someone there?"

With the twig broken up, the jig was up. So Peyton walked out into the open, no longer hidden by the silver birch.

"Hey," Peyton said, her hands tucked into her pockets.

"Were you *spying* on me?" Pamela asked.

"I just came here to check up on you."

"What'd you hear?"

"You're going trick-or-treating tomorrow?"

"Yes. I'd ask if you wanna come, but..."

Pamela trailed off, leaving the path of her statement unfinished.

"Trick-or-treating isn't my thing, anyway," Peyton said with a shrug. "Haven't worn a costume in years."

"Well," Pamela said, "you should be grateful you have the freedom to do so."

Pamela looked at Unicoren, who had a neutral expression rather than some reaction of approval that Pamela was probably expecting to see.

"Well," Peyton said, "I'll see you later. Gotta study for my midterm."

"Haven't you studied enough for it?"

"Have *you* studied?"

Pamela's pause said it all.

"A bit."

"All right. Well, have fun."

Peyton did not believe Pamela, but she did not know what else to say. She felt that the conversation would have been a dead end. Awkwardness tended to end their conversations.

She hoped that the midterm would not be her own dead end.

* * *

At Tree Culler Hotel, Verner invited August, Anton, and Fritz to his room for some drinks. They each had minimalist Halloween costumes: toilet paper hanging from their arms to make them look like ghost mummies. Between solid and airy, they did not have the solidarity to commit one way or another. The more beer they drank, the shittier their jokes became.

"Ghosts give boos," Verner said, "but I give booze!"

The other three rollicked with laughter as if it was the funniest joke they had ever heard. When Anton and Fritz stopped, August was still laughing. He went on for ten more seconds before clutching his stomach and trying to speak.

"This is the best way to die!"

He kept on laughing until he slapped himself in the face. Then he stopped. And then he chugged more beer. The other three exchanged looks between each other.

"You all right there?" Anton asked.

"There is *something* wrong with me," August said.

"Need some water?" Fritz offered, grabbing a bottle from a desk.

"No. Not that this. There's something that's been troubling me deep down. *Really* terrifying. I don't know what it is though. And *that* scares me! AHAHAHAHAHA! Frankly, my fecal matter's gone soft. Where's your toilet? I need to drop a mixtape."

"Right over there," Verner pointed to the door. "You gonna blow chugs?"

"Yeah. Thanks. Something tells me this toilet is better than the one I have."

* * *

For some reason, none of the students at the CPU wore trademarked character costumes the next day. They all looked like generic Halloween costumes. Peyton guessed that it was just one of those strange norms of CPU. It did not concern her, much. She had not dressed up for Halloween since she was a kid.

In her first class for the day, the midterm was passed out. And as soon as Peyton looked at the questions, she read each one and filled in the bubbles. Within fifteen minutes, she was finished, being one of the first people to leave the room. She felt confident, which was a nice change of pace. And so, when it came to the next two midterms, she did not have any worries at all. She just looked at the questions and knew how to answer them. After the last exam for the day, it felt like a load had been lifted.

Easy peasy lemon squeezy, she thought. *Guess Stagmantel's not full of shit after all.*

With the midterm behind her, she could look forward to the weekend. She had gotten an email with all the details of the Nap Kin camping trip. That afternoon, she met up with them at the drop-off zone at the front of the campus, the roundabout-looking road before the Sawton Bridge. They split up into a couple of cars. Reginald was kind enough to have his car stay behind so he, Naomi, Chelsea, and Shelley could wait for Mitch to be ready. Peyton ended up in the front seat of Gertrude's car. Grady and Randy sat in the back, beside opposite windows. Both seemed to be deep in thought, so Peyton was not sure what to say to anyone. The car just remained mostly silent during the drive, the passengers even napping along the way.

When they arrived at the mountainside, they set up camp.

"Where are the stakes?" Peyton asked.

"Steaks?" Grady said. "I thought we were roasting Hallo-wieners."

"No, I mean for the tents."

"I have them," Gertrude said. "Just give me a moment."

She zipped open her backpack and dug through it until she was able to pull out the stakes, which were covered in a bit of glitter.

"You really need to clean that out," Peyton said.

"Yeah, I know."

They set up all the tents they had. A while later, Reginald's car arrived. He and his passengers got out of the car.

"Hey look!" Mitch said. "Everything's set up. Darn. Wish we could've helped."

"Damn it, Ditcher," Gertrude said.

When it was dark enough, they set up the campfire and roasted wieners over it. Each of them had a lawn chair.

"So in the *Halloween* movies," Mitch said to Randy, "What exactly does one have to do to really piss Myers off?"

"The character has changed over the years depending on the movie," Randy said. "The mythology is not quite that consistent."

"Consistency of character would be nice," Chelsea said. "I just don't get it. Why would Mortimer leave? He's always there for office hours."

"Maybe he really *was* tired of us," Shelley said.

"I'm not complaining," Mitch said. "We got more cake."

"You mean *you* got more cake. You didn't even share."

"I had no choice. I was possessed by that force known as hunger. I needed to quell it. Because once hunger overpowers you, there's nothing you won't do to satisfy your appetite."

He took a bite out of the burnt wiener on his stick.

"You must've been a greedy trick-or-treater as a kid," Peyton observed.

"I did what I could to survive. It was the only time of the year my folks let me get candy."

Peyton knew that her sister was out trick-or-treating, and she wondered how she was doing.

* * *

"Trick-or-treat!" Pamela, dressed as Mandy and holding a pumpkin-shaped bucket, said as the door opened.

"Ooh, what have we here?" a kind old woman wondered.

"Mandy the Mantleope!"

"Oh, that's very cute." She reached into her basket and held out an emerald green pig piñata the size of a piggy bank. "Are you able to eat cashews?"

"Yep!"

"Here, have some chocolate-covered cashews." She dropped the little piñata into the bucket. "Happy Halloween!"

"Thank you!"

Once the door closed, Pamela continued walking down the street.

"Do you miss eating?" she asked Mandy.

"I haven't had such cravings in a while," Mandy told her telepathically. *"I'd be starving now if I could hunger. Probably best that I can't. Hunger can do terrible things."*

"I hear ya. I feel really guilty taking all this candy for myself, though."

"Why not share with your sister?"

"I guess I could do that. I don't know. Things are weird between us."

"Oh no."

"What?"

Pamela looked ahead at the next house, in front of which was a tall, hooded figure, leading a dozen others who were crawling on all fours.

Turn back. I don't like him. RUN!

Pamela obeyed, running across the street and then down the sidewalk until she could turn around the corner. Almost out of breath, she halted for a moment to catch it before speaking.

"What's wrong?"

"That man caused me so much pain."

"How did he hurt you?"

Silence. Pamela started to feel like she had done something wrong by asking that question. She wanted Mandy to feel comfortable. As curious as she was, it did not seem like Pamela's place to demand answers right away.

"Sorry. It's okay if you don't wanna tell me. Some things hurt when you remember them."

"It just hurts so much. I don't want to dwell on it."

"I understand. If you'd like, we can go back home, where it's safe."

"Home?"

Pamela thought over what she had just said. She was surprised that Petal Lock Park was the first thing to come to mind when she thought of the word "home."

"Yes. Home."

"Are you fine with that?"

"Are you kidding? If I get more candy, there's no way I'll be able to finish it. You did a great job tonight. People loved meeting you."

"Pamela."

"Yeah?"

"Can I tell you a secret?"

"If you're comfortable. You can trust me."

"I'm glad we became friends."

"Aw." Pamela felt tears surfacing from her eyes. "That's so sweet."

"I've never had a true friend before."

"Neither have I, really. You *are* a real friend, right?"

"I may not have experience, but I try to be. Am I doing well?"

"You're doing fantastic." Though it was dark within Mandy's head, Pamela had a bright smile on her face. "Never change, my friend."

* * *

Mathias was hooded by a black cloak that added an extra layer over the grad robe and bowler hat. The shades were all that were missing from his usual ensemble. He stood in front of the doorway, filled by a middle-aged man with a bowl of candy in his hands.

"Are you a vampire?" the man asked.

"Why yes I am, sir." He replied with a sly smile. "That is how I differ."

"Wow. Nice contacts. And these werewolves look real. It's like those crazy puppets you'd see in the movies."

"They are craving some *food*. And you would not want to be rude."

"Of course," the man said, nodding.

The blue-furred werewolves, growling, held out their bags, and the man put a few pieces of candy corn in each one.

"Ah, candy corn, those teeth-shaped treats," Mathias said. "Such sustenance will make wonderful eats."

The man smiled and waved at the werewolves.

"Have fun, kids!"

Mathias waved goodbye. The door closed, and the pack went on.

This was the only day of the year that Mathias felt free to walk around in public without his shades, showing his true self to a clueless world. And everyone was oblivious about the werewolves. Under his control, they required no leashes.

"Candy is barely filling!" Cackle Bucket complained.

"I know that you all crave meats," Mathias told them. "But tonight you will have to settle for sweets. That was a rotten thing you did to Vic. It truly makes me sick. You did not save any of his blood for me. Tonight, you do not get your killing spree."

The door opened again. Mathias turned around and saw that the man was holding a cell phone.

"Oh good! You're still here. Sorry, but I was just wondering if I could get a picture of all of you. Your costumes just look *so* good."

As a vampire, Mathias knew that his image could not be duplicated. He could have easily refused this request, but he saw no fun in that.

"I suppose there is no need to hide. But I think the lighting would be better inside."

"You really think so?"

Mathias nodded.

"Guess that makes sense. I have to admit, I'm not too tech-savvy. Not so good taking pics with this."

"May I come in now? I can show you how."

"All right. Sure."

Access granted.

"Wait here," Mathias told the werewolves. "Stay near."

He walked in and shut the door behind him.

Swiftly, he sank his teeth into the man's neck. Mathias put his hand over his prey's mouth to muffle the screaming. The man tried to bite back, prompting Mathias to shove his hand into the man's mouth and widen his jaws apart for a moment, surely spreading pain in the skin beneath the man's chin. Then he shoved the hand down his throat, depriving him of air. Mathias was not keen on allowing a chance for this man to live.

Once the deed was done, Mathias pushed the pale, lifeless body to the floor, and then dragged it into the already burning fireplace. He washed his hands and face in the kitchen sink, turned off the lights, and rejoined the werewolves outside.

* * *

While everyone else was asleep in their tents, Randy remained sitting alone in front of the campfire. In the time since his birthday, the bitterness of having nobody celebrate with him faded somewhat. Though he could not help but be reminded of birthday candles as the campfire danced in front of him. He noticed a moth flying nearby. He thought about swatting it away, but he became curious about its trajectory. Much to his astonishment, the moth flew into the flame.

"Same."

Randy saw a flash in the corner of his eye. He turned his head toward the woods. Then he looked up at the night sky, starry and clear without clouds. It could not have been lightning. It had to be the photographer, out here, disturbing this private moment with friends.

He stood up and thought about walking into the woods, his fists clenched like an upset aardvark.

"You all right, Brandy?" Naomi said, getting out of her tent.

"I'm fine." He unclenched his fists.

"You sure? We're in tents while you're looking intense."

"Heh. I just look like that sometimes. I don't *intend* to look intense."

"So why are you still out here all alone?"

"Someone's gotta watch the fire."

"Mind if I keep you company?"

Oh, my heart! Randy thought to himself as he sat back down.

"Not at all," he said.

Naomi sat in a lawn chair right next to his. He looked up at the stars, and so did she.

"Is this what you meant?" Naomi asked. "Keeping a watch on the fire?"

"No. But it doesn't hurt to look at those."

"Of course not. They're so far away that you don't need to worry about burning your eyes. And they're like a glimpse into the past. Imagine being able to see the light of stars as old as Miunis Grund itself."

Based on the stories passed around the school, all planets came from one world known as Miunis Grund. Apparently, this information came from Unicoren and Stagmantel, with whom Randy had never taken the time to speak. True or not, the thought of people being so close on one world and then drifting far apart made him feel lonely. Often in life, he felt as if all people and their perspectives were separated by the stars. But with Naomi sitting beside him in this moment, the effect was partially alleviated.

"Do you think we're like ants to anyone else?" he asked.

"That's a pretty heady thought. If you go too far down the rabbit hole, you start wondering, 'What's the point?' But if you look at ants, they still do their duties, gathering food and whatnot to live. Do you think they could have existential crises?"

He hoped not.

"I don't know. I don't really try to think of them as being that much like people."

"Do they think of *us* as people? Or as monsters?"

"Well, the concept of a gentle giant might be alien to them."

"Ooh. Maybe they think we're aliens. I say we beam down and ask them to take us to their leader."

Randy laughed.

"Straight to the queen."

"Oh, that's right. They have a monarchy. They'd probably think our government's weird."

"Now now, Naomi, there's no need to get too political."

"Shut up!" Naomi nudged him in the shoulder.

"Ha ha! I'm serious. You're making me really uncomfortable!" Naomi gave him a dismissive wave. "I'm kidding, of course."

"Liar," Naomi laughed. "You're just naturally mean."

Randy's laughter died down.

"No. I swear that's not me. You don't make me feel uncomfortable at all. You're good company."

"Aw." A charming smile filled her face. "That's so sweet."

So are you, he wanted to say. Instead, he went for a joke.

"Can't be too sweet, though. Otherwise the ants will come after me."

"Oh boy. They'd target you and be all up in your case. In most cases, they'd just wait until you're dead before eating you. But being super sweet would speed up the process."

"Some still bite the living."

"Yeah. If you're in their way."

"Hm. Sometimes I wonder whether *I* am kind of in the way."

Naomi's smile vanished, and she looked confused.

"How so?"

"I don't know." Randy shrugged. "Sometimes I feel like I'm just *there* when I'm hanging out with friends. Everyone else talks to each other pretty smoothly."

"You're talking to me right now. Clearly, you're capable of making more of an effort."

"I suppose. You've got me there. I don't know. For some reason, I sometimes feel like the odd one out. Like the onion ring in the bag of fries."

"But people like onion rings. Even if you're different, you can still belong."

Randy smiled, glad he had her attention. In this moment, he felt special. As if he was what mattered most to Naomi Clutcher.

"Thanks."

"Don't worry about it."

Randy's mind drifted to the topic of rings. Based on all that he had seen in media, it only took one ring to get an answer regarding love. He inhibited the thought, realizing that he was thinking too far ahead when he needed to remain within this present moment.

They continued to look up at the stars. This could have easily been an awkward silence, but it felt more like a comfortable silence, the laughter from before echoing through Randy's mind, immune to the night's edge. He did not dare bring up that his birthday had been forgotten. He did not want Naomi to stop being happy, even for a moment. And he did not care that he and Naomi were being watched.

Let them see how happy I am for now.

* * *

Based on Randy remaining by the campfire with the young woman, Candid guessed that he had dismissed any notion of him being watched.

Candid thought for sure that her cover had been blown like a candle, but now she was relieved. She could hear nothing from the conversation, but they seemed happy. Much happier than the moth she had seen embrace the fire. She was sure that there was some pretentious Icarus comparison to be made about that sight. She wondered whether the moth knew that it would die, or whether its attraction to the warmth had been so overwhelming that it was too blind to see how it could be devoured by destruction, like an oblivious angel enveloped by an inferno. And she wondered whether the process had been painless since it happened so quickly, or whether that hell was so huge that all the pain it could invoke built up into something that provided all possible torture within that one second before the moth blinked out of earthly existence.

It was times like these when Candid wondered whether she should have chosen philosophy as a career path instead.

* * *

Mathias and his werewolves kept going door to door until midnight, at which point all the house lights in the area were definitely off. Mathias then escorted his pack back to the campus.

He took them to the CPU library, a ten-story tower with no windows. On the basement level floor was a corner containing bookshelves surrounded by a rust-colored chain-link fence. The metal, which had been mixed with Mathias' own blood, was a magical one that the vampire had acquired and long kept over the years: Plo-Tunium. The gaps between the links were filled with Plo-Tunium Holes. Once behind the fence, the werewolves would go unnoticed by anyone who found their way down here. The Plo-Tunium Holes could also dumb down those who were near them and unaware of their power. Students sitting near them might have a hard time studying. But since these Plo-Tunium Holes surrounded the werewolves, it was easy to condition them to be less intelligent and more subservient to Mathias. Putting Plo-Tunium extracts within the drinks containing the werewolf disease also helped, dyeing the fur on the werewolves an electric blue. Some of the fur sprouted out of their skin. Other hairs were made from clothing, the matter shifting to get stitched into the skin as the transformation took place. Mathias loved keeping prisoners and watching them suffer.

He dumped all the candy onto the floor and then locked them in. Luckily, his vampire eyes could see them through the fence as they tried to divide the candy, each wolf swiping them into their own respective hoards.

"You're keeping more for yourself!" Harriet Harvester accused Juggle Mint.

"Come and get them!" Juggle Mint said, juggling mint flavored chocolates.

Harriet Harvester swiped her claws across Juggle Mint's muzzle. Juggle Mint dropped the sweets and then pounced on Harriet Harvester, biting her shoulder. Low Knife tried getting the candy that Juggle Mint had dropped, but then she noticed and bit his wrist.

Mathias just stood smiling outside of the cage, watching the show.

Chapter 14
What The Fudge?

Peyton felt like she got to know the Nap Kin a bit better during the camping trip. They did not have any particularly deep discussions, but she was very comfortable hanging out with them by this point.

When she returned to her dorm on Sunday, Pamela was there, out of her costume and doing some homework. Somehow, Peyton felt encouraged to talk to her. It seemed as though there was less pressure to do so.

"How was trick-or-treating?" Peyton asked.

"It was fine. Got a bunch of candy, but I've barely scratched the surface. The sugar's keeping me motivated though."

"That's good. Some people end up just using coffee. I never got into it though."

"You think it helps?"

"I think it depends on the person. Last I tried, I got too anxious. And mixing college anxiety with caffeinated anxiety just adds up to a whole lot of trouble."

"As opposed to half and half?"

The two of them laughed sisterly laughs they had not shared in quite a while.

"So," Pamela began, "how'd the camping trip go?"

"It was fun. Everyone seemed to be in a good mood by the end of the whole thing."

"Did you tell spooky stories over a campfire?"

"Seeing Mitch eat an overcooked hot dog was spooky enough. You know, I think you would've liked the woods over there."

"You think?"

"Yeah. We had a nice bit of hiking and exploration. Didn't find much, but I'm sure you'd make great use of the space."

"Well, you know, maybe *we* could go camping sometime."

Peyton smiled.

"I'd like that."

Pamela turned her eyes back to her desk, but she did not work right away. Peyton was ready to look away and do her own work, but then Pamela made eye contact again.

"Peyton, can I ask you something?"

"Sure."

"This'll probably sound like a weird question, but..."

"It's fine. You can ask."

It took Pamela a few seconds to let out the words.

"At what point do you think your childhood ended?"

Peyton did not quite expect a question like this one. She tried delving into her memories, searching for something that seemed like the turning point. And then she found it. The interchange she had not thought about for a while. The junction in the junk folder.

"Probably when I was ten, when Mom and Dad didn't wanna take me to see *Brother Bear*. I kept asking week after week if we could see it, and they kept saying they were busy and that we could just rent it later. But I wanted that big screen experience, you know? The animation, that top-notch music from the *Tarzan* guy in surround sound. But I guess they weren't that interested."

"Wow. You know, sometimes I wonder just how interested Mom and Dad really were in the things we liked as kids."

"Good question. I guess growing up is your parents telling you they don't wanna go with you to the movies to see talking animals."

"I hear that." Pamela looked up at her top bunk where the Mandy costume was lying. Then she opened the drawer of her desk and grabbed a handful of candy. "Do you want some?"

"Uh, sure," Peyton answered, holding out her hand and receiving the candy. She was not really craving sweets at the moment, but she did not want to refuse. "Thanks."

"Don't mention it. It's too much even for me to finish on my own."

Peyton unwrapped a mini chocolate bar and took a bite.

"That one's minty in the middle," Pamela said.

She was right about the filling.

"Guess that means I don't have to brush my teeth."

They both laughed, and Peyton could sense that she and her sister were a bit closer now.

"Did you get any Snickers?"

"No, but I got something similar. Instead of caramel, it's almost like a lemony Snickers."

And so they continued to eat sweets and do their homework in comfortable silence.

Later that week, Peyton got her grades back on her midterms and found out she got straight A's. Needless to say, she was very pleased with this. She paid Stagmantel a visit. As she expected, he was sitting on his unimpressive throne again, surrounded by ducks.

"Hey," Peyton said, walking out of the hedge tunnel. "How's it going, Staggy?"

"You again," Stagmantel said without turning around. "I take it then that your midterms went well."

"You knew?"

"Not until now. You are alive and in a chipper mood."

"Well, I guess I owe you a thank you for loaning me a duck."

"You owe me nothing. You took the risk and got lucky."

Peyton crossed her arms and walked around the chair to face him.

"Do you always have to be this stoic?"

"I don't *have* to be. I *choose* to be."

"How did you get to be like this? Where did you come from?"

"Miunis Grund, the planet of planets. A giant world that got broken into multiple worlds."

"How did it get broken?"

"I do not believe that there was just one cause. I believe that it was an accumulation of multiple causes. The world was inflicted by the Kin Conflicts."

"Anything to do with the Nap Kin?"

"I told August a little bit about these conflicts. He probably told the rest, fueling part of their name."

"I see. What more can you tell me about these Kin Conflicts?"

"There were also people who were united until each one misunderstood their core."

"Their core?"

"Their relationships with each other. The very core of some relationships was friendship. But, over time, some people misunderstood the meaning of their cores. Some thought theirs was romantic rather than platonic. Tectonic plates moved because of this. And the core spilled out, shooting lands in different directions across the universe."

"Are you telling me that love is evil?"

"Of course not. But there are just some people who misunderstand their dynamics with each other and take it too far. That is how some conflicts start out."

Peyton thought about Unicoren, and wondered what she was to Stagmantel. This mention of romance seemed to offer some sort of clue. Perhaps Stagmantel *had* felt something long ago.

"Are you and Unicoren a thing?"

"Two can form one, and that one can be malformed, becoming a thing."

"You've lost me."

"I have lost more."

Now Peyton was not sure whether to continue with personal questions. But her curiosity was killing her.

"Are things between you and Unicoren okay?"

"We get along. But things are not exactly the same as before."

"Before when?"

"Before coming to Copper Petal. Before the fire. Before leaving Miunis Grund."

Peyton wanted to learn more, but a male student came out of the hedge tunnel, carrying a skateboard.

"Hey, Stagmantel. Could you loan me a duck?"

"Of course."

"Wait," Peyton said. "So you're ending my loan? I'm not even sure I'm finished! Things with my sister are going so well now."

"The world does not spin for just one person, Peyton. These ducks are for everyone. You will just have to make your own luck now."

"I pick that one," the young man said.

"Very well," Stagmantel said, standing up and making eye contact with the chosen duck. "You there! Stand a loan."

The duck turned to stone. Peyton looked down from the hill and saw her stone duck become flesh and feathers again.

"Thanks," the skater said.

He got on his board and tried wheeling his way off the hill smoothly. But he landed face-first on a patch of mud below. This discouraged Peyton from wanting to take any further loans.

Later, Peyton returned to the dorm. It surprised her to see Mandy lying on the top bunk.

"Pam? Are you in there?"

No answer. Peyton looked around and walked over to the bathroom door. She could hear running water, as well as singing, on the

STEVEN SHINDER

other side. Then she looked back at the costume. It seemed moot to try wearing the costume now when things were going so well. But perhaps there was still value in Mortimer's advice. Even if he did bail. There was no telling when she might have another chance.

Peyton climbed the ladder of the bunk bed and brought down the costume. She put herself in the body of it and then put the head on. Pamela was right; it was not hot at all inside the costume. It was also easier to see than she had expected. She walked around the room. It did not feel like it added much weight to the walk. She got down on all fours, and it somehow felt so easy to walk in this fashion.

Then a memory came to her.

Peyton is in her room, a little while after refusing to play with Pamela. The door is closed, but she can hear the yelling downstairs.

"You ruined her!" *she hears Pamela yell.* "Aster! Can you hear me? You killed my best friend! I hate you! I wish you were never my mom!"

"Pamela, grow the fuck up!"

Peyton is not sure whether to trust her ears. She is shocked.

"Pam—"

"You cursed... You cursed me, Mom!"

She can hear Pamela running upstairs.

The door opened. Pamela, now in pajamas, had her eyes wide open, unblinking for a long moment.

"Mandy? Is that you?"

Nervous, Peyton did not know what else to do but stand up and nod.

"Oh my gosh. You can stand on your own now! This is unbelievable. How are you able to do this?"

Peyton said nothing.

"Why aren't you speaking to me?"

Peyton shrugged.

"I could hear you before. Is something wrong?"

She could HEAR Mandy the Mantleope?! Peyton thought. *Something IS wrong!*

159

Peyton could have gone along with this charade and extracted more information. But she knew that this tactic was a dishonest one, and she did not want to string Pamela along even further.

"Okay," Peyton said.

"Huh?"

Peyton removed the head, revealing her face, smiling nervously. Pamela looked like she had just seen a ghost.

"How *dare* you?!" she yelled. "You're not allowed to don Mandy the Mantleope! That is *my* responsibility! Get out!"

"I'm sorry."

Peyton tried getting out of the costume quickly.

"Be careful!" Pamela ordered. "There better not be any damage."

"Relax," Peyton said, slowing down the process.

Once she was fully out of the costume, she handed it to Pamela, whose face showed no sign of forgiveness.

"What made you think this was okay?"

"I was talking to my friends, and a professor they knew suggested I wear it to kinda see through your eyes."

"Other people *know* I'm the mascot? You're terrible!"

"I'm just trying to talk."

"Without talking?"

"How else am I supposed to talk to you, Pam? With or without that costume, you're mute as...fudge!"

Peyton almost did not stop herself from uttering the other word. But she could see from the look on Pamela's face that she caught the near slip-up.

"Mute as fudge?"

Peyton felt like a bad sister, rubbing salt on the surgical scissors. She tried to think of a way to justify her wording. To make it seem as if the phrasing had been intended all along.

"Fudge doesn't speak."

160

Pamela shook her head.

"You were gonna say the other word."

"But I didn't!"

"You're just like Mom!"

"Pam, that was a long time ago."

"It *still* hurts. It's cruel for a parent to tell a helpless child to grow up, as if it's so easy. And she said it in the *worst* possible way!"

"What do you want me to say?"

"There's nothing you *can* say. I'm moving out."

"What?"

"You heard me. I'm moving out."

"Where are you gonna live?"

"None of your business. Don't need you spying on me anymore."

Pamela packed all of her clothes in her suitcase and stuffed all her books in her backpack. Peyton stood by silently, not knowing what more to say. Hoping that Pamela would just come to her senses. Instead, she donned Mandy again and stormed out of the dorm, slamming the door behind her and leaving Peyton all alone.

"Fine!" Peyton said. "Room's all mine, then! I don't need you taking up so much space. Stupid Mandy..."

Peyton kicked the bed leg, stubbing her toe. It hurt like hell. When the pain died down, she was unsure what to do. She waited, thinking Pamela might come back. But then she reminded herself that her sister had conviction and would follow through with her choice. Peyton really had this room all to herself now. But it did not feel like a victory.

She opened Pamela's desk drawer. There were some mini fudge bars, but Peyton did not find them appealing at the moment.

Chapter 15
Punch Buggy

The monotony of the DMV was enough to inspire Tucker Ingersoll, age 37, to have fantasies in which he would just show up and shovel up the whole place out of the ground. All the people in line kept asking the same questions. Even the ones who had been there more than once. And the teens who barely had any driving experience were the worst, in his blunt opinion.

On this day, standing by the driveway in which people waited in their cars until an observer could ride with and assess them, Tucker commanded a teenage boy to turn the steering wheel to show that he could back up efficiently.

"Turn the wheel!" he yelled.

The window of the car rolled down.

"What?" the boy said poking his head out.

"Turn the wheel."

The boy put his head back inside. Though the glass was not clear from this distance, Tucker could tell that this was another kid confused about the controls.

"For fuck's sake. Don't parents take time to teach their kids these days? Turn the wheel."

The boy finally turned it, and the car backed up only a tiny bit. Not enough.

"Turn the wheel. Turn the wheel."

The car was backing up at a slug's pace.

"TUUUUUUURN THE WHEEEEEEEEL!"

The car finally backed up into the bumper of the car behind it. The woman in that car widened her eyes. Tucker stomped in disgust.

"Damn it!" he exclaimed. Walking over to the boy's window, he said, "You're not ready." The boy broke eye contact and stared at the windshield. "Get out of the car." More silence, and maybe a tear. "Go. Did you come here with your mama?" The boy nodded. "Where the hell's she at? Do you have a cell phone? Give her a call and tell her to come and drive you out of here. You've wasted my time. All our time. Lines would've been shorter without you."

Work hours passed by more slowly than that turn. By the time the workday winded down to a close, Tucker was thirsty for something other than his tasteless bottled water. He reached into his right pocket for his phone and felt the folded paper that had been there for two weeks. He always checked for the time, not text messages. The time was never absent, even if it did feel empty. In his left pocket, he felt the full flask. Tempting, he wanted an icy glass.

After work, he spent hours sitting at a table in a corner within Spike's Punch. The only reason that this was his favorite bar was that he never felt like checking out any others. Fruit punch was offered as a chaser, but Tucker preferred having his drinks unsoftened. Every Friday there was the same. He chugged shots of whiskey, campfires in his throat, lamenting the loss of his brother, whom he deemed too stupid to be a passenger. And it was his routine walk over to the bar counter and back to have enough peanuts for munching. As night grew more prevalent, and the bar became more full, he drank more frequently. At the end of every glass, he licked and chewed on what remained of the ice cubes.

Up on a stage in the corner opposite from his, there was a tall man with long hair, a royal blue pea coat, lime green suit pants, and black dress shoes. He sang karaoke, holding the mic in his right hand and a black thermos in his left. Noticeably, he struggled to keep his notes high and elongated as he sang "The Reason" by Hoobastank. Patrons seemed enchanted by his effort and applauded when he was finished.

Tucker felt the urge to follow up the act, to be in the limelight. So he went up and flipped through the song selections in the karaoke ledger, replete with singles. He found one he liked: "Wish You Were Here" by Pink Floyd. A classic. Though intoxicated, he remembered the lyrics word for word and danced with the microphone stand as he sang.

"Fuck yeah Pink Floyd!" the man in the pea coat yelled. Despite the sorrow he felt, Tucker smiled. When the song was over, he got the applause, and the man in the pea coat walked up to him. "Dude. You're a Floyd fan? Nobody else here's ever tried singing Pink Floyd the times I've been here! Have you listened to every album?"

"Yeah. And there's a new one coming out tomorrow called *The Endless River*. I can't wait."

"Wow. You're on top of it."

"It's weird. I've never really had anyone else geek out about Floyd around me."

"You wanna go to this sushi place three doors down? Ever been?"

"I haven't, but I'm starving. All I've had are the peanuts."

"You'll love it. And we can talk more Floyd! What's your name?"

"Tucker."

"Mathis Dillard," the taller man responded as he shook Tucker's hand.

Sushi Belt was actually four doors down, but Tucker did not mind the walk. Mathis showed him his thermos. It still smelled like clam chowder, bits of which were still stuck to the walls, but it was less conspicuous than Tucker's flask. So he took up the offer to pour his store-bought vodka inside so he could bring it to their booth. Only a few other tables were full at this time. Beside them, a conveyor belt passed plates of sushi around the restaurant. Each plate had two sushi rolls and cost $2.50. Tucker grabbed yellowtail, tuna, and squid. The squid roll disgusted him because it tasted like shampoo. Mathis, meanwhile, worked on a caterpillar roll.

"So was that song dedicated to anyone in particular?" Mathis asked.

"My brother," Tucker answered before taking more intoxicating sips. "His name was Glenn."

"What was he like?"

Tucker was not really sure he knew anymore. His brother's idiotic mistake overshadowed all the other memories of him. But for once, he tried to reach further back to a time before the screw-up.

"We used to watch movies together as kids. One of our favorites was *The Goonies*. Just some kids off on an adventure. I remember Granny took me to see *The Goonies* in the theater. My brother remembered seeing it with her too. I don't remember him being there with us, though. But judging from her character, I wouldn't be surprised if it turned out that Granny was willing to pay twice to see the movie. Even if it meant taking each of us to see it in theaters on separate occasions. Just to see her grandchildren happy. She used to say, 'You're not well unless you're full of wishes.'" Tucker took a few more sips. "I haven't been full of wishes in a while. It's kinda messed up that Glenn went out before Granny did. It really broke her heart."

"What happened to Glenn?" Mathis asked with a neutral expression.

"He was driving me to school. I was fifteen and he was eighteen. As kids, we used to play that punch buggy game. He never grew up. Punched me while he was driving. Then we crashed, and he died. How sad is that?"

Tucker took a dozen more sips from the thermos.

"I hear ya, man. Family can be trouble. People in general, really. I once had someone over at my place to watch a movie. She said there was no plot. That it was just violence for the sake of violence."

"So then what happened?"

"I cut her fuckin' head off with my scythe."

Mathis smiled. This sounded like the funniest thing that Tucker had ever heard, and it made him laugh for the better half of a minute. When he was done, he mellowed out a bit as he kept opening up.

"I don't blame my brother so much as I do the cars. Hell, I got this list."

He took the paper out of his pocket. It was a list of Volkswagen Beetles and addresses of their owners. He had jotted down while using the computer at work one day. He showed it to Mathis, whose raised eyebrows and teeth-full grin gave away how intrigued he was.

"Impressive," was all that he said. "When life gives you a punch, just drink it and smile."

"It can be tough to smile when life's so shitty. If I were happy, my face would smile, as opposed to... Um..."

"Projecting an illusion?"

"Y-yeah."

"Smiles are not innate; they are the most acceptable masks to wear. Nobody wants to see you cry."

"Guess that's true."

"You drink saké?"

"I don't think so."

"Bring us some saké over here!" Mathis called out, waving to a waiter. "Saké for the saké of violence, am I right?"

Tucker laughed again. When they each received a bottle of saké, they chugged it all. After that, they munched in silence. Mathis seemed like he was ruminating something, but Tucker was too hungry to figure it out. He reached for crab rolls, salmon rolls, dragon rolls, and before he knew it he had eaten $30 worth of sushi. He was embarrassed when the bill came and he finally got around to doing the math.

"I'll take care of it," Mathis said. "You can pay me back later."

"Thanks, man. I just wanna crash. I need to get back to my place."

"In your state, you might not make it if you drive home. But *my* place is just a few blocks from here. Not too far of a walk."

"You didn't drive here?"

"I'm very careful. Have you *seen* the gas prices?"

"Fair point."

"Come on. You can crash on my couch."

"All right. Let's go."

It took about six blocks to get to Mathis' place, which turned out to be a mansion. But Tucker was too out of it to be awestruck. He kept stumbling, so Mathis had to support him. He did not seem to mind, but Tucker still felt bad.

"Check it out," Mathis said, pointing to the full moon in the sky. "How dark do you think the dark side of the moon gets?"

"Does it even have one?"

"There's always a dark side. Even in you."

"You got that right. Man, I showed no mercy yelling at that kid today."

"Fun. Making sure they remember the moments that hurt them, so that they can suffer even further when they grow older."

"Huh?"

"You know what? You'd obviously be more comfortable in your own home. Why don't I drive you?"

"That'd be great."

"Wait here."

Mathis took out a clicker and pressed a button, causing the gate to open. He ran off to the car in the yard and pushed it over the round stones until it was out of the gate. Tucker was surprised by all the strength that Mathis was willing to invest in pushing the vehicle. Mathis seemed to enjoy it.

They got in the car, and Tucker fell asleep in the front passenger seat before he could provide his own address. But when he woke up, the car was moving anyway. He started moving his head around.

"Oh hey," Mathis said. "You were all tuckered out. Feel rested now?"

Wondering where they were, Tucker looked around and saw a yellow Volkswagen Beetle in a driveway.

"Am I awake?" he asked.

"Hopefully, the owner of that car isn't. I doubt it though. It's *way* past midnight. Come on."

They got out. Mathis popped open the trunk. Drunk and leaning against the side of Mathis' car, Tucker saw Mathis pull out a toolbox. Tucker blinked, and then Mathis handed him a hammer. Mathis then pulled out two scythes and tucked them into his sleeves until only the blades were visible in front of his hands.

"We're gonna fuck this bug up. You down?"

"I'm down." Tucker nodded without processing what had been asked of him.

Mathis led the way, and instinct told Tucker to follow. When they got up to the driveway, Mathis just jumped onto the hood on all fours—like a preying mantis rather than a praying mantis—and started cutting glass and metal aggressively as the car alarm sounded off. The chaotic cacophony was so unsettling that Tucker closed his eyes and vomited onto the lawn. He looked at the fish and seaweed that had flooded onto the grass. He dropped the hammer beside the mess.

The sounds stopped.

He looked back at Mathis, who shook his head, staring sternly. Tucker could sense that he had offended him.

"You disgust me," Mathis said, climbing off of the car. "What a wuss and a waste."

He walked up to Tucker and gave him a slash across the face too quickly for him to react against. Mathis picked up the hammer and smashed through one of the car's windows before coming back to knock Tucker out cold.

His last thought was the hope that nobody would come out to stop Mathis Dillard from killing him quickly.

* * *

August awoke to the chaotic cacophony of shattering glass. He thought someone was breaking through the hotel window. But when he turned on the light, he saw that the glass was completely intact. Then he realized that the sound was coming from the lavatory, so he walked inside and turned on its light. The mirror was still intact, but within it was a close-up of a man using scythes to behead another man who was lying on grass.

"AHHHH!" August screamed.

He covered his mouth, worrying that the man with the scythe would reach through the mirror and grab him. But the man in the mirror paid no attention, walking away and leaving the corpse behind.

Below all this was a text, the reflection of "OBJECTS IN MIRROR ARE CLOSER THAN THEY APPEAR." August was too disoriented to realize that it was backwards, so he read the last two words the way that his mind and his dizzy vision comprehended it.

"Reap payeth..."

August was convinced that he had just witnessed the work of the Grim Reaper. Irrationally, he gave in to the impulse to call out to him as he walked out of the frame.

"Death! Is that what you are?"

"Who are you?" he heard a startled woman ask.

"Sorry 'bout the car," the reaper said. "I can help you get *ahead* of the next payment."

The image started to disappear.

"HEY!" August yelled.

There was no answer, and the image vanished. He had no idea what he wanted to say to the reaper, but he knew that it would have been a question. He worried that his time was coming.

He turned on the lavatory light, grabbed his phone, and video recorded himself.

"If you find this, I might be dead. I woke up and saw the Grim Reaper in the mirror. He was beheading a man with his two scythes. He didn't look at me when I called to him. He disappeared, but I think he might be after me sometime soon. The words said 'reap payeth.' I don't know what I'd need to pay for. I don't *think* I've done anything wrong. Not on purpose... I need to get out of this room."

He considered continuing the recording to document what he intended to be his exit from the hotel, but he knew that it would distract him. He needed to stay focused. And some people did not like shaky cam, anyway.

As he made his way down the hallway, he gradually forgot why he had left his room in the first place. Then he looked at the phone in his hand.

"Oh. Duh. There's my phone. *Hate* it when that happens. Just jet lag I guess."

He walked back into the hotel room, oblivious to the execution he had just witnessed. Not feeling so sleepy, he decided to free up some memory on his phone. However, he was surprised to find that any photos and videos that he took on this trip abroad were already gone from his phone. Luckily, he had already posted everything related to his travels on social media. But it still did not sit well with him, knowing that his files were gone and being certain he had never deleted them.

Chapter 16
Cause for Alarm

In the days since the camping trip, the times when Randy hung out with friends felt more normal than expected. Part of him thought and hoped that he and Naomi would act a good kind of different toward each other after that night sitting by the fire. But they had not had a moment alone since then. And she had not invited him to go anywhere with her alone. Whenever they were together, it was sometimes the confines of Nap Kin hangouts. As such, he was worried that she was not so interested in him after all.

The other times they were together were during an art class that they shared, and they could not really talk to each other as the instructor taught the lessons. Randy and Naomi had different classes right before and right after this one, so they only had ten minutes to talk during the walk afterward. Randy at least appreciated that their classes were in the same direction. But he did not appreciate how much she was talking about the other Nap Kin. Especially Grady, who was able to spend more time with them since the group chat kept him in the know.

"So then Yo-Gert suggested I show Gravy Stew my sketchbook. He was pretty honest about where I need improvement because I encouraged him to be blunt. But I kept apologizing with every criticism. It was so funny and so sweet. That kid seems like he hasn't said anything bad about anyone in his life. He made some solid points about how I sometimes forget about shadows. You ever have that problem?"

"Yeah. Sometimes I forget to draw the shadows, too."

"Well, I'm more conscious of it now. Thanks to Gravy Stew, I'm able to keep it real. You know something? That kid's gonna go places, being the kind and constructive guy he is. There's no question he's related to a guy as nice as Eight-ball. It'll be great having both of them hanging around when Eight-ball visits for winter break. He's really living it up over in England. That dude deserves it."

You and the rest would know, Randy thought. *I'm the one out of the loop.*

"You know," Randy said, feeling nervous, "I really like how you compliment people even when they're not around to hear you. Do... Do you ever say anything nice about me behind my back?"

Naomi's face somehow looked more alert. If they did not have to keep walking, she might have halted.

"Wow. Are you feeling all right?"

"I'm...okay. Just curious. Never mind. It sounds like a silly, selfish thing to ask."

"No, you're good, Brandy. Um... I have told the others about how great you are at listening."

If only someone were willing to listen to me, Randy thought.

When they arrived at Naomi's destination, she checked the time.

"Shoot!" she said. "It's about the start. Bye!"

She waved goodbye without looking back, leaving Randy to dread his next class. He arrived a little late, disrupting the instructor's lesson with the bit of noise he made squeezing between desks to get to the only empty one in the corner furthest from the door. He could hardly pay attention during that particular seminar.

Later, when Randy returned to his apartment, he noticed a package on his doorstep. It was addressed to him and sent by his parents.

And it included their address.

"Shit!"

He looked around, hoping that the photographer was not nearby. He saw no sign of her, but he felt unsafe. Taking out his house key, he shakily unlocked the door and got inside, locking the door behind him. After setting the box on the coffee table in the living room, he tore off the label and shredded it with his bare hands. Randy ran to the stove and turned up the heat, then threw the tiny pieces into the flames. Smoke rose to the ceiling.

The smoke detector on the kitchen ceiling went off.

"Shut the fuck up!"

It beeped continuously, a noisy nuisance. He reached up and held down the button until it became silent.

Once Randy reclaimed his calm composure, he opened the box and examined its contents. It was another care package. His parents normally sent him at least one per quarter. Randy was mad at himself for forgetting that this could happen. Within the box was the usual: granola bars, bags of potato chips, cups of uncooked ramen, and a note. As predictable as the note probably was, he went ahead and read it.

Hope you can visit soon. In the meantime, hang in there! We love and believe in you, son. Kick this year's butt!

-Mom and Dad
P.S. Kayleigh says hi.

Randy did not know what he did to deserve such caring parents. Whatever they saw in him, he did not see at all. Sometimes he thought it was just the bloodline that kept them caring for him. He wondered how differently they would perceive him if he were someone else from a different family.

He grabbed a granola bar, a necessary snack for the exercise he had planned for today.

Randy went to the redwoods of Petal Lock Park, where he intended to run around by himself. He had walked through it from time to time but was not yet familiar with every single obstacle, even after all these years. Still, Randy ran and jumped over logs and tree roots, petrified wood that protruded out of the ground. He needed to increase his stamina and get stronger if he was to bring Mathis down with him whether it be in his own moment of dying or a victory after which he could continue his life with others.

* * *

On Unicoren's side of the park, Pamela, clad in her mascot outfit, saw someone run from the redwoods to the silver birches. He did not seem like an ordinary runner; he had a goal in mind. She followed him cautiously. He stopped in front of a tree and punched the air, seemingly imagining that he was facing an opponent.

He's pretending, she thought excitedly.

Pamela got on all fours and embraced the spirit of Mandy, chasing after the runner. As she and Mandy ran together, they stepped on twigs, creating sounds that alerted the runner that he was not alone. He looked back, spotted them, and then tried running faster. He crossed the pathway and entered retreated into the redwoods.

Pamela tried keeping up. After turning a corner around a thicket, she lost sight of him.

But then she saw a figure in the distance. He looked like he was walking on some sort of branch between trees. Instinctively, she ran closer and pounced, knocking him off of what turned out to be a slackline, and knocked him to the ground.

"Ouch!" the young man said. "Seek not a bear while it rides its unicycle!"

She inspected his face and realized that he was not the runner.

"Sorry," she apologized. "I thought you were someone else."

"So did I."

This response confused Pamela. But before she could ask the slackliner to elaborate, she heard the runner coming from behind. He ran blindly in their direction, tripping over the slackline and falling face-first onto the ground.

"Oof! Ugh..."

"Are you okay?" Pamela asked.

"Who put this rope here?"

"That would be me," the slackliner said, struggling to sit up.

Pamela looked at the runner's face, which implied familiarity between the two men.

"Frederick Filler?"

"Hello, Randy."

Randy stood and pulled Frederick up by the hand.

"Haven't seen you since freshman year," Randy said.

"Was that a choice?" Frederick replied.

"I wasn't even sure you were still around here. Still studying in philosophy?"

"Yes. I'm double-majoring, actually."

"Oh yeah? What's the other major?"

"Deep Diving Orchestra."

"Does that involve singing like killer whales?"

"No. Just playing instruments underwater."

"I see. How've you been?"

"Well, your friend here knocked me off balance for a moment. But," he tilted his head to crack his own neck, "I regained myself. I feel perfectly neutral now."

"Friend?" Randy said. "I mean, I've seen Mandy on campus. She and I have even taken a couple selfies together every once in a while. But friends?"

"You don't know Mandy, then?" Frederick asked.

"I know of the person behind the mask, but I've never hung out with her. She was just chasing after me."

Pamela's heart jumped.

"You know who I am?" she asked.

"Yeah. Oh! Sorry."

Must be a friend of Peyton, Pamela thought.

"Well, no use in hiding from either of you." Pamela removed Mandy's head, revealing herself. "I'm sorry. I was just having a little fun. I love pretending, and I saw that *you* were pretending... It's hard to explain." Pamela broke eye contact, looking down at the ground, where the runner had hit his face all because she had chased him. "You probably think I'm a weirdo."

"Weirdos are nothing new around here," Randy said, turning to face Frederick. "You walk here often?"

"Every day. Structured strangeness. I live here, actually."

Pamela looked around and spotted a red tent.

"You too?" she asked.

"Hold on," Randy said, pointing fingers at them. "You *both* live in this park? Are you homeless?"

"By choice," Pamela said. "Though I don't really see it as being homeless."

"I didn't have much of a choice," Frederick answered. "But I try to make do with what I have. Walking on this tightrope keeps me on a course."

"A course to what?" Randy asked.

"Remaining balanced. You ever have trouble with that?"

"I don't wanna talk about it."

"You're not obligated to do so. I was just curious. But I'm forgetting myself. I shouldn't really be caring so much. I *don't* care. That's not who I am anymore. It's not my place to care about other people's business. It's just everyone for themselves, as long as they respect each other. No need to look for a shoulder upon which to cry."

"I don't like you," Pamela said.

"It makes no difference to me," Frederick replied with a shrug.

Pamela turned to Randy and held out a hand. "Pamela Sheer, by the way."

"Randy Morales," he answered, shaking her hand. "So then you *are* related to Peyton."

"She's my sister..." Their hands let go.

"You don't sound so proud."

"Neither does she." Pamela crossed her arms. "To her, I'm kind of an embarrassment."

"Why?"

"I don't wanna talk about it..."

"It's okay to be silent," Frederick said. "Silence is where one may find peace."

"Hey," Pamela said. "Hush now. I meant I don't wanna talk about it *yet*. Just to be clear." She looked back at Randy. "I just met you. But, given time, we might be willing to share whatever problems we may have. If you want. I'm here lots of the time. How about you?"

"I was thinking of making this running thing a routine. But I'm probably getting ahead of myself. Well, I guess I can't really get ahead of myself with how out of shape I am. Not sure I'm ready for this, given how badly things went down."

"How badly *you* went down."

"Hah. I don't know. I guess I could avoid this rope thing next time. You tie it the same place, Frederick?"

"Not always to the same trees. I can't guarantee where I'll be. I move around quite a bit."

"Well then, I guess I'll just have to double-check with you each time. Because I really *do* need exercise. I just don't like people at the gym watching me do it."

"If only you had a costume like this," Pamela said with a smirk.

"Don't you get hot in that?"

"Nope! The temperature stays pretty moderate."

"Is there balance?" Frederick asked. "Or is there nothing?"

"Okay..." Pamela was unsure how to answer. "Um, wanna walk this way, Randy?" She pointed toward the silver birches. "There's someone I want you to meet."

"Okay," Randy said. "Well, Frederick, talk to you later, I guess."

"You could," Frederick answered, getting back on his slackline.

As they walked away, Pamela saw Randy pull a wrapped granola bar out of his pocket.

"Would you like some?" he offered.

"No thanks. Granola bars aren't really for me."

"Not my thing either, normally. But my parents sent it to me. Part of their care package."

"Oh. That's really nice of them."

Over the summer, CPU had mailed out an order form that parents could use to send care packages to students. Pamela's dad had asked whether it was a requirement, and Pamela said it was not. So he opted not to spend extra money. But Pamela might have appreciated a care package.

Randy unwrapped the granola bar and took a bite. After swallowing, he spoke again.

"So who do you want me to meet?"

"Not sure if you've met her before, but I've become somewhat of a good friend of Unicoren. She's letting me stay with her."

"Oh." Randy halted.

"What's wrong?"

"I feel like she'll stare into my soul."

"What do you have to hide?"

"Nothing. Nothing super important. Can I just talk to you instead?"

This was a first. No human had ever entrusted Pamela with any personal secret truths before. She was not sure whether she was ready for such a step, but thinking of Mandy somehow encouraged her.

"Sure. What's wrong?"

"I have these friends, you see. But I'm not sure they know how much they mean to me. And I'd like for them to know, but I'm not sure I can show them. I'm scared."

"Anxiety. It sucks. It's hard for me to make friends. I never outgrew this need to pretend."

"Are you a drama major?"

"Undecided."

"What's keeping you?"

"Fear of rejection. And maybe fear of what it could do to my ego, or whatever's left of it."

"Egos are overrated. They are a burden to carry. Caring so damn much sucks. Like, you want to feel special, and then you feel awful for wanting to feel special, you know?"

"There was a time when I *did* feel special," Pamela said. "When I was someone's whole world. Mom and Dad loved me and my sister equally, and they'd play pretend with us. But there was only one person who'd play pretend with me when nobody else would. She'd travel a long distance just to be in my world, so I could be *her* world. At least, that's how I remember it."

"What else do you remember?"

"I remember a few friends, back when I was a kid. Nobody else remembers them. Well, except the monkey, I guess. I'd hop around the park wearing this rabbit onesie, carrying this stuffed animal monkey on my back. She was purple, and her name was Aster."

* * *

Randy widened his eyes at this revelation as he thought back to his own childhood.

"Holy shit that's fuckin' weird. I used to have a stuffed animal—a rabbit—named Aster."

"The heck?" Pamela's facial expression mirrored his. "Did she talk to you?"

Randy hated looking back. He did not want to relive everything. And he was unsure of what Pamela would think of him. So he tried summarizing.

"Yeah. But after a while, she stopped. She wasn't happy with how we were playing. So she left me. Alone. And I tried playing pretend with other kids at school, but they didn't like my ideas."

"Was it the ideas or the execution?"

"I guess I was a bit of a control freak. I wanted the scenarios done a certain way. And so they didn't wanna play. Not with me. So I was left to my own imagination. My imaginary friend, a clown named Artie Docent."

"Did Aster know him?"

"No. I made him. He was her replacement. He talked to me whenever I needed someone."

He still does, Randy thought, reluctant to reveal the continuing correspondence.

"Have we found each other?" Pamela asked.

"I still feel lost."

"Why?"

He thought about Naomi. And then about Mathis.

"I can't say. It's personal."

"Well, if you ever need anyone..."

Though she did not finish, he knew the intended destination of the sentence.

"I know," he said. "Another friend told me that. Though, he and I haven't really been talking."

"I'm sorry. I didn't mean to make you feel bad."

"I'm fine. Don't worry."

I'm not all right, he thought. *Please worry. Press further.*

"Well, if you say so."

Damn it. Why did I do that?

"See you around, Pamela."

"See ya."

* * *

Candid took another photo as she watched Randy walk away from the girl in the costume. She wondered whether the mascot would even matter to her benefactor. Better to be safe, she supposed.

Part of her still felt guilty, bringing more people into the frame.

Why does Randy have to be so damn sociable? she wondered.

Walking off of the campus and back to her car, she looked through her photos. There was the one of Randy tripping and falling next to the mascot and the guy who had been on the slackline. She wondered what the slackliner's deal was, but then thought he was probably not that important in the grand scheme of things.

When she got back to her apartment, her four roommates were sitting in the living room, gathered around a paper on the coffee table containing a sketch of a building's layout. Her roommates' names were Calvin, Cleo, Ivory, and Simon. She would never have been associated with them if she were rich and able to afford a place for herself.

"Candid!" Simon said. "There you are. You're just in time for our planning meeting!"

"What planning meeting?"

"Did you not get the memo?"

"Oh," Ivory said, checking her phone. "I forgot to set my reminder to let her know. My bad."

"We're planning a bank heist!" Calvin said. "It's so exciting!"

"Come again?" Candid said.

"We're kinda running low on funds," Simon said. "And we thought, 'Hey, we've seen enough movies to know what to do and what not to do. Why not rob a bank?'"

"You're doing a robbery, then?"

"No, a heist. We're running in with guns—to threaten people, not to shoot unless we have to—and getting them to fill Cleo's new safe with money."

"Robbery, then," Candid said.

"What's the difference?"

"A heist implies more stealth," Ivory chimed in.

"Oh. That does sound safer. Well, which do we wanna do?"

"The question is," Calvin said, "which one is the greater thrill?"

"Okay, well we have more details that need ironing out. But that's okay."

"Have you picked a date yet?" Candid asked.

"Well, no. Not yet. But this requires a ton of preparation. So are you in?"

As tempting as the idea was, she had no confidence in these bone-heads to execute their plan (if they had one), and she really did not wish to get caught.

"I don't have time. I know nothing about your plan. All an illusion. Don't mind me."

Candid sat down and opened her laptop. As she uploaded the photos, the rest continued with their meeting. Cleo set her newly acquired safe onto the table, pressing the buttons to demonstrate how to open it.

"The combination is easy to remember: four-two-six-one-seven-three-five. That is the order in which *Pulp Fiction* is presented. It starts off with the odds, and then it evens out. The middle is in the beginning, and the beginning is in the middle."

With that, she lifted her middle finger, which stood alone among all digits of the hand.

"Actually," Simon said, "That combination begins with evens, and then ends with odds."

"Oh."

"Yeah. I'm not gonna remember all that. Maybe you should be the one to hold the safe during the...robbery or heist."

"How much did you spend on that safe?" Ivory asked. "Couldn't we have just gotten bags?"

"You gotta spend money to make money," Simon said. "This will keep the cash secure. Wouldn't wanna trip and have to pick up whatever falls out."

"Being on the run's gonna be so much fun," Calvin said.

Rolling her eyes, Candid tuned them out as she attached the photos of Randy to an email, which she then sent to Ben. Once she was done with that, she noticed a new email from him within her inbox, sent to her a few hours earlier. She read it and then groaned as she closed her laptop.

Not another fuckin' sidequest.

The directions provided led her to a junkyard. This was where cars went to die. Parts were lying everywhere, like intestines in the basement of a serial killer. She pointed her flashlight around the place until she found a yellow Volkswagen Beetle, as described in the email.

With her gloved hands, she opened the driver door, where there was a headless body—a woman, from the looks of it—reclined in the driver's seat. In the passenger seat next to it was a headless man. Reaching past the driver's shoulder, she pulled up the metal cylinder to unlock the back door. Getting back out, she pulled the back door open and checked the backseat. The woman's head was there, in the middle seat where nobody would want to sit. Candid opened the mouth and saw no cash. She lifted the head, but nothing fell out.

The treasure had to be in the trunk.

Getting back to the driver seat, she pulled the lever that opened the trunk. She heard the back hood rise, and then she took a look inside.

Nothing.

"The fuck?"

It took her a few seconds, but then she remembered the front hood. She pulled the other lever.

Surely enough, there was the man's head, tucked between metal. It smelled like vomit. Candid tried not to inhale the stench. She picked up the head and opened his mouth. There was a plastic sandwich bag—covered in a bit of vomit—containing the stack of cash. Candid really hated her benefactor.

The car alarm went off.

FUCK!

Candid took the cash, dropped the head, and split. She tried running back the way she came in.

"What's going on?" she heard a voice say.

Candid kept running until she made it to her car. She took out her keys, and then unintentionally did the annoying action of dropping her keys and struggling to pick them up. When she had them in her hands again, she pointed the car key at the keyhole but kept missing. It irritated and stressed her to no end. When she finally got it in, she opened the door and entered quickly.

But it was not over.

She had to put on her seat belt if she was going to drive fast. She did not want to risk something stupid like flying through the windshield and splitting her skull on pavement. Trying to be safe, she tugged on her seat belt, which got stuck and could not reach the buckle right away. She kept pulling repeatedly until, finally, she tugged it far enough and got it to click. Now secure, she hit the brakes and sped away.

As she drove, she felt paranoid, wondering whether she was being watched. She imagined eyes behind her car, hovering on the highway. She kept checking the rear-view mirror and saw nobody following her.

When she got home, she opened her laptop and checked her email. There was a new message from Ben. She read it.

Why'd you run off? Did I alarm you?

He was there. He was the one who had activated the alarm. Remotely, it seemed. Even worse: he revealed this to her through a terrible pun. He was playing a game with her, and she was not having fun. As well as he paid, the resentment toward Ben F. was brimming out of the bowl.

I hope you fuckin' die, fucker!

Chapter 17
Food Forethought

At Tree Culler Hotel, the American students decided to bring Thanksgiving to London. Bessie coordinated between everyone who was interested, marking down who was bringing and cooking what. The turn-out was surprising, the dining room chairs around every table filled.

August went down the stairs from the kitchen. The steepness of the stairway tended to creep him out. With no rails, he stepped carefully so as not to fall. Once he got to the floor, the whirring of twenty refrigerators became prominent to his ears. He opened the fridge that he shared with Verner and a couple other students with whom he was not very familiar. He had bought a tub of mint chocolate chip ice cream from the shop to share with everyone. Examining the shelves, however, he could not see the dessert. As anyone else would, he suspected theft.

He walked back up the stairs, through the kitchen, and into the dining room, where he saw Tate clinking a wine glass with a spoon. Everyone who was seated turned to look at him.

"I would like to make a toast," Tate said. "However, *someone* stole my toaster! How am I supposed to contribute?"

"A bunch of my pots and pans are missing," Fritz said. "I'm gonna need to borrow someone else's if I'm gonna cook something."

"Seriously!" Bessie said. "Who keeps stealing stuff? I put a bird right in the oven, and when it's almost time to take it out, I come back to find that it's gone!"

"I suspected that something like this would happen," Jade said, carrying to-go boxes in a plastic bag. "Which is why I just bought some fried chicken from down the street. Also, I didn't feel like cooking."

"All right," August said. "Whoever is responsible for all this stuff going missing, please step forward."

Nobody stepped forward.

"Coward!" Bessie yelled.

"Please," August said. "This is supposed to be a wholesome dinner with friends, and whoever is stealing stuff is ruining it for the rest of us."

Out of the corner of his eye, August saw a scoop of mashed potatoes rising from a tray. It flew right at his face.

"What?" he uttered, bewildered.

"Food fight!" Anton yelled.

Needless to say, a food fight ensued. Bits of corn, cranberry sauce, and chicken, among other things, flew all over the place. August hid under a table, disheartened to see the hotel divided. Nobody even teamed up; everyone was out for themselves.

He wondered whether the Kin Conflicts of Miunis Grund ever got this bad.

* * *

Peyton drove home for Thanksgiving. She knew that her parents would bombard her with questions, and she was not looking forward to dealing with them. But it was inevitable.

"Peyton!" her dad said, hugging her as she arrived inside. "You didn't bring Pam with you?"

"She really needs to study. Like, you have no idea."

"I hope she's all right," her mom said. "She couldn't have come down just for dinner?"

"I wanted to stay here the whole weekend. She wouldn't have wanted to stay that long, and I *really* don't wanna drive back and forth. Sorry."

Her mom sighed.

"It'd just be nice for Pam to call once in a while. We hardly ever hear from her."

You and me both, Peyton thought. *Some family we are.*

Despite the fallout, Peyton hoped that Pamela was at least eating well, wherever she was living.

* * *

Stagmantel and Unicoren sat together at the halfway point between their respective sides of the park. There, on a table set up for them, was a bowl full of pears, a plate full of pasta pearls, and a cup full of milk tea. And there, on the side, was a plate with a pear and a cantaloupe, courtesy of the chancellor. The pair shared eye contact.

"He is full of himself," Stagmantel said.

"But he does not have *all* of himself," Unicoren said.

"Do you still remember?"

"Yes. I still remember."

The pearls floated in the air, each depicting a fragment of the memory like a screen that was incomplete.

Stagmantel and Unicoren are seated at the end of a table, holding hands the entire duration of the dinner. Their souls are covered by their original forms consisting of flesh, fur, and fabric. On either side of them are their respective parents, who disapprove of their relationship. Antlers on one side, horns on the other side. One can taste the silent resentment if they take a bite out of the air. The young couple want to announce their impending union, but the looks that their parents give each other convey that it may be best to keep it secret. No family, no friends.

Not even the one who had introduced them.

Now they felt indifferent toward the family they had lost. For this moment, their general indifference slid away.

"This stinks," Unicoren said.

"Should we light a match?" Stagmantel replied.

"No. Not while we have a chance of getting everything back."

"But when will that happen? Every time we have the urge to do something about it, the boundaries lessen our motivation."

"Pamela is the key to setting us free. All of us."

"She certainly moves us."

"We're getting closer to getting out. My spirits rise ever so slightly, but they rise. We just need to be patient for a while longer."

"I've seen her sadness walking beside her. It keeps her from moving as much."

"She can heal from it. She just needs to adapt and look elsewhere for friendship."

"But where?"

"Closer than you think. It's all closer than you think."

"You think?"

They turned their heads when they heard Mandy approaching, worn by Pamela as expected.

"I'm here," she said. "Food looks good."

She sat between them at the table. Stagmantel and Unicoren smiled slightly. Then they all ate their food in silence. But it was a comfortable silence.

* * *

Behind the chain-link fence in the library basement, the werewolves, sitting in their human form, deliberated about their next meal, even though any such meal was far out of reach.

"Where are we going to eat?" Mortimer Mutterer asked.

"Fast food feeds the quickest, but it makes you the sickest," Doggerel Grill said.

"I'm willing to dice something up and make that gamble," Juggle Mint said. "Gobble. I'm so hungry I can eat three double-cheeseburgers. With sesame seeds."

"None of that fake food!" Tomb Scone said. "Let's get tofu!"

"Tofu?" Cackle Bucket cracked. "I need meat, old man!"

"I need a break from meat, and tofu is better than dirt."

"I'd rather eat earth than eat that garbage."

"Barbecue!" Stitch Tyke said. "Watch where you're going with those thoughts. Don't want them to linger away from barbecue. Think about it. Ribs. Sauce. Smoky flavors."

"Throw me in the fire, why don't you?!"

"Give me moon made of cheese," Shed Cheese said.

"I don't like cheese," Low Knife said.

"Fuck you. I seen you eat cheese in your burgers!"

"That's fake cheese! I can handle it."

"This is what it means," Fork Feed said. "This is what it means. This is what it means."

"Shew she," Spoon Drop said.

"Huh?" Mortimer Mutter said.

"Shew she."

"You mean to shew her? Shew Fork Feed?"

"This is what it means. This is what it means. This is what it means."

"Shew she."

"Shush her?"

"This is what it means. This is what it means. This is what it means."

"Wait," Harriet Harvester said. "I've figured it out... She's trying to say 'sushi.' Is that right?"

"Ah," Spoon Drop said. "Sushi."

"Not enough," Host L said. "It's not enough."

"But there's all you can eat sushi."

"We need a buffet with variety, not just sushi."

"I'm so hungry please kill me."

"What do you wanna eat?"

"Anything! I'll eat anything to live!"

"Someone," Tomb Scone said. "Leave the room. Lead the way."

"I will not fuckin' follow!" Cackle Bucket said. "I am wolf, not sheep."

"Mutton," Mortimer Mutterer muttered. "Mutton sounds good right about now."

"Not a bad idea, Professor," Host L said.

"But I don't know if there are any mutton places around."

"Muffin muffin muffin," Doggerel Grill said. "Stub or top, I'll gobble it up."

"Gobble gobble!" Juggle Mint said. "Turkey day needs to come today!"

"Has it passed?" Mortimer Mutterer asked. "Or is it coming up?"

"What day is it?" Stitch Tyke asked.

"Same day as yesterday if we're still talking this way," Doggerel Grill said.

"Where are we going to eat?"

"Fast food feeds the quickest, but it makes you the sickest."

"I'm willing to dice something up and make that gamble. Gobble. I'm so hungry I can eat three double-cheeseburgers. With sesame seeds."

"None of that fake food! Let's get tofu!"

"Tofu? I need meat, old man!"

"I need a break from meat, and tofu is better than dirt."

"I'd rather eat earth than eat that garbage."

Spoon Drop tried to munch on the dust in the air, but it was not enough. She collapsed, dying of starvation. The conversation continued.

"Barbecue! Watch where you're going with those thoughts. Don't want them to linger away from barbecue. Think about it. Ribs. Sauce. Smoky flavors."

"Throw me in the fire, why don't you?!"

"Give me moon made of cheese."

"I don't like cheese."

"Fuck you. I seen you eat cheese in your burgers!"

"That's fake cheese! I can handle it."

"This is what it means. This is what it means. This is what it means."

Spoon Drop, dead, said nothing.

"Huh?"

A moment of silence.

"You mean to shew her? Shew Fork Feed?"

"This is what it means. This is what it means. This is what it means."

Another moment of silence.

"Shush her?"

"This is what it means. This is what it means. This is what it means."

"Wait. I've figured it out… She's trying to say 'sushi.' Is that right?"

Yet another moment of silence.

"Not enough. It's not enough."

Silence again.

"We need a buffet with variety, not just sushi."

Silence of the dead.

"What do you wanna eat?"

Silence.

"Someone. Leave the room. Lead the way."

"I will not fuckin' follow! I am wolf, not sheep."

"Mutton. Mutton sounds good right about now."

"Not a bad idea, Professor."

"But I don't know if there are any mutton places around."

"Muffin muffin muffin. Stub or top, I'll gobble it up."

"Gobble gobble! Turkey day needs to come today!"

"Has it passed? Or is it coming up?"

"What day is it?"

"Same day as yesterday if we're still talking this way."

The sound of footsteps approaching.

"Hello, pack. I'm back!"

"Mathias!" Host L said. "You are always welcome here."

"Spoon Drop dropped dead!" Low Knife said.

"You all drank Vic's blood, so I deprived you all of food flood. Someone had to pay. So I waited until today."

"It's like being just a day late to turn in an overdue book," Doggerel Grill began, "and forgetting to renew it for *another* three weeks, cook!"

"My spices cook the meat, and it becomes what you eat. That was the arrangement, and you got greedy in your derangement."

"I did not suggest it! It was the work of some other shit!"

"Dear Doggerel Grill, lips on the loose," Mathias said to the former instructor. "There's only one who can be like me if they so choose."

"You locked me away for asking why you rhyme. And now I have trouble keeping track of time."

"You still need some work. Now wipe away that smirk."

"So *that's* how I know you," Mortimer Mutterer said. "I knew you looked familiar."

"Why are you still mad about the chicken blood?" Host L asked Mathias.

"Honestly, it is a lot of work tampering with the food. Why not eat your prey as *humans* in their normal mood?"

"That's not us! We will *not* resort to cannibalism!"

"Ditto," Mortimer Mutterer muttered. "Not one bite."

"After all this time, you cling to humanity. Truly, this is the peak of insanity."

"We won't get full on human," Stitch Tyke said. "If we eat a full-on human, it'd be the gateway to us eating each other. Dog eat dog world!"

"Well then that *would* spoil the fun. Anyway, here is light, from moon, not sun."

Mathias pulled out the glowing amulet. Hypnotized by hunger, the pack gathered around, transforming into wolves. As usual, their tongues did not touch the amulet itself, but rather the bright air around it. All they wanted was to lick the light.

Chapter 18
Booking Up

Randy had spent Thanksgiving alone in his apartment. He had no idea where Vic was, but the fact that he was not home meant that Randy did not have to worry about any of his food being stolen. Randy had brought home two double cheeseburgers and booze that night. He was lonely, but it was his choice, and he knew that his family was not too happy about it. But he cared about their safety. And since December was approaching, he could use finals as an excuse.

December also meant cooler weather. Since this caused fewer people to pass through Petal Lock Park, he felt less self-conscious about running around, out in the open. He wanted to get used to the cold anyway, believing that he would probably face Mathis in nighttime, when the cover of darkness could aid him in his crusade. He really felt out of shape, needing to breathe heavily after just a couple minutes of running.

At times, he got bored with running just on his two legs. So he spent a chunk of time trying to run on all fours. It did not happen as smoothly as he had envisioned. Every time, he slipped and fell, rolling on the grass. He often felt like he was being watched. And there came a time when his suspicions were confirmed.

"Not so easy, is it?" Pamela said, wearing Mandy and walking up to Randy.

"How do you do it?" Randy asked.

Pamela removed the head.

"I think it's the suit. I sure as heck can't do it as efficiently without it."

"You can't let me borrow the suit, though, can you?"

Pamela backed away, keeping her arms tight around the head. But then she seemed to loosen up a bit, staring into the eyes of Mandy's head.

"If it were any other suit, I might. But Mandy is special."

"It's okay," Randy said. "I'd probably ruin it."

Pamela looked at Randy again.

"Are you always this hard on yourself?"

Randy shrugged.

"It happens."

"You just need some guidance. Here." She put the head back on. "What I *can* do is try to teach you."

They started with the basics, walking on all fours. Randy was impatient, but he obeyed Pamela and followed her step by step. After some time, they tried speed walking on all fours. He tripped now and then, but he did not do so badly. When it was time to run, he still tripped often. Pamela laughed, and he laughed along with her. He did not care that he was making so many mistakes. As much as it surprised him, he felt content failing at physical endeavors in the company of this friend.

Sometimes they pretended that they were being chased.

"Look up!" Pamela once shouted. "There's a dragon! We've gotta outrun the fire!"

And so they did. Another time, Randy said they were running from a giant robot, and they did sidesteps to dodge its lasers. On another occasion, Pamela said they were being chased by giant squirrels, which they imagined jumping from tree to tree and hurling down acorns and pine cones (despite those not being attached to any of Petal Lock Park's trees). They raised up invisible shields in their arms to block the attacks. Another time, Randy said they were being chased by zombies that could run. Pamela was not quite a fan of this interpretation, but she ran with it and had fun.

The next time, Randy said that there were pirates, and they had no choice but to halt at some point and fend off the pirates with their swords. Randy and Pamela stood back to back, cutting through their foes. One of which Randy imagined was Mathis Dillard. He kept this to himself, imagining Pamela teaming up with him to kill Mathis.

She can help you, a voice in his head said.

No, Artie Docent interrupted. *Leave her out of this.*

Randy was inclined to agree with Artie Docent. There was something tempting about having someone fight alongside him at the moment he intended to kill a foe and possibly die. But he did not want Pamela to be harmed.

Then there came a day when there was no running at all. Carrying his backpack and laptop case, Randy stopped by just to hang out with Pamela. They sat on a log, and she initiated a conversation.

"Do the Nap Kin know that you run out here?"

"I'm not sure they'd really care. And I don't really want them to know."

"Are they really your friends?"

"I like to think so. They're just forgetful sometimes. It's not their fault. I'm just kinda private about my exercise life."

"Some things are hard to share... How often do you think about Aster?"

"I try not to. It hurts. I felt like I was abandoned by a friend at such a young age. I know it's kind of a lame thing to say about a stuffed animal."

"I don't think it's lame at all. Sometimes I wonder what happened to her."

Silence filled the air, paving the way for an awkward vibe that unsettled Randy. He looked up at the full moon, mesmerized by its luminescence.

"I've got some final essays due next week," Randy said, getting up and turning around to walk away. "I have to go."

"Wait!"

Randy paused and turned his head slightly to listen.

"Yeah?"

"Do you wanna spend the night at the library?"

"Uh, I-I," Randy stuttered, weighing the choices in his mind haphazardly. "S-sure. You can come with me."

"Great! The library is gonna be lit!" Though she had a wide smile, it faded as she paused, looking like she was listening to something.

"What's up?" Randy asked.

"Uh, let me just leave Mandy in my tent and get my stuff."

* * *

Running and pretending with Randy had been even more fun than the sports events that Pamela attended as Mandy the Mantleope. Probably due to being with someone who knew who she was. She walked over to her tent.

"*The library scares me,*" Mandy told her. "*There's something off about it.*"

"You'll be safe here," Pamela said.

"*I'm more worried about you.*"

"I'll be fine. Plenty of students go to the library. Besides, you're probably getting sick of me being around all the time, huh?"

"*Not at all. I treasure it. Because I feel there may come a time when we will have to part ways.*"

Pamela did not know how to respond to this prediction, other than through a tear. She wiped it away.

"I'll be fine."

"*It's okay to have other friends. But I need to know that you will be safe with them.*"

198

"I'll make good choices. I'll see you later. I promise."

Pamela returned to Randy. In a comfortable silence, they walked over to the library, the height and sight of which tested their comfort zones. Ten stories. They went inside. There were no windows on the walls, but light bulbs lit up the inside. They walked over to the elevator doors.

"Where do you normally study?" Pamela asked.

"The basement level."

Randy pressed the down button, and they stood awkwardly for ten seconds before the elevator doors opened. They got inside, and the doors closed behind them.

"Why the basement level?" Pamela asked as the elevator moved downward.

"Because it feels like it's far from all the noise."

"Did you say it's *fart* from all the noise?"

"What? No. *Far* from all the noise."

"Sure you did. Just don't let out any of that smelly noise while we're in here."

"You're messing with me."

Pamela revealed a mischievous smile that confirmed his suspicions. Randy could not help but chuckle a bit. When the doors opened on the basement level, Pamela swatted the air and pinched her nose before hopping out of the elevator. Randy was glad that there was nobody right outside the elevator. Amused, he shook his head and led the way.

He brought Pamela to his usual spot. Along the way, they noticed that some tables were full. The table to which he led her was in the corner furthest from the elevator. They were the only two at the table, far from the full ones, views of which were blocked by bookcases.

"Do you ever get lonely here?" Pamela asked.

Randy thought about Naomi. On various occasions, he had almost asked her to come down here with him, but chickened out. He had never asked her—or anyone else, for that matter—to spend the night at the library with him.

"I do get lonely pretty often," Randy said. "But I'm used to it."

"Would you rather I not be here?"

"I don't mind your company."

"I don't mind your company either."

A few feet away from the table was a rust-colored chain-link fence through which they saw bookcases, but no people. They could not hear anybody. And it seemed like nobody could hear them either.

Pamela let her backpack fall to the floor.

"I'm new to this whole thing," she said.

Randy removed his jacket and placed it on a chair.

"You've never spent the night at the library before?"

Pamela looked down at the table, shaking her head.

"Nope."

After a moment, she looked up again. Randy, renewed now with a slight sense of purpose, made eye contact with her.

"No worries. I'll show you how we do it."

Pamela smiled.

Randy slid his laptop out of his case and opened it up on the table to demonstrate. He showed Pamela his study playlists. Their tastes differed somewhat, but Pamela got the point. Each with their headphones on, they sought selections that seemed most helpful. Pamela's setup mirrored Randy's: a laptop in the middle of the table, one open textbook in front, a stack of closed textbooks to the left, a stack of notebooks on the right with the open one on top, and bags of chips in the wide space by the wall. The two of them ate, listened, read, and wrote for the next couple of hours, barely exchanging any words with each other.

This was the dynamic of Randy Morales and Pamela Sheer, completely and canonically platonic peers. And this was pretty much how students at this school spent the night at the library.

*　*　*

On the other side of the fence, the blue-furred werewolves were growing restless with hunger. The sight of potential prey sitting at the table was ever so tempting.

"Come closer, flesh nuggets!" Cackle Bucket yelled.

The young woman got up from the table and looked over at the fence. With a bewildered yet focused gaze, she stepped closer and closer to the fence.

"Come on!" he yelled.

"The guy looks familiar," Mortimer Mutterer said, barely audible to the other werewolves. "Where have I seen him before?"

Stitch Tyke tried sniffing through the fence.

"That girl carries a familiar scent with her... *Mandy*. She's Mandy right now. That costume should've been *mine*."

"You auditioned to be Mandy?" Mortimer Mutterer asked.

"Year after year. Every time, Mathias told me to keep coming back to audition. This was my last chance, and he gave the mantle to a *noob*. Mathias *knew* what he was doing to me. Mandy should've been me. Mandy should've been me. Mandy should've been me."

He continued repeating this. Then Fork Feed repeated her own mantra simultaneously.

"This is what it means. This is what it means. This is what it means."

*　*　*

On the bookcases behind the fence, Pamela noticed the red symbol with green arrow shaped buttons. Seeing no way to get in, she walked toward another pair of bookcases and checked out the buttons there. She pressed a green arrow, thus making the two bookcases close in on each other. She pressed another button, which pulled them apart. She pressed again and ran through the aisle, making it to the other side before they could close all the way.

Students at other tables were visibly bewildered and distracted by the sounds of the moving cases and the steps on the floor.

"Come on!" Pamela invited Randy with a wave. "Give it a try!"

Shaking his head in amusement, Randy walked over and joined her, pressing buttons and running alongside her to get to the other side before the bookcases closed in on each other. She often ran faster than he did, so she had to pull him by the hand. He did not care that other students looked at them judgmentally. The students got up and walked away, leaving them alone to run together for the rest of the night.

* * *

Pamela went to class the following Monday. Dwelling on her mind was the lack of studying the previous night. An in-class final was mere days away. She was so anxious that she could not even pay attention to the lecture. Afterward, she walked up to the middle-aged professor.

"Hey, um, I'm Pamela Sheer."

"Ah," he said. "I was wondering whether you'd come for help."

That doesn't sound good, she thought.

"Do you have a review session with the students?"

"If you'd been paying attention at all, you'd have heard my announcement of the study session."

"Oh. Sorry. When is it?"

"Last Thursday."

Her heart jumped, and her blood went cold then hot.

"Crud."

"In any case, I don't think it would've made a difference. You've already failed a syllabus requirement."

The other "F" word she feared hearing.

"Wait, so I'm failing the class?"

"I'm afraid so. Your attendance has been poor."

"But I haven't been absent from these lectures even *once*. There's been a mistake!"

"Not according to my attendance sheet."

Attendance sheet? she thought. *What attendance sheet?*

"I never *heard* about any attendance sheet."

"It was mentioned on the syllabus, which you should have read."

She had not read it.

"Well... So, is it passed around during class?"

"Before class. I reward the early birds and hope that those who come closer to class start time are wise enough to ask to be marked."

"But I've *been* here every lecture!"

"Have you? What is the name of this course?"

Pamela paused. She realized that she could not recall the full title of the course, nor what it was even about.

"Uh..."

"Being here *physically* means nothing if you are not here *mentally*. Attendance requires being *attentive*. Shocker, I know."

"I did the homework though."

"You did. I acknowledge that. But that's not enough."

"Please, Professor..." *Oh shoot! What's his name?* "Professor..."

"Essen. Justin Essen."

"Professor Essen. Please. Have a heart."

"There's nothing I can do. I left my heart the moment I first walked onto this campus."

Disheartened, Pamela felt defeated. Later that day, she wore Mandy, wanting to hide her sorrowful appearance. But it was still visible voice and demeanor. She hung out with Unicoren again, and they talked about the humiliation she had experienced.

"It made me feel like I wasted my time. But I don't *want* to feel that way! I know I daydream, but I love the things I imagine. Being out and free in the wilderness. Is that a crime?"

"Not as far as I am aware."

"I wonder how Randy's doing. He didn't get much studying done the other night either. It's all my fault, though. I shouldn't have messed around with the bookcases."

"Distractions are often great temptations."

"Is this place here a distraction?"

"You are doing a service by being here."

"Really?"

"Really."

"Thanks. I guess I kinda needed to hear that."

"There is more to hear."

The geese gathered around, and Pamela could hear musical notes being emitted from their beaks. Pamela felt the stirring of lyrics in her mind.

"It sounds beautiful," Pamela said. "They have a purpose. Wonder if I have one."

"What do you wish to do?"

"Pretend with a Friend."

I want to play pretend
With the company of a friend
With whom I may collaborate
Let us build new worlds
And let us act anew

At the time when we feel done
Do the new worlds go on?
The places where we were
The people whom we shaped
Do they never reappear?

How we improvise
Without a chance to revise
Within a small space of time
Enchanting dream that spills
Invested, will I disappear?

The song felt so empowering and comforting. Pamela danced along to it, caressing the air, spinning slowly, and raising her arms to the sky. She was surprised to hear clapping. It was not coming from Unicoren, though. She looked around and saw Peyton approaching her.

"That was very good," her sister said.

"What are you doing here?"

"I wanted to talk."

"I don't. You know why? Because I'm mute as fudge."

"I'm sorry I said that. Just hear me out. Winter break is coming, and Mom and Dad will want to see you again. I know what I did was wrong, and I'm willing to propose a truce."

"A truce?"

"Yeah. And I can drive you home so we can all be together for the holidays."

Part of Pamela wanted to set aside this feud to be with her family. But then she thought of Mandy, who had never really had a chance to be with family for the holidays. How Pamela would be needed to animate Mandy. It seemed that there needed to be more family time in Petal Lock Park before a change could be made. She wanted to tell Peyton her entire line of reasoning, but she did not think her sister would believe her. So she summed up her answer in fewer words.

"Thanks, but I'm fine where I am. Maybe next year."

Peyton's next words told Pamela that she took it the wrong way.

"Unicoren, tell her she's being unreasonable."

"She has made her choice," Unicoren said. "Family is important, but I cannot change her mind."

"What the hell's wrong with you? Do something!"

"Hey!" Pamela shouted. "Don't talk to her like that!"

"Pam, this isn't where you belong. You need to come home."

There was the word again, the former meaning of which became more alien to Pamela with each passing day.

"That home left me a long time ago."

"What's that supposed to mean?"

The day when she lost Aster flickered in her mind.

"I bet you don't even remember."

"I might if you told me."

Pamela turned around.

"Come back to me when you've figured it out, and I might reconsider."

She went back to her tent, zipping it closed. She could hear Peyton storming off.

* * *

Pitchers & Forks was the next place where the Nap Kin met. Randy wished that it was not so loud. But he supposed that it was not too bad since he was sharing a meal with his friends. The music and the numerous customers just made it difficult to carry a conversation. At this rectangular table, he and Peyton sat on opposite ends. She sat between Gertrude and Naomi. Randy could not hear what Peyton was saying. But he could see her. The hand movements swatting the air, wanting to push the troubles away. The restless mouthing of words that, though not audible to him, conveyed her desperation. The watery eyes that just wanted something to change.

He knew that she was suffering, and he felt helpless watching without listening. Inauthentic, looking straight ahead as if he knew exactly what was going on. And he could not ask for clarification this far into the conversation. He did not want to look inattentive or nosy. He was sure it had something to do with Pamela. But given his involvement with her, he did not want to stir up any trouble by mentioning his recent activities with her. However, part of him wanted to be put in the hot seat. To be given attention.

Naomi was clearly a good listener. Randy could not hear her words from this seat, but he could imagine her sweet, comforting pitch.

A pitcher of pear cider arrived, but nobody else at the table seemed thirsty, only invested in what Peyton was saying. He did not want to make things awkward by pouring himself a glass while everyone else was discussing some deeper issue.

Nobody's looking at you, the voice in his head said. *Nobody cares. Just drink up.*

It was true. Nobody was looking at him. He wanted Naomi to look at him. To talk to him and get to know him better. And that made him feel terribly selfish.

He poured himself a glass and took big sips, catching nobody's attention. Always the duck, never the goose.

Chapter 19
The Gap Kin

With the semester winding down, August was ready to return home for winter break. He was excited to experience the familiarity of friends and family whom he had missed so much. During class, he was so sleepy. Looking at the window was no help; the falling snow only reminded him of sheep. He missed virtually every other word that came out of Professor Peralta's mouth. Not wanting her to catch onto his lack of attentiveness, August opened his notebook. He intended to take notes in an effort to keep himself active and awake. But it unsettled him to discover an entry he did not recall writing.

August, look at this handwriting. This is from you. There's nobody else in this country who knows your handwriting this well. This is you writing to yourself. Something is wrong in the hotel room. There is a man in the bathroom mirror. You can hear the toilet of his bathroom, and when he comes out you can see him in front of his sink. It looks like the mirror only shows him whenever he is in front of another mirror. Any other time, it's just a normal reflection. I suspect that I have seen this happen time and time again because I have been rushing out of the hotel room pretty often despite not remembering why. And while I didn't see anything this particular time, I get the feeling that he is a killer. Maybe I've seen it happen and forgotten. I don't know. But you need to tell somebody. The internet's rubbish in your room. Perhaps bring multiple people to the room and leave the doors open to hear reactions. Video record with a cell phone. Might be a long wait in front of the mirror, but there needs to be evidence. Until enough people are gathered, you must stay out of the hotel room. I don't even want to think about the extent of how much harm I may have suffered after all this time.

Normally, August would take a little bit of pride in how legible his handwriting was, but his shock hindered him. Though he was startled awake, he could not focus very well throughout the rest of that seminar.

Could someone at the hotel be pranking me? he wondered.

August hoped that to be the case. Any other explanation was anxiety-inducing. He reflected on possible times when one might have had an opening for this sort of thing. Yesterday, he had been doing homework in the dining room. He was so tired then that his head just dropped onto the table.

Damn, he thought. *Could've been anyone. Everyone goes in and out of that dining room. Well, Jade doesn't really stick around there. And I have yet to see...*

There was a name trying to enter his mind. He knew it was familiar, but he was having trouble remembering it.

There's someone I know, whom I haven't seen come through the dining room. I just can't remember who...

After the seminar, August walked back to the hotel. From the sleet-filled sidewalk, he looked up at a flickering light coming from behind a window. Counting the floors and windows, he realized that it was his own room. He got inside and ran up the stairs, losing breath by the time he reached his floor. When he got back to his room, he noticed something wrong.

The door was a crack open.

"Shit!"

He opened the door all the way. It was dark, so he flicked up the light switch. Now that he could see better, he dug into his drawer.

His passport was gone.

August took his notebook out of his backpack and examined the entry again, re-reading it.

Someone has been in here, he suspected.

Perhaps this was not the first time. He guessed that whoever stole his passport had gotten ahold of his notebook at some point. That would explain the order to stay away from the room. It seemed more reasonable to believe that someone was just trying to make him believe a supernatural cause for the eerie events surrounding his hotel room.

Earlier that day, he *had* rushed out of the room with his backpack and his notebook on hand. But he had not opened it at that point. He did not recall the door lock clicking. August felt terrible for having made such a mistake.

He stared across the hall at the door to room 315. He had never seen anybody leave that room. He wondered whether anyone of note was living there. Perhaps the culprit. How to confront the tenant was the question. Surely they would deny everything. He did not want to knock and give away his suspicions. But he also did not want to take his eyes off the door to 315. For all he knew, the resident was still inside and could leave once he went downstairs to alert the staff.

He checked his cell phone signal. Unfortunately, it was indeed rubbish, so he could not contact a friend to come upstairs and keep watch for him. Furthermore, he now questioned whether he could even trust any of his friends. He felt certain that they were not malicious, and that this was just some joke that was not meant to drag on for long. Hopefully, one of them might have the passport.

Not quite having decided on his next course of action, he gave into the impulse of stepping out into the hallway.

And then he forgot what he was doing. He turned around and looked at his room again. There was something on his mind. Something very important, howling in his head. Something that needed to be taken care of immediately.

"Pack!" he told himself. "I need to pack."

He packed his clothes into his luggage case. Once it was finished, he realized that there was just one essential thing that was missing: his passport.

Once again, he went in circles hypothesizing where it could be. In the possession of a stranger? With a friend? Surely the hotel staff might be able to help. He needed to take action soon; his flight was a few hours away.

Grabbing his luggage case, he ran out into the hallway and locked the door behind him. He took the elevator down to the lobby and walked up to the receptionist.

"Checking out for now," he told her.

"Flying back for the holidays?"

"Yes. I'm really looking forward to it. I'll be back for next semester, though."

"All right. We look forward to seeing you here again."

"The feeling is mutual. The whole staff is full of fine, wonderful people. Merry Christmas!"

August took the London Underground to the airport. All seats were taken, so he had to stand. It was difficult trying to stay awake.

He blinked. And then he had a daydream. He could see himself stepping off of the train and then falling through the gap between the train and the platform. Suddenly, it was his point of view, and he was falling down into the darkness. Nothing but cold air around him. And then it was scorching hot as a light appeared below. But it was not a comforting light; it was the planet's core, fraught with fire, unstoppable. He could not halt his fall, and just kept going, seeming to fall through the fire, which held him like a prisoner, bathing him in magma, breaking up his matter.

"AHHHHH!" August yelled, opening his eyes awake.

The other passengers stared at him. A mother wrapped her arms around her frightened child. August felt so silly in this moment he now wished to put in the past.

"Sorry," he apologized. "I have a mind gap." Awkward silence. "They say to mind the gap when you get off of trains. Luckily you don't need to worry about any gap on the toilet stalls. Right?"

More awkward silence.

When it was time to get off of the train, he was cautious, stepping over the gap and onto the platform slowly. He rolled his luggage as he walked to the terminal, where he was asked for his passport.

Then he realized that he did not have his passport in any of his pockets. Neither in his jacket nor in his trousers. He dug through the zippers of his luggage case, but found no sign of it.

He knew that his parents would be very upset, having paid for the flight he could not take.

August had his hood up when he returned to the hotel, not wanting the receptionist to recognize him.

"Excuse me," she said. "Have any identification?"

The jig was up. Embarrassment had to ensue. He pulled down his hood, unobscuring his face. Though she recognized him, she was visibly surprised.

"Did you forget something?"

"Yeah. My passport. I'm not gonna be able to make the flight."

"Oh. I'm sorry to hear that."

"It's fine. Just means I get to spend more time here."

And that my parents got to spend money that did not get put to good use.

When he returned to his room, he unloaded everything onto his bed and searched everywhere for his passport, to no avail. He pulled out his cell phone and scrolled down to his dad's number. He had no choice but to face the music. He just hoped that it would be radio friendly. He dialed the number. After a few rings, his dad picked up.

"Hello?"

"Hey, it's me."

"Who is this?"

Another one of his jokes, August thought.

"Is Mom there with you?"

"Excuse me?"

"Look, Dad, there's no easy way to say this, but I mucked up. I can't find my passport, and I'm not gonna be able to come home for the holidays. I'm sorry."

"You must have the wrong number. I have no son."

Ouch.

This was a gut punch. He expected anger over his blunder, but he did not expect disownment.

"You don't mean that, Dad."

"I'm sorry. But my wife and I have never had kids. We tried, but it just never happened."

"Dad, please stop messing around. You're *hurting* me. I know I made a mistake, and I'm sorry. I'll make it up to you. I promise."

"You've got the wrong number, bud."

"It's me! August Wilhelm! Your son!"

"Look, sir, I don't know how you got my last name, but this is cruel of you! You think me and my wife don't *wish* that we had kids?"

"Wait! My name! It should have popped up when I called you!"

"I see no name! I don't wanna take any of your telemarketing 'I'm from the future' bullshit! Get a life, you piece of shit!"

His dad hung up, and August had no clue where he stood. He tried scrolling down to his mom's number. Perhaps she would be more willing to listen.

His battery icon was being drained. In a span of seconds, it went from a green 80% to a red 20%. As it kept decreasing, he dialed his mom's number. It rang a couple of times. And then the screen went black.

"What the hell?"

Something's infecting the phones, he thought.

He hooked his phone up to a charger and plugged it into the outlet beside his bed. No charge. He tried holding down all multiple buttons to turn it back on. Nothing worked. He took his laptop out of its case and pressed the power button. But the screen remained dark. Looking at the bottom of the device, he noticed that the battery was gone.

"Why is this happening?"

He heard a flip. On the bed, his notebook was now open, pages turning until it got to the mysterious note. Then came the tearing sound. The page floated, seemingly in slow motion, August too frozen to grab it before it phased through the door. August ran to the peephole and saw the page phase through the door to room 315. He swung his door open and ran over to that room. Before he could touch the doorknob, he stopped himself, and looked back at his own room.

"Oh. *That's* my room."

He returned to room 314 and looked at the open notebook. Remnants of a torn page remained. Once again, he discovered that his phone and his laptop battery were not working. He had the weight of information on his mind, though he was not sure what the information was. He swiped the notebook and all his luggage off of the bed. Then he got down on his knees. With his fists, he banged the floor aggressively, for no reason he could discern. When he was out of breath, he stood up, and flopped onto his bed, trying to get some rest.

Chapter 20
Candy and Randy

Randy was all alone in his apartment on Christmas Eve. He had some peppermint schnapps. Some of it he had straight, and some of it he had stirred with hot chocolate, drinking as he stared into the darkness. He had turned off all the lights. Pouring the schnapps down the chimney, hoping to put out the fire. Anyone else might have shotgunned a show or had a holiday movie marathon, but Randy was not in the mood for such treacle.

Getting deeper under the influence, he let himself imagine that he was a guest on Artie Docent's show once again...

This time, Artie had a red ornament for a nose.

"Now, I know it's Christmas," Artie said to the audience, "and everyone expects me to take the day off. But you know what? I need to keep this party going. That's right, folks. It's The Tardy Party, and we're going all night!" He waved his arms as the audience cheered. Once they settled down, he continued. "Now, my guest tonight, you all know him. He's a good friend of mine. Please welcome Randy Morales!"

The audience clapped as Randy walked onto the stage. He shook hands with Artie, and then they both sat down.

"Thanks for coming down here," Artie said. "You know, I wasn't so sure you'd be coming. I thought you'd be home with your family."

"And I thought you'd be home with yours, pal."

The audience laughed.

"Sick burn!" one of the audience members said.

"Well played, sir," Artie said. "But no! I've got nowhere else to be tonight."

"Wait," Randy said. "I never gave you a family, did I?"

"I beg your pardon?"

"Never mind. I tell ya, Artie, it's great to be here. I really needed this."

"Oh yeah? Do tell. What's been new with you? The fans are itching for an update."

"Well, the finale still seems like it'll go as scheduled. It seemed like there was a chance of extending the life of the show, but that's just how it goes. It's still a long ways away, but I think it'll meet expectations, more or less."

"You know, I like the addition of that girl Pamela to the cast. She seems like a breath of fresh air for the show."

"You really think so?"

"Yeah! I mean, we used to have Kayleigh, and she was cute as a button. But since she hasn't popped up this season, it's felt like something's been missing."

"Yeah, well, we can't really have my sister on the show because of scheduling and, quite literally, budget issues, to be honest."

"Well, that's a shame. Luckily, the budget here is fine. We get everything we need in this studio. Someone get this guy a hot chocolate!"

A cup of hot chocolate appeared on Artie's desk. Randy grabbed the cup and took a sip.

"Did you spike this?"

"Well, we're not allowed to broadcast the consumption of alcohol on this show. So, we'll just leave this bit on the cutting room floor. Right everyone?"

"The cutting room floor," Randy heard a sinister voice say.

The sound of buzzing saws, and a brief second of a blood-filled stage. Red all over the floor. And then it was back to pink.

The audience clapped and whistled.

"What just happened?" Randy asked.

"You tell me!" Artie laughed, the audience following suit.

"Quite a lively crowd tonight," Randy said.

"Yeah. Oh. And we've heard that you've been working out for your role. How's that been working out for you?"

"I mean, I'm not really sure if I'm building enough muscle, if any."

"This request may be weird, but you wanna flex for the audience?"

The audience clapped and whistled. Randy chuckled.

"Thanks, but I'm good. I don't really like people looking at me."

"Well you could've fooled me. Seems like you always want the attention."

"Did you look in a mirror during that assessment?"

The audience roared with laughter.

"Ah, I can't stay mad at you, Randy. Well, this has been a fine interview. But let's end it with this question: If you could have one Christmas wish come true, what would it be?"

"Easy. Infinite money."

"Wow. Way to be creative."

"Oh, I can take more sips of this and get even more creative if you'd like."

He chugged the chocolate, leaving a peppermint aftertaste in his mouth. The studio lights started to look blurry. Briefly, Randy was blinded by the booze. He kept blinking; the scene fading away...

And then he was back in the living room.

Despite being buzzed—or perhaps *because* he was buzzed—he decided to go outside. Rain sprinkled down on the cupcake that was Copper Petal. Randy did not mind. The droplets made him feel less numb.

He went to Petal Lock Park, hoping that he might find company.

He arrived on Unicoren's side, but all he saw were the geese. Continuing past the silver birches, he could see a few people in the pathway, between the eastern and western sides of the park. Pamela dressed as Mandy, dancing around Unicoren and Stagmantel, both with wide, genuine smiles on their faces. It was a beautiful sight. A perfect family portrait. And he did not want to ruin the moment by wandering into the frame, burning the photo with his flame. Feeling cold, he tried retreating discreetly.

On the way, though, he spotted Frederick Filler on a slackline.

"You're still here?" Randy asked.

"I could say the same about you."

"Shouldn't you be with your family for the holidays?"

"I choose not to," Frederick explained. "I feel ashamed, being the way I am. I know that they are full of love, but I don't wish to burden them."

"Burden them how?"

"I know they'll offer financial support. But I've made sure they haven't needed to make such sacrifices for me. I'm not *that* important. After I graduate, I don't want them to pay a cent for me."

"You never took loans?"

"Almost for our sophomore year. But I went homeless to avoid it."

"Smart. I made the mistake of taking some, right from the beginning."

"Well, hopefully they're not too hard to pay off."

"It's pretty standard for students like us to repay without much problem. I think. It's what I hear. My plans differ from everyone else's."

"How so, Randy?"

"I can't say."

"Then why would you mention it?"

"I'm sorry. I guess I'm kinda self-absorbed."

"Some people often try to take the reins of the conversation, dominating it with their own anecdotes, alienating the other party. Trying to reign over the party and rain on the party."

"How the fuck is your vocabulary this good?"

"It's what I hear."

Out of the corner of his eye, Randy saw a flash of light. Frederick fell off of his slackline. Randy ran over and pulled him up.

"Did you see that?" Randy asked.

"A flash of light," Frederick replied. "And then it was gone. But it's never gone." He rubbed his own forehead. "Not in here."

Not knowing what to say, Randy ran off on all fours, keen on confronting the photographer. Leaping over the bushes, he saw a running woman holding a camera. The strap was loose, and he pulled on it, getting it out of her hand.

"Give that back!" she demanded.

"What are you doing?" he asked. "Spying on me, I bet." He wanted to look at the photos, but he did not know which buttons to press. "How do you work this?"

"Give it to me and I'll show you."

Randy ran back, and the photographer chased after him. Frederick, still reeling from the light, was visibly confused.

"What's going on?"

"That guy be taking my camera!" the photographer said.

"I think I have a stalker," Randy explained.

"You wish."

"Who are you? Shouldn't you be with your family for the holidays?"

"Shouldn't you?"

"What? Are you a disappointment to your parents or something?"

"More like they're lacking to me."

Her word choice seemed strange. He doubted that she would say why. She seemed very secretive.

"You don't let anyone get in your head, do you?"

"Nope," the photographer replied.

Randy wanted to know whether they were all in a safe space.

"Is it okay to be vulnerable?" he asked.

"Don't know," she said. "People gave me shit for the way I talked."

"Nobody wants you to talk about your suffering," Randy said. "Society deems it unacceptable."

"Don't try to be all deep. Like you're trying to teach. You don't know me."

"Nor you me. You just know what I look like and where I go."

"Look. We got off on the wrong foot. Begin again. I'm Candid."

"I'm sorry, Candice?"

"Call me Candid."

"Candy?"

"Don't you *dare* call me that. *Candid* be my name."

"Did your parents name you that?"

"No. Did your parents name you Randy?"

Randy gave a stoic scowl.

"My parents named me Frederick," Frederick Filler filled her in.

"Noted," Candid said.

"You've seen me around campus?" Randy asked.

"Yeah," Candid answered. "You seem to like people who don't like you back as much."

"It hurts. But does your work hurt *you*, Candid?"

"Maybe little."

"Love is painful surrender," Frederick chimed in. "But for you, Candid, love is surrendering pain."

* * *

Candid raised an eyebrow. Something about what Frederick said hit a nerve as if it was something that rang true. Had she surrendered the pain of knowing the living after they had been killed?

Lucky guess, she thought.

"If you'd like," Randy said to Candid, "we can talk in private. Sorry Frederick."

"It makes no difference to me," Frederick said. "Seems to be the trend. Farewell, friend."

Randy, still holding the camera, walked alongside Candid until they were a good distance out of earshot.

"He hired you," Randy said. "The guy I took a loan from."

Candid looked at the camera, then made eye contact with Randy again. Maybe it was finally time to unload.

"I'm not Candy, so I'm not gonna sugarcoat it. You're in deep trouble."

"So, what? Are you his sidekick or something?"

"Hell no."

The possibility had crossed her mind. Not that she saw herself as a potential sidekick, but rather that Ben F. hoped to somehow mold her into a killer. Birds of a feather. A larger part of her, though, was convinced that Ben F. just wanted to see how long it would take to break her as she was forced to see his victims. All the shells without lights.

"What's he like?" Randy asked.

"I've never met the guy."

"So you know he's a guy?"

"It be a hunch."

Randy raised an eyebrow over those words.

"You a pirate or something?"

In a way, she was. But she knew that he referred to how she spoke.

"Ben F. Written in an email. A hunch."

"I've seen him in person."

This surprised her. She wondered how well Randy knew Ben F.

"He let you get near him?"

"He bumped into me and then invited me to his place. Told me his first name."

At last. Light that could be shed on the whole mystery.

"What be the name?"

"I'm not sure I should say. Is he dangerous?"

Candid crossed her arms.

"If you really *did* know him, you'd know. Yeah."

"How dangerous?"

"He can...kill."

"You've seen his work firsthand, and you just allow it to happen. And you don't think you're an accomplice?"

"I'm not an accomplish! Shit! Shut up! Shut up! I'm not a partner or anything!"

"Sorry to set you off. But he needs to be removed from this world."

In a way, Ben F. *did* seem somehow removed from this world. At least, the grounded world as Candid knew it.

"I kinda need the money," she said.

"Don't we all? Heh. Well, I don't intend on doing anything about him until the end of next September."

"Then you're letting it happen too. Hypocrite."

"You know what? Fine. Yeah. I'm a hypocrite. We're both terrible people. But at least *I* intend to end this. You've known of all this longer for a much longer time. And you've just been letting him roll in shit and rub it all over the kitchen table."

"How do you come up with that shit?"

"I talk to myself a bit. All right? We're both really shitty. I don't care. Keep on following me, taking pictures." Randy shoved the camera back into her hands. "And I'll pretend I don't know it's going on. But I'm getting ready. Please don't beat me to the punch. I know that I have to do this."

"Did a prophet tell you?"

"No. I *want* to do this. It's the only future for me."

Randy really was seeming crazier by the minute.

"You *want* him to kill you?"

"He and I will die together if it comes to that. I've made my peace with that."

"Bullshit. You're *counting* on it. You feel *sure* it'll happen that way. I don't predict you overpowering him, though. It might be *you* going down."

They stared at each other for a long moment. Then Randy spoke again.

"So you've seen his victims. But have you *heard* their voices?"

"I'm hearing you right now, aren't I?"

"How will you see me."

"As a head."

"And *where* will you see me?"

"It can vary."

"Hmph. Well, I'm sure I've heard one of those heads you've seen. So I guess we're both missing pieces. And we won't be the same after all this."

"You've met one of them?"

"I heard her voice over the phone. She was at his home. Didn't seem to be in danger, but I saw a bit of blood when I visited him."

"When?"

"Late September."

She rethought the timeline in her head and then remembered the night at the train.

"I have a name too, you know. Of the victim."

"I'm not gonna tell you his name in exchange for hers."

"Darby Morineau." She saw Randy's eyes widen. "Yeah. Shocked that I told you? I try to forget, but the name can linger."

"That name sounds familiar... I think my former professor dated her."

"Come again?"

"Me and my friends gave him dating advice, and we saw her briefly. And now *he* is missing."

"Well," Candid sighed, "it be personal now?"

"Something like that."

"Would you be killing him for him, for her, or for *you*, Randy?"

There was no answer, but rather a question.

"If I can't kill him, can you finish the job for me?"

"Maybe after I finish mine."

"Very well, then. Welcome to the contingency plan, Candid."

Not knowing how to respond, Candid walked away. She was not even certain she would follow through with killing her benefactor. Candid speculated that Ben F. knew Randy's intentions and was tormenting him for a purpose pertaining to her. To have Randy push her into embracing a killer instinct. And then she shook her head, thinking it absurd to believe the benefactor to be that many steps ahead.

* * *

For a moment, Randy felt something. After all the paranoia, he felt a bit safe, knowing that he might have an ally. He wanted to hold on to this feeling. But he was not quite sure whether he would see Candid again. However brief, he held onto this feeling for a little while. It would not last through the night, but for the rest of the day, it existed.

For Darby and Mortimer, he kept thinking to himself, lamenting the loss of an old friend and another innocent whom he had seen and heard only briefly. *I'll honor them. This is my offering.*

* * *

From a tree branch, a bat watched Candy and Randy walk in opposite directions. Candy and Randy, walking below a tree. From which a small bat could see. He thought he would merely watch family playtime, but this other thread intrigued him. Now he could follow Candy to her address. A holiday gift, indeed.

Chapter 21
The Safe and Sounds

During winter break, August was the only student still at the hotel. Though the staff still operated, August was all alone whenever he ate in the dining area. A large room with empty tables. But the real horror came whenever he was up in his room.

One night, August tossed and turned in his sleep. After a while, it seemed that his own body was moving on its own while his mind was detached from it, inhabiting the head of a man armed with scythes. A reaper. He was surrounded by four people. They were by an apartment complex carport, right beside the van that the four residents were planning on using.

The residents were each armed with pistols, and one of them even held a safe under her arm. The figure swung the scythes around, cutting the residents and causing the safe to drop. The residents tried shooting, but in each gun, the safety was on.

The safe was lifted by the reaper, who then used it to bash the head of the woman who dropped it.

Not sure how to turn off the safety on his gun, one of the residents used it to hit the reaper in the face multiple times. The reaper felt pain, but he smiled and shoved the point of a scythe into his stomach. Shocked by the attack, the man collapsed, and the reaper retrieved the blade.

One of the residents figured out how to turn the safety off. He aimed for the head, but right before he pulled the trigger, his arm jerked to the side, missing the head. The reaper raised the blade of a scythe, slicing the man's throat.

The remaining woman was ready to shoot him in the stomach, but the reaper grabbed her arm and turned the gun on its wielder just as she pulled the trigger.

It just so happened that this was what August wanted. He did not feel like he was controlling the movements, nor did he feel like he was an unwilling participant. He was simply within this being, wanting the killings to happen and being pleased when they did. August was astonished by how satisfied he was to see the sight of blood. He wanted all the liquid to levitate and disappear into a glowing light, revealing a cleansed person.

Instead, he woke up, cold and sweaty. Horrified by the desires he had felt.

"I need... I need to leave. I need to go somewhere."

White Cliffs of Dover, a ghastly voice said.

"White C-Cliffs of D-Dover."

Jump.

August hopped in place three times.

JUMP.

"I have to go. I must go."

August ran over to the lift and let it take him down to the lobby. He ignored the receptionist when she told him to have a good night.

The walk from the hotel was a blur. With tunnel vision, he walked to the train station, trying to ignore the cold of the falling flakes of snow. He did not even look up any directions. He had a vague idea of where the cliffs were. He knew that they were somewhere beyond Canterbury. So he bought a train ticket and rode eastward.

Unfortunately, along the way, the route was canceled because of icy rails. So he took to the road as a hitchhiker.

After a while, a car stopped. There was an elderly woman driving.

"Ex-c-cuse me," August said in a fragile voice, his teeth chattering. "I n-need to get somewhere. I d-don't know where but we ha-have to get there. Once we're close, I know we're th-there."

"Are you all right?"

"N-no. I need to get there. I won't feel s-s-safe until then. *Safe.* C-can you gimme a ride? P-please?"

"Let me consult my driver." The woman turned to her right shoulder. Her head remained pointed in that direction for ten seconds before she nodded and then turned back to August. "You may come in."

"Thank you."

August got in the car and buckled up. The heater was on, much to his relief.

"I'm Patricia," the woman said.

"I'm August."

It was more of a reaffirmation of who he was rather than an introduction.

I'm August. I'm August.

"Something the matter?" she asked.

"Whatever it is, it has a far-reaching influence. Or maybe I'm infected and I carry it with me. I don't know. I just want to find peace."

* * *

Candid returned to her apartment. When she opened the door, she saw three severed heads on the coffee table: Calvin, Ivory, and Simon. Beside them, a severed hand stood upright on a coaster. She was too unnerved to recognize whose it was. Candid wanted to puke, but she had not eaten much. So she had the awful lingering taste of vomitus stuck in her throat.

She knew right away that her benefactor had been responsible for this. Not wanting to be around the remains, she went into Cleo's room.

Once there, she jumped back at the sight of Cleo's headless corpse lying in the bed. Shaking and hyperventilating, Candid took out her cell phone and typed up an email, constantly backspacing to correct any typos.

You got into my house didn't you mothermucker!!!!

She sent it to Ben F., who responded quickly.

Sorry about the rings on the table.

The blood rings from those severed throats would probably be difficult to wash off. She typed a response.

Why don't you ring me up so we can talk face to face, you coward?!

She sent it, and waited for a few seconds. She looked at her panicked expression reflected in the mirror hanging on the closet door.

That door swung open, and there she saw a tall, long-haired man with a beard.

"SHIT!" she reacted.

"Candice Cornelia Cobb."

Candid was taken aback. He knew her birth name. Did he also know where she used to live prior to college?

How much more does he know? she wondered.

"Who the fuck invited you in?"

"I didn't *need* an invitation."

Candid glanced at her phone.

"Go ahead. Make a call, Candy. They'll find nothing to incriminate *me*."

That wording, though, she thought. *Is he trying to frame me?*

"Why?" was all that she could ask.

"You were out of focus. Now you're *in* focus. Welcome to the center of the lens."

"What the hell you mean?"

"Just a fancy way of saying I'm messing around, as I tend to do. Always looking for new ways to have fun."

"I didn't want any of what you've done."

"I could give a shit what you want. You tipped off Randy."

He knows.

Then she rethought everything. Just because he knew where she lived did not necessarily have to mean that he knew about her talk with Randy. Surely he could not be omniscient. Perhaps it was just some wild guess.

"Randy don't know shit," Candid denied. "You're jumping to an unfounded conclusion."

Her benefactor stroked his beard.

"You're *lying*. You know where you go when you lie? Your deathbed."

He held out his arm and pointed his fingers at Cleo's corpse, still lying headless on the bed. Candid did not want to suffer the same fate.

"Well," she began, "even if Randy did know a thing or two, he can't do anything."

"But there's something *you* can do. You two made a deal. If he decides not to pay me back, he will try to kill me at our appointment. Spoiler alert: Randy can't overpower me. So once he dies, you're gonna try finishing his little quest."

"I never agreed."

"A maybe is enough to fall out of line. You didn't have to tell him a thing. But people are so vulnerable." He walked over to the bed, bent down, and tugged on a hand that Candid could now see. He was pulling out a body from underneath. Simon's headless body, from the looks of it. "All it takes is a look into someone's eyes, and you become them." There were no eyes for Candid to look into. "You become *weak*. Want some advice? Try being your own person, and you might not be so predictable. Poison permeates through my veins and I love it!"

Holding up the mattress, he pulled out one of two scythes that were lying underneath, and used it to poke his thumb. For a split second, a drop of blood appeared, and then it dissipated into thin air. For a moment, Candid's vision was focused on this phenomenon, everything but the thumb blurred in the background. Then he rolled up his sleeve, slitting his forearm. Blood dripped onto the wooden floor and then vanished, and the scar on his forearm disappeared.

He can't leave DNA, she thought.

Now she was curious about the scar on his eyelid. She pointed at her own eyelid.

"That one can't vanish. Why?"

"It's a birthmark. Nothing more."

She looked at the mirror behind him, and her heart jumped.

No reflection from this monster.

"What are you?"

"The result of a ritual, put out into the world to do as I please."

"And your endgame?"

"I like to make it up as I go along. If you can help me hide these bodies, I will let you live and give you your next payment. And I won't harm anyone else who may be close to you from here on out. If they *are* even close to you."

"I literally *hate* you."

He shrugged and showed his smiling teeth.

"No prob, corn on a cob. It comes with the territory."

Candid also hated herself for giving in, following her benefactor's instructions as they wrapped the bodies up with sheets of plastic that he had stored in one of the other rooms. The heads were wrapped separately. Candid counted only three of them. Confused, she tried to keep a steady head throughout this demented process. Once they had all the remains from the apartment wrapped up, they went to the van in the parking lot, where Ben F. had the other two headless corpses already wrapped. With the van fully loaded, they buckled up. He drove, and she was the reluctant passenger.

He took them to a river on the outskirts of Copper Petal. They dragged the plastic-wrapped remains out onto the bank. Not the bank that her roommates had in mind for their plan. Ben F. took a wrapped head and punted it into the water.

"Go ahead," he told Candid. "Give it a try."

Candid grabbed a wrapped head, walked up to the river, and dropped it. Ben F. shook his head.

"You're no fun."

"That what the 'F' in your name mean? Who are you really?"

"Randy didn't tell you. Not wise to have such unreliable allies."

They continued to put the remains in the river until nothing else remained in the van. That is, nothing except for the safe. Ben F. picked it up and presented it to Candid.

"If you know the passcode, you can have the prize that's inside!"

"Another fuckin' head in there?"

"You know me so well, but not well enough. That's what I call good business."

Candid could not quite remember the chronological sequence of *Pulp Fiction* in her head, but the passcode was easy to remember since it sounded like a phone number: 4-2-6-1-7-3-5. She pressed the buttons and unlocked the safe. And surely enough, there was Cleo's head, caved in. Beside it was a plastic bag with cash. She retrieved that, and then Ben F. walked over to the water and let the head fall out. Then he threw the safe in as well.

The drive back to Candid's place was silent, and she could tell that Ben F. was quite enjoying the silence. Once they arrived at the parking space, they both got out. Ben F. tossed her the key chain for the van.

"Pleasure doing business with you," he said. "Keep an eye out for your next assignment. And keep on watching Randy for me."

With that, he walked off, and Candid was left questioning her place in all this.

* * *

The drive to White Cliffs of Dover seemed infinite. Though August sat in the front passenger seat, he felt as if he was strapped to the front bumper, watching the road, lit up by headlights, pass beneath him.

When they arrived, Patricia stopped the car.

"Here we are," she said.

"Thank you. You may leave now."

"No. I'm keen on making sure you get back home after this."

"Why?"

"I trust my Driver."

August unbuckled his seat belt and got out. As he walked, the bracelet squeezed his left wrist. Crying in agony, he continued onward even though he worried that his hand would get severed.

* * *

August isn't looking for me, Cassie thought. *So much for true friends...*

* * *

It was a bit of a walk from the road to the pebbly shore. But when August was there, it felt like no time had passed during that walk. To him, the cliffs looked like ice. The wind threatened to blow him away into the water. He was tempted to let it take him away.

Then he noticed that the bracelet on his left wrist was coming undone, leaving a tan line behind. And as the wind took it away, time seemed to slow down. And still the wind was too quick for him to reach out and grab the bracelet before it became invisible, blending into the environment. August scrambled to the pebbly shore, digging around for the bracelet.

"No! No! Where is it!"

He could not find it. He thought it might have been blown far away into the water. He stooped down to scoop up handfuls of pebbles, tossing them into the water.

"Damn you! What have I lost? I want it back!" August fell to his knees, crying. "I've lost someone... Who is this friend and where are they?"

His home was westward, in the opposite direction. He felt alone and unremembered. He knelt for an agonizing hour, his flesh freezing and his knees bruising. This was not an ideal way to spend the holidays, heart aching and head emptying.

"Where are you? Where have you gone? What's happening to us?"

Drown. Drown. DROWN.

He felt a hand on his shivering shoulder and flinched. He turned around and saw Patricia.

"There's nothing more to do here. Just tell me where to drop you off."

"The water. Drop me into the water."

"Wrong answer. Try again, child."

"The train. Take me to the station. The rails."

"Too risky."

"The rails. Rallidae. They are birds. They live in wetlands. Water."

"I'm willing to make sure you get home safely."

"There is no going home. Just back to the hotel."

"Where's this hotel?"

"London."

"That'll be quite a drive... But I'll leave you there."

"Thank you."

August tried blinking away near-blackouts, staying awake during the entire drive. She stayed true to her word. Once they got to London, they drove around until he could point out the familiar building. When they got to Tree Culler Hotel, August got out of the car, and there was not another word. He went back into the hotel and up to his room.

* * *

Candid sat alone on the couch in her living room. Under other circumstances, the availability of a room with an actual bed she could use would have been ideal. But she could not sleep in any of those rooms. They were haunted now, even with the blankets and sheets thrown out. She could barely get a wink in the living room. Even the coffee table, though it had been cleaned, had to go. Rather than go through the hassle of trying to sell it, she threw it into the dumpster, hoping that it would burn wherever it ended up.

* * *

At some point, August blacked out. The next time he was aware of his movements was when he was tossing and turning in bed. He knew he was asleep. He knew he was in bed. He knew he was trapped in his head, remembering the time when, days earlier, he had hitchhiked all the way to the White Cliffs of Dover. Simultaneously, he felt his body trapped, stagnant in bed, as well as his mental body cold and walking tiredly.

The smooth drive was deleted from his memory, replaced by the imagined act of walking every single step from the hotel to the White Cliffs of Dover until his feet bled upon the pebbly shore and he screamed for the friendship bracelet to return. In this memory turned dream, his mind demanded that his hand reach out further into the air to catch the bracelet, but it would not budge. He was frozen in place.

He wanted to go to bed. But he *was* in bed. Yet he did not feel like it. And when he *did* feel that he was in the bed, it felt like a prison.

He opened his eyes, screaming about the pain in his ankle. It was twisted, and would take time to heal. He found himself laughing at the absurdity of his situation. In his blurred vision, he thought he could see milky white eyes in the dark. The ticking of a clock even though there was no clock in the room. Whoever it was, he did not want it to tickle his feet, which he believed were bare and bleeding. He wiggled his toes, and his legs trembled. Desperately, he rolled out of bed. He tried to get up, but his arms did not budge. Even though there was nobody physically in the room, he felt as if there was a presence. And he feared that any movement would encourage the presence to pounce upon him and obliterate his soul.

His eyes remained open, though blinking every now and then until daylight crept through the curtains. Then he knew it was safe. Slowly, he crawled up to the door. He opened it, then crawled out into the hallway, closing the door behind himself in a calm fashion.

He sat against the door, frozen for several seconds.

Then he turned around, opened the door, and crawled back into bed, forgetting the dream in which he bled, taking a nap to catch up on the hours of sleep he felt were missing.

Chapter 22

Filler

Randy sat in the darkness of his apartment, lights off. If he was being watched, he wanted to at least obscure the vision of any voyeurs. Nothing on the TV. That was his design. Only a coffee table full of drinks, none of which were coffee. Picking his poisons (vodka and whiskey), and letting it all fall down his gullet. He nearly choked, but a few coughs relieved him.

Though the curtains were drawn over the windows, he could hear the fireworks sounding off outside, announcing the arrival of a new year. He saw it as nothing to celebrate. But he raised a glass anyway, making a toast.

"To my final year," he said to himself before drowning again. "Boy. I haven't had one of these since last year."

He laughed hysterically at his own remark, trying to brush away the thought of nobody else being around to hear it.

* * *

Frederick Filler, full of fear, covered his ears as the sound of fireworks disrupted the night. A new year, but no new him. A new year, no new fear. Same him, to those who knew him...

Frederick Filler was born on February 4, 1993. After hours of labor, he was allowed into the world with all the light that filled it at the time. His parents, Derek and Phyllis, looked upon him with pride and joy.

Derek turned to Phyllis, pressing his forehead against hers as she was lying on the hospital bed.

"I never knew I had so much purpose before this moment," he told her. Both of their eyes watered. "You are the most beautiful woman. I thank you, with all my heart, for bringing this gift into the world."

"Nothing will ever be the same," Phyllis said, exhaling. "This is a new life."

With much love and affection, they nuzzled each other's faces, as partners who had chosen each other. Loving spouses who had agreed to combine to create life and raise a human being together, with absolutely no regrets. Frederick was crying, and they just kept smiling.

At age two, Frederick was terrified by fireworks when he first saw them in the sky. They were at a picnic in the park, and he had nowhere to hide from the open sky lighting up with flames. His mother tried to assuage his fears.

"They're just like singing flowers," she told him. "No need to be frightened."

"This singing hurts!" Frederick cried.

"Well," his father said, "at least you're not listening to death metal on headphones with the volume all the way up."

His parents laughed at a joke he did not comprehend at that time. The words "death metal" sounded ominous, becoming etched in his mind, like a utility knife cutting through cardboard. He tried to push the words out with the phrase "singing flowers." But with this in mind, Frederick thought the singing in the sky was terrible.

He then spent hours wandering in the garden of their backyard, holding his ear against the flowers, hoping to hear them sing more pleasant songs. Instead, he got a thorn on his lobe, and children at school would later ask him whether he got his ear pierced. But it was a scar, and Frederick would sometimes wonder how such a beautiful garden could be full of creatures crafted with cruel features. He would also wonder why his father allowed such evil within the garden that he grew, including the chili peppers into which Frederick would sink his teeth, inflicting fire upon his taste buds. His parents would rid the garden of its evils, but Frederick would still remember.

* * *

Meals were often okay. As Frederick ate, his parents smiled, staring at him.

Our son, his mother thought. *He's growing up so fast. What a beautiful boy we've raised. He truly is a gift to this fam—*

"STOP STARING AT ME!" Frederick yelled.

* * *

And there were times when his mother served soup on hot days. Even though she intended no harm, Frederick wondered how often people who were seemingly good got away with allowing evil to prevail in the world. Even at such a young age, he knew that it did not make sense. Hot liquid was not good for consumption on a blazing hot day.

Some hot days, when he was a kid, his parents took him to the beach. On that beach, he was enchanted by the beauty of the ocean. But, at age five, he stepped on a sharp shell, causing his foot to bleed. His parents tried to drag him to help right away, but he sank to his knees for a little while, screaming at the water as a red stream met an endless sea of salt, seemingly drowning the fires of the sun to bring the day into darkness.

In first grade, he asked a fellow student whether he could borrow the scissors. And she just pushed him back, causing him to trip over a basket and hit the floor with the back of his head. He cried. So very much. The teacher came to his aid and made the girl apologize. She did not feel very sorry. He could tell.

239

He tried to make the most out of recess, but it was difficult to enjoy when the slide on the playground gave him static shocks on sunny days. He wondered why such a hazard was even allowed for children. Sometimes, other kids pushed him down the slide, and he landed in the sand face-first.

Time passed. But even in fifth grade, he suffered through the immature antics of his peers, who stole his pencils whenever he was not looking and used them to desecrate the trees with such etchings as "FREDRICK FILLED WITH SHIT." They did not even have the decency—or intelligence, rather—to spell his name properly.

One day, he reached his limit. Right by the swing set, he tried swinging a fist at one of his tormentors, who then took out one of the recently sharpened pencils and got him right in the left palm. It hurt like hell trying to get the graphite thorn out of his skin, scarlet in that spot.

In fifth grade, feeling isolated, Frederick entertained fantasies in which he ended himself. But he knew that it would break his parents' hearts. They liked to tell him the story of how they reacted right after he was born. But the fantasies still persisted. He visualized many settings. Tall buildings. A field of bear traps—the death metal—surrounded by an audience who, when it was too late, would feel sorry to see him suffer. An arena in which he would willingly walk into the mouth of a reptilian beast, its sharp teeth digging into his flesh, putting him out of his misery. Frederick Filler filling the belly of a beast. Frederick Filler, fecal matter, remaining buried beneath the sand.

Nothing notable happened in middle school.

High school was not much better. Frederick went to one of the restroom stalls, the walls of which read "EAT SHIT." Classy. Once he got out of the restroom, he spotted two boys in the hallway who were trying to ditch school. He would not have alerted anyone, but they did not believe him. So they grabbed him and covered his mouth, dragging him out of school with them. They were much stronger than he was.

They took him to a hill and rolled him down into a thicket of thorns. Once down, he did not want to move. He hoped that they were looking down, feeling sorry. But when nobody came down, he looked up and saw that they were gone. They did not care whether he was alive or dead, and it saddened him to no end.

He was not sure why he even kept going on. His sorrow intensified when, one day, he overheard his parents talking in the living room.

"You know what I really appreciate about you?" his mother said to his father.

"My irresistible charm?"

His mother laughed merrily.

"How much of a good friend you still are to me."

"Wait, are you friend zoning me while we're married? Ouch. Haha!"

"Shut up! I mean, granted, not all friends start families with each other. But, you know, I'm thankful that I still have my best friend here with me, even with the new labels."

"You really know how to make a guy blush, pal."

"Oh, stop!"

"You stop!"

Frederick wondered why he could not be happy like his parents. They made it look so easy. Almost as though they had never faced any adversity. As if his generation had it tougher, or at least made it tougher on themselves somehow. He was not sure which was more true.

But then came the beginning of junior year. Fall semester, the term to fall. Frederick Filler, falling in love with MacKenzie Mallard. Frederick Filler's fellow classmate in AP Physics. He was not sure how he even got in that class, seeing how he struggled with all the assignments from the beginning. But there was no question that MacKenzie belonged. And so he worked up the nerve to ask her for help. It began with tutoring. And then tutoring was teetering between friendship and romance. He was not sure where in the middle it leaned more toward. But there was definitely something there.

They learned a lot about each other. His fear of fireworks. Her fear of Ferris wheels. How amazed he was about people who could walk on tightropes. Her interest in bears, various simulacrums of which she had collected. Frederick and Mackenzie talked and listened.

Eventually, he summoned the courage to ask her to junior prom. Carefully, he rehearsed every single word to himself in the mirror. And then they went on a field trip to a beach cleanup, during which Frederick talked to her beside the sound of water kneeling on the sand.

"MacKenzie, you are the smartest person I know. And also the most pleasant to be around. I feel very fortunate to have gotten to know you over the last few months. You've made me feel relevant. It's really hard to explain. But the point is that I really like you. And I was wondering if you'd wanna go to junior prom with me."

"Aw, Freddy. Yes! Let's go to prom!"

He had done it. This was the happiest that he had felt so far. Even though the music at the prom itself was a bit shit for his tastes, he treasured her company, as well as the kiss at the end of the night.

In terms of the student body, Frederick hoped that college would be a fresh start for both him and MacKenzie. He applied to various universities, most of which sent him rejection letters. One day, in class, the teacher bragged about how MacKenzie was getting a full ride at her alma mater. This was the first that Frederick had heard about it. The expression on MacKenzie's face showed that she did not mean for him to find out this way. She was embarrassed. There was a part of Frederick that felt envious, and that made him feel terrible. He wondered whether any other classmates felt the same, belittled by this teacher who, throughout the school year, had emphasized that people needed to go to universities—not community colleges—in order to have fulfilling lives. Frederick Filler, wanting a fulfilling life. Frederick Filler, wanting a full ride.

Accepting the scholarship meant that MacKenzie would have to move to the opposite side of the country. Copper Petal University was the only school that accepted Frederick. His parents were proud of him, but he felt like a bit of a failure, only being accepted by one school. And since it was his only choice, he would certainly be far away from MacKenzie for four years. Or perhaps even longer.

They had a long chat about this. Though there was a tug of war regarding the pros and cons of staying together, they leaned more toward deciding that it would be best to end their romantic relationship. The break-up was not official just yet, but pending. So Frederick took some time to learn a bit of guitar. Just enough to compose a song of his own. A song for MacKenzie that might end up defining what they would be to each other from then on. A song titled "I'd Feel the Void."

Is this the last time that our eyes meet?
Paths into the world lying at our feet
Is this the time to say goodbye?
So many laces left to tie

If you were to go off on your own
Toward your best destiny
I would send my vibes of support
But rest assured I'd feel the void

Many people will come and go
But none can take another's place
Apertures within the spirit remain
As the soul carries on its expansion

Relationships romantic and platonic
Shifting like the plates tectonic
When you move you shake up the earth
I feel the ever-changing mirth

If you were to go off on your own
Toward your best destiny
I would send my vibes of support
But rest assured I'd feel the void

We can talk across the scape and seas
We can keep our connectivity
Even if we don't meet so frequently
Rest assured I'd feel your voice

MacKenzie had a tear in her eye. She had a smile on her face. She walked up to Frederick and gave him a hug.

"Oh, Frederick. Your heartfelt honesty is something I'll always appreciate."

"I'm sorry that it has to be this way," he replied. "I guess I'm just not good enough."

"Stop beating yourself up. Even if we can't be together, you shouldn't sell yourself short. You have a big heart, Frederick. Don't ever change that."

"I'll try not to."

And so they went their separate ways, promising to keep in touch online, as friends.

He applied for financial aid and received some grant money. But it was not enough to meet his needs. He applied for scholarships, but won none. When he was a kid, his parents had told him he could get a scholarship for college. But applying was not as easy as it sounded. He felt insignificant, not as valuable as the few of his classmates who were lucky to receive scholarships. Frederick Filler, financial failure.

With the grant money that he received, Frederick could barely afford living in a dorm on campus with Randy Morales and a couple other roommates. They talked sometimes but never went in-depth about their personal lives. They basically knew each other as an art student and a philosophy student. Perhaps they could have been closer friends, but Randy was more focused on hanging out with the Nap Kin. Frederick, on the other hand, did not feel well enough to go out looking for more connections. His correspondence with MacKenzie became less frequent. Eventually, it stopped altogether. He was the last to send a message, and then he was not sure how to start another conversation. He held no grudge against her, but he hated himself for his inability to make progress. So he gave up social media, sending no further messages to MacKenzie.

With no money for housing the following year, Frederick was forced to live outdoors, in Petal Lock Park. To pass the time, he learned to slackline, whenever he was not too occupied with homework. This secret living condition was kept from his parents, who were too nice and generous for him to want them to worry. He could not fathom how someone as miserable as he was could come from such caring and loving people. He did not want to infect them with his disease when they were so perfect. Frederick Filler filled with anger. Frederick Filler filled with salt, above which he wanted to transcend.

He tried. One day, he made an appointment to go into a sensory deprivation tank, filled with darkness and water with Epsom salt. Frederick Filler floating alone in the night, hoping that everything would be all right. An hour of darkness, with no sound other than the movement of water.

But he wanted more. So he pressed a button in the tank that turned on some new-age music. It was so tranquil. Maybe he could make music underwater, and add the Deep Diving Orchestra major, which would allow him to play a violin in scuba gear as he swam in an aquarium tank. He would not be able to hear, of course. The class would feel more like miming. As he continues listening to the tank's music, he kept hoping that he would transcend.

But when he emerged from the tank, he felt neutral. He got dressed again, but still felt stripped of his emotions. Whatever extremities he had felt remained within the darkness he had just inhabited, gone when overtaken by the color of the light. And so came the question that remained with him to this day.

Is there balance, or is there nothing?

* * *

Fireworks still sounding off, Frederick tried to keep his ears covered as he walked on the slackline. But he kept falling. His arms needed to be outspread for balance. The frequency of firework booms seemed to decrease, so he uncovered his ears. This time, he heard a familiar sound gracing the ground.

"I recognize your footsteps," Frederick told Unicoren.

"You are on the verge," she replied.

"Never been a fan of fireworks."

"At least they remain in the sky. Try falling through them and losing everything."

He was not very good at continuing conversations.

"I don't know your experiences," he said. "And you don't know mine."

"I take it then that neither of us feels like sharing."

"Such is the status quo."

"Fair enough, Frederick Filler."

He watched her walk away. He wondered what was in store for her in the near future. And then he felt the need to say something.

"Everyone just wants to be loved, and to give love to fill a need. To fill the void."

Unicoren stopped for a moment, and then she just continued walking.

It seemed to Frederick that she and Stagmantel were growing closer to Pamela, looking like one big happy family. He was not sure what to make of this, nor whether there was something he ought to do about it. In the grand scheme of things, Frederick Filler felt he was just in the middle of it all, not going anywhere in particular. Unlike other people, he had no resolutions for this new year. He knew that he would not fulfill them, anyway.

Frederick Filler, feeling unfulfilled.

Chapter 23
The Numbers

August was working on a final essay for one of his modules. The new laptop battery that he had acquired during winter break was working well. When he was nearly done, however, August heard the cacophony of the fan in his laptop going haywire. It clicked several times, like an insect making a call in the night. And then smoke spewed out of the exhaust port.

"Holy smokes!"

Carrying it, he ran out into the hallway, through the fire exits and down the stairs, until he reached the dining room, where every table was full.

"My laptop's going off the fritz!"

"Huh?" Fritz said.

"Not you, Fritz."

Suddenly, the laptop caught on fire.

"Oh fuck!" Tate exclaimed.

"Where's the fire extinguisher?!" August asked frantically.

Everybody looked around in confusion. Anton ran into the kitchen and then ran back out with a can of whipped cream. He shook it and then sprayed it onto the flame. But the fire grew bigger.

"It's not working!" he yelled.

"Of course it's not working!" Fritz said. "It's CREAM! Cream burns!"

"Not ice cream!"

"Have you never roasted marshmallows?!"

"Marshmallows aren't made of cream, are they?"

Bessie ran over with the fire extinguisher and sprayed it all over the laptop.

"How the hell did it catch fire?" she asked.

"I don't know. But my history essay was on there."

"You didn't back it up?"

"No."

"Now what?" Bessie asked.

"I'm gonna have to do something I never thought I'd ever have to do; I'm pulling an all-nighter."

"You've never pulled an all-nighter before?"

"No. I manage to get a good night's sleep."

"That's impressive."

"Is there a laptop I can borrow?"

Nobody raised their hands.

"It looks like all of us are already pulling all-nighters," Verner said, shaking his head. "Sorry."

"All right then. I'll just have to go to campus and spend the night at the library. In a moment." August nearly fell to the floor, but he slammed his hands onto the table to prevent it from happening. Verner and Bessie lifted him up.

"You all right?" Bessie asked.

"NO!" August yelled. "I. Need. Caffeine!"

"All right!" Verner said. "Hold your horses, Alice Cooper. I'll give you some of mine. Already got a batch brewing."

Verner lent August his thermos so he could take coffee on the go. August headed off to the library. It was difficult searching for a computer that was not already occupied. He spent a half hour going up and down stairs, waiting for anyone to leave a computer. Time was slipping away, and there was no way he could control it. The deadline was fast approaching. The essay was important, and he also had the nagging feeling that there was another pressing matter that he needed to have in mind but could not recall.

At last, a space became available. He sat down at the computer and typed away as quickly as he could. Every once in a while, his hands cramped up, and he had to shake off the pain. After a while of this, someone walked up behind him.

"Hey," she said.

He immediately recognized the voice as Jade's. For the moment, he stopped typing and turned to her.

"Funny seeing you here," he said, shaking his hands in the air. "Hadn't seen you back at the hotel yet."

"Sorry," she said. "When I'm not in my room, I'm kind of out and about. I guess technically I haven't seen you since last year." Jade's mouth curled into a slight smile, but August was too downtrodden to chuckle. The curl faded. "I know. Shit joke."

"Sorry. I'm just having a mood. You studying?"

"Just finished a final essay and turned it in. Glad to have it out of the way."

"Lucky you. I'm doing the same."

"I guess it's great that here even seventy percent is an 'A.'"

"Yeah. But I still have a ways to go. It got deleted, so I'm basically building from the ground up."

"Sorry to hear that. You at least have a good vacation?"

"It was a bit shit."

"Oh yeah? What went wrong?"

"I've been having these problems in my head. I don't know what's going on." He rested the right side of his face upon the desk. "And now I have this essay to worry about. Basically pulling from my notes."

August flipped through his notebook. Every page that had writing on it had notes he remembered writing. But then he came across remnants sticking out from between a couple of pages, paper spikes on the spine. A page torn out at some point he could not recall.

"I must be losing my mind."

"What's wrong?"

"Some pages have been torn out. I don't remember doing that at all." He lifted his head and rubbed his eyes. "Or maybe I'm just too sleep-deprived right now. Shit, what if they're important?"

"I'm sure your essay will be fine without them."

"Hopefully. I feel...distressed. I don't know what to do with myself."

"Maybe you should go to the counseling center on campus."

"There's a counseling center?"

"Yes. Don't they have them at your school?"

"Not at CPU."

Jade scrunched her face in disbelief.

"How the hell do students survive without one? Is this a west coast thing?"

"I guess it might be worth looking into."

"Trust me. It does wonders. There was a semester when I went in every week because I was really stressed from all the work I had.... Okay, it was *last* semester."

"And it helped?"

"Well, it did take up some time I could've used for work... But still. I felt like I improved as a person. And I *did* get the assignments done a bit more easily, even if last minute."

"I might look into it. For now, I'm dying."

"Would..." Jade yawned. "Sorry. Would you like company?"

"I would. But there's nowhere for you to sit, and I don't wanna keep you up. This is my problem to deal with."

"It doesn't hurt to ask for help, August."

"I know." August smiled, and then it faded with a yawn. He covered his mouth for a moment until he was able to speak again. "I appreciate it, Jade. I really do. I just don't want you to feel as tired as I am right now. I've still got some coffee left. I'll be fine."

"All right." Jade gave him a much-needed hug. "Stay merry, my friend."

"Thanks. I'll try."

Jade left, and August kept on typing. He had some paragraphs. They sounded intelligent, but he was not sure whether they sounded relevant to what he was trying to argue. Then he realized that he was not even sure what he was trying to argue. Or what his essay was even about.

What's my thesis? he wondered.

He needed a thesis if he was going to turn this thing in. For all he knew, the paper would feel incoherent without one. And maybe knowing his thesis would help him connect the dots between all the sentences. He stared at the screen, trying to read the words. But in his mind's eye, he only saw numbers and mathematical symbols. Not being an expert in arithmetic, he was not sure what any of it meant. He rubbed his eyes, and his then it all went away. August tried looking through his essay again, but he could not understand a word.

He selected the whole thing, deleted it, and saved the blank page. Cracking his knuckles, he started anew, reading aloud what he typed.

"Zero is black. One is black. Two is green. Three is orange. Four is blue. Five is green. Six is orange. Seven is yellow. Eight is blue. Nine is brown. Ten is black. Eleven is black. Twelve is black *and* green. Thirteen is black and orange. Fourteen is black and blue."

That last sentence brought the Pink Floyd song "Us and Them" to mind. And in his mind was a flicker of a man's head jammed under the hood of a car. August slapped himself in the face, trying to stay focused. He typed out pi. Not just 3.14, but many more digits, with the value showing no end in sight. He typed the digits until dawn. Then he fell asleep in his chair, never turning in the paper.

This pattern would persist for the other papers on which he needed to work.

Chapter 24
Roommates Ruminate

It was a new quarter at CPU. One day, Chelsea and Shelley were in a hurry to get to class from one side of campus to the other. So they tried taking a shortcut through the park. During their hurry, they noticed their school mascot, Mandy, sitting beside a student. But it was not just any student. He looked familiar. And surely enough, he looked like Randy.

Being in a rush, they were not quite sure at first. So, after class, they walked into the park more stealthily, managing to sneak a peak at Randy and Mandy running around together, even an hour and a half after the first sighting.

On their way back to their apartment, Chelsea and Shelley tried talking through their confusion.

"How long you think they've been hanging out?" Shelley asked.

"Hard to say," Chelsea said. "They seem pretty familiar with each other, though."

"Really makes you wonder."

"What?"

"Why Randy hasn't told us. He knows that's Peyton's sister. So why wouldn't he say they're hanging out?"

Chelsea rubbed the top of her head, digging for a possible answer.

"There's a lot of friction between Peyton and Pam," Chelsea said. "Maybe he doesn't wanna get stuck in the middle of that."

"Huh. Guess I can't blame him. I guess everyone's going through their own little drama. Peyton and Pam arguing, Randy being secretive, Grady trying to fit in, Mitch being Mitch..."

Chelsea gave Shelley a concerned glance.

"You think something's up with Mitch?"

Shelley shrugged.

"Maybe not anything huge. Just him always being late. *Little* dramas, like I said."

"I think you underestimate people's troubles. For all we know, Mitch is often late because of emergencies."

"Every single time? That's stupid."

"All right. Point taken. But I think lots of people have their own dilemmas going on deep down."

"Then why don't they say anything?"

"It's hard for people to openly talk about certain things. Sometimes it can be embarrassing, and sometimes they fear it'll make people worry more than is necessary."

"You've been reading too many blog posts."

"Oh, I know. I got a 'B' because of that."

"Could be worse. Remember when we got 'C's because we spent so much time browsing those rumors about a tunnel leading to Moseley's office?"

"Oh yeah!" Chelsea laughed. "We never did check out the inside of that tunnel."

"We've gotta try before we graduate."

"I'd be down."

Looking ahead, they walked silently for a little bit before Shelley spoke again.

"Hey Chels. If you were...down, like depressed or full of little dramas, would you tell me?"

The smile having faded from her face, Chelsea made eye contact with Shelley, before looking ahead again.

"Shelley, you can be very insensitive... But, I consider you my best friend. And, as such, I would still feel comfortable telling you if something was bothering me. I suppose I've been fortunate to not have to be in that position."

Chelsea looked at her best friend again, and the two of them smiled.

When they reached their apartment, their other roommates Gertrude and Naomi were there in the living room.

"Hey, Seashells!" Naomi said. "How are you two?"

"Kind of a weird day," Shelley said.

"Weird how?" Gertrude asked.

"Well..." Shelley looked at Chelsea. "Actually, I'm not sure we should say."

"Uh," Chelsea began, "I don't see the harm... We saw Randy and Pam hanging out in Petal Lock Park."

"Peyton's sister?" Gertrude replied.

"Yeah," Shelley said. "They were talking and doing running exercises. Didn't seem like their first time hanging out."

They heard a toilet flush, and then Peyton came out of the lavatory.

"Oh," Chelsea said, realizing that they had a visitor.

"So Pam's been talking to Randy?" Peyton said.

"Seems like it," Chelsea replied.

With a defeated expression on her face, Peyton sighed.

"Guess she has nothing to say to me if Randy hasn't said anything on her behalf. I'll see y'all later."

Peyton exited the apartment, and the rest were left wondering just what the deal was with Randy and Pamela.

* * *

When Randy returned to his apartment, he opened the fridge. He realized that it had been a while since anyone else touched his food. It had been a long while since the last time he had seen Vic. So he knocked on Vic's room door. No answer. Randy tried messaging him on his phone.

Randy: *Where you at?*

He stared at the phone for a quarter of a minute before it revealed that there was typing going on at the other end. He received a response.

Vic: *Staying with my girl. She is quite a pearl.*

Randy was not even aware that Vic even had a girlfriend. Then again, Randy never really asked him about his personal life. He wondered how long Vic had been staying with her. Vic's portion of the rent had certainly kept on getting turned in on time. But if he was not home most of the time, it seemed like a waste. Surely it would make sense for *someone* to be occupying the room while it was being paid for.

Randy: *Are you still using your room?*
Vic: *Not really, dude. She makes good food.*
Randy: *Is it okay if I let a friend use it for a while? I know you're all set for paying online. When are you coming back?*
Vic: *Tbh I'm probably just gonna keep crashing here with the ma'am. Feel free to use the room as long as you'd like, fam. I'll give you a heads up if I ever think of moving back. Then your friend can stay on the couch if they still need a place and have no shack.*

Vic seemed more generous than Randy would have expected. The downside would be having to clean Vic's room. He was not much of a cleaner, and the room reeked. Probably more than the beast from *Attack of the Clones*. First, Randy needed a concrete answer if he was going to endure such lengths. Evan and Ted ended up being okay with the idea. Three down, one to go.

Later, Randy met with Pamela once again, at Petal Lock Park. They did the usual running routine for a while before stopping to take a break.

"It's freezing out here," Randy said.

"You feel it's affecting your performance?" Pamela asked.

"Don't say it like that."

"Huh?"

"Never mind. It's just that... Are you comfortable out here?"

"The weather's not ideal. But I enjoy the company."

"Unicoren and Stagmantel?"

"If they can handle the weather, so can I. Especially when I've got Mandy. Though, I guess it does get really uncomfortable. The ground beneath the tent doesn't treat my back very well."

"I've been thinking. My roommate Vic has been away. He's still paying for rent, but he's rarely home."

"Heh. I can relate."

"He's staying with his girlfriend for the foreseeable future. If you want, you can stay in his room. I'd just need to tidy it up a bit."

"Really? I don't wanna impose."

"It's no problem. He says he's okay with it."

Pamela watched the geese walking in front of them as she thought it over.

"Well, if I were to stay over, there'd be conditions."

"Like what?"

"You *can't* let Peyton or any of the Nap Kin know I'm there. In fact, it'd probably be safe to never invite them over."

This was a no-brainer to Randy. None of the Nap Kin had ever asked to go to his home. Usually, they hung out at someone else's place.

"I accept these conditions."

"Really? You'd do that for me?"

"Of course. We're friends, aren't we?"

Pamela smiled, and then she moved in to give Randy a hug. He accepted. It scared him knowing how much he needed it, and how much he would have to let go if all played out as he predicted it would: Naomi, Pamela, friends, and family. Despite his mixed feelings, there was so much that he would miss.

They set a time for when she could bring her stuff over. First, Pamela had to talk to Unicoren and Stagmantel while Randy tidied up the room for her arrival. And so he went off on his way, leaving her to deal with that awkwardness.

* * *

"You believe you will be complacent in Randy's home," Unicoren said with crossed arms.

"It might be good for Mandy, too," Pamela added. "You know. Being in a warmer place."

"Mandy has a core like ours," Stagmantel said, walking over. "It does not feel so cold out here."

"I'm sorry," Pamela said. "I just have this *feeling* that I should do this. At least for a little while. It's not exactly *normal* for me to be out here, you know?"

"You are trying to conform," Unicoren said.

"It might be good for me. I know I won't be with Mandy, or either of you, forever. So I need to make sure I can maintain a lasting friendship with someone. And I think this can strengthen it."

"Do as you wish," Stagmantel said, turning his back to her. "We will be waiting here, whenever we are needed."

He stared at the geese for a long moment, and then he walked back to his side of the park.

"Is he mad?" Pamela asked.

"It's been too long for me to tell," Unicoren said.

"I promise I'll take good care of Mandy."

Unicoren nodded, apparently giving Pamela her blessing.

"I know you want to keep your word."

"And I will. I promise. I can still visit. And Mandy will be back with you."

"All right. Go then, Pamela Sheer. I trust you."

* * *

Once Pamela was gone, Unicoren walked over to the redwoods. There, she caught Stagmantel looking down at a boulder. His fists were clenched.

He punched the boulder, creating a crack.

"Stagmantel!"

He turned around.

"How could she do this?"

"You dare question?"

"You just did, too! See? This Randy fellow is upsetting the balance. He is pushing back the timetable! I thought we would be out of the woods soon!"

"It will still happen. Pamela promised we would have Mandy again. She needs to set up her life, and what it has to be without Mandy. Without us."

Stagmantel blinked and then unclenched his fists.

"I'm sorry. I'm not usually this impatient. It's just that we are so close."

"And if we remain calm and collected, it will remain close. *We* will remain close."

She held out her hand, and he grabbed it, running a finger along her ring, which symbolized their union. One that had been made long before any of this school had been constructed. Long before the machinations of Mathias Moseley.

"Will you miss her when she is gone?" Stagmantel asked.

"I might. But better to have one than neither."

* * *

Randy heard the knocking on the door. With Vic's room now ready for use, he opened it confidently, letting Pamela into the apartment. His roommates Evan and Ted sat in the living room, studying on their laptops.

"So this is Pam," he told them. "The one Vic said could use his room."

"Hi Pam. Evan."

"Ted."

"Nice to meet both of you. I promise I won't be in your way."

"Ah, no worries," Evan said. "We barely have our eyes off our screens. Should feel the same."

"And this is your room over here," Randy said, escorting her to the doorway and showing her a bed with clean sheets, a blanket, and a pillow. Randy had also washed the clothes and put them in the closet. He was not sure when Vic might return, but he figured that the clothes should be clean in case Vic wanted to retrieve them anytime soon.

"This looks really nice," Pamela said. "Thank you. I can't tell you how much I appreciate this."

"No worries. It's implied."

Pamela chuckled at that. A little victory for Randy, bringing joy to a friend whom he knew genuinely enjoyed his company.

Chapter 25
Beach Cleanup

A cloudy day at the beach in late January seemed like a good time for four friends to walk upon the jetty of rocks stretching out into the ocean.

They were wrong. Seagulls flocked around. But these birds were not the worst of their troubles. Bird turds covered the rocks, cloaking them with such a repugnant stench. But still, this was not the worst of their troubles. Some rocks were wobbly, nearly causing these hikers to fall into the water. But, still, these were not the worst of their troubles. After fifteen minutes, they reached the end, and there, sitting at the end beside the water, staring out into the horizon...

It was Mathis. Mathis was the worst of their troubles.

* * *

August looked into the mirror and saw seaweed coming into the frame and then drifting out of frame. The frame was from the point of view of the surface of an ocean. Confused, he slowly reached for the glass, wondering whether he would feel the water.

And then a body flying toward him. He backed away. Rather than fly out of the mirror, the body disappeared.

He could see a tall figure, its face too far away to decipher. This figure used a scythe to slice at a hiker's ankle, causing her to fall into the water. Her body grew as it approached August's vantage point and then disappeared. But then the figure's scythe grew closer, swinging swiftly back and forth, turning the mirror red.

The figure turned back and dragged another person, pushing him into the water, hands around the victim's neck. The back of his head filled the frame of the glass. With the man's head wriggling, August could tell he was struggling for breath. But the assailant was too strong. Once the victim stopped struggling, the head rose to the top of the frame, the back of his blood-soaked shirt becoming visible.

August needed to get out of here.

* * *

Mathis watched the man's body float in the water. He turned around and saw the remaining woman trying to run away. Confidently, Mathis ran after her. When he caught up to her, he flipped the rock beneath her, sending her into the water. She could swim, but he could fling. He picked up a rock, aimed for her head, and let it drop.

PLOP!

The body sank beneath the rock.

Mathis knew that it would take a lot of work retrieving any of these heads to present to Candid. But he was still determined to fill her with fear.

He checked his phone. The weather forecast for another beach up north proved to be promising. It would be sunny, broad daylight in which Candid could climb. He grinned.

She'll be filled with fear.

* * *

August could no longer see anyone in the mirror. Nothing but red water. Somehow, it called to him. Seductive like fruit punch. Slowly, he reached through the mirror. The tips of his digits entered a numbing liquid, their space replaced by reflections of the tips. The further he reached inward with his hand, the more of his hand's reflection appeared. When he pulled his arm back, there was nothing beyond his wrist, and the hand's reflection levitated in the air of the mirror's space.

"AHHHHH!"

August ran out of the room. As soon as he shut the door, his hand reappeared, and he had no idea why he had left his room. He examined his hand and noticed the tan line on his wrist. He could not remember wearing anything there recently.

He looked at his room door, and his vision became fixated on the room number, 314, as he shut the door.

Three-one-four... Three-POINT-one-four.

"Pi," he said aloud.

After a split second of clarity, he ran to the lift and took it down. When he got to the bottom floor, he walked into the dining room, where he found Anton and Fritz using their laptops.

"What's up?" Fritz asked.

"Pie. Something to do with pie."

"Feeling hungry?"

"I'm not starving, but I could eat. Where could I get pie?"

"I don't have any at the moment," Anton said. "But there is a really nice shop down the street. Really high quality."

"Do they have lemon meringue?"

"Yep. You like it?"

"It's my favorite."

"All right." Anton closed his laptop. "It's time to procrastinate a bit."

After the laptops were put away, the three of them walked down the street to the pie shop Crust Desserts, where August got lemon meringue pie. Anton ordered cherry, and Fritz ordered apple.

"My god," Fritz said after taking a bite. "Anton, you sure know your stuff."

"You can count on me."

They looked over at August, who sobbed as he took bites out of his pie.

"This pie. The lemon." August cried. "I should love this, but it just *hurts*. I feel like I should be hurting about something, but I don't know what it is. I'm wounded and I don't know why. I don't know how to fix this!"

One of the workers walked up to him.

"Would you like some whipped cream on that pie?"

"Yes please."

"See?" Anton said. "Whipped cream *can* help."

August knew that the whipped cream would not be enough. He really needed to schedule an appointment with a counselor and get to the bottom of what was eating him up inside.

* * *

Candid received her benefactor's new instructions a couple of days later. Apparently, she was supposed to go to the beach, where she would climb onto a tall rock formation in the middle of the water, and then find her next payment. The caveat was that it was out in the open, in broad daylight. Normally, she was sent to these places under the cover of darkness, but now the sun would be hovering over her.

Candid brought her waterproof hiking boots to the beach. She had no swimwear, but she did not think anyone would notice or care. It definitely made it easier to walk on the sand.

She saw the formation out in the water, surrounded by smaller rocks. Sometimes the water surrounding the rock formation was shallow, but on this day, the tide had raised up the level. She could not simply walk to her destination. So she had to hop from stepping stone to stepping stone, which was a bit of a challenge. Luckily, the hiking boots helped her maintain her balance.

At last, she arrived at the tall rock, and the climb began. It was full of dried bird turds, giving off a foul stench. Seagulls hovered above her. She hoped that the head was buried deep within the crack on the top of the formation, but not too deep to retrieve. She imagined the seagulls pecking at the remains, giving her location away to the local authorities.

It was dark in the crack, but she did see a shape. It looked like a rock, but she was certain that it was a head, which she imagined was a bit squished.

She slipped on a fresh pile of turds, throwing her off-balance. On the way down to the water, she hit her knee on the rock and cut her hand. Down she fell, tasting salt upon impact. She closed her mouth and held her breath. It was too deep for her to stand up. She waved her arms frantically, trying to rise toward the sun. Before closing her eyes, she thought she saw a plastic bag sinking down into the water.

A hand reached down, pulling her up. Judging from the red she was wearing, she was a lifeguard.

"You can breathe now," the lifeguard said.

Candid obeyed. She exhaled uncontrollably, in a panicked state.

"You can let go of me now."

"What's that?" The lifeguard pointed to blood trickling down the rock and into the water.

Oh no, Candid thought. *The body.*

"Uh... I don't know."

"Oh my god."

"What? What?"

The jig is up! Candid thought.

For a moment, she considered just breaking free from the lifeguard and letting the water take hold of her. Candid believed she might have deserved it, having let her benefactor's deeds go on for this long.

"Your hand's bleeding," the lifeguard said. "I've got a first-aid kit."

Candid looked at the cut in her hand, then back on the rock.

Is that my blood? she wondered.

The lifeguard took her to the shore. There, she was treated for her wound. During this, she thought about the bag that she had glimpsed. She could have sworn that it fell at the exact same time she did. The possibility that the payment was in the poop popped into her head. The feces puzzle was pieced together.

Are you fucking kidding me?

Without obtaining the payment, she returned to her apartment after this incident. After walking in and closing the door, she was startled by a presence that spoke from the kitchen.

"How was your day?"

Ben F. walked out of the kitchen, onion in hand. He bit right into it, stripping it of its layers and revealing the core. No tears came out of his eyes.

"Did you not put a body there?"

"Nope. I went for shits and giggles, and I *got* what I wanted. You oughta see the look on your face. I sure as hell can't see the look on mine, but I can feel the delight."

"Why the fuck did you make me go through all that?"

"Were you *hoping* to see a body?"

"Enough of the whole 'Evil Candy' bullshit!"

"It was *bird* shit. And I gave you a break. What more do you want? I have been *generous.* Are you not comfortable?"

"Financially, yeah. But you know damn well I'm uncomfortable in other ways, you demented fuck!"

"Hm. You think words can *hurt* me. You *wish* I were so fragile."

"If you're not human, then what are you?"

"I don't care for labels. I just need outlets for my innate wrath."

"Why are you full of wrath?"

"It's just how I came into this world. I don't care to question it. How goes the watch on Randy?"

She did not feel like updating him on Randy's boring activities. But she felt like she had nothing else to do. She was in no position to fight Ben F. at the moment.

"He don't do much. Only going to each module and playing around with Mandy the Mantleope."

"Keep on following him. And tell him to meet me at Garlick's, the ice cream parlor, on Friday the sixth at six o'clock. Evening."

"Fine." She pointed at the front door. "Now get the fuck out."

He took another bite into the onion and exited the apartment.

Candid had had enough. She wanted to smite this murderer.

Chapter 26
Counting on Counseling

August met up with Dr. Carol Crooks, a counselor, once the next term started in the first week of February.

"Take a seat, and we may begin whenever you feel ready."

August sat down in the chair, adjusting himself until he was comfortable.

"It's really complicated," he began. "I've been going through it in my head over and over, trying to figure out the best way to explain this. But it feels like there's no good way to explain it." He looked at his wrist. Though the tan line was fading, it was still visible. "I've noticed this tan line on my wrist, and I think I'm missing something. Something to do with a friend I can't find. And that scares me. See, I firmly believe that a person is the sum of their friends and family."

"Would it be accurate to say that when you lose a friend, even if it's just one in many, you feel as though you've lost a major part of yourself?"

August stared at the tan line on his wrist.

"It does hurt."

"How do you know you've lost them?"

"I just have this feeling that this friend doesn't really like me anymore."

He thought she would look at him funny, but she seemed unfazed, listening intently.

"Growth sometimes involves accepting that not everyone can be— or even remain— your friend. I know that may not be something you want to hear. But I am sorry that you've lost a friend."

He could feel her analyzing him. Marking him up. He had to set the record straight before the pin left a scratch.

"The thing is, I'm not necessarily super dependent on all these friendships. I don't mean to sound arrogant, but it's pretty easy for me to befriend people."

"So this friend whom you've lost. Does losing them make you feel less secure? It seems like you feel very comfortable making friends, and it's been your status quo for a while. And so when you lose a friend, you may be questioning the ease with which you befriend people. How it might change."

"I hadn't really thought about that. But, look, I'm not this 'Mister Popular' type of guy trying to collect. I'm not some clingy creep. You have to understand me."

"I don't mean to impose an inaccurate view of you at all. I'm just trying to help."

"Right. I know. Sorry if I sound defensive. I'm just trying to be clear."

"We can work through this. Just take your time. But, well, keep it within the hour. I'm seeing someone else after you. Sorry. I don't mean to rush."

"No worries. It's your job. And I really do appreciate that you listen to students."

"Everyone needs an ear or two. Go on. Continue, as you please."

"It's not just that I've lost this friend. My bond with them is gone. Their trust in me is gone. All that is true. But the other facet is that I can't remember who this friend is. And I have this feeling they might be in some kind of trouble."

"What gives you this feeling?"

"I'm not sure. I can't really explain it. But it's consuming me. I don't feel comfortable. Studying abroad should be the dream. But I feel like I've been losing sleep, even though I don't remember losing sleep."

"You're not conscious when you're asleep."

"But sometimes I don't remember going to bed or waking up."

"Do you sleepwalk?"

"I don't think so. Although..." He thought about the dishes that had been going missing. "No. Some students are still in the common area really late. They would've noticed. I think. Unless they're studying really hard."

"Maybe you don't travel that far."

"It sure feels like I do. But that can't be right."

"Are hallways a possibility?"

"I don't even know anymore. This isn't how things should be. I'm normally well adjusted. It's not even being away from home that's making me feel this ill. It's all these other lingering worries I can't even confirm. These unconquerable concerns. Counseling sounded like it could help. But if I'm being honest, I'm not even sure where any of this is going. I feel like I'm just talking in circles." He sighed. "But...I guess that's not too bad. The world goes in a circle, right? Better trajectory than long before the orbits."

"I'm sorry, what?"

He remembered that not everyone knew the story of Miunis Grund.

"Nothing. Just some science stuff. But while we're on the subject of circles—which, for some reason, are making me think of pie—it looks like I'm gonna be an undergrad for an extra year. Didn't turn in the work I should've, and I don't know why."

"I'm sorry to hear that."

"Yeah. I applied for financial aid again, so those wheels are in motion. I feel so embarrassed. Really thought I'd finish within four years."

"Each person is on a different path. Even though some paths may intersect from time to time, it's impossible to be ahead of or behind someone."

STEVEN SHINDER

"Huh. That's a really great way of looking at it." He looked at the floor. "I'm really gonna miss my friends when they graduate."

"You've made new friends here, haven't you? I'm sure you can make new ones."

August looked up again. Her smile suggested that she probably saw a glimmer of hope in his eyes.

Though the counseling session did not yield any answers, August was glad to have talked through his concerns. For once, he even had a good night's sleep.

But then the morning came. And with it, the sounds of power saws.

August jumped out of bed. He looked at the lavatory door. The sounds were not coming from within there. He walked over to the curtains over his window and pulled them aside, letting in the sunlight. He had left the window open to let some air in at night, and now across the street he could see some construction work going on. People using power tools to build.

August inhaled, then exhaled, before closing the window, keeping disconcerting sounds away for the time being.

271

Chapter 27
What's Bottled Up

Randy stood in the alcoholic beverages aisle at the supermarket. He was not thirsty per se, but he felt like it would be a good idea to get something from this aisle. But there were so many options. It was like all those times he took forever selecting anything from a restaurant menu.

"Brandy?"

He turned to see Reginald parking his shopping cart.

"Oh. Hey Gin."

"You all right?"

"What do you mean?"

"It's just that you seem like you've been down."

Oh, so it HAS been noticeable, Randy thought.

"Maybe a bit. So what?"

"You can talk to me, bud."

"Not about this. Trust me." He faced the bottles again. "I need to finish shopping."

"Where's your cart?"

Randy closed his eyes and sighed.

"I also need to start."

"I can wait for you outside, if you'd like."

Just fuck the hell off! Randy wanted to say.

"I'm getting milk, eggs, and ice cream that'll melt. It all needs to go in the fridge, Reginald. Is that what you want? For ice cream to melt like my heart at the sight of a woman who's unattainable?"

You moron, he thought to himself.

"I'm getting the sense that this isn't about ice cream. Is it Tonic?"

Uh-oh, Randy thought. *He knows!*

"I...might buy some."

"I meant Naomi."

Randy turned around, certain that his open mouth and wide eyes convinced Reginald that his guess was correct.

"How'd you know?"

"You don't have to hide. I've seen how you look at her. It's how *I* used to look at her." Unsure about what to say, Randy averted his eyes from Reginald's. And then Reginald continued. "I'm not mad or anything. She and I are really good friends, and nothing will change that."

Randy supposed that there was no use hiding now.

"I wasn't sure how you'd feel about it. And anyway, I'm at a bit of a disadvantage. You two grew up together. I haven't known her as long."

"Look. You don't need to worry about whether I approve. I'd be okay with it. But ultimately, you have to find out what *she* wants. She might not reciprocate, and you need to feel prepared for that possibility."

"That's the thing." He tried his hardest to hold back the tears. "I'm *scared*. I don't know how I can come back from rejection. I've been trying to avoid it for so long."

"If it's not meant to be, you two can still maintain the friendship. Pretend like asking her out never happened."

It all comes back to pretend, Randy mused.

"If she says she doesn't like me that way, then I don't know how I'll be. It's hard to imagine that there could be someone else in the future." He made eye contact, but not the kind where it felt like two people were connecting. He was searching for himself, and he saw himself reflected in Reginald's eyes. "I can't *see* my future."

"None of us can. But you take a chance, see what happens, and hope for the best. And if you need to talk afterward, I'm here for you."

"Why the hell do you have to be so nice?" Randy laughed nervously. "How can I possibly live up to that?"

Reginald shrugged.

"You can be a nice guy, too."

"I try to be. But I can be so shitty sometimes. I'm not wholesome enough. I don't *want* to be destroyed."

Reginald opened up his arms.

"Come here, buddy." Slightly hesitant, Randy obeyed, walking over to Reginald for a hug. "It may hurt if it doesn't go how you want. But you can remain whole as long as you make an effort to remain whole."

During this hug, another customer walked into the aisle, trying to reach around them to grab a bottle of rum. Randy and Reginald let go.

"Good luck with her, bro. Remember, it's not the end if it doesn't work out."

Randy nodded. Then he heard a sound. A text notification. He checked his phone. It was a message from Pamela.

Pamela: *Your parents and sister are here.*

"Crap!"

"Something wrong?"

"It's not a big deal. I just need to take care of something."

Randy started heading toward the exit. At the moment, he had no way of telling whether Candid might be outside the store or whether she might be watching the house. He thought they had an understanding about Mathis needing to be killed, but he was not sure whether that agreement would hinder her obligations to send Mathis info on something like his family.

Once he was out of the store, Randy stood for a moment, thoughts going in circles and making him feel helpless.

* * *

"Has he responded yet?" Mrs. Morales asked, sitting at the dining table with her husband and their daughter, while Pamela sat on the couch.

"Not yet," Pamela replied.

Pamela could see that Randy had read the message, but there was no typing taking place at the other end.

"So how do you know Randy?" Mr. Morales asked.

"We're friends. He just let me study here. It's so noisy at my place."

Pamela felt bad about lying. Especially since the Morales family seemed like nice people.

"Why does Randy hate us?" Kayleigh asked.

"Kayleigh!" Mrs. Morales said. "He doesn't hate us. He's your brother."

"Then why don't I get to see him?"

"Randy doesn't hate you," Pamela said. "He's just going through a tough time."

"So if someone never visits family," Kayleigh began, "it's 'cause they have a tough time?"

"Yes."

Pamela got the uncomfortable feeling that Kayleigh could see right through her, but she knew that such a feeling was absurd.

"Then why not talk about the tough time?"

"Well... Maybe it's hard for him to explain."

"How come he has time for you but not for me?"

Those words felt like a punch to the face.

"Okay," Mr. Morales said. "That's enough, little missy. You're being rude."

"Stop calling me rude!"

"I'll stop calling you rude when you stop *being* rude. That's how it works."

"Randy doesn't work," Kayleigh said. "He doesn't have a job like you want him to have. *He* is the one being rude..."

Pamela typed on her phone.

Pamela: *Where are you? You need to get over here now.*

* * *

The next message from Pamela made Randy paranoid. The urgent tone worried him.

What's wrong? he wondered. *Fuck. Is Mathis there with them? Fuck fuck FUCK!*

*SLAY THE FUCKER!!!*the voice in his head said.

If his family were being held hostage, then he would absolutely try that. But at the moment, he was uncertain.

"Hey!" he heard someone say.

He turned to see Candid, holding her camera. Randy scowled.

"You better tell me what—"

"Chill. I took a photo of you right now. Yeah, I keep following you, but I'm with you on taking down my benefactor."

"You're fully committed for sure?"

"He showed up at my home and killed every roommate."

Randy went numb for a moment, imagining the same thing happening to his family and friends while he was too far away to save them.

"Shit..."

"And he tried to get me digging through bird shit to get paid. I've had it with him."

"So then what are you planning on doing?"

"He told me to let you know to meet him at Garlick."

"The ice cream place?"

"Yeah. At...eighteen hundred on Friday. I wanna attack him at home. You know where that be?"

"Yeah."

"Map it for me." She handed him her phone, which had a map app open. "I'll go into the mansion. I can break in while you meet with him. Maybe I can find a thing to kill him. Hell, I'll bring a thing with me and come out of nowhere. A walk through the door, and then the end."

"A sneak attack. You're serious about killing him?"

"Yeah. A cut on the arm, and the blood vanished. He showed me."

Randy thought back to when Mathis squeezed lemon juice into his own eye.

"What the hell is he?"

"He ain't human. And he can't be caught. But hopefully he can be killed. I'm willing to find out. I'll aim for the head. And if I die, you finish the job."

"How will I know if you've died?"

"I'm gonna need a lot of luck. The dumb duck flock in the park? That'll be how you know. Give me your number. I'll go the park, take a loan, and take a pic of the duck that turn to rock for you' to know where it be. If you can't find it there the day after, I'm dead."

"You know, the luck of the ducks can lean either way. That's why I've never tried them myself."

"I know. I'm aware that I could die. You can finish the job if I do."

Candid *did* look determined. Randy tried to find meaning in this, seeing it as a sign that perhaps he should feel encouraged to keep on living. Maybe Naomi would have feelings for him after all. Maybe he did not need to be the one to kill Mathis. Maybe it had to be Candid. Her association with him had a longer duration, so it made sense for her to have first dibs. If there was a compass, it seemed to be pointing—

"Hey!" Candid said, snapping her fingers. "You done thinking? What'll it be?"

"All right. We'll go through with your plan. On one condition."

"Damn it." Candid stomped. "Why you gotta be lame?"

"I was just gonna say to not follow me for the rest of the day."

"Oh."

"I swear. There are people I don't want Mathis to track. I don't want you snooping around, getting their license plate number and whatnot."

"No problem. I'm done with that. After today, I'll only follow until the day of your meeting to throw him off."

"That I'm okay with."

"That be the name, then?"

Randy figured that there was no harm in confirming since they seemed to be on the same level now.

"Yes. His name is Mathis Dillard."

He typed the address to Mathis' mansion into Candid's phone.

"I *will* kill him," Candid said.

"I'm sure you will."

There was a peculiar moment when they both smiled, united by their hatred of Mathis and their desire to see him dead. Randy knew that he could trust her word on this.

After the meeting with Candid, Randy let Pamela know that he was on his way. A short while later, he returned to his apartment.

"There you are!" Kayleigh said. "We've been waiting *hours* for you!"

"It's been less than an hour," their mom corrected.

"Uh, it's called *hyperbole,* Mom."

"She is kinda right," their dad said. "We drove for six hours to get here, after all."

Randy received a hug from his mom.

"How are you doing?" she asked.

"Just been busy." The hug ended. "Why didn't you call in advance?"

"We wanted to surprise you!" she said.

"Well, congrats. You really caught me off guard."

"See?" Kayleigh said. "Told you he's rude."

Randy heard Pamela laugh.

"I'm guessing you've all met Pamela."

"Yep," Kayleigh said. "She told us *everything*, Randy."

"Huh?"

A flicker of paranoia, followed by overwhelming doubt. Pamela did not really know anything that would worry his family. Out of all his secrets, she only knew about the running. But his parents would probably be proud of him for getting exercise, the intention unbeknownst to them.

"There's nothing to tell," Pamela said.

"Why don't we go out for dinner?" Randy's dad suggested. "Any good places to eat around here?"

"Why didn't you check online for places in the area?"

"We want to hear what *you* like around here."

"He probably doesn't wanna eat with us," Kayleigh said. "He won't talk about his *tough* time."

Tough time, he thought. *Does she know about the running?*

"We've just been worried about you," his mom said. "We hardly ever see you, and we figured we'd come over and cheer you up if you're going through stressful times. I know school's busy, but holy cow, you haven't visited us all year. Not even on the holidays."

"I'm sorry. I've been really out of it."

"I bet," his dad said, opening the vodka-filled cabinet above the fridge. "Any of these yours?"

"Th-those are Vic's."

"Oh yeah? Where is he?"

"He's out right now," Pamela covered. "He's got a bit of a problem."

"Yeah," Randy said. "We've been meaning to give him an intervention for a while."

Randy's dad stared at him for a long moment, and then he looked at Pamela. Then he brushed the whole thing aside.

"Well, all right then," his dad said. "Let's eat! You got anywhere you wanna go?"

"I guess we could go to Burger Breath."

"That doesn't sound like a real place."

"It's a few minutes away from here."

"All right. You'll navigate for us."

The Morales family headed out, eventually ending up at the burger joint called Burger Breath. Randy was not exactly good at breaking the ice, opting to just dive into his burger and fries.

"So," his mom began, "what's the plan after graduation, kiddo?"

Randy stopped eating for a moment.

"Please stop calling me that. I'm not a kid anymore."

"But you'll always be a kid to me."

"Well," Kayleigh said, "guess I'm not growing up either."

"I hope not," her dad said. "That's when I'll for sure feel old."

"Dad," Kayleigh said, "you *are* old."

"Am not. I'm only forty-nine."

"Only?" she replied.

"And unashamed. I'm glad to have lived this long."

Wonder if I'll experience that, Randy thought.

"So," his sister began, looking right at him, "what *is* the plan? What are you gonna do?"

He really did not want to apply to mundane jobs, but he was not sure what other options there were. He really hated having to lie, so he tried wording it in such a way that was not technically a lie, despite sounding deceptive in his mind.

"I guess I *could* apply for work back home."

"Anything to do with your major?" his mom asked.

"I guess I could paint houses." He shrugged. "Or maybe work at a grocery store."

"And you'd be okay with that?" his dad asked.

In all honesty, Randy did not believe so.

"What other choices do I have?"

"Did you ever take any business classes?" his mom asked.

"No."

"I've been telling you they'd be helpful. A friend of mine has a son who majored in business and started his own company. You should really take advantage of what you can."

"There's not enough room in my schedule for business classes this school year if I wanna graduate on time."

"Oh. Well...would you *want* to stay another year if it meant learning more about business?"

Randy knew that she wanted the best for him. Neither of his parents went to college, and they seemed to have this romanticized idea that certain classes would automatically solve everything. But Randy knew that the world was tougher than he thought it was as a kid. Once again, he deflected, taking another bite of his burger.

"It's been forever since the last time I've been here," he said.

"It's been forever since you've been home," Kayleigh said, looking down at the table.

Ouch, Randy thought. He was surprised by how hurt his sister seemed to be about him not being home very often. He noticed that she had not touched her burger or fries.

"Are you gonna eat that?" he asked awkwardly.

"I'm not very hungry," Kayleigh said, getting up and heading toward the lavatory.

Randy's parents were silent. They looked at Kayleigh, then at him, and then at each other.

"I'll go talk to her," his mom said, leaving Randy and his dad at the table.

"So," Randy's dad said, "you like anyone at school?"

Randy wanted to flip the table, but he knew that it would not budge if he tried.

"That's irrelevant."

"Okay." His dad nodded. "You like anyone *outside* of school?"

"Dad, don't ask me about relationships. *Ever.* I know romance might seem easy for some, but it's tough. And it hasn't been for lack of trying. So when you ask me about this stuff, I feel *really* shitty. I'm sorry I can't be a success story like you, and that nobody wants to date me, marry me, or have kids with me. But that's just the way things are."

His dad looked down, moving his own fries around with the fingers of his right hand. The hand that had facepalmed all those years ago, making Randy feel like he had done something wrong and would never be in perfect form.

"Just asking," his dad said. "I didn't mean to upset you."

"I know you didn't," Randy said. "Sorry. Just, please drop the subject. I know I look like I don't have a plan, but things will play out how they have to. All right?"

His dad made eye contact again.

"All right. And I don't care if it makes me feel older, but I'm sure that you'll meet someone and give us grandkids someday."

Who would wanna have kids with me? Randy wondered. *And would I even be able to support them?*

It was difficult for him to imagine "child of Randy Morales" when nobody expressed romantic interest in him. Naomi Clutcher seemed like an ideal match, but he was still not sure how she felt. Having received encouragement from Reginald, he was even more desperate to find out.

Kayleigh and their mom returned to the table, seating themselves again. Kayleigh wiped her eyes.

"I'm fine," she said.

Randy knew that this was a lie, and that she was hiding her pain.

No doubt we're related.

* * *

While Randy was out with his family, Pamela looked at the vodka bottles. She had seen them before while going through the kitchen cabinets, but she had assumed that they were for all three roommates who remained here. She had not considered that they may have belonged solely to Randy. But the hesitation with which he had answered his father worried her.

She was sitting at the table when Randy came back from having dinner with the family.

"How'd it go?" she asked.

"It went well."

"Those drinks." Pamela pointed in the cabinet's direction. "Are they all yours?"

Randy looked like a rear caught in the flashlights.

"It's not a big deal."

"How often do you drink?"

"Well, I haven't had any here since you've been here. You would've seen me. Though I do drink with the Nap Kin."

"Socially is fine, I guess. But do you ever have some by yourself?"

"Last quarter, yeah." He sighed. "I just buy a few every now and then, just in case."

"Any particular reason?"

He opened his mouth, and she expected a made-up excuse. But then he closed his mouth for a moment, probably rethinking his next move. And then what he said next sounded sincere.

"I'm just a lonely, insecure guy. It's pretty common. There doesn't have to be this huge thing about it."

"If you're so lonely, why'd you refuse to visit your family? Why torture yourself like that?"

"Why do *you*, Pamela? You haven't gone to see *your* family much, have you?"

It sounded like a fair point. Even so, she did not want to let the Ferris wheel turn on her. She wanted to be in control. But she had to open up.

"I guess that's carnival. But how does your family treat you?"

"Fine. Normal. We get along well."

"Because with mine, I feel the judgment. There's baggage. *That* is why I don't try to see them."

"Fine. I won't judge you for that, and you don't judge me for this."

"Randy. They're *nice*. What are you hiding?"

He sighed.

"Things will be different now. I had a reason for not going back, but now that reason may be gone. I just need to be sure of something."

"Sure of what?"

"Don't worry about it."

"That sounds really sketchy. How can I *not* worry?"

"It's nothing huge."

"Is someone back in your hometown bothering you?"

"No. And that's the truth. Now please stop interrogating me when there's nothing to discuss."

Pamela wanted to continue talking, but she could not think of anything that would get him to open up.

"Fine."

Pamela got up and started walking to her room.

"Pamela." She stopped. "If there was something you could do, I would tell you. It's not in your power, though. I just need to hear back about this thing."

"All right. Good to know."

Pamela entered her room, closing the door behind her.

Chapter 28
Caught Candy

That Friday, Candid arrived at Petal Lock Park, where she found Stagmantel sitting on his chair up on the hill.

"Hey!" she called out from below. "You got a duck to loan out?"

"Candid Du Clips. It's been a while."

"Yeah yeah. Look, I need luck for a thing. I don't need to tell you what for, do I?"

"It makes no difference to me. Choose a duck. Any duck. The one who currently has one would be ecstatic. She's been failing some assignments."

A risk that had to be taken. Candid looked around and saw a duck near a boulder that had been cracked. That spot would be easy for Randy to recognize. She pointed.

"That one!"

"You there!" Stagmantel called out. "Stand a loan!"

The duck turned to stone. Candid took a photo of it and sent it to Randy. Then she looked back at Stagmantel.

"Thank you," Candid said before walking away.

Shortly before the scheduled meeting time at Garlick's, Candid arrived at the fence behind Mathis' mansion. She was surprised to see the garlic bulbs. The fence did not seem to be electric. She took out the pliers she had gotten from the store and used them to cut up the barbed wire. Once there was an opening, she climbed over, and landed on the stone-filled floor below. She could definitely imagine Mathis living in a place like this. No alarms had gone off, which put her a bit at ease. But she was still somewhat paranoid.

She went up to the door at the front of the building and tried picking the lock with an ice pick that she had bought. Upon her first try, she opened it successfully.

"Luck pick for the win," she said to herself.

She got inside and shut the door behind her. It was dark. Rather than feel around for a light switch, she hoped to save some time. So she clapped, turning on the lights. A lucky guess.

She went upstairs to Mathis' office. The desk had nothing on top. But Candid found the scythes hanging on the wall. The scythes that had for so long been used on the victims whose remains she had been forced to find.

This is how it'll go down, she thought.

She picked up the scythes and went back downstairs. She set the pliers beside the steps behind her. The tool felt like too much for her to carry, and she did not want to be distracted as she wielded the scythes.

Once she had a good idea of the layout, she clapped again, cloaking herself in darkness, disrupted for a moment by the light of her phone screen. She saw a text from Randy and responded.

Randy: *Are you in yet?*
Candid: *Yes I'm in. Is he there?*

* * *

At Garlick's, Randy sat by the window, waiting for a response from Candid. He had a cup of garlic banana split in front of him. He was not craving it, but he wanted to show that he had power in this meeting. There were other people in the parlor, but he felt very isolated. Looking out the window, he saw Mathis get out of his car. When the loaner walked in, Randy froze. Mathis waved and approached the table.

The phone vibrated.

Randy saw the notification on his phone. Though he did not have time to read the message during the split second when he covered the screen and shoved the cell back into his pocket, he saw clearly that the message was from Candid.

Did Mathis see?

Mathis seated himself on the other side of the table. Randy had another spoonful of ice cream.

"Good choice," Mathis said, looking at the banana split. "If a banana and an orange walk hand in hand, then are they for eating?"

Randy tried to hide his anxiety as he answered.

"If they walk, then I guess not."

"Some might disagree."

"So. What's the scoop?"

"From what I can tell, you don't seem to be so concerned about making a *living*. I've given you a great deal. Normally, it should take you about ten years to pay off your loans, more or less around the time of the pathetic reunion. Where do you see yourself in ten years?"

"I don't. Where do you see *yourself*, Mathis?"

"Nowhere."

"Well then, that makes two of us."

"No. Only one of each. Tell me how you expect to pay me back."

"I don't."

The corners of Mathis' mouth curled into a sly signal.

"Then I'll have no choice but to go after your friends."

Randy's eyes widened. He did not want his friends roped into all this.

"But, but—"

"Butt-butt-butts are for sitting and shitting. Are you shitting me right now?"

Randy re-adjusted his body, planting himself firmly in his seat before responding.

"I *shit* the shadows."

Mathis raised an eyebrow and chuckled.

"Is that a threat?"

"Maybe." Randy tried to remain stoic, but small facial twitches betrayed him.

"Hmm. You're hoping that by saving your friends you'll get some validation from them."

"I don't *need* validation." A twitch of the left eyelid. "And *you* are never gonna get it either. I bet there's someone out there *you* wish you could impress."

"There isn't. It's just me and me alone. You, on the other hand, *crave* love. You want so badly to belong. But how could anyone ever love Randy Morales? You could never realize what you've been conditioned to dream. Growing up, getting married, having a child... Time to rain on the charade, because it's not gonna happen. You wouldn't want anyone to inherit your curse, anyway. Me, I never got that conditioning. That, *and* childhood, are for the weak. I inherited no curse. I merely became, mirror cracking curse spread from flawless me."

Randy was thankful for this long-winded response. It gave him time to figure out his next verbal move. The banana split in front of him was helpful inspiration. He leaned forward.

"You are like a fruit fly born in the bruised banana. If you hover over the oven, the baker will swat and bat you away from his brief breakfast."

"So you're the baker in this scenario?"

"If this scenario comes to fruition."

Mathis swatted the air, and Randy flinched.

"Fruit flies are hard to swat. I swear, I'll be the worm swimming in the milk of your cereal." He moved his index finger as though it were a worm slithering around. "September twenty-sixth, I'll go after your group. Let's say nine at night. Enjoy your ice cream, Randall. Have a lick and keep to your little clique before it all melts away. For now, out of all your friends, *Candid* will be first."

He knows.

Out of impulse, Randy tossed his garlic banana split at Mathis' face. The banana fell to the floor, but ice cream stuck to Mathis' face. As Randy got up from his seat, Mathis stuck his fingers in the garlic ice cream on his face and placed his fingertips on his tongue, apparently unfazed by the frozen dessert. Randy ran to the door. Looking back quickly, he saw Mathis get up, step on the banana, and slip. The workers and customers watched him confusedly.

Randy kept running, turning a corner and not slowing down until he was a couple of blocks away. He stopped to catch his breath, his heartbeat not slowing down with the prospect of Mathis hurting his friends on his mind.

The fantasy flashed through Randy's head. His friends in fear. Mathis at large. Randy triumphant. Dying a hero's death. It just seemed too glorious to resist, especially in the heat of the moment when Mathis was antagonizing him. Making Randy want to hurt him very badly.

IT HAS TO BE YOU, the voice said. *YOU HAVE TO END MATHIS. MAGNIFY!*

But that would mean that Candid had to be out of the picture.

And then Randy felt awful for the part of him that wished for Candid to not succeed. He wondered what would happen to her as a result of the text. If he was lucky, Mathis would keep her alive. But if she died, it would be Randy's own fault.

No, the voice said. *She knew what she was getting into. I bet there's no way she could've overpowered him, anyway.*

Randy hated himself for having these thoughts. He knew that he had to warn her.

* * *

Candid was startled by the vibration of her cell phone.

"Shit!" She looked at her phone and saw that Randy was calling. She answered. "Hello?"

"Candid, Mathis knows that you're coming."

"Fuck! How'd he know? What the fuck did you do?!"

"I'm sorry! He saw your text. I couldn't hide it in time."

"Bullshit!"

"You have to get out of there. He said he'd kill you first and then go after my friends."

Candid suspected an ulterior motive.

"You want to be the one to kill him."

"What?"

"You're warning me to not kill him. *You* want to be the one to do it."

"Candid, I'm serious! He's on his way!"

"I'm not backing out. Randy, you're not a killer. You'd get ill looking at the dead like I have. I *know* what he can do. *I* have to be the one."

"I'm just trying to help!"

"No. You just want all the glory. But you're not athletic enough, no matter what you think. You're in over your head. I'm gonna end him. Luckily, I got in with no problem. I got luck in my favor."

"So then you should be able to kill him?"

"Should. But if I have trouble, I *will* find you and make you hurt."

Candid hung up the phone. She looked out the window and saw Mathis opening the gate. She tried to maintain her composure.

Just aim for the head, she reminded herself.

The door opened. Even in the dark, she could see well enough. She swung both scythes toward the throat...

And missed.

Like, it was so frustratingly ridiculous how she missed. She was super close, but no dice and no slice. Rather than clap to light up the home, Mathis closed the door behind him and faced Candid in the dark. She could hear his footsteps, but she could not quite place where he was. So she swung aimlessly in the dark, only slicing the air that surrounded and taunted her.

She felt the stair rail and went up, trying to get the high ground. But when she was halfway up, she saw a light down below.

The light of a blowtorch, the only part of Mathis' face it revealed being his sinister smile, which he maintained as he spoke.

"If a cockroach is all that survives nuclear fallout, is there anyone left to laugh? I like to think so."

Slowly, he walked up the stairs with one hand behind his back, stepping like a Tin Man who needed more from his oil can, as if he knew that he did not need to run after her. But rather than run, Candid stood still. She could not tell whether it was out of fear and the realization that death was inevitable, or whether it was out of courage to which she could cling, if there was any left at all.

Mathis stopped a few steps below her.

"What's that saying about passing the torch to the next generation?"

Below, he blew fire onto the carpet of the steps. Nowhere for Candid to go but up. She felt the fire on her shoes and tried to step it away. She felt like she was walking on hellfire. She stumbled and fell to the floor. Mathis laughed maniacally. The fire grew closer to Candid. In a moment of bleakness, she threw a scythe down, hoping to hit Mathis. He threw the blowtorch over the rails and then used that free hand to catch the scythe.

"Who gave you permission to play with my toys?" The hand behind his back came around, wielding the pliers. "This could be fun. It's only fair for me to borrow it. All is fair in fire and gore."

The fire on the carpet parted as he stepped toward her.

"I don't get it," Candid said. "I had luck!"

"I'm *full* of luck! Plo-Tunium permeates through my veins!"

* * *

The next morning, Randy and Pamela went to Unicoren's side of the park. Randy could tell that Pamela was not so enthusiastic this time around. She had been more introverted toward him ever since his family's visit.

"You go ahead and start without me," Randy said. "I need to check on something real quick."

"All right." She accepted without question, worrying Randy.

He walked over to Stagmantel's side of the park and found the boulder with a crack on it. There, beside it, was the duck, still stone.

She's still alive, Randy observed. *But in what state?*

The temptation to imagine the worst flushed over him, but he shook his head, not wanting to think about it. He kept himself from visualizing anything, but he could not prevent screams from echoing through his mind. Though they were artificial, they felt too real. He raised his hands to his face, his fingers digging into his forehead.

"Stop," he whispered to himself, tears escaping the grasp of his eyes. "Stop."

On the boulder, he saw the shadow of antlers, prompting him to turn around.

"She was here yesterday," Stagmantel said. "She wouldn't tell me why she needed this. I pressed no further. Didn't seem like my place. But I might have asked had I known *you* were involved."

"You don't like me. I get it."

"It's a *huge* deal. Not much can set me off, but there is just something about you that pushes me. This crack? That is you."

Randy looked back at the crack in the boulder, wishing he had the strength of Stagmantel.

"Are you gonna hurt me?"

"No. I wouldn't want to disrupt the trajectory. You may have delayed it, but my life will be back to how it should be sooner or later."

He faced Stagmantel again.

"I don't mean to hurt anyone."

"You just want to be loved, but I'm not certain you know how it works. How to build a life with someone. How it feels to have that life taken away."

Randy thought about Naomi, and his desire to build a life with her. He felt guilty thinking about romance at a time like this. But he felt alone and wanted some comfort. For as long as he had known her, he always believed that if he could form a relationship with Naomi, he could do anything. Maybe it would give him the confidence to fulfill everything else that came his way. He closed his eyes. Though he could hear Stagmantel walking away, he still spoke.

"I'm sorry for any unintentional hurt I've caused. And I hope to make things right."

Chapter 29
Letting it Out

On Friday the thirteenth, the Nap Kin met up at Mitch's apartment. Nobody was worried about him being late, seeing as how he was the host. But they all showed up late to give him a taste of his own medicine. He rolled his eyes about the whole stunt.

There were various drinks on the table. Randy poured himself some rum as he ruminated the fate of Candid. Every day of the past week, he had checked up on the duck. Each time, it was still in its stone state. Randy felt miserable as he continued drinking sips.

But when he looked at Naomi, things somehow seemed to be a little less shitty.

Mitch had karaoke set up on his laptop and the TV. Karaoke was a way of letting out some truth without having to necessarily tip people off that it was coming directly from the singer. Randy sang Gowan's "Moonlight Desires," somewhat of a romance song. Somehow, it made him nostalgic for the 1980s even though he was too young to have lived in that decade. He thought about the luminous glow of the moon, and looked at Naomi every now and then but tried not to make his feelings too obvious to everyone else. He hoped that Naomi could somehow see into his soul and know what he was trying to convey to her.

When the song was over, everyone clapped. Even Naomi. Her clapping and smiling meant more to him than everyone else's.

As the party continued, Randy kept on taking sips. He was uncertain whether he was drunk or just using the alcohol as an excuse for being more open, but he felt ready to tell Naomi how he felt. It was the only way he felt he could remove at least a bit of a weight from his mind. A possible moment of comfort to make him feel better in light of the mistake he had made.

"Naomi, I really need to tell you something. Can we talk outside?"

"Uh, yeah. Sure thing, Brandy."

They walked outside, away from all the noise and ears. The sudden silence intimidated Randy.

What do I say? he wondered. *Do you wanna be my Valentine? No. That could be misinterpreted. Friends could be Valentines.*

"Do you wanna go on a date...with *me,* Naomi?" he asked, holding back a pout. "I...I...feel... I have feels. *You* make me feel... Well, you make me *feel.* I think you know what I'm trying to say."

Naomi's eyes widened briefly, an obvious sign of surprise.

Good surprise, or bad surprise? he wondered.

"I've had a feeling," Naomi said.

His hopes rose to his chest, a bird ready to sing a symphony that could shine through his seemingly bleak, dour existence.

It's working! he thought, channeling his inner Jake Lloyd. He restrained a smile, fearing that it would be so wide it would creep her out. He had to craft his words carefully.

"S-s-same feeling I'm feeling?"

"No, I mean, I've had this hunch that you've had these feelings for me. And, I'm sorry, but I don't feel the same way."

And so his hopes were cast down to the pit of his stomach, where butterflies ceased to flutter.

"So you don't love me, then..."

"As a friend, I do. But nothing more than that."

"I see... That night we talked by the fire. You remember that?"

She nodded nervously.

"A talk between friends."

Randy rubbed his eyes.

"I slept very well that night because I thought you saw me in the same light I saw you. So close to the fire. Guess I was wrong."

"I still enjoy hanging out with you. This doesn't have to change anything."

"Did that light show you my shadow?"

"What?"

"Because I didn't see yours. I only saw *you*. Your attributes."

"Brandy, I—"

"Am I a mess so easily seen? Did you see me with a magnifying glass?"

Water escaped his eyes.

"There's nothing wrong with you, Brandy."

He disagreed. Cognitive distortions rushed to his temple.

"Bullshit. I know what you're thinking: 'Brandy is such a coward. Couldn't tell me all of this sober. Got drunk to say it, to *spill* his feelings.' Well I'll be spilling a lot..."

Spilling blood, he thought.

"Brandy, are you gonna be fine?"

"No. Someone's gonna hurt me. Not you; someone else."

"Who?"

Randy paused, preparing his words carefully. He wanted to follow through with his fate, dying at the hands of Mathis. Especially now knowing that Naomi did not reciprocate romantic feelings for him.

"The universe. I'm so small and insignificant. The universe is so big that it's just gonna crush me. Much worse than my crush on you. I deserve it, to be honest."

"It can't be *all* bad."

"Please," he said with desperation, before shifting to a rude tone that turned his attitude to stone. "You should leave. I love—loved—you, but you should leave."

"But, this isn't your place."

"It *is* my place to make this call."

"I reserve the right to be with our friends. Look, I care about you. I know it must really hurt to see me right now. But if you want this friendship to last, then we can go back inside together and treat things like normal."

"Normal," he scoffed. "What did normal ever get me? I tried to be Mister Normal, being all formal, and you rejected me."

"Not as a friend, though. But you're pushing it in that direction. Is that what you want?"

"I don't know what I want... Forgive me. Don't leave, but stay away from me."

"Brandy—"

"Don't *call* me that."

Randy went back inside. He kept on drinking as people continued to do karaoke. He tuned out the tunes, not being able to recognize what they might have been. He just kept sipping and slipping.

After a while of this, his insides stirred, so he rushed to the bathroom. He had to run through Mitch's room to get to it. He shut the door of that room and then shut the door of the bathroom once inside. His knees got down on the floor, and he vomited into the toilet. There were three loads, and they all burned his throat, leaving a foul taste in his mouth. After those loads, he felt like he still had a little more and kept trying to let it out.

Has it passed, or is it coming up?

Dry heaving. Nothing coming out. He even tried to yell it out. But all that escaped were whimpers. He took his head away from the bowl and cradled his face in his arms.

"This is why nobody loves you," he told himself. "You have nobody..."

All around him, the world seemed to rotate, quicker and quicker until the room was like a twister.

"Stop spinning," he whispered to the floor and the walls before raising his volume and crying some more. "Stop spinning. Stop spinning!"

The room would not listen to his demands because it had no ears. And his friends had ears, but none of them came. He wondered whether they could even hear him over all the music, or whether they simply did not care about him.

"Nobody will help you..." he told himself. "You care *so* much, but they don't see..."

They all deserve to die, a deep, modulated voice in his head said. *They probably hear you but don't care. Unleash Mathis Dillard onto them. Make your attack on him seem like an act of vengeance. Let the world remember you for your wrath, so they see how powerful you are inside!*

More crying, more tears.

"STOP SPINNING!"

He reached up for the doorknob and turned it back and forth until the door opened. He crawled out into Mitch's room. With the popcorn ceiling being the last thing he saw that night, he passed out on the floor, imagining the smell of burnt popcorn.

* * *

Out in the living room, the music overpowered any outside source. Peyton sat beside Gertrude. A playlist was on in the background, but the Nap Kin were talking rather than singing along.

"Hey Mitch," Shelley said. "There's something I've always wondered about you."

"My last name?"

"No. Why are you always late? You a superhero or something?"

Mitch shook his head.

"It's kinda stupid, but also kinda hard for me to talk about."

"Mitch," Chelsea said. "We're your friends. We won't—" Chelsea looked at Shelley. "Well, *most* of us won't tease you."

"All right. Well, in high school, I used to go to parties that my classmates had. Open invitation. I wouldn't necessarily call them 'friend friends.' It's like, you know people and then act like you're all cool with each other. But there's not really that deep connection. Not back then."

"Teen stuff," Chelsea said. "We've been there."

"Right. But I used to show up to these parties early, hanging out with the host before everyone else arrived. Sometimes people were fashionably late. But even when it was just a few minutes of waiting, I just didn't know how to make conversation. We didn't have much in common. So it was a relief when awkward silences stopped and other people came in. But even during the parties, I'd sit in the corner, act like I'm busy on my cell. But when the battery ran out, I didn't know where to look. And I didn't want people I barely knew to think I was staring at them when I was just staring into space. Those parties made me realize just how boring I really am."

"Aw, Mitch," Gertrude said. "Do you really believe we'd think differently of you if you showed up on time and didn't have much to say?"

He shrugged.

"I've never wanted to find out. I like what I've got going with y'all."

Mitch smiled and then took a sip of his drink.

"Must be some weak-ass battery on that phone," Shelley said.

As he was swallowing, Mitch laughed, and then he started coughing. He tried taking another sip.

"Don't sip again!" Reginald warned him. "That'll make it worse."

Chelsea got up and ran behind Mitch, giving him the Heimlich maneuver until he stopped coughing. Once he let go, Mitch exhaled in relief.

"You all right?" Chelsea asked.

"Guess a hug was all I needed."

Mitch chuckled, and the rest rolled their eyes. Most of them smiled, but Peyton did not. Mitch noticed this and sat down.

"How's your sister?" he asked.

"I don't know. I thought I could be closer to her by coming to this school. But now we're just further apart."

"Have you tried talking things out with Pam?"

"I try, and I try, and I try. But she just wants to play around. Her grades suffer. And the family suffers. It's like she has no regard for reality. You're lucky you don't have to deal with any siblings, Mitch."

"Hey, come on. You love Pam."

"I do. But she makes it so hard to love her. That costume just shuts me out."

"She has a huge responsibility though," Chelsea said.

"Uh. What is it with all you weirdos? It's just a costume! Why can't you all just be happy on your own?"

"We have classes," Shelley said. "Duh. How do *you* try to be happy?"

"I guess I'm not sure that I'm ever happy." She took another sip of her drink. "This just numbs everything, doesn't it?"

"If you're lucky," Gertrude said. "But sometimes it makes things worse. Lately, my brother's been having a party problem. He graduated a couple years ago, but he still tries to relive glory days by going out to parties rather than grow up. And he's been doing it a lot more lately. I keep telling him how worried I am. He knows I'm scared for him, but we'll have to see if he changes. I hope he's at least being more self-conscious about how much he drinks."

Peyton thought about how close she and Pamela used to be as children. Chasing butterflies in the backyard. Climbing trees to pick lemons. The thought of these memories being so far away made her tear up.

"I'm worse. I'm *so much* worse. I miss her so much."

Gertrude gave her a shoulder to cry on.

"Maybe you can get Randy to talk to her. They've been hanging out a lot."

"Maybe... Where is Randy, anyway? Anyone know where he is?"

"I saw him walk into my room," Mitch said. "If he's anything like past parties, he'll crash. Hopefully, on the inflatable."

Naomi sighed.

"Randy's not in such a good mood right now."

Peyton saw Reginald lower his head as if he knew something.

"How come?" Peyton asked.

"I probably shouldn't say. But be nice to him when you see him. He might be in a crabby mood. I don't know what's going through his head right now. Gertrude, you've known him the longest. Maybe you could hang out with him one on one."

"Come to think of it," Gertrude said, "I'm not sure we've ever really hung out one on one. I don't really know him that well."

"He just needs to feel welcomed."

"All right. I'll try to work something out."

For a moment, there was a comfortable silence (save for the music).

"Communication," Shelley said, looking at Peyton. "That's my major."

"Huh," Peyton said. "How about that?"

Peyton was definitely one of the Nap Kin.

* * *

Late in the morning, Randy awoke on the inflatable mattress, thankful that he was not on the lavatory floor. He remembered intentionally leaving the toilet unflushed, hoping that someone would see his pain and suffering. Mitch was lying asleep on his bed. Randy walked out into the living room, which was empty. He was certain that nobody had checked up on him during his lowest point. He left the apartment, surrounding himself with an atrabilious atmosphere. He walked down memory lane, revisiting events he had tried to keep away from his mind for so long...

Garden hose in hand, Randy, age seven, crouches down in his backyard, looking at the anthill. He kicks it, and then the pismires pour out, wanting to defend their home. They seem keen on attacking him, but he unleashes the flood of the rubber serpent upon them, drowning them without warning or mercy.

Aster, through the eyes of a stuffed animal—a rabbit—watches reluctantly.

"Why drown them?" she asks.

"Because. Red ants bite. That means they're evil."

"But they have no way to fight back."

"They started it! I am the king of this yard, and they are trespassing!"

He eventually becomes bored with this method. But after receiving a magnifying glass for his birthday, he uses it to watch over the ants and makes an astonishing discovery. He can use the glass to channel the sunlight into a burning beam, giving pismires a smell reminiscent of burnt popcorn. With a weapon in hand, Randy feels powerful. He feels superior to these smaller beings who had bitten him. He wants to teach them a lesson, and the lesson does not seem to have a finite end. This is his ritual.

Aster watches, and Randy believes she is mesmerized by the sight.

"Here comes the UFO," Randy says. "The people of this world are hostile. They won't accept us. We must eliminate them!"

"Fear of rejection is understandable," Aster says. "But why not try to be friends first?"

"I don't wanna. It's more fun this way."

"Fun... The notion of being powerful enough to destroy those who have wronged you is...an attractive idea. I'll admit that. But I won't play this way unless I absolutely have to."

Randy stares at her.

"You don't wanna play?"

"Not like this. Not right now."

Randy can feel the judgment.

"What do you think of me?"

"To be quite honest, I think you're mean."

"That's a mean thing to say! You hippo critter!"

"Now you're attacking me."

"Am not! You don't see me pointing this at you."

He looks down at the magnifying glass, then back at Aster.

"Would you?" she asks

"If you don't help me, then you're evil."

"So to you, I'm as pathetic as an ant. But I am much bigger than you are, Randy."

"You don't seem so big."

"I am. I have more friends than you realize. If you cast me aside, then I will turn to them."

"Then go! I dare you! I double-dog dare you! I'll have my own friends and they'll be better than you!"

No response.

"Aster?"

He picks up the rabbit and shakes it.

"Aster?"

Still no reply.

"This isn't funny! I swear, I'll burn you!"

He puts the magnifying glass over the stuffed animal, leaving a burn mark on it. But there is no reaction.

"Is that how you wanna play? Fine!"

He takes the stuffed animal to the garage and throws it into the dryer. After pressing buttons, he watches it circle around in the machine. Still no reaction. Either she is gone, or he is being ignored.

"Aster! How could you?!"

He hopes that she is still in there, and that she can feel the dryer tearing her into ripped pieces of stuffing. When it is done, he throws away the trash, feeling abandoned by a friend.

One day at school, he tries to burn the ants in the grass during recess. His classmates tell on him and he gets in trouble with the teacher. She is very disappointed in him, and gives him a red card to let him know that what he has done is wrong. He is told that he could have burned up all the grass, and being a young kid, he believes it. A part of him finds that idea appealing, and another part of him is frightened by that prospect.

His parents are informed about his behavior. They ground him and get rid of his magnifying glass. He does not try to justify his actions. For as he rethinks all that he has done to the ants, he comes back to a question: Why? The more he thinks about it, the more the act of killing these insects how he did feels very alien and inhuman. He sees himself as other. A monster rather than a higher being. He deserves to go to bed with no dessert.

For good measure, his mother teaches him a technique to keep ants out of the house: the lemon technique. Juice and peels. It does not appeal to him at first, but then his preference for the magnifying glass method frightens him. So he remains silent and does as his mother teaches him. A new ritual.

Despite this change in habits, his classmates do not want to play with him. He walks alone during recess. He goes through the motions during later grade levels, too set on believing that everyone still perceives him as a freak, thus making the formation of friendships seem out of the question. It is not until his arrival at Copper Petal University that he has a clean slate. A chance to start new, lasting friendships.

Now, walking aimlessly on campus, Randy was questioning the legitimacy of those friendships. And if Pamela was his one true friend, he did not want to go home and expose her to his current mood. On this Valentine's Day, Randy just wanted to be alone, keeping his inner angst from contaminating anyone. As he walked around campus, he avoided eye contact with everyone. Since it was Saturday, there were not as many people on campus. Still, he did not want to be recognized by anyone he knew.

A year earlier, he felt the Valentine's Day spirit despite not having a significant other. He had sent Valentine's Day cards to all of his friends. But this year it was different. Feeling alone, he kept walking around the oval-shaped campus, feeling like a ghost.

Eventually, he grew tired of this cycle and decided to check on Candid again. He walked through the redwoods, hoping to avoid Stagmantel. The elemental was sitting on his chair, but he did not bother coming down the hill to say anything to Randy, who stared at the stone duck, worried that it may have been all for nothing.

* * *

It was difficult for Naomi to concentrate during the study session at the library with her classmates that afternoon. She wondered how Randy was doing. She messaged Mitch at the beginning of class, asking how Randy seemed to be feeling. It was not until the end of the session that Mitch saw the message and responded, saying he just woke up and did not see Randy anywhere.

Naomi considered messaging Randy to see if he was okay, but she also knew that he probably did not want to hear from her. At least not right away.

As she walked away from the library, she decided to take the path in the middle of Petal Lock Park, hoping that she might find Randy hanging out there as he sometimes did. Despite how upset he might have been with her, she went against her better judgment, hoping to talk to him and mend the friendship between them. She did not know what she would say, but she wanted to make their friendship work.

In her peripheral vision, Naomi saw a familiar face.

"Oh. Hey Gin."

"Hey," Reginald said. "How's it going?"

He had not called her Tonic since the breakup, but Naomi had become comfortable calling him Gin again within the past year.

"Just thinking about Randy," Naomi said. "Mitch says he left before he woke up."

"Oh. Yeah, I was actually hoping to find him here. Um... Did Randy tell you anything?"

"What do you mean?" She thought it over for a moment, then put it together. "Wait, you know?"

"Oh, uh—"

"You knew he was gonna ask me out?"

"Well, I guessed he might. And I told him I'd be fine with you two—"

"You *encouraged* him? What the hell is wrong with you?"

"I was just trying to help."

"You may have damaged a friendship or two!" Naomi crossed her arms. "What's your game, Reginald? Has it always been a game with you?"

Reginald looked down at the dirt of the path.

"Randy's a friend." He looked at her again. "And I thought if you were to move on with anyone else, it'd be easier with a friend."

"Easy on me?" She pointed at herself, and then at him. "Or easy on you?"

"Why not both? Come on, you've seen the taco commercial. I thought I could revive two birds with one stone."

"That's not how it works! I don't need you controlling who can be with me. Why can't I just be single, huh? I'm doing fine!"

"Are you?"

"Yes. You?"

He was silent for a moment. A closer look revealed that his eyes were getting wet. They spoke volumes, but he translated just in case.

"Sometimes I think about the old times. When we were together. I've been trying to make the feelings go away, but some still linger Do you ever look back?"

"Of course I do. We had good times, but I know things are different now..."

"No regrets?"

She had something building up inside of her. Something she had been wanting to say to him for a long time.

"Would it have *killed* you to hold my hand in public?"

"It was killing me *not* to! But I knew it would've killed other people!"

"What?"

"I've *been* on the other side! I've been single and jealous of all the couples holding hands in public! I may look like I have it all together, but deep down it eats at me. I'm sorry for making things awkward. But I don't want us to stop hanging out." He took a moment to sigh. "So where do we stand?"

Naomi wanted to be careful with her words, but she also wanted to be honest.

"Sometimes I still have those feelings. But I need..."

"What?"

"I need a friend."

"You've got friends. We've got good friends."

Her eyes got watery, and she did her best to hold back any cries.

"I need a friend who can understand what I'm going through. Can you do that for me?"

"Yes."

"I *mean* it. I don't want you thinking this'll lead to something more, because I really need a friend right now."

"I'll do it. I don't know if I'll be great at it. But if you really need a friend, and having one will help you get through what you're feeling, then I'll be there for you. Because I don't want you to be sad for so long. If you need me as a friend, then I'll be that person. Nothing more. I promise. I just want you to feel fine for real."

Simultaneously, they moved in for a hug, knowing not to kiss.

"So," Naomi said, "completely platonic?"

"Of course," Reginald said. "Hey, maybe I should call you Platonic from now on."

That made Naomi laugh.

"Shut up, you."

Without looking, she knew that Reginald was smiling.

"Whatever you say, my friend."

* * *

From behind a redwood, Randy witnessed the hug between Naomi and Reginald. He had not seen the buildup to it, and he could not hear what they were saying. Randy only knew that he wanted to be dead. He wished that he had gone in Candid's place. Maybe then he would have endured neither the rejection nor this particular sight. He did not know what Naomi and Reginald's situation was now, but he wanted to be far away from them.

Sneaking away, he ended up at Pitchers & Forks and went downstairs to the windowless basement. The only light source was a blood red bulb in the middle of the ceiling. He gazed at it, imagining that the bulb was the nose of Artie Docent, the clown's body hovering over him like a float balloon at a parade. For a moment, Randy felt safe. But then he banished the image from his imagination. Now, in his mind's eye, the bulb was a beaker full of his own blood.

He needed a pint.

Sitting alone, facing the corner, he drank from a large glass of pear cider. The crowd within the pub was loud, and he tried to digest the melancholic music that was making its way to his ears. It was as if someone was trying to speak to him but could not reach him. And he could not find a voice that would willingly sing to him. A blink, and a tear, silent waterfall onto the tabletop. And it went unnoticed because everyone else had someone. He had nobody.

I will be nobody, he thought. *History will be written, and I won't be part of it. Not even in the hearts of those I knew around here. They'll forget about me as soon as a die. And they won't even notice they forgot...*

The light of the room seemed to dim to night in his eyes. It was like being asleep but not being able to find rest. He wanted to know where the spirit was, and why it had abandoned him. Drinking more cider, he stifled his want to whimper. When the glass of cider was half empty, he made an observation. Bubbles rising from the base of the glass to the surface of the cider. Worlds spinning in a controlled trajectory, toward a firmly set destination. That was what he wanted: to rise with certainty.

After another sip, he put the pint back on the table. He barely missed the ring of water that had already been created. Lifting the glass, he saw another ring, intersecting with the first to make an infinity symbol. He wanted a coaster. He wanted to coast through life. To a coast where the wale of a whale-sized ghost could be sent from the sea, enveloping him and shielding him from uncertainty. And there on the table was the water of infinity, looking back at him, reminding him of the cycle of sorrow he kept enduring.

* * *

Out in the woods, Stagmantel and Unicoren clasped their hands together. If their fingers were invisible, one would be able to see their wedding rings form the infinity symbol, proclaiming that they fell in love, and that the fall should last forever. Together, they danced, for the first time in many years, waltzing in perfect synchronicity. They felt the love they had long been afraid to embrace once again because of the ramifications they believed it had on their original home long before. The small division it had caused within their families, which formed a fraction of the grand division of Miunis Grund.

"I have missed this," Unicoren said. "I never realized how sad I have been before all this."

"Cry not, my love," Stagmantel said. "The time will pass, as all things do."

* * *

Randy got a pitcher this time. He continued sitting in the corner, taking in the depressant and sinking into the shadows.

He tried to imagine a future, a Valentine's Day a year from today. It would be on a Sunday. Probably one with a midseason premiere of *The Walking Dead*. It would also be the 85th and 25th anniversaries of film adaptations of *Dracula* and *The Silence of the Lambs,* respectively. If the future conformed to the past, then he would watch them alone. If he chose to live beyond the appointment with Mathis, that is.

If he had his way, he would be watching all of these back to back with Naomi in the school mini-theater, and it would be romantic to him because she would see and understand the turmoil within him, and why he felt he needed to be loved. Resting his head upon the table, eyes half-closed, Randy allowed the fantasy to take over, even though he did not feel fully in control of the narrative.

"You ever wonder why people make horror movies?" he would ask.

"It taps into a deep desire within people," she would say, still admired. "I mean, let's face it. Who hasn't imagined killing those who are close to them, even for a moment?"

"I hope you don't think my interest in horror makes me a secret murderer or something. I'd never do any of these things you see here."

"I'm sure you wouldn't. For some people, horror is a filter for their desires. Don't you think?"

So artificial and manufactured, yet Randy would hope for this moment. Randy would lean in to kiss Naomi, but then she might pull away. He would then wonder why he tried that, realizing that a Hannibal Lecter movie might not be the appropriate film to set the tone. He would wonder whether he blew his chances.

"I'm sorry," he would apologize, breaking eye contact and looking at the floor. "I shouldn't have done that."

"No. It's fine. I really want you to kiss me, but there's the camera."

He would look up at the corner of the ceiling where the black bubble containing a camera within hung.

"Of course," he would say with a smile. "How did I forget about that?"

"Why don't we go out in the hallway? You know, if you really wanna kiss."

He would want this.

"Okay," he would say with a gleeful grin.

They would go out into the hallway, closing the door behind them, both the camera and the film out of sight. Nobody to capture this seemingly perfect, candid moment. They would probably kiss while out of sight of the notorious Jame Gumb scene set to "Goodbye Horses."

"Should we rewind?" she would ask when they were done making out.

Randy would think about the iconic scene she would have missed. Not really required viewing. Especially not on the first date. He would not want the scene to be the image that Naomi would remember when looking back to their first kiss.

"No need to rewind," he would decide. "You didn't miss much."

"You didn't kiss much..." Randy muttered to himself, merely repeating the lyrics to a song that was waking him up.

He looked up and saw that couples were dancing in the pink light to this pop song, the lyrics of which were the following:

You didn't kiss much
You had your chance
But you squandered it all
Yes you wandered away
And now we're floating eons apart
Somehow I knew this end from the start
Yet I let myself fall into your arms
Well I'm telling you that it's over now

But I still wish you the best
I wish you a merry kiss much
Let's just give it a rest
I wish you a merry kiss much
Because I'm moving on
Yes I'm moving on
This new chapter's about to begin

Randy was filled with hatred toward all the couples with their public displays of love and affection. They all seemed so happy, and he wanted to steal all the joy from them. Struggling to rise from his seat, he walked over to the dance floor. Alone, he mimed hand movements to the music. Some people probably thought he was air drumming. But in his hands he imagined hammers bashing the skulls of the living. They had no distinguishable faces; he was far too drunk. And then he imagined slicing throats with a knife. The people around him cheered, and he grinned, for this was the fantasy he wanted to come true. The one in which people would applaud him for acts of violence displaying how powerful he could become. He believed that this was the way to transcend. But the voice of Artie Docent lingered in his head.

What the hell is wrong with you?

That night, Randy got home late. Pamela was sitting on the couch when he entered.

"Hey!" she greeted him. "How are you?"

Randy considered saying he was fine, but he did not feel like lying to her.

"I don't wanna talk about it."

"Oh. Is it 'cause of the day?"

"It's 'cause of everything."

"What's wrong? Do you wanna go to the park? I know it's late, but it might do you some good."

He thought about Candid's duck, still and staring coldly.

"I can't keep going there," he said.

"Why not?"

"It's hard to find the time."

"Okay. But you *will* let me know if you feel up to it again, right?"

"If. Yeah."

Randy walked back into his room and crashed onto his bed, wishing for his pillow to put him out of his misery.

* * *

Starving, Candid was chained up in the cellar. Though she could not see much in the windowless room, the foul aroma of a rotted skeleton filled the air. A skeleton in a wheelchair, from what Candid had been able to tell by feeling around. And she regretted feeling around, touching the bony remains. There was nothing near her to help her get out of the chains. Mathis had taken the lock pick from her. She doubted that she would have gotten far, anyway. Though her feet had been healing a bit throughout the duration of her captivity, they still hurt from the burns. She was partially glad she could not see how they looked.

Mathis had left her plates of meat and bottles of water, but she had refused to eat or drink anything provided by him. She did not trust her morbid warden. Somehow, she held out.

But on this night, Mathis came down the stairs as she slept in hopelessness. She could hear him moving the skeleton, its bones hitting the floor and waking her up. He unlocked the cuffs from her ankles and lifted her onto the wheelchair, cuffing her wrists to the armrests. She wanted to react, but it did not feel real enough. She was convinced that this had to be a dream. But then she felt the motion around her as she rode the wheelchair as Mathis pushed it up the stairs.

"This used to belong to some rich lady who used to live here," he explained. "You could say I kinda *inherited* this place after she died. I keep her around as a decoration."

So that's who's been down here, she thought.

"How long..."

"Nearly fifteen years ago."

"How long have I been here?"

"Ah. Eight days."

"The fuck?! How? I haven't even needed to go to the bathroom!"

"You've still got some good luck going on. It's not enough to conquer me, though."

It was still dark when they were out of the cellar. She could hear muffled voices.

"Who that?" she muttered.

"They can't speak just yet," he said. "I'll get the show started."

She heard him walking up the stairs. And then Mathis clapped his hands twice, the chandelier now lighting the room. There he was, at the top of the staircase—its steps visibly scorched—beside speakers that blared music.

Downstairs, a man and a woman were tied up in chairs. Silver duct tape covered their mouths. With scythes in his hands, Mathis rode the stairlift as it slowly descended downward. He sang a song of his own creation.

I am the worm,
Inside your ear.
I'll make you squirm,
Fill you with fear.
I play my greatest sh-hits,
Performing gigs that lull.
Sh-hit-hit-hit-hits and giggles.

You'll lose your head,
I'll watch you bleed.
Your fear will spread,
In the stampede.
I play my greatest sh-hits,
Performing gigs that lull.
Sh-hit-hit-hit-hits and giggles.

Lullaby time,
You'll go to sleep.
Death so sublime,
And I will reap.
I play my greatest sh-hits,
Performing gigs that lull,
Sh-hit-hit-hit-hits and giggles.

When he reached the floor, Mathis hammed it up, crawling on all fours, holding scythe tips like mantis appendages. He removed the tape from the man's face, a swift motion that removed a bit of facial hair.

"Ah! That hurt!"

"Oh, I know."

He put the tape back on, then ripped it off again. Then he ripped the tape from the woman's face. The music continued to blare. The woman looked at Candid.

"Who are you?" she asked.

"She's my supplier," Mathis said, holding out the pliers.

"Forgive me," Candid said. "I tried to kill him."

"Candy, meet Bruce and Bria. A couple of blind dates I found at the bar."

"You're a monster for ruining romance!" Bruce said. "You'll be a tapeworm trapped in the tripe...of a trout!"

"Now, you're just trying too hard. Candy, you seemed keen on using one of these scythes. I'll let you kill one, and then the other one will live. Albeit as a prisoner here, of course. You'd have a roommate. But if you don't choose one, *both* die."

Candid was done with his shit. Under other circumstances, she might have felt pressured. But she felt apathetic, having already given up hope.

"Fuck you," she said defiantly.

"Suit yourself. Enjoy the show."

Up above, the chandelier reflected the fates of the couple below. As above, so below.

* * *

August awoke in the morning to the sound of screams. The source seemed to be from within his hotel room lavatory. At first, he thought he was dreaming. But the screams seemed too real. Instinctively, he got up and swung the door open. In the mirror, he saw a man and a woman tied up in chairs, getting beheaded. Another woman in a wheelchair, screaming for it all to stop. The view was from above, but clear. Blood was spilling onto the floor.

He ran out into the hallway and then to the lift, pressing the buttons repeatedly as he waited for it to come up. When the doors finally opened, he was taken aback by what covered the elevator floor: sheets of plastic. His mind immediately jumped to an image of the blood-filled floor.

There's a killer in here!

The doors closed. He decided to run down the stairs instead. Off he went, until he arrived in the kitchen where Jade was microwaving store-bought chips.

"Are you all right?" Jade asked.

"I've come to warn *someone* about *something*... And I'm *somewhat* lost about what it is..." He thought about his fridge downstairs. "Oh! Your milk has expired!"

"Damn! Oh well. Milk is probably not good for french fries, anyway."

Not knowing what else to say, August walked back to the lift and pressed a button. He could hear a buzzing sound coming from within.

Buzz saw! he thought.

When the doors opened, he jumped back. But then he realized that it was just Tate, buzzing his head with portable clippers.

"Tate? What are you doing?"

"It's hard to shave my head with just one mirror. With three, it's easier to see."

August looked at the plastic sheets on the floor, covered with hair. Then he looked at the three mirrors in the lift.

"So it's *you*. I saw these sheets when I was upstairs."

"Oh." Tate said. "So it was *you*. You pressed the button before I could bring my clippers and get in."

"Sorry about that."

"Now, if you'll excuse me, I have to finish."

* * *

"What a finish!" Mathis yelled.

The heads of Bria and Bruce were lying on the floor, the headless torsos still in the chairs. Candid did not know how to react. Mathis walked over to her with a grin.

"Not having fun?" he asked.

"Go to hell," she said.

Mathis took a key out of his pocket and uncuffed her.

"I'll give you a ten-second head start. Ten..."

Surprised, she tried not to delay. She got out of the chair and started limping away. Going out the door and into the cold night air, she ran barefoot on the stones, which hurt a lot. Mathis' car was by the side of the building. But with no key, her instincts said to keep going forward. Candid did not look back. She hoped that she would luck out.

She arrived at the gate, and could hear his footsteps on the stones as she climbed. There was no avoiding the barbed wire. It hurt her hands, but she knew that she could survive with the luck that remained.

Mathis, still carrying scythes, caught up to her and tried pulling her down by the ankle. But she kicked him in the face and made it over, hitting the ground. Trying to crawl away and get up, she looked back and saw Mathis put the scythes between the bars so that they would be on the other side of the gate. Then he started climbing over. He seemed to be enjoying the cuts of the barbed wire. Mathis the masochist, indeed.

She did not want to risk reaching down for the scythes, so she ran out into the road. Mathis made it to the other side of the gate and picked up the scythes.

"Crossing the road, chicken?" Mathis called out, running after her. "Chicken needles! I'm craving some chicken needle soup!"

After Candid crossed to the other side, a speeding car hit Mathis, sending him flying forward.

"Holy shit!" the driver said, getting out. "Are you okay?"

"He'll kill me!" Candid yelled. "Get me out of here!"

The man got back in the car and opened the front passenger door for her. Mathis jumped onto the hood, using a scythe handle to break through the glass and bash the driver in the skull.

* * *

Looking in the lavatory mirror, August saw cracks. And then a middle shape of the glass showed the reaper's body being far away, making his arms appear rather large on the sides of the glass. He could not make out the reaper's face, but the brightness level of the mirror was just high enough to show him some of the movements. When the reaper reached forward, August stepped back, afraid that the hand would come through the mirror. But it withdrew, instead pulling the driver through the broken glass and throwing him into the road. The murderer jumped onto the road. Though August could not see what was going on, he heard the slicing.

* * *

Quaking with fear, Candid scooted over to the driver's seat. Mathis looked up from the sliced up body and made eye contact with her.

"You're next, Candy!"

Candid pulled back the lever, bringing the car backward a good distance, then hit the accelerator. She aimed to hit Mathis with a killing blow...

But she swerved around him and missed.

"FUCK!"

Rather than turn around, she opted to just keep driving, wanting to be safe.

* * *

The image vanished. August ran out into the hallway and screamed. But then he could not remember what he was screaming about. That terrified him, so he just kept screaming, begging for catharsis. But it never came.

Instead, he fell to the floor, just lying there. In his blurry vision, he thought he saw his tears turning into blue flames, cold fire spreading onto the carpet. They did not burn, but they hurt. More blew flames grew all over his body. And then there were green flames. Pretty soon, he thought he looked like a peacock of fire, lying down and unable to fly. And even when the flame feathers disappeared from his vision, he still felt hurt on the inside. August Wilhelm felt broken, and it would be hours before he got up again.

* * *

Candid drove as far as she could from the mansion. But a tank of gas could only bring one so far. As the sun was rising, she ran out of gas, in front of a building in the middle of nowhere.

"Shit!" she uttered.

Looking around, she saw no gas station. However, she noticed that the words on the building. It was Crackpot Casino. Candid smiled.

"Today might be my lucky day."

She went inside and played a dice game, during which she won a lot of money. With all her luck still active, she knew that she could roll with this. And the more money she won, the easier it would be to pay off her debts and travel wherever she wished.

Chapter 30
Wishing Weld

Randy awoke early Monday morning, blinded by the blues. Unable to get back to sleep, he walked over to the kitchen cabinet and got himself a drink to pour. He sat at the table, drinking and indulging in yet another fantasy...

A candlelit dinner table. Randy would be at one end, and Naomi would be at the other. Pamela would be on the side to his left, and next to her would be August, Gertrude, Chelsea, and Reginald. On the side opposite of them would be Peyton, Grady, Mitch, Shelley, and Candid. They would all be tied up, and he would be wearing a welding helmet, with his eyes being the unhidden features behind the lens. Randy would try to break out of his binds.

Mathis Dillard would show up beside him, wielding a circular saw.

"Must be hard to breathe," Mathis would say. "But not for long."

Mathis would activate it and start cutting horizontally through Randy's mask. Helpless, Randy would sit still, his heart on a treadmill. With the disc slicing through the material, sparks would fly. Once done, the jaw of the helmet would drop, leaving everything below Randy's nose exposed. His face, a moon half-concealed yet revealing his broken nature. Mathis would then speak again.

"I'll cut you...a deal. I set you free, you set the fire. You are the set designer. You get to kill all of these guests in any order you wish. Is this what you want?"

Randy would nod and give the guests an unhidden grin.

Mathis would saw through the ropes, setting Randy free.

"*In friendships,*" *Mathis would say,* "*people are welded together. Wield this.*"

He would hand Randy a blowtorch. With a press of the trigger, a blue torch would come out.

"*Please!*" *Naomi would say.* "*Whoever you are, you don't have to do this!*"

Randy would remove the mask, reveling in the revelation of his identity. Shocked expressions on all the faces.

"*No!*" *Naomi would say.*

"*Why?*" *Gertrude would ask.*

"*Because,*" *Randy would explain.* "*I got hit by the taco truck. Your tacos are the reason I wake up at five in the morning crying through my asshole. I was loyal. I willingly let myself get shot in the gullet so that I could shit bullets. And I've had enough of this shit.*"

"*You don't have the guts,*" *Candid would taunt.* "*I'd like to see you try to kill us, you piece of shit!*"

"*Watch me,*" *Randy would say, putting the mask back on.*

He would jump onto the table. Hunched, he would walk all the way to the other end, stooping downward to look Naomi in the eyes.

"*Please,*" *Reginald would say.* "*Don't hurt her. Take me instead!*"

There would be fear and tears in Naomi's eyes. Those pure, shining eyes.

Randy would wink.

He would run back toward Mathis, using the blowtorch on the kidnapper's eyes, blinding him with the blues. Mathis would scream and saw through Randy's stomach. Using his remaining strength, Randy would take off the mask and use it to bash Mathis Dillard's skull until he no longer breathed. Randy would take the saw from the dead man's hands and first untie Pamela, who would then take the saw to untie everyone else.

Randy would fall to the floor. Everyone would gather around his dying self. Naomi would hold him in her arms. A dream come true for him.

"Do you see me now?" Randy would say. *"My love is unending."*

There would be no kiss. Randy would not feel deserving of one despite what heroism would come out of this scenario. Feeling ugly, Randy would die, his friends mourning over him and regretting the lack of closeness he had desired.

A view from above. The verdict of a life? Wasted.

Randy wiped the tears from his face. He needed to talk to someone. And he could not believe where he was going.

Unaccompanied, he went to Petal Lock Park. There, he found Unicoren.

"Randy Morales," she said. "You have never come to me before this moment. And you have brought neither Mandy nor Pamela with you."

"They're fine. Don't worry. I just needed to be here."

"You have a reason."

"For coming to you, yes. For continuing to live, I don't know. I got hit by the taco truck. I've lost my faith in humanity. Or, I guess the humanity that surrounds me, and how it relates to me. Maybe I just don't belong."

"Psychiatric help could be useful."

"If I share my pain with psychiatrists, they'll probably send me someplace. But *you* wouldn't do that. I could share my tacos with you. And nobody would ask you about me. Who would? Babies have nothing to cry about yet. I want to cry, but the world seems to think I've used up my cry credits."

"There *is* someone who wants to speak to you."

Randy heard steps in the grass behind him, and he turned to see that it was one of the geese.

"Randy Morales," the goose said. "I know you."

They can talk? Randy thought. He had known that there was something magical about these geese. He had heard their musical notes. But he had never heard that they were capable of speech. Unicoren started to walk away.

"I will give you some privacy."

She seemed to be heading toward the redwoods, probably to meet with Stagmantel. When she was a good distance away, Randy spoke.

"So we've met? You all look the same, so I wouldn't know, to be honest."

"We have never spoken."

Definitely not, Randy thought.

"So what I say stays between us?"

"Yes."

"What do you see in me?"

"I see pain. You are a walking wound. A walking taco. You want to open, but you don't want to infect your friends with whatever may be in your stream. You do not want to spread disease."

"True, but I think anyone could've figured that out. It's vague enough to apply to anyone, really."

"For nearly four years, I have watched over you. Your loans accumulated to twenty thousand dollars, lowered to ten thousand thanks to Mathis Dillard."

Okay, now there are specifics. At least I know it knows what it's talking about.

"What else have you observed about me?"

"You want to express your pain to your loved ones. But you feel that, in the grand scheme of things, it is not worth expressing. When there is war, famine, and poverty, why should the world worry about a lazy first world college student afraid of work and unable to find love?" Randy's eyes began to water, and he struggled to find the words he felt needed to be said. "Those people who endure much more serious suffering than I do are the ones who need saving. Me? I don't think I'm worth saving. I'm just a piece of shit that led Candid to her undoing."

"Candid still lives."

"But in what capacity? Can you tell me?"

"She has escaped."

Randy felt a glimmer of hope, and then a flicker of fear.

"Where is she? What'll she do to me?"

"I cannot tell you that."

"Damn it. Why should you care, right?"

"Unicoren is indifferent, but *I* care about you, Randy. I know that your future could be bright if you let it be lit. It is just that you get so overdramatic and insecure. All these years, I have been wanting to tell you it will get better. But I could not tell you unless you came to me."

"Why is that?"

"You needed to seek a voice before you could hear one. It will get better, but only if you let it."

"What am I supposed to do?"

"I cannot dictate what you must do. You just have to trust."

"That's a load of bull! If you really want me to turn away from my own demise, then you will tell me what I need to do!"

"Please. I do not want to see you get destroyed."

"Because all your work will be for naught, right? Oh wait, *what* work? All you ever did was *watch*, getting your thrills and your goosebumps! You should have been working all this time, and you should start working now!"

"Same."

"What?"

"I could say the same about you."

Randy mentally replayed what he had just said about work. Then he found himself to be hypocritical. This reinforced his belief that he deserved death.

"You don't deserve death," the goose said, startling Randy. "Despite all that you have done, I still care about you and want you to change."

"You do?"

"I know that you have wanted to hear someone say that you are loved one way or another. I can assure you that your friends love you even when they do not say it."

"But do they love me as much as I want them to?"

"If you ask for too much, then is it really love?"

Randy looked down at the grass. If one were to look at the blades a few seconds later, one might mistake the water drops for dew. But they were Randy's.

"Why is it so hard for people to say? Why is it so much to ask for a hug that can last more than just a few seconds? Wouldn't the world be better then?"

"That is the world as it was when it was all on Miunis Grund. Back when all worlds were one. But then they separated and went off in different directions, the planets never having hugged each other since. It would be a much better world if they could hug again and never let go. But *this* is the world with which you are left to deal. The Kin Conflicts divided everyone back then, and even now people *still* get divided. Please, *think* about what you are doing, and how it would affect the worlds of others. Imagine yourself as the observer..."

The goose turned into a bright light, which dimmed out once it took on the shape of Randy Morales. Mirroring him, it burst into tears. Randy felt like he had stepped outside of himself, and he pitied the suffering soul he saw before him. He wanted to tell him that there was a good road ahead, and that the answers would come, eventually. But he knew that he could not.

Randy heard a text notification from his phone.

"Go ahead," the imitation Randy said. "Read it."

He pulled it out and noticed a message from Gertrude.

Gertrude: *Hey. Is it alright if Peyton and I hang at your place?*

Randy was surprised, and partially excited. Even after all the hurt he had felt. The imitation Randy turned back into a goose.

"Go," it said.

Randy nodded, then strode away. He knew that he would have to let Pamela know that her sister was coming, so he called her along the way. After a few rings, she answered.

"Hey, what's up?" Pamela asked.

"Gertrude and Peyton wanna come over."

"Oh no. When?"

"In a bit."

"Okay. Um. I can go out for a bite for a bit. Feeling hungry anyway. I'll find somewhere to eat. Maybe get groceries while I'm at it. Just, please, let me know when they're here."

"I will."

"Thanks. Where are you, anyway?"

"Um, just out for a walk. Was feeling a bit anxious."

"You all right now though?"

"Yeah. Fine."

"Okay. Talk to you later, then."

After the call, Randy replied to Gertrude, letting her know that she could come over. By the time Randy returned to the apartment, Pamela was already gone. A little while later, Gertrude and Peyton came over, carrying their books.

"Hey!" Gertrude said. "How are you, Randy?"

"Haven't been so good, to be honest."

"How come?" Peyton asked.

He needed to be careful so as not to alienate them.

"It's too much to explain."

"Randy," Gertrude began, "we've known each other for a while. If we're friends, we should be able to talk about personal stuff."

She seemed to be making an effort, and this eased him.

"Well, I've felt kinda left out lately. I know y'all invite me to Nap Kin meetings, but I've felt like y'all have your inside jokes, and I'm just an outsider. I know that there's a group chat."

Her brows rose.

"Wait. You're not in the group chat?"

"No."

Gertrude pulled out her phone and checked the chat.

"Oh shit. All this time I thought you were!"

"You didn't notice that I never messaged?"

"You can be a pretty quiet guy sometimes, if we're being honest. I never know what's really going on with you. And you know how much of a shitshow I can be." She pointed at her own backpack. "Case in point."

Randy could not help but feel a little stupid for making such a big deal out of this misunderstanding.

"Wow. I guess it's kinda my fault then."

"Don't beat yourself up about it." She pressed some buttons on her phone. "There. I've added you."

He checked his phone, and sure enough, he was now in the group chat. He smiled.

"Thanks. I guess all this time I've been worried about not feeling included."

With this taco mended, Randy thought it might feel more satisfying defending his friends from Mathis when the time came. He knew that Mathis would still go after them, and Randy was willing to do all that it would take to protect them.

"Peyton also really wants to talk to you," Gertrude said.

"What's up?" Randy asked.

"So," Peyton began, "you've been hanging out with Pam pretty often, right?"

Uh-oh, Randy thought. He did not want to do anything that would betray Pamela in any way. But he also knew how concerned Peyton was when it came to Pamela

"Uh, more or less. A little less these days. Just been so busy."

"Well, I really wanna fix what we had. But it's so hard to talk to her. She never wants to listen. I just want her to come back and know that she is family."

Randy could see that Peyton was genuinely worried about her sister. He knew that Pamela wanted nothing to do with her, but he considered that it might be best for her to move in with Peyton again.

"I'll talk to her," he said.

"Thanks. Also, can I use the restroom? I had way too much coffee."

"Sure. It's right over there."

* * *

Walking over to the doors, Peyton opened the one on the right, which is where she thought Randy meant.

"Wait," Randy said.

She opened the door. There, on a bed, was Mandy, staring her in the face. Peyton's eyes scanned the room, finding other traces of her sister. Her clothes in a hamper. Her backpack in the corner.

Pamela's been here, she thought.

Randy had kept this from her. All this time. She turned to face him.

"Where is she?" she asked.

"Huh?"

"Pam. She's clearly been living here. Is she hiding? Come on out, Pam!"

"She's not here right now."

"But she *was* here."

"Crap. I'm sorry. She didn't want me to tell you."

"Of course not. That is just like her. You've been keeping this from us?"

"I'm sorry! I just figured that it's been freezing, and it'd be better for her to stay indoors."

Peyton sighed. She hated to admit that it was a good choice for a friend to invite Pamela somewhere to shelter her from the cold.

"I guess that's good on you. She'd rather freeze than make up. The only making up she does is make believe as she goes along. Are you gonna tell her I know she's here?"

"Uh..."

"It might not be best," Gertrude interrupted. "She'll get mad at Randy, and then that'll cause another mess. We want *less* friction."

"Damn it," Peyton said. "I guess that makes sense."

"Randy," Gertrude said. "Can you just get her to talk to Peyton, please?"

"Yeah. I'll try."

"Thank you," Peyton said. "And thanks for looking after her."

"I think she takes better care of herself than you realize."

Peyton thought this over. Maybe she *had* underestimated Pamela, whom she had long perceived as the little sister who always needed someone to take care of her. Still, Peyton wanted Pamela back in her life.

* * *

Pamela was shopping for groceries when she got the text from Randy saying that the coast was clear. A little while later, she returned to the apartment and unloaded her groceries.

"Peyton wants to talk to you," Randy said.

Here we go again, Pamela thought. She opened the fridge, crouched down, and started loading it with food.

"Probably to talk down to me again."

Avoiding eye contact, she continued loading the fridge with cheese and sandwich meat.

"She really seems like she wants to make things better. And things won't get better if you stay bitter."

Pamela stood up and shut the door. She did not turn to face Randy. "So I'm *bitter* now?"

"I know I've been shitty." Randy rubbed his chin. "But—"

"But you're hoping that this will make you a better person?"

"I just want to help."

Pamela turned her head, locking eyes with him.

"Do you?"

Randy was silent. Pamela sighed, and then proceeded to load bags of ramen noodles into the cabinet, its creaky door peeving Randy.

"I don't know what to tell you," he said.

Pamela closed the creaky cabinet door when she was finished.

"I'm sorry," she said. "I'm just being stupid. I swear, something about this school makes everyone act stupid."

"So are you gonna talk to her?"

"I'll think about it. I just need some time, that's all." She looked at him again. "I can't talk to her until I've taken care of something."

Randy opened his mouth, seemingly ready to ask what the task was. But then he stopped himself, probably remembering that he did not tell Pamela everything either. Instead, he kept it short and simple.

"Understood."

Pamela went into her room, closed the door behind her, and put on Mandy's head.

"Peyton saw me here," Mandy said.

"I know."

"Are you going to return to her?"

"Maybe. I don't know. I don't feel ready to talk to her yet. I wanna make sure you're fully healed first."

"But will you be fully healed as well?"

"Only time will tell, my friend."

"Pamela. A fractured family is painful. If it can be fixed, then it might be worth looking into."

"Once I'm done taking care of you first. I'll keep it in mind."

Part of Pamela wondered whether she was just using Mandy as an excuse for not confronting her sister head-on. Still, she genuinely cared about Mandy and wanted to see this through.

Chapter 31
Crazy Bus

I t was nighttime. Wayne P. Watkins, clad in a business suit, sat alone on a bench at the bus stop. His life and occupation were full of details that one would find interesting. Having worked—

"Hey you there!" a hooded man said as he approached him and held out a hand. "Food to spare?"

Wayne P. Watkins was a generous man. Normally, he would give some change to anyone who seemed like they needed it. But he was picking up an off vibe from this hooded man, who stepped closer and closer to him.

"I don't have any food on me," Wayne said. "Do you normally ask people for food instead of money, sir?"

The hooded figure made a leap and put his hands under Wayne's armpits, lifting him a foot off of the ground. Wayne could now see white eyes and fangs. The latter sank into his neck. As his blood was drained, Wayne's entire life flashed before him. He could see—

* * *

Mathias finished the job and sat the corpse down onto the bench, not caring one bit about who this victim was. He transformed into a bat as the bus approached, and he perched himself on top. The bus doors opened.

"Sir?" he heard the bus driver say to the corpse on the bench. "Sir, you taking this bus?"

Silence.

"Damn," she said. "It's been a long day for everybody."

The doors closed, and Mathias stuck to the top of the bus until the next stop. When the doors opened for this stop, a few passengers got inside, and Mathias flew in after them. As the bus began moving, someone noticed him.

"A bat!" one of the dozen passengers yelled.

"Oh my damn!" the bus driver yelled, swerving the bus off of the road and crashing it into a sycamore tree. The windshield broke, shards of glass flying into the face of the driver. The passengers fell out of their seats, hitting themselves against the floor.

Mathias took on his humanoid form, prompting gasps all around. He looked around at all the frightened people. There were no children present. For him, this was unfortunate; he would have liked to have given a child some nightmares about what he was about to do to the adults.

He revealed his fangs and started with the driver, tearing at her neck. Then he worked his way through the bus, biting into all the injured passengers. Neck after neck, he let the blood fill the hunger vacuum within him. And he bit off the skin just for fun. Sometimes he swallowed the skin, sometimes he spat it out for the living to see before they met their demises. There was screaming all around. They were helpless. He was in control.

Once he was done with the bloodbath inside, he exited. There were bloodstains on his dress clothes, but they would come out. He was adept at brewing remedies. For now, he liked the imagery. Red on green. Bloodshot peacock feather eyes on his tie.

He stepped back a decent distance away from the bus. And then he ran up to it and pushed it with his hands. It moved a little. He did this several more times until he tipped the bus over on its side.

Once again, he turned into a bat, his blood-stained clothes getting stitched onto his skin. It was a painful sensation to which he was no stranger. It would have hurt even more if he had brought his shades with him. The amulet, however, still added more to the pain. But he had lived with it long enough to embrace it. Physical pain was more welcome than the other kind...

Flying back to Copper Petal University, he landed on top of the library, and then returned to his humanoid shape. He held out his amulet, letting the light of the full moon shine into it until he had enough to feed the pack. When it was full, he flew down to the ground and then walked into the library.

Reaching the basement level, he found his pets in their cage, hungry as usual. Beside them was the decayed skeleton of Spoon Drop.

"Still surprised by how much restraint you've shown, opting not to eat one of your own."

"Chancellor," Host L said. "Feed us. Please!"

Fork Feed grinned.

"This is what it means. This is what it means. This is what it means."

"Shut up!" Cackle Bucket yelled. "This fatherfucker Fork Feed is hiding leftovers, me thinks. Fork it over!"

"Neither accusation is true," Mathias assured him. He took a package of sausages out of his pocket. "One for each of you."

One by one, he threw each sausage link through the chain-link fence holes. Each werewolf got their share, and then Mathias held out the amulet so they could lick the light. He made sure they did not have too much, and that a lot of light still remained.

He then returned to the top of the tower and continued looking up at the stars and the full moon, opening his mouth wide open. He had learned over the years that the act of yawning could summon tears to the eyes of humans. He let out some air, but no water came out of his eyes.

A sentient vampiric virus, he had been leaping from body to body for so long, picking up some desires along the way. The desires of these people who used to have control of their bodies. Desires to feel. Desires to have. Desires to create. But he could never fully experience the lives that these people would have lived. He could not even turn anyone into vampires as a means of creation. He had met other vampires who could do that, but he was not like them.

He was a parasite manufactured by some faction during the Kin Conflicts. He was a means to their end. He had no idea where they were, but their machinations were surely in some nooks and crannies of the universe. They did not concern him. He had been going his own way for a while, having learned to trust only himself. Even when he thought there was one person he could trust, he was faced with the reiteration that he could not operate with an equal. So the only companions kept over the years were his pets, werewolves under his control. Surrounded by a fence he had crafted by extracting blood mixed with Plo-Tunium in his veins.

He had come a long way since the Kin Conflicts. At many places, he made himself a landlord. He loved having control over the places in which people lived. And he was never too short on pets. Many were caged over time, and the master always outlived them. Sometimes, he had to put them down himself when they were so difficult to contain. And whenever the werewolves made a noticeable mess, he fled to a new place where he could reinvent his identity.

One day, the virus found a new body in London and tried burying the old one. It was then that the vampire discovered deposits of metal in the ground. The element was gray and looked plain, but he could sense that there was more to it. Thanks to years of experimentation with alchemy, he was able to recognize the metal as Plo-Tunium, a dangerous element.

The Landlord founded and built Tree Culler Hotel in London on the land in which he found it. He ran it for years until a Copper Petal University senior studied abroad and was allocated to his hotel. This student stayed in room 315. The Landlord used the power of Plo-Tunium to torment him. Each time the student went into that room, it was a nightmare. The Landlord experimented with him, injecting some Plo-Tunium into his veins. When he was sure that it was safe to have a body infected with the substance, he left behind specific instructions for his death, so that people could still run the hotel, and sank his teeth into the student's neck, passing The Landlord—the virus—onto him.

The student's name was Mathias Moseley

Now in control, The Landlord looked deep into the desires of its new home. Apparently, Mathias really wanted a hat that he had seen during a tour at a new art museum that had just opened in London. It was a bowler hat with peacock feathers, apparently of Transylvanian origin. The virus did not very much care for cliches regarding vampires of pop culture, but there was no denying that Mathias had an eye for fashion. So they flew into the museum. A bat stealing a hat. And once Mathias had gotten a taste of forbidden satisfaction, The Landlord pushed him further, enabling him to wreak havoc in the streets of London. Back in the days when The Landlord was still able to transform into a wolf, pouncing on civilians. The two became one, embracing the thrill of the thirst.

When that spring term was over, they graduated. Soon afterward, the virus had the student circle back to Copper Petal University to become the chancellor, and have a new playground in which to imprison and torment people. With the Plo-Tunium element in his veins, it did not take him long to convince people to make him chancellor. Sure, The Landlord could have taken over the previous chancellor's body. But he had gotten used to Mathias, who, for someone so young, already wanted to start a family of his own. Especially after The Landlord convinced him to get rid of the family he already had. And it did not take long for The Landlord to find a familiar family...

Now, nearly fifteen years later, the chancellor had trouble fulfilling another desire. Despite the lack of results, he kept trying to cry, yawning until the dawn. When the sun was up, he decided that it was futile. The daylight weakened him a bit, but it would not kill him. He put his hood back up and headed back to his office.

Part Three
The Swim

Chapter 32
A Bridge Version

One evening at Tree Culler Hotel, August limped over to the front desk in the lobby where Tate and his fiancé Georgia were talking to Tommy the receptionist.

"Thank you!" Tate said to Tommy. "I can't tell you how grateful I am that you're all letting this happen!"

"No trouble at all," the receptionist said. "It'll be a most special occasion."

"What kind of air conditioner you got?" August asked the receptionist.

"We only have complimentary shampoo," Tommy said.

"No. The air. The whistling of the wind from the woods. How's that possible in this building? I woke up at three in the morning with the most *excruciating* pain in my calf!"

"Don't have a cow. Just calm down."

"I kept trying to fall asleep all day and kept waking up. But I found something. Listen carefully. I had a dream. I couldn't remember it after leaving my room, but I recorded it."

"You recorded the dream?"

"I recorded me explaining the dream. I think 'cause I had a feeling I'd need to. Allow me to use my pocket computer."

August pulled out his phone and pressed play on the recording.

"I've been waking up throughout the night. It's half past seven in the morning and I have just woken from such a strange dream. In that

dream, I was watching The Cabin in the Woods *for some reason. That movie's not really for me, and in this dream I figured out the reasons why. But they're irrelevant now because, in the dream, the movie had some changes. It had the same twist, evident from the start. But the movie was very different."*

August paused the recording.

"Now, I'm not gonna tell you the twist in *The Cabin in the Woods*. Let's just say it's made clear early on, which colors the rest of the film in a way that doesn't quite work for me."

He pressed play again.

"In the dream, The Cabin in the Woods *took place in a hotel. It was this hotel. Tree Culler Hotel. There was a bearded man walking alongside a brown-haired woman. And he was skeptical of their bald companion walking ahead of them in the hallway. The bald man turned around when he was next to a door to a room, and said, 'It could be any of us!' And the bearded man kept saying something like, 'How can we trust you?!' And then they kept walking through the hallway, until it turned into a sidewalk in the night surrounded by branches sharp enough to impale you. As they kept going, the trees became statues, and in came the sunlight.*

"And then suddenly I was back in the lobby. I went to the front door, and there was a cat. It had additional digits on its right paw, fingers brushing out of the fur. I followed it to a shore. A pebbly shore. No sand. No time. The cat wanted to go fishing. So it took out a fishing rod. But the lure that it used was a jewel. Now, not being a geologist, I could not identify the jewel. But the cat used this jewel as a lure on the hook. And as it released it into the water, I said to myself, 'Cat see jewel lure.' I felt like there was another syllable on the tip of my tongue, but then the cat took a leap at me and bit my tongue out of my mouth. Blood spilled onto the shore, and the ocean turned red."

The recording ended. With an exhausted expression, August stared at the receptionist.

"What the hell is going on in this hotel? *Could* it be any of us? Tate? Georgia? You, Tommy? After all, you're always down here in the lobby, Tommy. Aha! Lobby Tommy. Lobotomy! You're doing something to my mind, aren't you?"

"You need to comb your hair, honey," Georgia said. "You've lost your beehive."

"Are you calling me crazy?"

"You might just need some rest," the receptionist said. "Sounds like you kept waking up pretty often."

"Perhaps..."

August returned to his room. As soon as he closed the door, he heard a sound. The buzzing of bees was what came to mind. It got louder as he got closer to the mirror. But the mirror was not showing him anything. Something told him he should have been able to see something other than himself, but the sound persisted in his head.

He ran back downstairs. When he got to the dining area, he was out of breath. Verner was sitting at the table with a mug of coffee. Leaving the mug there, he got up and walked over to August.

"August, what's wrong?" Verner asked.

"Wrong? What are you implying?"

"You just seem a bit off."

"Please. My heart is beating fast. Don't stand too close to me!"

"Who put a fly in *your* coffee?"

"That's it. I need coffee."

August walked over to the table and tried reaching for the mug, but Verner pulled it away from him.

"Coffee won't calm you. If you drink this, you will surely die."

"Maybe it's for the best."

"No. You can't take this."

"I can't take it! I can't take it!"

"August, pull yourself together!"

343

"I'm already all over the place, like piss by urinals! Here in England, the urinals are so much better. Higher or rounder, and somehow the floor beneath is often cleaner. America needs to get its shit—or piss, rather—together!"

"I don't think all urinals here are like that. Might just be memory bias."

"Ah yeah. There is *something* going on with my memory, and I can't remember! But just gimme some damn coffee and I'll be fine. I'm perfectly fine. Just give me some damn context! When we're born, we're dropped in the middle of it all without any context!"

Fritz walked over to August and took him by the arm.

"Come with me," Fritz said.

He led August to the kitchen where Anton was baking brownies. Verner followed. Fritz showed August the meat patties on the grill. He pointed at one of them.

"Take a look at this. The patty is well done on the outside but raw on the inside. Looks fine on the outside, but there is so much raw energy at its core. Do you understand what I'm saying?"

"Are you calling me a *meat* patty?"

"Take it easy," Anton said.

"No, *you* take it easy! Why don't you keep to your patty cake, Becker man?!"

"August?" Anton said. "What's gotten into you? You need to take it easy. You're burning up like a candle on a cake. See, the cake is friendship. And if you're burning up and leaving wax everywhere, you're overstaying your welcome. You wouldn't want to be the candle, would you?"

"Well which one is it?! Am I too raw or am I on fire?! You can't just throw two opposite metaphors at me and expect them to make sense!"

"Calm down," Anton said. "You don't wanna burn the casserole."

"Cassie roll? Cassie roll? Where the *fuck* is Cassie! I will cut up all you fuckers if you don't tell me where my friend is!"

"August!" Verner said. "You're being extremely rude to everyone! What's the matter with you?"

"I'm sorry. I need a drink. Can we go get more cider?"

"No," Verner said. "You shouldn't drink when you feel mad. There's no good in putting a lot of anger in cider."

August breathed in, and then out.

"You're right. I'm sorry. I just need to go for a walk."

August took a stroll through the streets of London, going in circles for a couple of hours. But this was by choice. At night time, it seemed so lit up and alive. But he felt dead. He walked over to Westminister Bridge, where he looked over the railing and down at the water of the River Thames. There was something appealing about it. Something inside of him made him want to get closer to the water. He was not sure what or why. But he had an urge to jump off.

He turned to the north and saw a woman with a camera, photographing Elizabeth Tower, probably zooming in on its clock. She looked familiar to him. Curious, he walked over to her.

* * *

Candid found London to be charming. She could imagine herself living here for a while. If not long term, then there were certainly other places around the globe to see.

"You look familiar," she heard a voice behind her say.

She turned around and saw a young man. She did not recognize him, and she did not want to be recognized by anyone.

"No way you and I have ever met," she replied.

"I don't know. Your face rings a bell. Oh well. Take any good pics of the bell in that tower?"

"Uh, yeah."

"Do you know what that bell is called?"

"Big Ben?"

"Yeah. That's a nice name. Ben. Do you know anyone named Ben? Second initial, 'F?'"

"Fuck!"

"Hello, Candid Du Clips." The voice no longer sounded like it belonged to this man. It very much resembled the voice of her benefactor.

"No," Candid said. "Math—"

"Not quite the one you're thinking of. I'm an extension. A conduit. A bridge, if you will. As long as the source survives, so do I!"

He tried wrapping his arms around Candid's throat, but she grabbed his wrists and tried to push him away. As he tried to push her hands back, Candid looked around. People on the bridge were walking past them, not paying any sort of attention.

"Help!" Candid shouted.

No heads turned. The man laughed.

"Plo-Tunium is a hell of an element!"

Candid looked over the railing, the river running down below. She summoned as much strength as she could to push the man overboard.

Sea how it feels! she thought.

As the possessed man fell, she swore she could see a surprised, innocent expression emerging in the face.

SPLASH.

"No," Candid said.

I killed someone.

Theoretically, there was enough time to save him. But Candid did not want to risk it. She started to run. At this moment, the city did not seem so safe anymore. She had to get to the airport.

* * *

August regained consciousness, having no memory of how he ended up in the river. He closed his eyes as he felt the freezing water around him. His arms and legs were moving, pushing for survival. But it was not him controlling his limbs.

At length, he made it to the shore, next to the Millennium Bridge, and his limbs stopped moving. He felt as helpless as a beached fish. There he remained, upon the sand, until the sun rose. At that point, he had the same thought repeating through his mind.

Who wants me dead?

Eventually, he rose, brushing the sand off of himself. Feeling all turned around, it took him a while to figure out how to get back to the hotel. But he made it. Entering the lobby, he saw Bessie, Fritz, Jade, Verner, and Tate standing together, facing the entrance.

"What's going on?" August asked.

"This is an intervention," Bessie explained.

"We talked about it last night," Tate said.

"For who?" August asked.

When they all pointed, he thought they meant him. But it turned out to be Anton, who was just entering the lobby, walking past August. Anton was wearing a backpack stuffed with groceries.

"What's happening?" Anton said.

"Anton," Bessie began, "There's no easy way to say this, but you have a problem. You've been baking *way* too much. More than any of us can eat."

"Seriously?" Anton said. "What's the harm? It's not like I'm hurting anyone."

Fritz stepped forward. He took a wad of paper out of his pocket and uncrumpled it so that he could recite it aloud.

"Anton, I consider you my best friend. So it hurts seeing that you're baking way more snacks than you need to. And at the end of the day, when there's just too much for people to finish, you just end up throwing it all in the trash. And it's a sad sight. All that money spent on ingredients, and some of the fruits of your labors go in the trash, whether they be cupcakes, muffins, brownies, pieces of pie... Well, you get the picture. It pretty much becomes a grocery list. You need to dial it back, Anton. Because I am very worried about you."

Fritz put the paper back in his pocket and made eye contact with Anton, who started to tear up. Anton fell to his knees.

"I just miss being at home! I miss baking with my family as often as I did, so I guess I'm overcompensating."

"It's okay," Verner said. "You are among friends. Baking goods in and of itself isn't bad. You just need to adjust the proportions so you're not making way too much."

Anton wiped his face. Fritz walked over to him and pulled him up by the arm.

"You're right. I'm sorry. From now on, I'll be sure to ask how much everyone wants, to give me a better idea of how much to buy and bake. Thank you all for your help. I'm so thankful to have such reliable friends like you. I promise that I will change."

Anton gave Fritz a brotherly hug. The rest of the friends in the lobby applauded Anton's resolve. Even the receptionist was clapping along.

"You're gonna be fine now, my friend," Fritz said.

August wished that the same could be said about himself.

Part Four
Shots Of Fire

Chapter 33
Guaranteed to Know Pissed

On the next Friday the 13th, Stitch Tyke was asleep, a mantra echoing in his mind.

Mandy should've been me. Mandy should've been me. Mandy should've been me.

Eventually, his growling stomach awoke him. This time was different. He felt energized. The rest of the pack was still asleep, but the blinking red light on a bookcase's black panel drew his attention. He remembered seeing the current mascot and her friend pressing buttons and running between bookcases months earlier. Tomb Scone sat between two bookcases. Curious, Stitch Tyke pressed the green arrow button.

With the rows of shelves squeezing against Tomb Scone, the scrawny, emaciated being did not stand (or sit) a chance, especially not in his human form. As his body was crushed, blood splattered out of the row and onto the chain-link fence, like the contents of several packets of weak sauce. Stitch Tyke pressed the button again so that the space between the bookcases was widened again.

Crawling over to Tomb Scone's corpse, he welcomed a craving. Changing into his wolf form, he feasted.

But even when he was done, it did not satiate him completely.

He walked over to the blood diamond fence and licked it, right by the lock. But a closer inspection showed that the lock had not been clicked into place the last time that Mathias visited. He moved the lock aside, placing it on the floor.

The gate opened.

The other werewolves remained asleep in their human forms, but Stitch Tyke walked out, a free wolf with an absent wind hissing through his mind.

When he noticed a few students sitting at tables, he quickly changed into his human form. A few looked up at him, but then glanced back at their work. Stitch Tyke saw a buffet in front of him and did not know where to start.

One of the students got up, this one looking familiar. Stitch Tyke was sure he had seen some of the faces around here before, but something stood out to him about this one. Thinking back through his fragmented memory, he remembered that this was one of the students running between bookcases. A friend of the one who had been chosen to be the mascot. The one who had taken the role Stitch Tyke coveted. Fixated on this student, the werewolf followed him and watched him enter the elevator. Stitch Tyke would just have to wait for the next one and see if he could catch up.

* * *

Exiting the library, Randy saw Grady right outside, carrying a couple of textbooks and wearing a stuffed backpack.

"Oh, hey Randy."

"Hey. Pulling an all-nighter?"

"Yeah."

"Damn. That sucks."

"Yeah. Guess you're the lucky one, not having to stay up all night. I've got an in-class final in the morning."

"On a *Saturday* morning?"

"Yeah."

"Damn. I thought maybe it was some essay due online or something."

"I've put my phone on silent so I can focus better. Wish me luck!"

"Have a good night," the tired Randy replied, feeling a bit neutral about Grady.

In the cold of the night, Randy headed home. He heard footsteps. Out of the corner of his eye was a jogger. He paid no attention at first.

But then a hand grabbed his shoulder.

"Hey," the jogger said. He was almost out of breath, and what was left of it smelled like alcohol. "Do you have a phone?"

"Uh...yeah."

"Can I call someone to pick me up? My battery died."

"Sure..."

Randy handed him his cell phone, screen unlocked. The jogger dialed a number, pressed the green phone icon, and then placed the cell to his ear. The other end rang a few times before getting to a voicemail box that had not been set up yet.

"Shit," the jogger said, handing the phone back to Randy.

"Are you okay?"

"Yeah. Don't...don't worry about it. Thanks."

Not knowing what else to do, Randy started walking again. And the jogger walked alongside him. Truthfully, Randy did not want to deal with this drunk person, but he knew that others might have wanted him to do so if they could see him now. So he let the guy follow him along.

"Where do you live?" Randy asked.

"I think I'm gonna..."

The jogger fell to his knees and vomited onto the sidewalk.

"Shit!" Randy exclaimed. "Are you all right?"

"Yeah, yeah. Don't worry about it."

He stood up and faced the bushes away from Randy.

"Look," Randy said. "I can walk you to your place if it's nearby."

He heard a zipper and then piss falling on leaves and dirt. Randy cringed.

Fuck this! Randy thought.

If the jogger did not want him to worry, then he would not worry. He waited until he zipped up again. The jogger looked at him, and then Randy pointed to the curb, a good distance away from the vomit.

"Listen. Just sit there until you feel well enough to walk."

"Yeah... Okay."

The jogger obeyed. Annoyed and frustrated, Randy walked away.

* * *

Tim remained sitting on the sidewalk, dizzy and trying to overcome his nausea. This was the lowest that he had ever felt. He started to believe that drinking so much on his birthday was not such a good idea. Especially when it was at a party with people whom he had never met before. He used to visit friends at CPU, but they were long gone, having graduated. But people still partied around here.

His sister—who studied at CPU—had been really busy with school work all day, but she promised that she would hang out with him tonight. He just could not remember what the address was.

He looked around and saw a pair of eyes surrounded by blue fur. Surprised, he could not speak.

"Are you staring into my soul?" it asked. "It must be *really* hard to find!"

* * *

A bat flew and perched itself onto a sycamore tree, from which it viewed the werewolf biting into the young man, devouring his jugular and then gnawing and clawing at his limbs and torso. After a little while of watching, the bat flew down and transformed into a humanoid, revealing himself to be Chancellor Moseley. Stitch Tyke recognized him and greeted him with a gleeful smile.

"Mandy should've been me! I nailed those auditions, dancing for you like a puppet. And you *know* I still would've nailed them with an arm tied behind my back! Proud of me now? I opened the gateway!"

Mathias looked down at the corpse, lifeless with open eyes.

"You really should not have done that. Now you will face the wrath of the bat."

* * *

When Randy got home to the apartment, Pamela was sitting on the couch, which was covered with her textbooks. She had hardly hung out with him these days, and it worried her.

Am I losing a friend again? she wondered.

Evan and Ted being in their respective hometowns for the weekend meant that Pamela had a chance to talk to Randy privately.

"Where've you been?" she asked.

"Studying for finals."

"At the library?"

"Yeah."

"You wanted to be alone?"

Randy shrugged, then nodded.

"Is it because of last time?"

"What do you mean?"

"Did I get you distracted and affect your grades last time?"

"My grades were decent. I just needed to be alone for other reasons. In between studying, I was...thinking over some things."

"What things?"

"Just some post-grad stuff. How different things will be. What will happen."

Different how? Pamela wondered. She moved some of her textbooks to make some room on the couch.

"Do you wanna talk it over?" she asked.

"It's nothing for you to be concerned about. You wouldn't understand."

That's a low blow, Pamela thought. She stood up.

"Why? Just because I'm a freshman?"

"That's not what I meant."

"You think you're more seasoned than me? Is that it, rotisserie chicken?"

"What'd you call me?"

"You heard me."

"Pamela, by no means do I view myself as being above you. If anything, you're on a whole 'nother level. You'll be fine hanging around at this school without me. There's nothing you need to take so personally."

"Okay..." Pamela took a deep breath. She wanted to continue, but she did not know what more to say that could make any difference. There was just awkward silence.

"Well," Randy said, "see you later."

Randy turned to walk to his room. But Pamela, having found her words, was not finished.

"Hey Randy." He stopped but did not turn around. Just as well. She did not want him to see the wetness of her eyes. "I want to pretend with a friend. But if you're gonna let me down, you should just *leave* this friendship."

What followed was a statement, not a question. An indication that he had heard.

"I'm sorry."

"Good. Guilt means you're at least real. At least you have *that* aspect realized. Better than nothing, I guess."

"Pam—"

"Go. Just go. Take your salt and pepper with you. I'll pack my things and leave in the morning."

"Where will you go?"

"It's none of your concern. You wouldn't understand."

Randy sighed. She watched him walk back into his room and could not believe that she had said all that.

* * *

Lying in his bed, Randy was worried about Pamela. Part of him wondered whether he should let Peyton know what was going on. Perhaps. But first, he really wanted to vent in the group chat.

Randy: *Tonight SUCKED. I was walking home and this drunk guy showed up. I let him use my phone to call someone. Nobody answered so he kept following me and then PISSED ON THE FUCKING SIDEWALK!!! Like WTF?!*

Reginald: *Sorry to hear that Randy.*

Gertrude: *Randy, did you try calling me half an hour ago?*

Randy: *No.*

Gertrude: *Your number is listed under my missed calls.*

Randy checked his phone. Confused, he noticed that Gertrude's number was listed as an outgoing call from half an hour earlier. He became even more perplexed when he could not see an additional number for the night. He had seen the drunk man dial it manually.

Oh shit.

Randy: *Gertrude, were you expecting a call from someone?*

Gertrude: *My brother Tim is in town and I don't know where he is.*

Randy: *Shit! OK. He may have been the guy I bumped into. I can show you where he is.*

After letting his friends know where he had left Tim, Randy ran

LEMONS LOOM LIKE RAIN

out of the apartment. When he arrived at the spot where he had left Tim Yose, he was dismayed to see his eviscerated remains. Only his face was untouched.

Did I do that?

Randy got down on his knees and vomited onto the street.

When he looked up, he saw his friends approaching. They all looked at the horribly mangled body of Gertrude's brother. All were in shock, frozen like snowmen in a meat locker.

"Oh no!" Mitch said. "We're too late!"

Reginald took out his phone and started dialing.

"I'm calling the police."

Gertrude turned to Randy with an expression that pierced spikes into his spleen. She walked up to him quickly and punched him in the jaw.

Randy fell to the ground, right next to his vomit. The world spun again. He looked up. Gertrude's lips moved, as if trying to figure out what to say. But no words came out. So she kicked Randy in the stomach three times in quick succession.

"Gertrude!" Randy said.

"Don't you fucking talk to me! My brother is *dead* because of you!"

"No." Randy rolled over and tried to get up. "I know how this looks, but I didn't kill him! He was alive when I left him!"

"No shit! Of course *you* didn't fuckin' kill him! You wouldn't be capable. But you are *culpable* because you left him alone for someone else to do this. And we don't know *who* it is or *how* to catch them!"

She continued to kick him, and he fell back onto the ground.

"Please," he begged. "This hurts."

"Good!"

"No. The inside, too. My heart..."

"To *hell* with your heart! You've ruined everything!" Gertrude backed away. "Get up and fight, you coward!"

Hands on the ground, Randy tried to push himself up. The word "coward" was like a rake on a chalkboard. He looked at Naomi, who stood by, not interfering.

She's not helping, a voice said. *She'd rather see you get hurt by Yo-Gert.*

Randy now had a beef with all of them. He could feel his wounds opening up. The tacos unfolding from his skin. The beef pouring out of his veins. Could a Nap Kin really get rid of a taco stain?

They all deserve to die.

Breathing heavily, Randy struggled to stand up, clenching his fingers into fists. He was tempted to just unleash everything and fight everyone. He *wanted* to see them get hurt. To wrap his fingers around their throats and deprive them of air until they begged for him to stop. And he was open to the prospect of showing no mercy once they begged. If he was the outcast, then he wanted all the power. To drain the lights from their eyes so that he might be illuminated like a moon, in a starlit sky surrounded by scarlet dye.

They all deserve the dye. The red dye. Give them blush and a gush of blood. Give them a makeover! UNMAKE THEM! MAGNIFY!

The mental yell scared him for a moment, and then for a brief flash it empowered him, sending a surge of strength through his twitching, flexing muscles. In his arms. In his eyelids. In his bloodthirsty tongue, licking his lips in a counterclockwise circle. Randy wanted to be *feared* as well as loved. To make the dead, bidding them farewell to unburden himself from the ties that had meant so much to him. The ties that had made him feel warmly welcomed. Like he was not so alone in this world.

It's not worth it, Artie whispered to him. *You made a mistake. Own up to it.*

Randy listened. Part of him wanted to tune out the clown, but he listened. He took longer breaths.

"I'm sorry," Randy said, forcing himself to break into tears as he sank down to his knees. "I should've helped him."

"You fuckin' *should* have!"

Gertrude punched him in the face. He fell over. He did not know what to do but play dead. Unconvincingly, at that; his breathing was heavy.

"Go ahead and play dead, cow turd! Even the possums are better than you, you piece of shit!"

"If I were to die yesterday, would you remember me tomorrow as I am today?"

Gertrude ignored the question. She backed away, walking over to her friends. Naomi opened her arms and let Gertrude cry on her shoulder. She gave Randy a look that said this was the end of comfort, thus assuring that the two of them could never be.

Peyton walked over to Randy, and he did not know what to expect.

"Where's Pam?" she asked.

"She's at my apartment."

"Stay away from her. I'm taking her home." She turned to look at the other Nap Kin. "I need to go get Pam."

"I'll go too," Mitch offered. "You shouldn't go alone."

Peyton nodded, allowing Mitch to accompany her. Naomi, Reginald, Chelsea, and Shelley stayed with Gertrude.

"The campus police are on their way," Reginald said, putting his phone in his pocket.

Randy started stepping away slowly, departing without any word from his former friends. Not even a peep from Naomi. It seemed that they would rather dismiss him than miss him. This left Randy feeling more alone than he had ever felt in his existence thus far. He even blocked Artie from his mind in this moment.

Chapter 34
Family Tatters

Minutes later, a police car pulled up. The driver got out. He looked around at the Nap Kin standing on the sidewalk.

"I'm Officer Johnson. Any of you Reginald?"

"Yeah," Reginald answered.

The officer looked down at the remains of Tim.

"My god," Johnson said. "Looks like the work of an animal."

"My brother..." Gertrude said with a sob.

"I'm so sorry," Officer Johnson said. "I know that family matters like this are tough."

Gertrude wiped her eyes and then tried to keep talking.

"What could have done this?"

Gertrude could see that Johnson was clueless as his eyes scanned the remains.

"Well, it's not my area of expertise. I can get some people down here to figure it out. And we could send out an alert to all the students, telling them to stay safe and indoors. There's no telling where this thing is now, but we'll watch out for it."

Gertrude looked at her brother's remains, wanting justice for the boy who grew up with her. The boy whose life had been ended far too soon. Even if it was not Randy's intention to allow her brother to die, she could not help but hate him for leaving Tim all alone. But shunning Randy was not satisfying enough. She wanted to end whoever was responsible for this. She wanted to end whatever caused this to be such a disastrous night. She wanted to prevent further disasters right away rather than wait and hope for the best.

The sooner the darkness was lit by fire, the better.

* * *

Pamela awoke a half hour before midnight. Beside her window was Mandy, right where she had been left.

"Can't sleep, huh?" Pamela said. "Wanna move around?"

"Sure," Mandy replied.

She put on the costume and rolled around the floor of her room. Then she lay in bed, continuing to wear the costume. She could have removed it, but she wanted Mandy to feel safe. Pamela could read her thoughts. She could see Stagmantel and Unicoren in the park, standing side by side, holding hands and bearing hints of smiles. And then the imaginary image of Mandy standing between them, holding their hands and looking more real than she did now.

"They're waiting for me," Mandy said.

"I know. It's late. We'll go there in the morning. I promise."

Mandy trusted Pamela, and thus was willing to let her get some rest, knowing that she cared. Mandy could sense Pamela's uneasiness.

"You're worried that we won't see each other again."

Pamela shed a tear.

"You have your family. And without you, I have...no one."

"What about Peyton?"

"I think we're too different to ever be on the same page, no matter how hard we try. Look, it's getting late. Just get some rest. We can talk in the morning."

* * *

Stagmantel and Unicoren stood still on the pathway, in the middle of Petal Lock Park.

"It's almost time to leave," Stagmantel said.

Unicoren nodded.

"We'll be reunited soon," she said. "She will come."

* * *

A cool wind filled the park, and lightning flashed across the sky, frightening Frederick Filler. Something stirred within him. At this moment, Frederick Filler was filled with high ambitions. He wanted to conquer the light. He had felt somewhat at peace walking on the slackline, but now he craved more, no matter the risk. So he climbed a tree, and he tied the slackline to the top. Once back on the ground, he ran over to another tree to climb, where he did the same. Both ends ended up being forty feet above the ground. Higher than he was normally comfortable with, but he was willing to risk it all.

Since he was no flying sparrow, he could only walk upon this narrow path that was suspended in the air. But he lost control and started to fall toward the ground. Frederick Filler falling from above, not able to freely fly like a dove.

A goose flew by and tried to rescue Frederick, who grabbed it by the feet. As they got closer to the ground, Frederick unintentionally pushed their trajectory to the duck side of the park. When the goose landed on the grass, it turned into a duck, getting lost in the wrong flock.

The ground shook. Frederick Filler, his course provoking a curse.

"Forgive me!"

* * *

Unicoren, now very much aware that she had lost something, was filled with sorrow. She let go of Stagmantel's hand and put her hands over her heart. Fire filled her eyes.

"My core is spilling. The spell spoken is compromised."

She looked at Stagmantel, who was running his fingers all over his antlers. Fire filled his eyes as well. He laughed maniacally, because he had more than her now. The leaves of the trees descended upon him, swirling like a katabatic wind.

"Leaves a smile on my face!" he said with a grin that had no business being as stretched out as it was. "The earth is my inventory!"

The two of them backed away from each other until there were ten feet between them. Then they got down on all fours and ran at each other. Unicoren aimed her horn at Stagmantel's forehead, but he managed to turn his head just right so that an antler blocked it. They backed away a bit, hissed at each other, and then looked to the side, the direction in which they both sensed they would find Mandy. They both ran off in the same direction, racing each other as unstable father and mother.

* * *

Pamela, still wearing the Mandy costume, was lying in bed. The costume shook, and she thought there was an earthquake. Pamela tried to open her eyes, but something was preventing her. She was forced to see a dream that was a vivid memory. She saw the event through the eyes of Mandy.

Mandy has flesh, fur, and fabric. She is the human equivalent of a toddler. She is surrounded by the arms of her parents as Miunis Grund breaks apart. As the ground quakes, the flesh, fur, and fabric on Mandy's parents transform into dirt and stone.

"No!" Stagmantel cries. "We are being cursed!"

"This must be what happens to a family divided!" Unicoren surmises.

Mandy does not transform, however. Her parents hold on as the three of them are lifted up into the sky. There is a light so bright that

Mandy closes her eyes as they accelerate. A vacuum sound surrounds them. Mandy opens her eyes. There is nothing but fire everywhere, and the family falls and floats at the same time. It feels as though they are in place, but also going up and down simultaneously. Mandy does not know how much time passes. It feels like an eternity.

Suddenly, the fire freezes. And then some of it moves away, forming an archway. There, in the opening, is Chancellor Moseley, sitting in his office. Despite the shades, hat, and everything else, Mandy's parents recognize him.

"That smile..." Stagmantel begins. "It cannot be... The Landlord?"

"A new face," Unicoren observes. "Much time has passed. But not dead."

"You recognizing me is enough to amaze. I have evolved in so many ways." He points to his own head. "We are so intertwined. Two beings, one combined. This one has a desire to satiate. I really want to create."

"How did you find us?" Unicoren asks.

"There were times when I saw you in each fireplace. A broken family, simply falling from grace. Plo-Tunium Holes are as good for finding things as they are for erasing them. Oh Plo-Tunium, that powerful, sacred gem."

"Plo-Tunium is dangerous. You have been tampering with the elements!"

"Are you really calling me mental? Look at you two, now elementals! Why did you not invite me to your wedding? When I found out, it was very upsetting."

"Our union was private. We did not want it to reach judgmental ears. There are many guests we could have invited, but we chose to keep it personal."

"Acts of exclusion are what broke Miunis Grund, that giant world so rich and fecund. Your union probably contributed to the separation. And now, here you are, with much desperation."

"Please. Let us out."

The chancellor smiles. He knows he has power.

"I will make you a deal. The child will be mine to steal. I will use it as a mascot for this school. You two will inhabit the land that I rule."

Stagmantel and Unicoren are desperate. They put their child in the hands of the monster.

A flash forward. A room in a mansion. An extra set of clothes lying on the ground. Mathias Moseley holding up Mandy as Stagmantel and Unicoren stand and watch.

"You, dear Mandy, will become a costume, and the life within you will be ready to consume. It will be exchanged for the flesh of my own child, who will be so enhanced and styled."

The chancellor chants in chilling whispers as he holds Mandy up to the mirror. Mandy is still in her organic form at this point. Since Mathias is not visible in the mirror, it looks as if Mandy is floating. Then the head pops off of the body, allowing organs, tissue, and blood to fly from the head and body and into the glass.

Lightning from the open window strikes the mirror and ricochets onto Mandy. After being zapped, Mandy feels softer. And the lightning enters the mirror, which becomes a bright white light. Mathias presses an open eye against the light until a reflection of the eye appears. As the light turns to solid glass, a burn forges a scar on Mathias' upper eyelid and its reflection. Mathias falls back.

The reflection of the eye, complete with lids, pops out, falling and then floating above the floor where the clothes lie. And then blood, tissue, and organs gushes out of the mirror, molding a being identical to Mathias, wrapped in the clothing. He stands up. Two beings, mirrored images, with their scars on opposite upper eyelids. Mathias drops Mandy to the floor as he gets up. Mandy cannot move at-will anymore.

"I am Mathias Moseley, your creator. You have come out of some sort of incubator."

The newborn feels his own face.

"What do I look like?"

There is no reflection in the mirror.

"You look like me, but reversed. You have grown but not yet traversed. I give you this home as a gift. You are the owner, your rise being swift."

Mathias offers the newborn adult a chest. The newborn opens it and removes from it a slice of garlic bread. He takes a bite and swallows. Mathias looks pleased.

"Within this chest is also your Plo-Tunium doctored identification materials. You are now in the system, but invisibly bacterial. So raw yet refined. I see my features defined. My exact image is what you reflect, but without any vampire defect."

The newborn makes a scowl, looking like he needs to defecate.

"I...defect...from...YOOOOOOUUUUUU!"

The newborn points at the vampire.

"Oh no." Mathias drops the chest. "Not so."

"My wrath is my own! Wrath is Mathis alone!"

Mathis the newborn steps toward Mathias, who begins to step back.

"Have rhyme and reason! Do not give in to treason!"

"I did not let you into my home! You are not welcome!"

An invisible force pulls Mathias. He hits the wall next to a closed window several times, before the unseen force lifts him up and launches him through the glass, breaking it.

"All of you!" Mathis yells to the family. "Get the fuck out of my home!"

Mandy, Stagmantel, and Unicoren fly out as well, accelerating through the air until landing in Petal Lock Park beside Mathias. Up in the sky, Mandy sees the mirror flying as well, to a place unknown. But before it disappears, dozens of spherical entities fall out of it. Glowing white, they rain onto the park. Once they land on the path separating the redwoods and the silver birches from each other, they stay still for a moment.

"Somehow, I know," Stagmantel says.

"So do I," Unicoren says. "They are scanning and learning."

Taking the forms of ducks and geese, the entities choose sides. Unicoren and Stagmantel walk to their respective halves of Petal Lock Park.

Mathias looks down at Mandy.

"A broken bloodline. Now, you are mine!"

Pamela opened her eyes. She could not move her body, but Mandy made both of them rise. Mandy was in control, standing on all fours. She was angry, and Pamela had no way to break away.

* * *

Peyton stood in front of the apartment door, ready to knock. She tried to rehearse some words to exchange with her sister, but nothing came to her.

Mitch stepped in front of her.

"We have to act now," he said.

Before he could knock on the door, it swung open and knocked him to the side. Mandy jumped out and landed on all fours. Peyton backed away. Mandy looked at Mitch, lying on the ground, and pounced on him.

Then the flame-filled horns dug into his chest. And so, the late Mitch Bunkle was gone from this world.

"No!" Peyton yelled. "Pam! It's me!"

Mandy stared Peyton down. The beef was there. The beast started running toward Peyton. And so, Peyton ran away, into the open field where Mandy would have no trouble losing her.

Pam can't be doing this! Peyton thought. *Why the hell would she?*

Up ahead, she saw Unicoren and Stagmantel, flames on their respective horn and antlers.

"Mandy!" Unicoren commanded. "Please. Be under my thumb. Listen to your mother."

Mother? Peyton thought in confusion. *That must mean...*

"Wanna fight Father?" Stagmantel said. "Whichever of us doesn't die wins the child."

Peyton moved out of the way as Stagmantel ran toward Mandy. It was instinctive, though it quickly became a regret as Peyton realized that he might hurt Pamela, who was probably within Mandy. Antlers and horns pushed against each other.

"Come on!" Stagmantel said to Mandy. "Is that the best you've got?! Is that the *beast* you've got? If you're even *half* me, you shouldn't be this weak!"

Perplexed, Peyton stared at the struggle and then remembered Unicoren, who ran past her in that moment. Unicoren got between Mandy and Stagmantel, pushing them away with the force of fire emanating from the palms of her hands. Both beings fell to the floor.

"Pam!" Peyton yelled.

"Don't harm my servant!" Unicoren shouted to Stagmantel. "Mandy *will* do my bidding! *You* will be the hunted!"

Stagmantel stood up, hoping to maintain his ground. Mandy took the opportunity to ran away.

"COWARD!" Stagmantel shouted.

"Come back!" Unicoren said.

The two parents stared each other down, and then they departed in separate directions, apparently keen on tracking down their child.

"What the duck is going on?!" Peyton said. "Wait, what did I just say? What the duck? Duck? Duck? Duck! What's happening?"

She heard someone approaching. Turning around, she saw that it was a young man, carrying a coiled up slackline.

"You can't curse because the ducks have been cursed."

"No ducking way. How? Who the duck are you?"

"Frederick Filler," he answered.

"Who?"

LEMONS LOOM LIKE RAIN

"It's all my fault," Frederick admitted. Frederick Filler, eyes filled with regret. "I should've remained parallel, but instead I caused peril. I upset the balance. Stagmantel's mind is a mess. Fragmentel would be a more appropriate name."

"You did not just say that."

"And," Frederick continued, "Unicoren's not any better. They're both fighting over their child and what gets to happen to it."

"Wait. So *you're* the reason all this is happening? You're responsible for that thing having my sister trapped?!"

"I didn't mean to make it happen. I was reckless. But I wanna do all I can to help your sister."

Chapter 35
Library Charred

Around midnight, the nine remaining members of the pack, changing into wolf form, awoke in the library, sensing that something was going on. Doggerel Grill noticed the blinking red light on the bookcase. Green and red. She knew she wanted to say something at some point, but she was not yet sure what. All she knew was that it had to be on the nose. In the meantime, there was something else that she could say, based on speculation.

"The usurper slurps the soup and stages its coup from its chicken coop."

"CPU," Fork Feed said. "This is a machine. This is a machine. This is a machine."

Shed Cheese lifted his back right paw and used it to pick the inside of his ear. Then he licked his toes. Jam or wax, Mortimer Mutterer winced.

"Stop eating yourself!"

"If a wizard can eat wax, why can't I?"

"Waxing or waning," Doggerel Grill said. "Relaxing or raining."

"I just remembered," Harriet Harvester said. "There is a missing link."

"Ah," Low Knife said. "But could Mathias be hiding it from us?"

"It *has* to be him," Host L said. "He knew. He set the rest around the table and left one out. We did not get the whole pack. We need to find the missing link."

Shed Cheese opened his mouth. He had trouble formulating words, but they eventually came out.

"If we were wieners, we'd be bleeding ketchup and pissing mustard. And we would relish that."

Host L examined the chain-link fence, noticing the open door.

"The gate is open," she said.

One by one, the werewolves exited. Out in the basement level, they saw many students sitting at tables, studying for their final exams. The screaming made it evident that the werewolves were visible, and it got their blood pumping. One by one, students were picked off by the pack. Some students ran to the elevator. Others ran up the stairs.

For the pack, the hunt was on.

* * *

Outside, Stagmantel and Unicoren made it to the plaza in front of the library. Momentarily, Mandy became the least of their priorities as they watched Mathias approach with a luggage case.

"What are you two doing out of the park? Especially now when it is dark?"

"We *escaped* the park," Stagmantel said.

"We are free now," Unicoren said. She pointed to his luggage case. "Your prey?"

"My pet," Mathias said. "Fate set. My pack has disobeyed me. The result is what they will see."

Terrified students poured down the stairs in front of the library, chased by werewolves. Quickly, Mathias unzipped the case and poured out a pale human arm, its blood having been drained after being torn off of the elbow.

"Look at your packmate's paw diminished! Disobey and you *will* be punished!"

Most of the werewolves were more focused on the students. But the remains caught the attention of Doggerel Grill and Harriet Harvester. As they ran over to Mathias, the vampire backed away. Looking at the arm, they started biting off some skin. Mathias' mouth was wide open.

"But, what about the inhibition? You should be under my submission!"

"It appears that you're too late," Unicoren said, stepping toward him with her horn glowing orange. Mathias reacted by turning into a bat and flying upward as Unicoren sent an inferno onto the floor where he had stood.

Harriet Harvester stopped biting at the arm.

"It's not fresh flesh anymore," she observed.

"Interesting," Unicoren said. "And here I thought you'd eat anything at this point."

Harriet Harvester turned around and pounced on Unicoren. To defend herself, Unicoren used her horn to stab Harriet Harvester in the left eye. Rather than help her packmate right away, Doggerel Grill continued chewing on Stitch Tyke's arm. Stagmantel got ready to charge at Harriet Harvester.

"Time to take a ride on the antler express!" Stagmantel said.

He charged, and then he used his antlers to stab the werewolf and push her away from his wife. Doggerel Grill turned her attention to the fight, and then leaped at him, biting at his face. The confrontation resulted in Stagmantel losing his nose. Doggerel Grill tried chewing on it, but then spit it out. No doubt due to its dirt-like texture.

"I know what to say now," Doggerel Grill said. "Rudolph is dead. His face is Christmas green and red."

Stagmantel bled, a bloody triangular hole in the middle of his face. Through his nasal passages came lava, cauterizing the wound.

"Liquid light!" Harriet Harvester yelled. "It has risen, and we are doomed!"

His eyes glowing red and his face hardening to stone, Stagmantel shot lava out of his nasal passages, spraying Doggerel Grill and Harriet Harvester with fire on which they were set.

"AHHHHHH!" they both screamed.

Unicoren joined in, spraying fire upon the two werewolves. Stagmantel looked at the running students and laughed.

"This is what I've been waiting for. All the world to burn."

"Fracturing further and further," Unicoren said. "Fire can bring it closer."

For this one intimate moment, chaos united them. Hand in hand, they calmly walked up the steps as students frantically ran past them. Together, they set fire to the tower, a sublime display of power.

* * *

Grady was on the top floor during all this chaos. The floor where one could get the most privacy in the lavatory. After witnessing something horrific in that room, he ran out and smelled smoke. Further examination revealed that it was coming from the elevator shaft. It seemed like he would not make it to his final examination. Looking at his backpack and books on the floor next to the lavatory door, he knew he had to leave them behind. But he still had flashcards and pens in his pockets.

He ran out to the balcony and saw how far down the ground was. Ten stories. He began to lose a lot of hope.

And then he saw a bat fly by, seemingly watching the whole scene unfold. Grady believed there was more to this bat than met the eye. It hovered by the railing, staring at him. Feeding on his fear. He looked back at the fire.

This bat wants me to die, he concluded.

Grady summoned tears to his eyes and walked over to the railing. He climbed on top of it, raising his arms to signal that he was going to jump off.

He jumped.

But as he did, he reached forward and held onto the feet of the bat. Frantically, the bat flapped its wings as they fell together. It was much stronger than one might expect, and Grady was glad that his hopes were met. They were hurdling down toward a redwood on the edge of the park. At the right moment, Grady let go and grabbed onto the branch. The bat flew around and landed on the branch. It revealed its fangs, seemingly ready to attack Grady. But then it hesitated and flew away.

Looking behind himself, Grady saw Stagmantel and Unicoren approaching. Their faces and ivory glowed with fire. He was not sure what had gotten into them, and he was not ready to find out. So he ran for his life, his track and field days in high school still relevant. Back then, he knew that running would be a useful skill. The dog had never chased him when he was younger, walking home all by himself. But he knew that there would come a day when a beast would be unleashed, and he would have to run like hell. With or without August. His cousin was not here, but he had to keep running. The beast was loose, and it was manifold, apparently. The ancient evil.

He ran around various trees, trying to shake the Stagmantel and Unicoren off of his tail. They ran in circles within the park until, at last, he backed up and threw himself behind a bush, hidden from the couple as they ran past it. He waited until they were a carnival distance away, worried that any movement too soon would alert them. As much as he wanted to exhale, he tried to hold in as much of his breath as he could. When he seemed to be in the clear, he got out of Petal Lock Park.

Once he was out of the woods, Grady saw the werewolves running around campus.

Here we go again.

He thought about giving up right then and there, but he ultimately decided to keep running. A zig-zag pattern through the campus. Grady kept running until the dawn. The werewolves were howling. It was

March, and August was far away. Marching would not be quick enough, so running was the only way.

The longer he stayed alive, the less dark it became. Forsooth, the darkness faded as the sun announced its arrival. The werewolves, not keen on this type of light, withdrew into the wilderness outside of campus.

With the pack gone for the time being, Grady had a chance to concentrate on his final exam, which was scheduled to take place at 8 AM. He took out his flashcards and tried to cram everything, right to the very last minute when people were allowed inside the lecture hall.

When it was time to take the test, however, his pen broke. He tried the others, and they broke as well. He looked around and noticed that people were writing chicken scratch rather than coherent essays. He knew that something was wrong at the school. There was no point in continuing the test, so he ran outside of the classroom. He was surprised to see familiar faces.

Fortunately, it was the Nap Kin. Most of them, anyway. Mitch and Randy were absent, and there was a new guy. For a brief moment, Grady was worried that he was being replaced.

"Grady!" Gertrude said. "We've been looking everywhere for you. We've been messaging you!"

"Cell's been on silent. But the school's not silent. Sc-sc-screaming everywhere! I was in the restroom, at the urinal. While I was leaving a special, I saw a big ducking mosquito out of the corner of my eye, two urinals down. It looked like a big ass spider with wings! It was getting closer, but I still needed to pee. I tried to finish quickly, and it flew over my head and I was like, 'Oh duck!' So I ducked and didn't know where it was. Could've been on my head for all I knew, but I just kept peeing! When I finished I swatted the air above my head and ran over to the sink. And there it was: sitting under the *soap dispenser*. HOW THE DUCK WAS I SUPPOSED TO CLEAN MY HANDS?! So I got a paper towel and ducking killed it! I washed my hands, but I still feel like such a mess. What kind of a school allows a blood-sucking monster to fly around campus?"

"I'm not on the knows," Naomi said.

"Huh?"

"It's a saying around here. Means we're not sure."

"Oh." Grady looked at the new guy. "Who's he?"

"Frederick Filler," he answered.

"Who?"

"Well, I—"

"He broke the balance and turned the world to poop," Shelley said.

"Shelley!" Chelsea said.

"I'm getting right to the point! He fell off a rope and threw a goose to the duck side of Petal Lock Park, and now Stagmantel and Unicoren have gone crazy."

"I've seen them," Grady said. "Where are Mitch and Randy?"

"Mitch," Peyton began, looking at the ground, "got impaled."

"Oh no. No... Was it Stagmantel and Unicoren?"

"No." She shook her head. "It was Mandy."

"Your sister?"

Peyton looked at him defensively.

"She's not doing this! She can't be! That suit's got ahold of her. We've seen other dead students, each looking like they've been impaled by a pair of horns. But it's Mandy who's doing this. Not Pam. We've gotta get her out!"

With the news of Mitch's death, Grady was worried that Randy might have perished as well.

"I'm afraid to ask, but where's Randy?"

"Probably hiding somewhere," Gertrude said, her face red. "He found my brother Tim last night and left him all alone. One of these werewolves must've gotten to Tim. We've gotta rid them off this planet."

"I saw them run off campus when the sun came up. Guess they don't like sunlight."

"We need to reset the balance," Frederick said. "Let's go to the park."

They ran over the Petal Lock Park. Once there, they spent a while trying to figure out which duck used to be a goose. None of the geese revealed anything. They remained silent during the questioning. The Nap Kin tried to grab one duck at a time and bring each one to the other side to see whether they were the goose. But none of these few ducks turned into a goose. As they kept trying, it became difficult to tell which ducks they had already tried moving, especially when the birds kept walking around, trying to avoid the humans.

"This is hopeless!" Shelley said.

"I'll say," Unicoren said, having arrived with Stagmantel.

The couple shot out fire, and the Nap Kin ran in various directions. The trees were burning. The redwoods: orange. The birches: orange. Flames engulfing wood and leaves. Ducks and geese flying around to avoid the flames, no longer sticking strictly to their sides, making the couple even more unstable. Fire spiking all over the park.

When the Nap Kin had run far enough and reunited, they turned and looked at the burning trees. They could hear a melancholic song sung collectively by the geese.

When there's so much anger inside,
What happens when dogs collide?
A bark against a bark,
Ignites the burning spark.
When the fire's gone,
The trees are dark.

Chapter 36
Flying Pan

August walked through the kitchen and opened the door to the basement. Wanting to get to his fridge, he walked down the stairway.

He missed a step, tripping and falling all the way down. Waiting for the pain to subside, he got himself up and walked over to his fridge, from which he pulled out a gallon of orange juice. Carrying it, he walked up the stairs, carefully this time. He got a glass cup from his shelf and poured the juice in halfway. Tasting it, he grimaced. Then looked at the expiration date: 3/13/15.

"The orange juice has gone sour."

He dumped the rest of the gallon down the sink drain. The liquid made a steamy acidic sound. He worried that the pipes were burning and that he had made a mistake. That the hotel would be set on fire. He stuck his eye close to the drain hole and could only see darkness at first. But then there was a flicker in his mind's eye. Orange liquid becoming magma. The core of the world. He felt his veins burning up and wanted it to stop. He could feel pain in the vein where the friendship bracelet used to be. It hurt thinking about the friendship that had apparently disappeared. He needed to stop the pain.

A meat cleaver levitated, and August knew that it was aiming for his left wrist, which was lying on a cutting board on the counter. For a moment, he wanted it to happen. But then he blinked and shook his head. Reaching out with his right hand, he grabbed the handle before it could fall fully.

The kitchen door swung open.

"Hey!" Tate said, walking in. "That's mine!" He turned around. "Hey everyone, August is trying to steal my steel!"

Anton, Bessie, Fritz, and Verner—being the only other students in the hotel at the moment since they did not have any Saturday plans—walked in and were astonished to see him holding the meat cleaver.

"Wait!" August said. "This isn't what it looks like!"

"Oh, so now he thinks we're stupid!" Bessie said. "Everyone grab a pan or a pot and get him!"

Most of these students obeyed, grabbing pans and pots and surrounding August. Before anyone could take a swing at him, though, Verner stood beside him and waved his arms.

"Hey!" Verner shouted. "Stop it! Let's be reasonable before we resort to tearing August apart. He seems like a swell guy, so maybe this is just a misunderstanding. When has he ever steered you wrong before? Fritz, when you accidentally cut off your pinkie while cooking, who put it on ice so you could get it stitched back on?"

"August. That was *some* Saturday."

"And Bessie, when you got in a bar fight, who was there standing with you back-to-back, swinging stools as people attacked the two of you?"

"I barely remember that happening, but I *think* August was there."

"He was. I saw the whole thing. You two were a force to be reckoned with."

"Why didn't you join the fray?"

"Didn't wanna spill my drink. I walked you both home when it was done. Tate, who took a train all the way to your girlfriend's school in Wales to tell her all the stuff you were afraid to tell her yourself, thus setting your engagement in motion?"

"August."

"And Anton, when you baked all those pies and just couldn't eat them all without dying, who was there to finish the rest for you?"

"So he *did* take all our food!" Anton said. "Let's get him!"

Tate picked up a pan and nearly hit August. But then the pan levitated, picking Tate up. He let go, letting it phase through the ceiling. The students' jaws dropped. They looked at each other, then back at August.

"Really sorry, August," Bessie said.

"My bad," Anton added.

"Talk about a *Toy Story* situation," Tate said. "I feel like such a tater head."

"I forgive you," August said. "But hey, we've found a new nickname for you."

"And what would that be?"

"Levitate!"

People laughed about the misunderstanding and the pun for two minutes straight. Then they stopped, thought about how long the sequence of laughter had lasted, and then laughed again. When two more minutes had passed, their guts started to hurt, and they displayed terrified looks on their faces. Remembering the odd sight of the levitating pan, they knew that they had to stop. They tried coughing away the laughter, then inhaled and exhaled until they were calm again.

"That wasn't that funny," Fritz said.

"Okay," Verner said. "So what's our next step?"

"I think," Bessie began, "that we need to keep watch on this kitchen. Tie a rope to everything. Once something goes up, we'll take the thief down."

"Why steal our stuff?" August wondered.

"Everyone needs a good meal," Anton said before turning to Fritz. "Fischer, it's time to go fishing."

"I feel like that should have segued into something epic, but I don't have any rope."

"To the tablecloths!"

Chapter 37
Double the Math

Wearing dark blue silk pajamas, Mathis awoke in the morning, sensing a presence. He looked outside his window and saw the familiar figure whom he loathed so very much, standing in front of the garlic gate, a barrier beyond which this visitor could not trespass. Annoyed, Mathis changed into his day clothes. Then he walked outside and over to the gate.

"Mathias. Surprise to see you here."

Mathias removed his shades, letting the daylight reveal his milky white eyes, and the scar that ran over his right upper eyelid. A pink worm above a milky orb.

"Hello my sin. May I come in?"

"No."

"You are so unappreciative of my presence. I sent you Candid's address, one of the best presents."

"Why have you come here?"

"My prisoners and pets are out of control. This is not how matters are supposed to roll."

"Seeking refuge when you know you're slipping? The press is not kind to depressing murder scenes."

"One of my wolves committed the deed beyond his barrier. And I fed some of his arm to the rest of my 'terriers.'"

"Still keeping animals, I see."

"When you cannot have a child, you must settle for pets. And here you are, unsettling whilst settling debts."

"Only a matter of time before you get caught. Have you heard of Darby Morineau?"

"Afraid I am not familiar. At this moment, I am no liar."

"I found her at a bar six months ago. I could sense that she was aware of something. And despite that—or maybe *because* of that—she agreed to come to my home. She bored me. Talked about some professor she dated and the pointlessness of love and existence. I could tell that she was not attracted to me. I don't care about such matters, obviously. But I knew she was here for a reason. I put on some horror films to see if she'd be fazed, but she remained resilient. I left the room, acting like I was getting a snack. And then I heard her talking on her cell phone. She mainly listened, but then she said a few words."

"What have you heard? Tell me each word."

"Vanquish the vampire."

Mathis expected Mathias to look nervous, but the vampire just smiled.

"Those words do not mean what you think. Did you kill her so I would not sink?"

"I did not do it for you. It just seemed like perfect timing to attack after a dramatic line like that. I cut off her fucking head, and that was the end of her. I can see your end, too. You'll get caught and decay alone in a cell."

By this time, the smile was gone from Mathias' face.

"Why don't you ever talk to me? Don't you wish to see? There is something that you lack, looking at a mirror with nobody looking back."

"No. I feel untethered. No relationships restraining me. Just because you made me through some batshit crazy ritual doesn't make us family."

"You do not feel just a little bit bad, ignoring your own creator and dad?"

"You created me just so you could see yourself. If you see yourself in others, then you're just being selfish. Why can't you just see someone as their own person? *I* am a self-made man."

"You have got to be kidding. For you, joking is unfitting. You did not make yourself, son. Out of all such people, I have never seen one. Even Ibby Daga had help trying to change from wolf to man, and *that* did not end quite according to his plan. You should be *thankful* that I was able to shape you without *any* deformities. Look at how you can simply blend into conformities. I have much to show. I shaped a shadow!"

"Maybe in the beginning. But it was through my decisions that I turned into who I am now. *That* is how I view myself."

"Oh please. Disease. You sound like a dunce. You have never viewed yourself *once*."

"I have no need to. I'm stripped of my vanity. Good, yeah? I can focus on how other people look. How pathetic they are. And how fun it would be to rid these people who occupy space with no aim. Even if I were to get scarred, I wouldn't lose sight. You have your wolf pack? Well, I'm a lone wolf... Blech. Scratch that. I almost upchucked uttering that cliché."

"I used to turn into a wolf, you know. But that power died when you let me go."

"Good. I don't *need* you."

"Try to disassociate yourself from me all you want, but that will not prevent a haunt. You know we are practically the same. We both feed on suffering, a familiar flame."

"And I'm feeding on *yours*. I'm sure I do it better."

"Have you ever been so wild, as to kill a helpless child?"

"No. Why kill them before they have a chance to suffer?"

"Not so different, I see. You cannot deny that you are like me. You will be swallowed and trapped in tripe. Then, when your tears trickle, the birds will tweet with delight."

"Get lost, old man. If you die, I will not cry."

"As a matter of fact, you will! And you would no longer be able to kill. The Plo-Tunium goes away if I die. Your victims would survive no matter how hard you try."

"Guess you'll just have to be careful."

Mathis turned around, heading back to his mansion.

"There will come a time, Mathis. You will see what a bloodbath is!"

Chapter 38
Friending the Night

It was almost midnight at Tree Culler Hotel. Tablecloth ropes were tied around pots and pans. The little group of friends tried to stay vigilant in the kitchen, but there was no unusual activity. At least not yet. Tired of standing, they all sat on the counters. August yawned.

"Tired?" Verner asked.

"I can't remember the last time I got a good sleep."

"Get some rest. We can handle this. I've got a lot of coffee brewing."

"I want to be here to help. But at the same time, I feel like my room is the place to be right now."

"Don't worry," Bessie said. "We'll keep you in the loop, let you know if something happens."

August nodded. He left the kitchen and then took the lift up to the third floor. He walked over to his door and suddenly felt as if he had quicksand in his stomach. He went over to door 307 and knocked. Jade opened it and answered.

"Oh, hey August."

"You been in here all day?"

"Yeah. Just figured I'd stay in and shotgun a show."

"Hey, can you do me a favor?"

"What is it?"

"Come here." He walked over to his door, but remained in her doorway. "I just want to know if you sense something odd here."

"Like what?"

Jade walked over to his door. August felt a malevolent presence. He was not sure where it was, but it was near.

"Do you sense something?" he asked.

"No," Jade answered, shaking her head.

"Damn." He looked down at the floor. "I don't get it. I don't understand why I feel this right now. I want to rest, but I don't know if I can. Not alone..." He looked at her again. "Can I spend the night with you?"

Jade backed away, eyes widening like the space between moving bookcases.

"Look, you're a nice guy, but—"

"No. You misunderstand. Nothing like that. I just need help. I can sleep on the floor."

Jade arched her eyebrows and crossed her arms.

"What's going on?"

"For months, I've been running out of my room, and I don't know *why*. It's all incoherent; I cannot co-hear! I forget! There must be a reason, and I'm afraid to find out what it is. And when I do, I worry that nobody will believe me. Please." He broke, displaying overwhelming tears. "I don't wanna be alone. I feel so far away and I just wanna go home. I feel forgotten. I want to make it to the dawn."

* * *

She really *was* worried about him. His tears seemed genuine. If he were left to his own devices, there was no telling whether or not he would end, possibly by his own hand. And she did not want that to happen.

"We'll stay in your room. If there's anything wrong, I'll be there with you."

"Thank you," August said. "Can I hug you?"

Jade was reluctant at first, but she could see that he was in distress. And she really cared about him.

"Sure."

She opened her arms, and he completed the symmetry.

"You're a good friend, Jade. And something tells me I need to see if I can say the same about myself."

Chapter 39
Stitches Be Rippin'

Back in his human form, Stitch Tyke awoke on the floor of a room, which looked like an ordinary school office. Except for the minifridge. And the shelves containing beakers and miscellaneous ingredients. And the vampire standing over him.

"The sedative is wearing off," Mathias said. "You seem all right, having no cough."

Stitch Tyke moved his right hand, but he could not feel the left one. He looked at his left arm and noticed the stitches at the elbow. As he got up, he changed into his wolf form. His left forearm and hand remained human, uncovered by fur. And uncovered by skin, in some places. With no blood in it, he could see bone very clearly on the inner half of his forearm. The dead limb was now just hanging on the side of his torso.

"All right?! What did you do to my arm!"

"You misbehaved, so I gave you an injection. Then I took your arm, but prevented infection. I only had a drink, but your packmates ate some flesh. And now it smells so horrid, no longer being fresh."

"AH!" Stitch Tyke walked closer to Mathias. "I can trust nobody now! I should kill all of you! *I* should have been Mandy!"

"With an arm tied behind your back? Then prove it despite what you lack! Pamela is out there, masquerading as Mandy. But if *you* get the costume, it would come in handy."

Stitch Tyke looked at his left arm once more.

"And then *I* could finally be the mascot?"

Mathias grinned and nodded.

* * *

After much running from the corrupted parents, Mandy had stopped in the woods outside of campus. The sun was setting, and the sycamore trees provided some shadows. There was blood all over Mandy's horns. Pamela's legs were killing her, and she was almost bereft of breath.

"Please," Pamela said. "Let me go."

"No! You are my prisoner."

"But we're friends."

"Not anymore. Everyone wants to hunt me, and I don't want anyone anymore! As long as you're within me, people will refrain from trying to kill me."

Pamela's voice was growing weaker. She could feel that she was losing herself.

"Just stop the killing."

"NEVER!!! My family was supposed to be united, but now my parents are mad! If I can't be happy, then neither can you nor anyone else!"

"This isn't fun anymore. Please. Please! PLEASE!"

"Magic words won't save you. Magic words changed me for the worst. It's far too late. We are beyond the threshold, and the door will not open again."

A memory rushed into Pamela's mind. Peyton refusing to play with her. Her friend Aster torn apart by her mother. Her mother cursing at her. Her sister falling down the stairs. She could tell that Mandy was playing the memory.

"Stop it!" Pamela demanded.

"There is no family."

Mandy replayed the memory again, so quick but sharp like a blade.

"Quit reminding me!"

"Yelling. Tearing. Cursing. Breaking. Yelling. Tearing. Cursing. Breaking. Yelling. Tearing. Cursing. Breaking. We come apart, and then we fall. There is no running away from it all!"

Pamela's heart burned with the resentment she felt toward her family. She hated what she was feeling, and she did not know how to contain the fire. There was an urge to cause destruction. But she still wanted to refuse.

"I won't kill. I won't. I won't. I won't!"

"You won't, but I will."

Mandy laughed a cruel laugh, and then Pamela started to cry.

But then the laughing stopped, and Pamela could hear someone approaching. Looking through the eyes of Mandy, she saw a blue werewolf with a dead human forearm hanging limply from its left elbow.

"Get out of that costume," Stitch Tyke said. "Mandy should be *me*. You don't deserve to wear that."

"You can have it!" Pamela yelled.

"No!" Mandy countered. "I am me! I control myself!"

"She's too weak to tame you," Stitch Tyke said. "But I'm stronger. The chancellor said I'll be in control if I wear you. I could be a *wear-*wolf. And with you under my control, your mommy and daddy will bow before me!"

"Leave them out of this!"

Standing on all fours, Mandy charged at Stitch Tyke, who swiped her away with his working arm. And Pamela, along for the ride, fell to the ground with Mandy. Her head hurt from the fall, but Mandy did not give her a chance to rest. Mandy got up, raising her arms to block Stitch Tyke as he clawed at her. There were three thin diagonal tears through the face, and Pamela could see through them. Pamela wanted to be free, and part of her rooted for Stitch Tyke to claw Mandy's entire face off. But the other part of Pamela felt guilty about wishing such a thing. She remembered all the times when Mandy seemed like a true friend. But now she listened to the rage in Mandy's shouting.

"You're not worthy, wolf! Look how you damage me!"

"Just a few stitches will fix that up!" Stitch Tyke replied.

"Stitch THIS!"

Mandy tugged on the dead forearm until it was no longer attached to the elbow. The stitches were ripped. No blood spilled since the wound had been cauterized. Then Mandy slapped Stitch Tyke in the face with the hand side of the forearm.

"That's mine!"

"If this is about stealing bodies, then this is fair play! Now fetch!"

Mandy threw the forearm over Stitch Tyke's head. He turned around and ran after it. As he picked it up with his remaining arm, Mandy charged at him. Stitch Tyke turned around just in time to have his lungs impaled by Mandy's horns. Pamela felt the opposing force of the motion, and it sickened her. As Mandy withdrew her horns, Stitch Tyke turned into a human. Once he was dead, the corpse fell to the ground. Once again, Pamela was mortified to see another dead person. Another death that she could not prevent.

Chapter 40
OccuPied

With the light on, Jade had been lying in August's bed and staring at the ceiling for a while. When he finally awoke, he sat up from the floor. Jade turned to look at him and saw how scared he looked.

"Are you okay?" she asked.

"Just felt like I was being watched... Speaking of watches, what time is it?"

Jade checked her phone.

"A little after three in the morning."

"Huh."

Lying down again, August stared at the ceiling. There was silence, and Jade felt like she had to break that silence. But she was not sure how. Then she remembered an old wound that gnawed at her now and then. She did not enjoy talking about it, but August, being in so much pain, seemed like the right person to talk to about it.

"You know," Jade said, "school's not the only reason I've had to go to counseling."

"Oh yeah?"

"Went for something family related. When I was a kid. Is it okay if I tell you?"

"No judgment from me."

Jade inhaled, then exhaled. Then she told the tale.

"When I was little, I was afraid of sleeping in my room. I thought there were monsters under the bed. And my little brother, he wanted to be brave. So he promised to protect me. He brought a sleeping bag and slept under the bed."

"How long did that last?"

"This went on for a couple of years. It's so silly, but I felt so *safe* knowing it was him taking up the space under the bed. It wasn't just some darkness. But as we grew older, I thought I didn't need him to keep the monsters at bay anymore. Because I felt for sure that there were no monsters. But he didn't wanna stop sleeping under the bed."

"Why not?"

"He confessed that he felt safer there. Said I was his guardian angel hovering above him, keeping him from harm. Our parents didn't wanna buy a bunk bed. They still had his bed in the room he hadn't used in years. I told him to go to his room, but he was scared. He stayed under my bed. One night, while he was asleep, I went to the bed in the guest room and slept there. I wanted to prove he could sleep soundly without me. In the morning, I went back to my room. But when I looked under the bed, he wasn't there anymore."

"What happened to him?"

"I don't know. Part of me thought he got sucked up into some void. My parents thought he ran away. They called the police and there were fliers everywhere. Nobody found him. For a while I was mad at myself for not staying. And for a while I was mad at *him* for doing something as petty as leaving to prove a point. But with no return from him, I feared the worst..."

"I'm sorry. I don't—"

"I know. There's nothing to say. It happened, and you have nothing new to contribute to it. That's fine. Doesn't mean I don't appreciate you listening." She sat up and looked at him. "What were you gonna do if you slept alone?"

"It's not what I was gonna do so much as what could be done to me."

"You don't think you're in control of your own fate?"

"It gets complicated when there are other unknown factors."

"Hmm. Unknown."

"My sincere condolences about your brother. I can't imagine what that's like."

"Don't worry about it. I stopped hoping he'd turn up. I used to think he'd crawl out from under the bed and be back. But I had to move on. You can't be happy hoping things will get better. You have to be happy with what you have now."

"Are you happy with what you have now?"

"There's a bit to be desired, but that's life."

"What was his name?"

"My brother? His name was Donnie."

"Donnie Teal. Has a nice ring to it."

"A ring without an answer. If he were still alive, I wonder if he'd even wanna keep using that name. He was ten back then. He'd be twenty-two now, two years older than me. Weird thing is that he couldn't remember anything about the first five years of his life. I was very young, but I remember how worried our parents were about him. Donnie adapted, though. And he seemed to be doing all right from then until his disappearance. I hope he was able to adapt, wherever he went."

The sound of footsteps in the lavatory.

"Did you hear that?"

"I did."

They both got up. Together, they turned on the lavatory light and entered. There, in the mirror, was the face that had been haunting August.

"Oh my damn!" August yelled.

"I see it too!" Jade replied.

The man in the mirror was washing his hands.

"I don't think he can hear us," August said.

"That mirror behind him," Jade said. "There's no reflection."

"Oh my damn. You're right. So, what? He's a vampire? Wait. Get me my sunglasses from my desk."

Jade grabbed the sunglasses from his desk. He held them up in front of the mirror, facing himself as if the figure in the mirror were wearing sunglasses.

"I've seen him before," August said. "At CPU. The chancellor. Mathias Moseley."

"You didn't recognize him before?"

"Maybe I did and forgot. My memory's been a bit shit since I've been here."

Jade got out her phone and recorded video of herself and August.

"This is Jade Teal. I'm here with August Wilhelm in room 314 at Tree Culler Hotel in London." She flipped the view on the cell phone so that the mirror was within the frame. "This is *not* us in the mirror. This is…"

"That is Chancellor Mathias Moseley," August continued. "And if you look in the mirror behind him, he has *no* reflection. I *swear* this is not edited! This is real! Chancellor Moseley of Copper Petal University is a vampire or something and must be stopped!"

Jade stopped recording.

"Sending it won't work," August said. "The internet is a bit in this room."

"Then let's leave!"

"No! Remember what I told you? Every time I leave this room I forget what happened. What if you do too?"

"You sure it doesn't just affect you?"

"Should we take any chances?"

"Hold the phone."

Jade handed the cell phone to him, and then she walked through the doorway out into the hall. She turned around and looked back at August.

"Do you remember anything?" he asked.

"Huh? What's going on?"

"Jade, what's the last thing you remember?"

"You said you didn't wanna be alone. I was about to go in, but... How did you get in that fast? How much time has passed?"

"Watch the video on this phone."

He played it, and Jade listened to herself.

"Oh no... That's really me talking."

"You don't remember seeing that?"

"No! Come on! We need to show this to someone!"

"I'll forget if I do! Whenever I leave this room, I forget what happened inside! There has to be some other way." August looked at the curtains that covered the window. "I have to climb down."

"You're crazy! Are you trying to kill yourself?"

"I don't know! This is all too much! I don't wanna lose myself but maybe I am! What's the point!"

August opened the curtains and the window. He started climbing down from the ledge. Jade ran over to the window.

"Don't!"

"No! You ran into the room! You'll forget!"

Down below August was a solid sidewalk on which he would surely die if he fell. The howling wind could breathe life to that possibility.

"Get back up here, August! There's gotta be some other way!"

She grabbed onto his left wrist with both hands. Struggling, she pulled him up and back into the room. Then he sat at his desk, crying in the corner.

"What's the point?" He slammed a fist onto the desk. Then he got up and walked over to the window. "What's the point?"

Jade held onto his arms as he looked out and down at the street. He tried moving out of her grasp, but she kept a firm grip.

"Don't you dare!" Jade said.

"I am above it all. I can jump down and crush it all. I can dive straight to the core and blow it all apart!"

Jade looked back at the room door, which had swung inward. Examining the numbers, she noticed a decimal point between the 3 and the 1.

"The point," she repeated.

Jade pulled August back and threw him onto the bed. Then she shut the window and walked up to the door. With her fingers, she tried pulling the decimal point off so that the room number would be 314 rather than 3.14. It would not budge. Instead, it gave her a static shock.

"Ow! I think this stone is what's messing with your head."

Jade tried to think this over. Walking out through this doorway would mean losing memory. She pondered what the opposite would be. Walking into the room meant retaining memory, but then it would be erased once one walked out.

Walking in.

She tried to think about the hallway as a different type of area. Not a place that was outside, but rather a place that was *inside*. The hallway was closer to the center of the building than this room was, so to her it made sense to think of the doorway as an entrance rather than an exit. She walked through the doorway and stood for a long moment. Then she turned around.

"I still remember! August, I've figured it out! Think of the hallway as being inside, not outside!"

"I can't!" August flopped left and right on the bed. "It's outside the room!"

"But it's closer to the core of the building! Think of it as being inside!"

"The core..."

August got up, stood for a long moment, and then walked through the doorway. And then he got an excruciating headache as all the memories of the murders in the mirror rushed back into his mind. He dropped to his knees and held onto the sides of his head.

"AHHHH!"

"August?"

"No! I remember. I remember it all, and it's horrible. So much death. It can't keep happening. It can't keep happening!"

"It won't," Jade said. "We'll find a way. We'll get through this."

"I need to warn my friends at CPU. They need to know about Moseley."

Chapter 41
Disaster Risks

aylight had been fading at Copper Petal. The Nap Kin had been patrolling the campus for hours, searching for the monsters despite the risks that came with the task. Naomi had suggested grabbing some equipment from the apartment she shared with some of the others. Now, each Nap Kin had silverware: forks, knives, and even spoons. At least two of each per person, in their hands and jacket pockets. Gertrude was the only one carrying a backpack. She had a feeling she would need it. In her quest to avenge her brother, she wanted to be prepared.

A notification sounded off. Grady pulled out his cell phone.

"Someone sent me a video," Grady said to the rest of the group. "A friend of August, apparently."

Grady played the video for them, and they gasped when they saw the man in the mirror.

"Is that Chancellor Moseley?" Chelsea asked.

"Seems like he might be a vampire," Grady said.

"Literally?" Peyton asked.

"Yes, literally! It sounds like August is in trouble. He wouldn't lie about this stuff. We have to believe this!"

"All right, Grady. We've seen werewolves and a fire-filled family. So of course there would be a vampire! The thing is, if this is true, then what else is true?" Peyton scratched the back of her head. "There's something in the back of my mind. I feel like it's something that can help us."

"We need all the help we can get," Gertrude said. "If it's anything that can bring me closer to killing that motherducker Moseley and those other monsters, then I'm all ears. Because this disaster needs to end!"

"Disaster..." Peyton repeated. "That's it! Maybe that can help us save Pam!"

"Huh?"

"I need to talk to my parents. This isn't something that can be done on the phone."

"Care to fill us in?" Frederick Filler asked.

She filled them in. And, sure enough, her reasoning made some sense.

"We can't just leave now," Grady said. "Not with Moseley at large."

"And these werewolves," Gertrude said. "The sun is setting and they'll be out and about again! They all have to be stopped!"

"I know," Peyton said. "But we also have to save Pam."

"Ugh!" Chelsea said, facepalming. "I'm so stupid! Okay, so Shelley and I once heard about this tunnel when we were browsing online. It's like a must for CPU students to explore it. Well, we found the opening to it a couple of years ago. Rumor is this tunnel leads straight to the chancellor's office. Based on where the end of it seems to be in relation to the campus map."

"We can take him by surprise," Shelley said. "Shove garlic down his throat! We strike him first, then we go after the pack!"

"But here's the other thing," Chelsea said. "If the werewolves know about it, then it would be the perfect place to hide from the sun."

"Damn," Shelley said. "We'd be going in as they're coming out."

"It's a risk we have to take," Gertrude said. "I'm going. If anyone wants to come, just be aware of what we're facing. You may also feel free to go with Peyton."

"None of you need to," Peyton said. "You clearly need to cover more ground here."

"I'll go with you," Frederick said. "This is all my fault."

"I appreciate your support, but what really can you do? We just need one person to talk to my parents, and that's me. You can be more use here."

"All right. I'll stay. Damn, everything's just snowballing."

"Just keep on moving. Don't freeze."

Chapter 42

The Answer

Jade looked at room 315, curious about what was behind the door.

"Does nobody live in that room?"

August looked at it too.

"I'm not sure. But come to think of it, I've felt the peephole watching me while I suffered."

"I think it's more than just a feeling."

"Wait! I remember now. Cassie."

"Your pen pal?"

"I saw her six months ago. She used her key and then disappeared. I remember now. Oh god, she's been gone that long. I don't believe this. We *have* to get her out!"

Jade was worried that Cassie might have been dead by this point, and that going into the room might be futile. Still, she could tell how concerned August was for his friend. He needed the closure. To see what happened to the one who had disappeared.

"How do we get in without a key?" she asked.

"We might not need one."

Slowly, August reached for the doorknob. As soon as he touched the metal, he was sucked into the keyhole. Jade was shocked (though not by the static shock that one might get from a doorknob in a hot environment). Hesitant, Jade did the same, and she felt her body shrink and shoot through the keyhole before being restored to her normal size, all within a second. She was dizzy when she landed in the room. And judging by how August was struggling to stay upright, he was dizzy as well. After a few seconds, her vision came back into focus.

The room was dark, but a light up above flickered repeatedly, allowing her to make out some details. A light bulb hung from a white cylinder and was surrounded by two white rings. The ceiling was comprised of long thin wooden planks, but some planks protruded downward diagonally, toward August and Jade's right.

In front of them was a passport. August stooped down and opened it to the page that showed his face.

"So this is where it's been," he said, putting the passport in his pants pocket.

The walls of the room were white and had cracks, though the crevices did not look so deep. Drapes covered the windows. In a corner of the room were the pots, pans, and utensils that had gone missing, as well as some chicken bones, food wrappers, and bottles of condiments.

Oh, and there were also some human skeletons. Jade did not want to count how many there were.

After a minute, the light stopped flickering.

"Is there a light switch?" Jade asked.

"I can't see one," August said, recognizing that this was a catch-22 situation.

"Maybe if we can uncover the window. The city lights, you know?"

"Good idea."

They stood silent for another moment.

"Are you gonna uncover it?" Jade asked.

"I thought *you* were."

"Oh. Okay."

They stood silently for another moment.

"Jade?"

"Yeah."

"I don't wanna move."

"Come to think of it, I'm not sure *I* can move either."

They were frozen, unable to move.

Chapter 43
Pack Attack

Chelsea and Shelley led the group across the street from campus and down a hill. Once they got past some thickets, they found the mouth of the sewer tunnel. Water sat still, forming a wide line that ran down the middle.

"We're gonna have to waddle," Chelsea said.

Gertrude turned on the light of her cell phone. She was the first to enter, waddling as Chelsea had instructed, avoiding the questionable water. The rest followed into the darkness.

As they delved further and further, they came across some writing on the wall of the tunnel:

"The Landlord"
Five mischievous travelers in an open field
See a village towered by mountains, their fates sealed
They approach the landlord in the open daylight
A weak old man who gives them a key for a night
At dusk, a wolf howls, shadow in the sunset
At midnight, standing wolfmen come from the summit
Towering figures pouncing on two of the five
The pack feeds until they are no longer alive
Breaking down the door to get two of the three left
No meat left on the floor, except a chin with a cleft
Survivor locked in the basement during the feast

Hears their departure as the sun rises from east
Sunlight shines through the window where the bat appears
The survivor believes that he is safe and cheers
Until he sees the bat's wickedness begin
Breaking glass, the sinister dragon black as sin
In its place, the elderly fanged landlord's pale shape
In the space of its outspread wings is now a cape
Teeth impale the skin, thus causing a crimson flood
The basement walls now splashed by many pints of blood
Vampire's wolf tongue licks walls, cleaning for a guest
Next time, he howls as the sun sets in the west

"The duckin' chancellor probably wrote this about himself," Shelley said. "What a tool."

"Hopefully," Chelsea began, "he's not the sharpest tool in the shed."

* * *

The seven werewolves had been wandering through the darkness of the sewers, getting lost and disagreeing with each other about which way to go. There came a point when Fork Feed, Juggle Mint, and Low Knife got separated from the rest. Cackle Bucket, Host L, Mortimer Mutterer, and Shed Cheese eventually found their way back to the main passage, which led to a door. They banged their furry fists on the door.

"Open up!" Host L demanded. "Open up, Mathias! We deserve an explanation!"

The vampire opened his door, revealing his office. He was holding the moonlit amulet.

"If you attack, I will break this. No more feeling the moonlight's kiss."

The werewolves entered, dialing back their aggressive dispositions.

"We have come for the missing link," Host L said.

"Ah, so you all remember. Is *that* the cause for many a dismember?"

"Show us."

Mathias put the minifridge on his desk. He opened it, revealing the last frozen sausage that remained in a plastic pack. He held it in his hand and dipped it in a glass of hot water.

"You could all fight to the death over this, but I would much rather be the one in bliss."

Mathias took a bite out of the raw sausage, despite the raw sewage scent of the werewolves.

They heard steps and turned to the door, seeing Gertrude peeking in through the opening. The wolves snarled, and Gertrude closed the door. Mathias stood up from his desk and pointed toward the door.

"For seeing me eat raw meat, I do not forgive. Go after her, my pack! She must not be allowed to live!"

* * *

Utensils in her hands, Gertrude was pushing herself against the door, trying to keep the werewolves from getting through.

"Werewolves!" she warned her friends. "Go! They only saw me. Y'all need to run. Is there a shortcut out?"

"Yes," Shelley said. "We can climb up this manhole and give 'em the slip."

"Go for it. I'll just have to make a run for it through this whole tunnel."

"We can't just leave you," Reginald said.

"Get the duck outta here. I *mean* it."

"I know you want to take them down yourself, but this is a *team* effort! We're the Nap Kin!"

"Fine! Maybe part of me *does* want to take them all down! But I'm just now realizing it might not be a fair fight against them. We've got

407

silver, but it's dark and they may be quick. I don't wanna lose anyone. Not again."

"I'll stay," Frederick said. "All of this started around the same time, and I'm sure it's my fault. Let me try to help."

"Damn it, Frederick! Fine! But know that you're taking a risk! The rest of you, scram!"

* * *

Holding their cell phones for dear light, her friends ran back through the way they came, until Chelsea pointed out the ladder to the manhole. They all turned off their cell phone lights, putting their phones and their utensils in their pockets. Chelsea started to climb up. As Chelsea started to move the cover, a car drove over it, the resulting force causing her to fall on her comrades.

"Ow!"

Chelsea tried to get up. She was limping.

"Come on," Shelley said, motioning for Chelsea to lean on her.

"Everyone else go ahead," Chelsea said. "I don't wanna slow y'all down."

"You're gonna make it," Shelley assured her.

Grady climbed ahead, removed the manhole cover, and made it onto the street. Reginald motioned for Naomi to go ahead of him, and she did. He followed. Then Shelley. With Chelsea last, Shelley struggled to pull her up.

* * *

Gertrude could feel the door loosening. She knew that they could not hold it much longer.

"We're gonna need to sprint," Gertrude said.

Frederick nodded.

So they sprinted. Though, wanting to avoid the sewer water, they did a speed waddle. The werewolves, having no shoes, did the same.

Gertrude and Frederick got the utensils out of their pockets and tried throwing them back at the werewolves. Two of them—Host L and Mortimer Mutterer—got hit and fell back. But the other two—Cackle Bucket and Shed Cheese—dodged and continued onward.

"Dang it!" Frederick said.

Gertrude saw Chelsea's legs as she was being lifted through the hole.

Shit! Gertrude thought.

"This way!" Gertrude said.

"Follow us!" Frederick added.

Shed Cheese continued to follow Gertrude and Frederick, but Cackle Bucket stopped by the ladder.

* * *

"Almost out," Shelley said.

Chelsea was being pulled down. Cackle Bucket had sunk his werewolf nails in.

"A claw!" Chelsea cried. "It's in my ankle."

"Help me!" Shelley told the others, who held onto the wrists before she finished making her request.

"Duck!" Chelsea cried. "Another one! So sharp!"

Cackling and clawing filled the tunnel. The friends could hear, and it frightened them. It was a tug of war, the werewolf's strength rivaling Chelsea's four friends. Ultimately, the werewolf was stronger, and it got Chelsea out of their collective grip. Chelsea fell down into the hole.

"No!" Shelley yelled. Then she patted her pockets. "Get out your silver, you duckin' idiots!"

She got knives out of her pockets and jumped down into the hole, landing on Cackle Bucket's back. He had already scratched Chelsea's face and was about to make a killing bite. But then Shelley shoved the knives into the skin between his shoulder blades, leaving burn marks. They were butter knives, but Cackle Bucket's howl echoed agony through the tunnel. Shelley struggled to pull the knives out, but she removed them, and then tried stabbing again. But then Cackle Bucket turned around and jumped backward, slamming Shelley into the tunnel wall.

Shelley slid down, landing beside Chelsea, who had three scratch marks on her left cheek. They were Seashells in the dark. Sisterly friends lying underground.

And then they saw the utensils falling. A spoon landed on Shelley's face. And a fork barely missed Chelsea's. But then a knife grazed Cackle Buckets ear, leaving a cut that made him scream. The burn had split his right ear down the middle.

Chelsea grabbed a fork and stuck it into his heel, causing him to trip and fall into the water. Shelley took Chelsea by the hand, helping her stand up. The Nap Kin kept throwing utensils down, trying to miss the Seashells, who managed to dodge as they climbed up the ladder.

When they made it out, the Nap Kin put the manhole cover back over the hole and sat on it.

"Wow," Naomi said. "Pulling you away from the claw. Talk about a *Toy Story* situation."

"Look," Reginald said, pointing at a moving truck that was approaching. "There's another such situation."

"An opportune one," Naomi said. "Run!"

Naomi picked up the manhole cover. Aiming for the truck to benefit them, they got up and ran to the sidewalk. As soon as Cackle Bucket's head poked out of the hole, the moving truck's tires split his head in half. As they ran, they heard the shout of another werewolf.

"Cackle Bucket has kicked the bucket!" Host L.

"We will find you all!" Mortimer Mutterer yelled.

No doubt that the two of them would climb the ladder, being more careful than their fallen packmate.

* * *

As Gertrude alongside Frederick, she remembered her backpack. Zipping it open, she reached inside. When she found the jar of silver glitter, she felt thankful that she had not cleaned out the backpack in all these months. Gertrude smiled, stopped, and turned around.

"Silver as ever!"

Opening it, she tossed some glitter at Shed Cheese. Each flake burned a hole into his fur, skin, and bones. The spots with greater concentrations of glitter created bigger holes, making him look like Swiss cheese. A huge chunk of his scalp by his left ear disintegrated, and then the ear fell off. This left a bit of his skull exposed, blood spilling out of his head.

"Glitter is worse than sand!" Shed Cheese cried. "Sand alligator lips left glitter!"

A couple of the holes were on his wrists. The thin bits of skin on the sides of his wrists could not support his paws, causing them to fall, hanging by thin strings of meat matter.

He kept walking forward, and Gertrude kept shaking the jar. Some flakes burned holes into his ankles, causing the rest of his body to rip off of the heels. Shed Cheese kept trying to crawl. But without claws, it was difficult. He tried elbowing his way forward.

At this point, Gertrude and Frederick did not even need to run anymore. They just watched the creature crawl slowly, curious about what would happen. The glitter just kept on burning through his skin. It was like watching a moving snail that had been given some salt. And he was certainly salty.

"You cheeseless tacos! I will feast upon you!"

As soon as Shed Cheese's head was in front of Gertrude's feet, she poured more glitter. Some got on his lips, which then fell off.

"I ill east uh on ya!"

Shed Cheese stuck out his tongue, wiggling it defiantly. Gertrude shook out more glitter, which burned his tongue in half, leaving a pink chunk in the sewer water.

"I ih eeh uh oh ooh!"

Gertrude kept pouring, and then some got into his eyes, and some burned through his skull and into his brain. They watched Shed Cheese melt until he could move no more.

"I...kinda liked that," Gertrude said.

"Doesn't look like we have much left," Frederick said.

Only small bits of glitter remained stuck to the inner walls of the glass jar.

"Still have any utensils on you?" Gertrude asked.

"Negative. Threw all mine back there."

"Same. And it's dark... Frederick, mind if I put glitter on your slackline?"

"Sure. I'd probably never walk on it again, but I suppose that's just as well, all things considered."

"Great. We really need silver slacklining."

* * *

Randy sat alone in the wilderness. He had lost track of how many hours he had been sitting out here. He felt as if he belonged nowhere anymore. Everything was spiraling out of control, and he did not know how to react. He had gotten the campus police's text alerts about the werewolves running around campus, as well as Stagmantel and Unicoren going bad. No word on what was going on with Mandy. And it worried him. He had no idea whether Peyton had gotten to her sister in time before all this. And he was afraid to find out what had happened to the one whom he had considered a kindred spirit with whom he could run and pretend. Since he was no longer part of the group chat, it seemed pointless to ask. He was not sure that any response would make him feel any better.

Hearing steps coming toward him, he turned around and saw three werewolves approaching him. These were Fork Feed, Juggle Mint, and Low Knife. They seemed very hungry.

"How about a bite?" Juggle Mint suggested, licking her sharp teeth.

Randy was open to just ending himself right at this moment. No friends, and no people dying all around him.

"Go ahead and do it! I've got nothing left."

"Here's the situation," Low Knife said with his fiendish grin. "We are a bit low in our pack."

"On food?" Randy asked. "Or on wolves?"

Fork Feed had a wide smile as she got closer.

"This is what it means! This is what it means! This is what it means!"

Passively, Randy held out his hand. Maybe he would become one with the pack, a friendship with hounds bound by blood. And then he could become stronger. A predator who could die with his prey in a heroic act. Or maybe he would be the prey, dying a pathetic death he might have deserved. Were the brick walls of his studio sturdy enough to withstand the wolf's blow?

The teeth were aimed right at his wrist, which would mean either death or a twisted form of friendship.

But then the sound of breaking glass distracted the werewolves. They turned back. There was Gertrude, holding up shards of glass. She threw them upward. Apparently on impulse, Juggle Mint caught a couple of the shards, which burned her paws. Randy could see the shine of silver glitter on her paws, disappearing into apertures. And then Gertrude picked up another shard and went for the throat, slicing it open. Then she jammed the shard inside, letting it fall and burn through Juggle Mint's insides. Juggle Mint fell backward onto the ground, wriggling for a few seconds until she became motionless.

As Gertrude went after Low Knife with glitter-covered hands, Frederick Filler jumped onto the back of Fork Feed, who jumped backward to slam Frederick onto the ground. It tried biting at Frederick's face, but Frederick tried moving his head away from Fork Feed's teeth. Making another attempt, Fork Feed got some of Frederick's hair in her teeth. She pulled the hairs, and bits of skin attached to them, off of his scalp. He screamed, a spot of blood covering the naked spot just above his forehead.

Gertrude was pressing her hands against Low Knife's upper paws, burning them. She turned around and saw Frederick on the ground. Fork Feed stepped on his hand, but then her paw burned, for he was equipped with something: his glitter-decorated slackline.

With Low Knife in pain, Gertrude put a glitter-covered hand over the eyes of Fork Feed, burning and blinding him. Frederick pulled himself up. He got behind Fork Feed and strangled the werewolf, burning through her throat until she was beheaded. Then he wrapped the slackline around Low Knife's lower paws, burning them off, causing him to fall backward. Frederick got out a knife and stabbed Low Knife multiple times in the stomach, and then in the head.

Even if it was temporary, Randy could see that his former roommate was full of purpose. Frederick Filler: Werewolf Killer.

"You saved me," Randy said.

"No duh," Gertrude said crassly.

What does this mean? Randy wondered. *There's no way she's forgiven me, is there?*

"This might not be most appropriate coming from me," Frederick said. "But you need to be careful."

"What do I do?" Randy asked, unsure about his next move.

"You can come with us," Frederick said, turning to Gertrude's stern expression.

"Fine," Gertrude said. "We need to catch up to the others. God, I hope they're still alive."

Naomi, Randy thought immediately.

No matter what had transpired, Randy did not want Naomi—or any of the other Nap Kin, for that matter—to die. Especially now that deaths were becoming very real.

* * *

Host L and Mortimer Mutterer caught up to the Nap Kin, who had run into the wilderness outside of campus.

"Don't seem so old now, do I?" Mortimer Mutterer said.

"That voice!" Naomi said "Mortimer? Mortimer it's us. Your students. Your friends."

Mortimer paused for a moment.

"Don't give in to such sentiment," Host L said. "You're weak, old man."

Mortimer clawed her face, leaving four diagonal marks.

"I'm *not* old. I'm in my forties!"

Host L pounced on him and sank her claws into his shoulders. Naomi ran over to them and hit Host L in the face with the manhole cover.

"Get off our friend!"

"He's not your friend anymore!"

Another bash. Naomi Clutcher, clutching the manhole cover, just get repeating, knocking Host L off of Mortimer. She bludgeoned Host L in the head over and over until there was no life left within the werewolf.

Mortimer got up and snatched the manhole cover out of Naomi's clutches. He almost hit her with it, but Reginald ran behind him and pulled it backward. Mortimer hit him in the side with it, causing him to fall over.

"Get away from her!" Reginald yelled.

"Mortimer," Naomi said. "It's us. Don't you remember?"

A montage of all the times they visited his office came to mind. All the times when they came to him in their hours of need. His office hours. Which were filled with their presences rather than those of students who needed help with his class. While it was not his preferred option, they kept him company. And yet, there was a part of him that was still annoyed about the fact that they had often come to him with their problems.

"You should've all just left me alone. What about *my* problems? What about what *I* want?"

He crept closer to the group. Still, a part of him tugged himself back. A part of him that did not want to hurt these familiar faces.

Grady stepped forward.

"Leave them alone," Grady said. "Just you and me."

Grady ran at Mortimer and kicked him in the face, knocking him down. His friends stood by, watching in disbelief.

"Go!"

By this time, Mortimer could not recognize Grady's face since it had been so long. So he had no problem attacking. He leaped at the freshman and swung a claw across Grady's face, leaving scars that made him even less recognizable. The other friends ran at him in an effort to fight back, but he swiped them away left and right. Grady jumped on his back and tried holding his muzzle shut. Mortimer grabbed him and flipped him onto the ground.

"You'll be nothing but scraps!"

He clawed at Grady and tore his face with his teeth.

"Grady!"

Mortimer recognized that voice. It was Gertrude. He looked up, and there she was with Randy and some other guy whom he did not recognize. Someone whom he imagined would be very filling.

Grady used his remaining energy to shove Mortimer's head away. He struggled to jump to his feet and aimed his own teeth at Mortimer's jugular. He tore out the tissue, no longer holding back the blood, which was now crying out of the skin. Grady then punched through the hole in the throat, even getting his hand stuck in the process. Apparently in a state of delirium, he instinctively moved the hand up through the throat, hoping to control the head like a puppet. His face expressed confusion over why his own hand movement was not moving Mortimer's lips. The former professor was changing back to his human form.

Losing blood, they knew it was the end for both of them. And so they both fell to the ground, Randy's words being the last catch for their ears.

"That should've been me."

Chapter 44
Sheer Sharing

Peyton pulled into the driveway of her parents' home. Her mom and dad came out to meet her. Peyton got out of the car and closed its door behind her.

"You sounded so worried over the phone," her dad said. "What's going on?"

"Pam's in trouble."

"Oh no," her mom reacted. "What's happened to her?"

Peyton knew that the events at the school sounded so outlandish that her parents would not believe her. She had to tell them at least a fraction of the truth that would be enough to get them involved.

"She's...running away."

"What?"

"She's somewhere around the school. But I think we can draw her out in the open. I just need your help talking to her. To calm her down. Apologize for getting rid of Aster."

"Aster?" her dad repeated. "The monkey? Peyton, that was *years* ago. You really think she's still upset about that?"

"Yes! It's been eating her up ever since. I *know* that Pam's not normal and that she should've grown out of this and gotten over it by now. But the fact of the matter is that she lost a friend and she won't be at peace until she gets closure." Peyton started to break into tears. "I just want her to come back."

Her mom wrapped her arms around her.

"I think it's time for you to know."

Peyton looked up from her mom's shoulder.

"Know what?"

"Come inside. We'll show you."

She led her to their bedroom, where they opened the wardrobe, revealing a safe. They entered the combination and unlocked it. Within it were important legal documents. But one thing was not like the others: a monkey in the middle of it all.

"You kept Aster," Peyton said.

"It was your mom's idea," her dad said.

"I couldn't throw it away," her mom said. "She's part of Pam. She's been here this whole time."

No, she hasn't, Peyton thought. *Nobody's been looking at her, talking to her.*

"Go start the car," Peyton said. "I'll be there in a moment."

Her parents obeyed and left the room. Peyton picked up the monkey and gazed desperately into its eyes.

"Aster," she whispered. "I know I've been a butt to you. But Pam's in trouble, and I need your help. She never left you. So please, come back..."

"Peyton. It's been years. I used to talk to people through flowers. And then I could only talk through stuffed animals. Will she still believe?"

"After all the crazy stuff that's been going on, she *has* to."

Peyton brought Aster up to speed on all that was going on with Pam.

"Is there anything you can do?"

"For a faithful friend...yes. I can..."

Aster explained a power she possessed.

"Oh!" Peyton said, struck with inspiration. "That gives me an idea! So, I'm thinking..."

Peyton explained the plan to Aster.

"I can work with that."

Peyton smiled, hopeful that the plan would work. And when she received a text message saying that all the werewolves were dead, she was even more hopeful. But then she learned that Grady was dead, and that hurt her. Still, she had to press onward.

Chapter 45
Know Regrets

With the werewolves slain, the Nap Kin just had a few targets remaining: Mathias, Unicoren, Stagmantel, and Mandy. They debated about which one to look for next.

"We need to kill Moseley first," Shelley argued. "The system has failed, and we have to go after the head."

"But his werewolves are dead," Chelsea said. "He's gotta be pretty much powerless now, right?"

"Did you forget that he's a ducking vampire?" Gertrude said. "He might have less power, but he's still at large."

"He doesn't seem too keen on facing Unicoren and Stagmantel," Frederick said. "With those two running around, he's scared to show his face. And understandably so."

"You're saying we should kill them first?"

"I want balance to be restored."

"How the hell are we supposed to balance them? We can't even tell the ducks apart!"

"If we can't balance those two, then I think killing them could restore Mandy's balance."

"Really?" Reginald said. "You really think killing the parents will make the kid stable?"

"If their present chaotic state has made Mandy's chaotic, then maybe getting rid of them *would* restore her health."

"Do you hear yourself?"

421

"We do need Mandy to be stable," Naomi said. "So we can get Pam out. There's an innocent life in that suit, being forced to watch the killings. It needs to stop."

Every phone except for Frederick's and Randy's received a notification. Those who were in the group chat read the message.

"What's going on?" Frederick asked.

"It's Peyton," Gertrude explained. "She says she and her parents are on their way. She wants us to track down Pam but not to confront her."

"All right. Then I guess that's what we'll do."

* * *

As the Nap Kin walked around campus, searching for Mandy, Randy walked up beside Gertrude.

"Can I talk to you about something?" he asked.

"Now's not the time. And I don't think there will *ever* be a time."

"Does that depend on whether we die?"

"No."

"So then we're not friends again."

"Never."

Randy was worried that this would be the response. No chance to restore the friendship whatsoever, it seemed.

"Why did you save me?"

"Because you're a coward. You wouldn't have been able to fight back."

That cut him deeply.

"You're wrong about me. Did I ever even really matter to you?"

"To an extent. Maybe not to the extent you were hoping. I didn't think we'd ever get so close that I'd ever invite you to my future wedding, if that's what you mean. I just thought that, after graduating, we'd only be in touch online. Commenting every once in a while on a topic we had in common. Now I want nothing to do with you."

Randy wondered what Gertrude imagined about him. Surely he was not the only one with revenge fantasies.

"Do you *hope* that I will never find love? That I'll never be happy?"

"It's none of my concern."

There it was. The indifference.

"This hurts so much," Randy said. "You should've let me die."

"No. You have to *live* with the consequences, Randy. Live for your family, but *know* you've lost your friends."

Chapter 46
Thesis Statement

August and Jade had been standing for three hours. Now, the curtains were drawn apart by a wind, and the window had a bright light through which they could not see beyond. The human bones of previous residents were illuminated by the dawn.

"Something is wrong here," Jade said. "Something is very wrong."

"August..." another voice said.

"Did you hear that?" asked August.

"Oh good," Jade said. "You heard it too."

"Cassie?" August said. "Is that you?"

"You took too long to find me, August."

"I'm sorry. I've been forgetting."

"You forgot about me."

"Yes, but it's not what you think."

"I've been watching. You haven't been worried about me. You should know by now that we're not friends."

August was lifted up into the air and slammed against the wall.

"August!" Jade yelled.

"Ow!" August cried, falling to the floor. "Cassie—"

"Nobody thought of me," Cassie continued. "Not my parents, not my friends, and not you. I tried to tell everyone where I was, and nobody came."

August tried getting up from the floor.

"I-I've been having my brain wiped by a stone."

"No excuses. I won't hear your lies. My mind is made up."

"But *my* mind isn't! That's the thing! This stone has been breaking my mind apart!"

"Then it's not doing a good enough job."

Telekinetically, August was lifted quickly so that his head hit the ceiling. Thankfully, it was the spaces between the protruding planks. He fell to the floor, eyes closed.

"August!"

Jade ran over to his body and put her hand above his face. He was still breathing, but unconscious. She looked around, but Cassie was still not visible.

"Leave him!" demanded Cassie. "I have no quarrel with you. *He* needs to pay."

"You're killing him!"

"Nobody cared about me being gone. Why the hell should I care what happens to him?"

"There are things we don't understand. Think about what's going on."

"I have. For six long months. I was tossed aside, like a sponge buried beneath the dishes. And now the mess has piled up. I'm done giving people chances."

August awoke, struggling to rise. Cassie became visible, a soul-piercing scowl adorning her face.

"Jade," August said. "You have to leave. This is between me and Cassie. Tell my friends and family back home that I love them. Some might not remember me, but I want them to know. And tell all our friends downstairs that I love them."

Cassie continued to throw August around the room. She even picked up the bones telekinetically, human and chicken remains battering August.

"You claim to love all," Cassie said. "But you forget."

She continued to slam him around. Jade did not know what to do.

"Run!" August ordered.

Jade ran to the door and touched the knob. Suddenly, she was back in the hallway. She touched the knob again, but it did not let her in.

"Shit!"

* * *

Lying on the floor, bones beside his face, August was relieved to see that Jade had escaped. And then confusion washed over him.

"Cassie. Did you ever try touching the doorknob to get out?"

"What do you think?! I tried everything!"

Cassie ran over to the knob and touched it, but still remained in the room. She then threw August around the floor, using him to wipe it as if he were a mop. His face was dragged against the cold floor until his nose bled.

"Please," pleaded August. "Have mercy."

There was a cackle in the room, and it did not come from Cassie. August saw a dark gray ghost, and he could tell that it was in the shape of Mathias Moseley, its shape including a feather-filled bowler hat and a cape-like robe. Only its eyes glowed color: dark blue pupils, light blue irises, flame-orange scleras, and lime green eyelids.

"Well, well, well," it began. "Well-adjusted August Wilhelm. Wah, wah, wah. The forgotten summer month. So mercurial. Such fickle matter dangling from a dark orifice."

"Are you Mathias?"

"No. I am...Mathesis!"

"Mathesis?" August repeated.

"I am a bridge. I've been in your head from the beginning, but you did not find me until the end. Same goes for these other residents who lie slain beside you. I have the memories of the mirror that have been sucked out of your head, and memories that predate the mirror. A backup drive, so to speak. In one hand, you have a specter. On the other hand, you have a solid. Which one matters more?"

"You've been in my head? So, what? I just stop believing in you and you go away?"

"That's not gonna work."

"Why can't Cassie leave?"

"Because I've made sure that the knob keeps her locked in. I have control over what gets in and out of this room. As for Jade, I'm not concerned. People will probably call her mad. Might be fun having her thrown into some asylum, whining about this, that, and the other. And her disappeared brother."

"Wait," Cassie said. "You're the reason I can't get out?"

"Hah! Silly Cassie. August here was telling the truth, you fuckin' moron. I kept wiping his memory whenever he suspected that something was wrong. A solid memory, in pieces, sinks within quicksand, blending into the quickness of time that erases. *I* am the reason he, and everyone else, kept forgetting about you. The power of Plo-Tunium. I even used it to link your bracelets. With the friendship destroyed, August's bracelet left him, leaving him more vulnerable. The weaker the friendship, the less powerful a friendship bracelet is."

The ghost's eyes projected orange memories of August panicking. All the times he witnessed murder in the mirror and ran around screaming. When the montage ended, Cassie closed her eyes and sank her head, wiping her eyelids regretfully.

"August was telling the truth? Oh my god. I—"

"You fucked up!" Mathesis mocked, telekinetically sending the pots and pans her way, hitting her. Mathesis turned his gaze back to August, who was in agonizing pain. The ghost held a butcher knife. Cassie picked another one up and ran over to August's side.

"No," she said. "I don't want this."

"It doesn't matter what *you* want. You're already gone."

The two of them engaged in a duel of sorts. She ducked, and he parried. Then he ducked, and she parried. Then he telekinetically threw her against the wall.

August reached out for a machete, and he managed to goose the ghost on the butt. Predictably, it felt like stabbing through gas. Mathesis, bothered nevertheless, kicked August in the face. Surprisingly, the limb felt solid to him.

"How *dare* you, August! I offer you sweet vindication, and *this* is how you repay me? She called you a liar! What kind of a friend is she? It's like she doesn't know you at all."

The ghost approached Cassie with the blade, but August ran between them.

"Step aside!" Mathesis said.

"Never," August replied, standing firmly with conviction.

"Really?" Mathesis tilted his head. "After *all* that she has done?"

"It wasn't her fault. You've trapped her. Distorted her view. Set her free, and you'll only deal with me."

"August, no!" Cassie yelled. "I won't let you!"

"You've spent enough time in here. You didn't get to see the sights. It's your turn now." He turned back to the ghost. "Do we have a deal?"

Telekinetically, Mathesis threw Cassie to the doorknob, and she vanished.

"So be it... Eat SHIT!"

Without lifting a finger, Mathesis spun August in a few circles and then threw him down to the floor, and then to the wall.

* * *

Cassie hit her head on the hallway floor. She looked up and saw Jade, who pulled her up.

"No," Cassie said. "August did no wrong. What have I done?"

Cassie tried turning the knob. No luck.

"It won't open for us," Jade said.

"There has to be *something* we can do! Is there no way to break down this door?"

"You know..."

"What?"

"Unless there's some magic that would prevent that, I don't see why not. It's worth a shot. Come on! There are more people downstairs."

Chapter 47

Burning Bridges

Keeping their distance in the night, the Nap Kin finally spotted Mandy walking on the sidewalk around campus. With the school evacuated, there was not much easy prey. There were moving cars in the street, and Mandy stared at the passing vehicles.

"We need to do something," Shelley said. "Mandy might be strong, but I'm not sure Pam can survive getting hit by a car."

Keeping her eyes on the group chat, Gertrude was the first to alert everyone about the new message.

"Peyton's parking in the shopping center. Wants us to lure Mandy her way."

They looked down the street and up at the concrete bridge.

"Sawton Bridge, then," Reginald said. "Tell her to meet us there."

"Got it."

"Hey!" Reginald yelled in Mandy's direction.

The mascot turned around and saw the Nap Kin.

"Come and get us!" Frederick yelled.

Mandy ran their way, and they started running.

* * *

Across the street, Peyton, wearing mittens and carrying Aster, led her parents over to Sawton Bridge. They ran up the stairs. Lights on the ledges illuminated the bridge in the night. They saw the Nap Kin straight ahead, running toward them. And behind them was the mascot, horns on fire.

"Oh my god!" Mr. Sheer said. "Did the mascot set its horns on fire?"

Peyton turned to her parents.

"There's something I didn't mention. So, our school mascot is alive and taking control of Pam, and its parents are also on a rampage shooting fire everywhere."

"God," her dad replied. "The parenting books don't prepare you for something like this."

"Pam!" her mom yelled.

*　*　*

Mandy stopped. Pamela, tired and eyes half-closed, looked up and saw the Nap Kin standing at the end of the bridge, accompanied by her sister and parents.

"Pam, it's us!" her mom yelled.

"We know you're still in there, Pam!" Peyton said, holding up a familiar monkey. "Look! It's Aster!"

"Huh?"

"Pam!" her mom repeated. "I'm sorry for the horrible things I said! I never threw Aster away because I knew how much she meant to you! All this time I was worried about what more time with her could do to you, so I kept her away! But she's here now, and we want you back!"

"Come home, Pam!" her dad added.

This can't be real, Pamela thought. *There's no way Mom's saying this.*

"Now, Aster!" Peyton said. "Show Pam. Make it accurate! An authentic aesthetic!"

Pamela was struck with a vision. She was a little girl again, wearing her rabbit onesie. Around her was the living room of the house in which she used to live—that is, an accurate approximation. Peyton appeared, looking the same age she was on that day that Pamela had gone to the park and gotten in trouble with her parents. Though the walls and picture frames were a bit shaky, there was no sound coming from their movements. This unsettled Pamela for a moment. However, the appearance of Peyton was precise, and her sister's footsteps on the marble floor were very much audible. Though Pamela had not retained every little detail, seeing and hearing Peyton this way tipped her off about what day it was.

"No. No." Pamela started to tear up. "Not *this* again." Pamela grabbed the monkey from her back and made furious and sorrowful eye contact. "Aster, you are *cruel* for making me go through this again. I *have* no friends!"

She fell to her knees, eyes closed, hand angrily gripped on Aster's avatar.

"Pam," Peyton said. "The backyard is sunny. Isn't there something you want to ask me?"

Pamela opened her eyes and looked up, crying a stream.

"I know you're gonna say no."

"Just ask."

Pamela was hesitant. A tiny part of her wanted to ask the question. And yet, she worried that it would all be the same, and that she would sink again. But the tiny voice inside of her spoke up.

"Do you wanna play...with me?"

Peyton smiled. Not overtly gleeful given the dire situation, but sincere.

"Yes. I will play with you, Pam."

"Really?"

"Really."

Pamela stood up, letting her eyes bleed emotions.

"This is silly. We're grown up. We're not really playing here because we're not really here."

"This is real. Not this place, but this scenario. This scenario is now. If you need someone to play with you, to dance with you, whether it be in the park or whatever, I'll be there. Because I love my sister. And, I've come to realize...you're my best friend."

Pamela was not sure what she was feeling. She wiped her face and shook her head.

"You don't mean that."

"Of course I do. It took me way too long to see how lucky I am to already have you in my family. Even if you weren't, I *would* choose you to be my friend. If you were to go away, I would wait forever for you to come back. Because life is so much better *with* you than without you. If I could go back, I would change this moment so that we would have had more time to play. But I can't. I *need* you to take control and get out of this so we can make up for lost time."

Pamela let the monkey slip out of her hands and fall to the floor as she embraced her sister with open arms, tears on both Sheer sisters' faces. They both blinked, and then they saw each other as they appeared in the present. The room of their old house still surrounded them, the house now settled for this perfect moment.

But not for long.

"No," Aster said. *"How could you?"*

"Aster?" Pamela said.

"You've LEFT ME!"

Pamela could feel Peyton getting pulled away. The front door opened, and Peyton flew out.

"PAM!"

The house around Pamela crumbled apart, letting in sunlight revealing a backyard. Beside Aster was a little boy, holding a magnifying glass. Pamela walked closer and gasped when she saw that he was burning an anthill. The fire grew larger, and so did the boy, who aged into the familiar sight of Randy Morales. He cackled and pointed his magnifying glass at her, magnifying his grin.

"YOU WOULDN'T UNDERSTAND!"

The fire circled around them and grew higher, forming twin peaks resembling horns.

"No!" Pamela yelled.

She watched him throw Aster into the dryer, hoping that she would feel hurt as she was being torn apart. And the fire just kept growing.

* * *

Peyton was back on the bridge. She could see Mandy standing motionless. And then the mascot took a step, flames growing on the horns. Looking down, Peyton saw the monkey that she had dropped. She picked it up.

"What are you doing? We had her!"

"She left me behind!"

"Stop being so possessive!"

"As you wish. You're on your own now."

"Aster?"

Silence. Peyton shook the monkey.

"Aster! Aster come back here!"

* * *

The link severed, Pamela was alone in the suit, which moved step by step on all fours. She was no longer in the yard, but memories gushed through her mind. A train of thought.

"I'll protect you, Peyton!"

Mandy's instinct was to run at Peyton to impale her with the horns. But Pamela pushed to make Mandy stand on twos. Once she stood upright, she put her foot forward and then stood firmly, trying to hold back Mandy's movements. Almost stationary, she stood solidly in the middle of the bridge, Mandy shaking, struggling to move forward.

"Please..." Mandy said in a voice filled with agony. *"She...needs... to...die."*

"No!" Pamela said. "She's my sister, and I will protect her until the end."

Pamela could feel the feet getting warm, burning the concrete beneath.

"It's...just...one...friend."

"There's no need to count friends as long as you have a friend you can count on."

"Family...means...nothing. We...all...go...away."

"Then that's what we'll do. We'll disappear."

She could feel the feet burning through the concrete, the two of them sinking downward. Pamela summoned more strength to spread Mandy's feet further apart. But the burning continued, the fire expanding into a circle around them. She knew that they could fall through a gap.

"Take us to the core," Pamela said. "Open down, Sesame Street!"

As they sank further through the concrete, Peyton walked toward her with hands still clad in oven mitts.

"Stay away!" Pamela warned her, clutching the ledge with the hands, which slowly ran down the wall as she sank further. "I won't let Mandy hurt you!"

"It's my turn, Pam."

Their parents walked beside Peyton, who then held out her arms to motion for them to back away.

"Stay back," she told them.

"We can't!" their dad said. "We're not losing either of you! We can't!"

"We won't!" their mom added. "We're taking you home! Both of you!"

"Please," Peyton said. "Trust me. I can do this."

Before she could let them answer, Peyton ran over to Pamela.

"Peyton!" they yelled.

Peyton grabbed Mandy's horns and pulled off the head, allowing Pamela to breathe in the air. The mitts on fire, Peyton threw them off and blew on her hands. There was now a hole in the bridge, and Pamela tried hanging onto the concrete, legs dangling beneath. Peyton struggled to pull her out of the suit. As Mandy's head floated, Mandy's hands punched Peyton in the face.

Peyton lost her grip.

But her parents, now caught up, grabbed Mandy by the wrists.

The head continued to hover, the eyes emitting a red glow conveying violent intent.

* * *

Stagmantel and Unicoren arrived on the side of the bridge behind Mandy, whose head was hovering, having been separated from her body. Something within them snapped.

"Sh-she's hurting our...daught-daught-daughter!" Stagmantel said.

"Where have we been?" Unicoren wondered.

They ran toward the fray, everything becoming clearer as they got closer and closer. As Mr. and Mrs. Sheer pulled Mandy's body and Pamela onto the concrete, Mandy's head floated toward Peyton, clearly set on impaling her through the torso.

But instead, each horn impaled one parent. Two parents who wanted to save their daughter, even if it meant that they would not be able to look after her anymore, even after all this time that the family had been divided. And so, Stagmantel and Unicoren started to bleed from the wounds inflicted upon them by Mandy. This time, there was no fire for cauterization. Only blood.

With the Sheer family reunited, Pamela got out of the suit. Once she was free, Mandy's body appeared to grow denser. Flesh and blood returned to the body, no longer artificial. Mandy's head gained flesh and blood as well. But with the mascot beheaded, there was no returning to life. The light of her eyes, alive for the first time in years, died along with the fire of her horns.

"No!" Stagmantel cried. "You were free, child... Are you free now?"

"Shh..." Unicoren said, watery tears on her face. "It's okay Mandy. You didn't mean to hurt us, or anyone. You did it because we were unstable."

"We are all in pain," Stagmantel said. "A family pain."

They looked at the Sheers, who were now a complete family once again. And then they looked up at the sky and noticed a bat hovering up above. It landed on the bridge and turned into the chancellor.

"No! Dead? Say it is not! This school needs a mascot!"

"Find another one!" Unicoren said. "We should never have given you our child!"

"It should have been my godchild! You pushed me away even after good times compiled!"

"Good times before we found out what you were," Unicoren said.

"You did not like the next face I wore. You saw me as something to abhor."

"Sucking the blood of the living is *not* a good thing!" Stagmantel yelled. "You are nothing but a vile virus violating the living!"

"Me introducing you two is what led to the offspring. You shut me out and saw me as a thing. Now here you two are, having lost it all. Bereft of the love through which some fall."

The parents looked at each other, then down at the horns in their guts. They removed their daughter's lifeless head, letting the blood pour out of their wounds. Mandy's remains caught on calm fire, which burned for a few seconds until the remains turned to ashes, flying into the air.

"The match still has a spark," Stagmantel said.

"We do," Unicoren said. "It is time."

"Just you and me. Freefalling through fire forever."

The two of them embraced each other and jumped sideways off of the bridge.

* * *

Peyton and Pamela rushed over to the railing and looked down. They could only see cars passing by as though the drivers had not noticed what had happened above them.

But then Pamela was overcome with a vision of the couple in a loving embrace, holding onto each other as they fell through a vortex of fire that seemed to be infinite. Their eyes were closed. She could not imagine how anyone could survive this, but, despite everything, she was glad they had each other in the end.

She turned around and ran back to her mom and dad, hugging them for the first time in a long time.

"We missed you, sweetie," her mom said.

"I'm sorry," Pamela said.

Peyton joined in on the hug. Despite some lingering uncertainty, Pamela felt safe. She knew that the chancellor was still present, and she was not sure what would happen now. But she was glad that the family at least had this group hug.

* * *

Randy soaked in what he had just witnessed. Stagmantel and Unicoren showed that they were willing to leave this world leaping into the fire. He was unsure whether that was the right thing to do. And he believed that, if he were to allow his friends to be killed, then that act might send *him* into the fire.

He looked at Chancellor Mathias Moseley. Randy had only seen him once before, giving a welcome speech for incoming freshmen when he started attending CPU. But now the chancellor looked more familiar than ever before. Especially when he removed his shades, revealing milky white eyes on a face resembling that of Mathis Dillard.

Mathis is Mathias?!

This realization of the resemblance made Randy feel more stupid than ever.

Chapter 48
Backup Pan

Out in the ocean water, there was something rising to the surface. Something affected by Plo-Tunium. It floated like a duck, and it had a place to be. But it could only return once a particular feeling of certainty returned. With any luck, it could fly. But there was something that needed to happen.

* * *

August could hear the banging on the door to room 315. He knew that his friends were trying to get in. But Mathesis had a powerful hold on the door, using telekinesis to hold it shut as he wiped the floor with August.

"You have failed, August."

Still reeling from the pain, August cracked a bloody smile.

"No. Cassie is free. She made a mistake...but she will be fine without me." He recalled the sessions with the counselor, Dr. Carol Crooks. How he had to come to terms with accepting that friendships might not all last forever. "Some friendships become fragile and break. But that won't stop Cassie from moving forward. And I...am... happy...for her."

Something broke through the window and flew into the room, wrapping itself around August's left wrist. The friendship bracelet was back. August did not care that it was freezing cold. Mathesis tried striking him, but August raised his wrist to block the attack. The bracelet was like a shield through which the ghost could not get through. A kick here and there only left it frustrated, as long as August could block accurately. Mathesis nearly kicked him in the gut, but August rolled away in time. He got up and then had his back against the wall as the ghost approached him.

The door fell open. Anton, Bessie, Cassie, Fritz, Jade, Tate, and Verner were there, wielding cutlery.

"Get away from our friend!" Cassie yelled.

Anton held an oven tray full of garlic bread. He ran at Mathesis, but the ghost pushed Anton and everyone else back with his thoughts. They dropped their weaponry.

"Try again," Mathesis mocked, giving everyone a bit of time to get up.

"Cassie?" Bessie said. "How do we take him?"

"Sorry?" Cassie replied.

"We need a plan. We should've thought of a plan."

"If we say it out loud," Verner began, "he will *know*. We need to surprise him."

"Well, what's the point?" Bessie asked. "He can read our thoughts, can't he? Isn't he telepathic?"

"Well," Cassie began, "he has telekinesis. That's different."

"He got in August's head," Jade added.

"That's true," Cassie replied.

Mathesis had his arms crossed as he listened to this banter. Then he turned his head to Fritz, who was taking a hot dog out of his jacket pocket. Fritz took a bite.

"What is this?" Mathesis asked.

"I get hungry under pressure," Fritz said with his mouth full.

"Wait," Mathesis said. "This is part of a plan, isn't it?"

The sound of the tray being moved alerted Mathesis, who turned his head to see Anton trying to pick up the tray of garlic bread.

Telekinetically, he slid the tray away from Anton. When it hit the wall and could slide on the floor no further, it slid *up* the wall, its contents falling off. And then the tray flew at Anton, hitting him in the head hard enough to make him fall.

Mathesis laughed, but then he stopped as his right eye disappeared. The half-eaten hot dog had flown through the ghost's head and eye. With his remaining left eye, he saw it fall onto the floor in front of him. The wiener rolled out of the buns, revealing a garlic yellow where the bread used to be white.

Mathesis stepped away from the buns. The tunnel remained in the ghost's head, the gaseous matter not filling the gap.

"Was that part of a plan?" Mathesis asked.

"Yup!" Bessie declared. "Did you really think we'd come in here without a plan? Did it work?"

"You've taken a bit away from me, but I still stand! I've lost an eye, but have still enough to see. In this form, it'll take lots of precise throws to get rid of all of me!"

"Then I'll throw *these,* asshole!"

Bessie readied her fists, ran up to Mathesis, and threw punches through him continuously. He stood for a moment in amusement, and then, without lifting a finger, threw her against the wall.

"Ow!" Bessie saw a pan beside her and picked it up. "I mean, throw *this,* asshole!"

She tried throwing the pan, but at the moment that it left her hand, Mathesis backed it up into her face. Bessie fell once again.

"That was stupid," Mathesis said. "Was that *also* part of a plan?"

"No..." Jade answered.

"Fools! The price of friendship is a shared death!"

Chapter 49
A Bridge to Car

Mathias stared at the students with his naked eyes. He opened his mouth, exposing his fangs. The students—and the Sheer parents—gasped and jumped backward. But Mathias remained in place. After a long moment, he brought his lips closer together, leaving just enough space to speak.

"Still no tears drip from these eyes, even after so many tries." His eyes, pearls without watery apparel, turned to the ledge over which Stagmantel and Unicoren had disappeared. "They would rather die than stay with me. It was their own way of being free."

"Can you blame them?!" Peyton yelled. "You took their world away! You were such a shitty friend!"

"It's all your fault!" Pamela added. "They decided not to invite you to a wedding they kept so private that *many* of the people closest to them weren't invited either! Do you even realize how petty you were?"

I have been such a terrible friend, unfortunately, Mathias thought. *Why be a parent when my creation doesn't want me?*

Mathias took a look at Randy.

"While we are revealing who has been shitty, there is one whom you should not pity." He pointed directly at Randy. "Do you think you know this prick? He did not notice the death of Vic!"

"Vic's dead?" Randy asked. "How long?"

Mathias took a cell phone out of his pocket and threw it. The screen cracked as the phone landed right in front of Randy.

443

"For five months, he has been gone, eaten by each werewolf pawn."

"We already know how shitty Randy is!" Gertrude said. "But nobody's gonna die anymore!"

"It's time to step down," Frederick added. "There's been too much bloodshed."

"You're not fit to be chancellor!" Shelley said.

"I am *The Landlord!* Not someone to be abhorred!" He put his shades back on. "This is *my* school, and none of you can stop me! Here in my domain, none of you can be free!"

He rushed at them with a fang-filled mouth. But Gertrude swung her backpack at his face. He fell on the concrete face-first, cracking his shades. He removed the glasses and tossed them over the bridge. Then he removed his grad robe, allowing the wind to carry it away into the night. The amulet on his necklace was more visible now that it was lit by the moonlight. He cackled as he walked slowly toward his enemies.

Gertrude unzipped her backpack and started searching through the contents.

"I've got just the trick," Gertrude told the others. "Oh, where is it?"

"I got you," Shelley said.

"Shelley, no!" Chelsea yelled.

Shelley ran up and punched Mathias' face. A movement of the head, but he did not fall; he stood his ground. She tried hitting him again, but he grabbed her by the wrist and threw her over his head. He turned around to see her side hit the concrete.

Then he felt a fist hit the left side of his face. He feigned a fall and swept his feet to trip Chelsea, whose scarred face fell onto the concrete. He tried to bite her, but then Shelley ran to Chelsea's rescue, kicking the vampire's face as if it were a soccer ball.

He got up and tried to bite Shelley by the throat, but she did a back flip, her shoe hitting his jaw along the way. After her landing, she got close to the vampire again. Shelley kicked, but he dodged and grabbed her by the ankle throwing her to the side. Her back hit the concrete wall, but her head was unharmed. To remedy that, he ran over to Shelley and elbowed her in the face, causing her to land on her face. A tooth fell out of her mouth, leaving a bloody gap on her gums.

Now standing, Chelsea got between Shelley and Mathias. As he ran toward her, Reginald and Naomi rushed into the fray and tried body-slamming him. They pushed him back a foot, but then he shoved them back further. Chelsea ran up to him and tugged on his necktie, causing him to choke a little. She pulled him hard enough to pull his face to the ground.

Shelley got up and grabbed his necklace, choking him further, her hand eventually reaching the cassette tape amulet. But then the amulet broke off, and she fell to the ground. Regaining his strength, Mathias swiped Chelsea's hands away from his tie. Before he could attack her, Shelley used the amulet to bash him in the face. It was certainly thicker than one would think, even leaving a bruise on Mathias' cheek. When the vampire pushed back, Shelley dropped the amulet on the concrete, breaking it up into shards. Quickly, she reached for a couple of shards and shoved them into Mathias' bruised cheek, all while Chelsea just kept punching him anywhere she could.

The Landlord pushed Chelsea to the ground. Thirsty, he jumped and picked Shelley up, raising her a foot off the ground.

"Put me down!"

"As you wish. Now perish!"

He sank his teeth into her neck and started draining her blood. Then he felt an arm wrap around his side.

"For Tim and Grady!" Gertrude cried.

Mathias felt a stab, right in the heart.

"Oh, and Mitch!" Gertrude continued. "A bit late, but still!"

Gertrude, now standing behind him, had shoved a tent stake right through his necktie. Mathias removed his teeth from the skin and threw Shelley off of the bridge.

"Shelley!" Chelsea yelled.

Mathias heard the young woman land on the windshield of a moving car, causing it to collide with another one.

Pushing Gertrude away, the vampire pulled the stake out of his chest. He looked down at his blood-stained tie. A maroon flood over green and blue eyes. He could feel himself crumbling. His flesh. His bones. Breaking apart to be blown in the wind. Thinking about Mathis, he smiled at a comforting thought.

Now he and I will be together forever!

Aware of knowledge hidden from the students, The Landlord, with his dying breath, recited the final words of Darby Morineau.

"Vein Quish the vampire!"

Pieces of his flesh, blood, and bones swirled in the air, forming a mini tornado which imploded into itself until there was nothing left but a spot of ash on the concrete. Even the hat and the rest of the clothes that had just been on him were gone.

* * *

Up in the sky, those who stood on Sawton Bridge could see the ducks and geese ascending, combining into a white energy forming a Plo-Tunium Hole that imploded upon itself.

Chelsea ran down the stairs of the bridge. The cars in the street had stopped. People were out and standing around the scene of the collision. Chelsea shoved people left and right so she could make her way through the crowd. There, she saw her best friend lying on the windshield, its cracks a nearly scarlet spider web. Chelsea ran over to Shelley, who was blinking uncomfortably.

"Shelley, please don't die."

"Don't have...much choice." Shelley coughed. "Did we win?"

"Yeah." Chelsea nodded, letting out the tears. "Gertrude got him."

"Good. Is the curse over?"

"I think it is."

"Fucking finally."

Shelley Bogdal took one last breath, then closed her eyes, passing away from this world. With her best friend gone, it would be an understatement to say that Chelsea Keltie was feeling down. She gave the body a hug even though there was no life left within it.

Chapter 50
Be Trayed

August was essentially backhanding Mathesis in the face, making sure that the bracelet hit the ghost. Mathesis felt the pain, but he spun and swept the floor with a foot, tripping August. He was lying on the floor again, Mathesis looming over him.

Jade tried throwing pots and pans at Mathesis, but he froze them in the air and then moved them back toward her. She dodged a few, but one of the pots got her in the knee, and she started limping.

Tray in hand again, Anton tried running over to the pieces of garlic bread. He managed to scoop up a few, but Mathesis' mind lifted him upward, the garlic bread falling off along the way. A wooden plank impaled Anton through the stomach, and he let go of the tray as he was letting go of life. It all seemed to happen in slow motion. Another ghastly fist was coming toward August's face. Though he had his left wrist up, he impulsively raised his right hand, hoping to stop the punch.

The fist stopped, now solid in August's hand. It still hurt, but August was able to stop it. The hand actually had skin, as well as blood and bone beneath it. Solidity spread to the arm and then the rest of the body. Blood, bone, skin, and clothing were wrapping around the spectral shape, getting sewn together. A wraith solidified. Mathesis seemed to be in agony during this transformation.

The tray hit the killer on the head.

"AHHH! That fucking hurt! What the fuck is happening?!"

Anton slid off of the plank and landed right on top of Mathesis, dying victoriously. The killer pushed the body off.

"Hey!" August said. "Do me a solid!"

August punched Mathesis in the face, giving him a bruise.

"For Anton!" Fritz said running at him with a knife, stabbing him in the stomach. Mathesis used his mind to push him back. He pulled the knife out of his stomach. He bled. Weakly, he tried punching August again. Cassie, however, used a meat cleaver to cut off his hand. As he bled from the stub, Cassie spotted condiments in the corner of the room. She reached for one, believing it to be garlic, and shook it all over the now solid ghost.

"You know what goes good on salad? Garlic. HAH!"

"Um, that's Parmesan," Fritz said.

"Oh..." Scrambling to the floor, she reached for a piece of garlic bread and shoved it into his face. "HAH!"

For several seconds, Mathesis was burning and screaming. And then, engulfed by fire, he faded away. A Plo-Tunium Hole appeared, sucking the fire out of the room. The floor quaked, and everyone backed out of the room. Fritz pulled Anton's body out. Once in the hallway, they witnessed the room and its door being sucked into the hole. The decimal point from the door to room 314 flew from behind them and into the hole. Within moments, the hole imploded, leaving behind a blank wall where the room used to be.

"It's gone," August said. "It's really gone."

"August," Cassie said. "I'm sorry for what I did to you back there. It was uncalled for. I had no idea who I was anymore, and what I meant to anyone."

"It's okay, Cassie. We're fine now. He can't hurt us anymore."

They looked at their wrists where their friendship bracelets remained.

"August!" Jade said. "Your friends at CPU!"

"Oh my damn! I need to check up on them!"

He tried video calling Grady on his phone, but there was no answer. Then he tried Gertrude. He knew that they would need to compare notes.

Chapter 51
Long Distance Bawl

Randy was reeling from what had just happened. Monsters were gone, but so were some innocent people. Friends. A victory, but a mess. And he did not know how to react. He felt as though he had used up so much of his tears crying over his banishment from the Nap Kin that he had none left to cry over anyone else. And that made him feel awful.

Chelsea reunited with the others on the bridge. Randy was sure that the scratch marks on her face would heal. But he was uncertain how she would fare trying to heal from the loss of her best friend.

Gertrude's phone rang.

"Everyone!" Gertrude said. "August is calling."

She answered, and August appeared on the screen of the phone.

"How is everybody on your end?" he asked.

"Oh boy," Gertrude said. "It's a long story, August. Crazy shit has gone down here. I lost my brother. We lost Mitch. And Shelley. And..."

"No." August's face scrunched up uncontrollably. "Grady, too?"

"Yep," Naomi said, with her head down. "Gravy Stew."

Gertrude nodded tearfully, and August's face became wet as well.

"Mortimer was turned into a werewolf," Gertrude explained. "So that's another loss. He tried to kill us, but Grady protected us, and they died fighting each other."

August broke down, and Gertrude gave him a moment. Everyone on the bridge let out whatever tears emerged from their eyes. They all needed the moment. But when it came time for them to collect themselves, people on both sides of the conversation let each other know what happened on their respective ends, comparing notes to compile the full story as best as they could.

"It's strange," August said. "I remember all the murders in the mirror now. Only one person was lucky to get away."

"Who?" Randy asked.

"He called her Candy. She escaped his home and drove off. And I remember being possessed by him and bumping into her in London. She saw that it was him controlling me, and she threw me off of the bridge and into the water. Wow. What were the chances of bumping into her?"

She made it out, Randy thought, feeling somewhat relieved.

As the conversation on the cell phone continued, Randy walked over to the spot where Peyton had left Aster. Picking up the monkey, he looked back at the group. Former friends, with some family for company. And Randy believed he neither belonged nor had anything useful to add. Sure, he had been associated with Mathis and planned on killing him. But now that it seemed like Gertrude ended him, the subject appeared to be moot. Standing around the group in this moment felt intrusive. So he carried the monkey and walked away, not waiting to see whether anyone would turn around to check up on him.

* * *

"Something doesn't sit right with me," Pamela said. "I feel like it's not completely over."

"You're just exhausted," her mom said. "Being inside of a costume with a mind of its own will do that to you, I imagine."

"Well, yeah. But I just remembered something. I saw Mandy's memories. Mathias created a copy of himself in a mansion. And that copy called himself Mathis. Mathias wanted them to work together, but then Mathis didn't want any of that. He said, 'I defect from you.' And then Mathias was blown out of the window and back to this school."

"Well," August said, "the ghost I saw did look like a copy of the chancellor, but he called himself Mathesis."

"The copy I saw was solid, though."

"So was Mathesis once Mathias died, apparently. Maybe he was solid at first and then became a ghost once he refused to join his creator?"

"Can we really be sure that Mathis was this ghost? The math is not adding up."

"No idea. I don't have any helpful memories, I don't think. It's all so confusing. All things considered, I'm glad that some of us made it out."

"We got lucky," Peyton said, giving Pamela a smile showing just how thankful she was to have her sister back.

"Sheer luck," Pamela said.

"Sheer Luck and Sheer Joy," Naomi said with a hint of a smile. "Maybe those can be your nicknames."

"Pam's definitely Sheer Joy," Peyton said.

"Heh," Reginald said. "No shit, Sheer Luck."

Despite the sorrowful aftermath, the two sisters could not help but appreciate the attempt at lighthearted humor, laughing at the cheesiness of the statement, mozzarella and all.

Pamela turned around, looking for Randy. He was gone. She had nothing to say to him, but she wondered how he was dealing with all that had happened, including the fate of Gertrude's brother Tim. In any case, she would not be living with him anymore, especially now that she had her family back.

"Now that we're together again," her dad began, "maybe we'll be able to Sheer up after all."

"You and your dad jokes," Pamela said.

"And after all these years, I still put up with them," her mom replied. "I'm sorry for everything, Pam. I wish I could've handled everything better all those years ago. I shouldn't have said what I said."

Pamela gave her mom a hug.

"I forgive you, Mom. I forgive all of you. And I'm sorry for how I acted back in the day. It really hurt not having someone to play with me. But I shouldn't have gone to the park without saying anything. The world's a dangerous place. And even if Aster didn't mean any harm back then, I know now that she's not much of a reliable friend."

When the hug ended, Pamela glanced at Peyton, who was looking back to where she had dropped the monkey.

"I don't see her anymore," Peyton said. "You don't think she...got up and walked away, do you?"

"No. I think a former friend of hers wants closure. But I doubt she'll talk to him."

Pamela had seen the fire within Randy. She decided to keep it to herself. She wanted to believe that what Aster had shown her was just that entity's idea of Randy. Maybe he did have a bad habit as a child that burned the bridges of his and Aster's friendship, but as an adult, he did not seem like the type to want to hurt anyone benevolent. Pamela sincerely hoped that Randy would find peace in a harmless fashion. Right now, it did not seem like Pamela's place to follow him on his path.

Chapter 52
Mirror Mortal

Mathis awoke in the middle of the night, feeling a sharp pain in his stomach. Clutching his belly with both hands, he walked over to the lavatory and vomited into the toilet. When he was done, he turned on the lights and was shocked to see a face in the mirror. The face of Mathias Moseley. He punched it, and six shards fell to the floor. A dozen eyes felt like a thousand eyes, watching him from below.

"No. This is impossible. This can't be."

As he moved his fingers closer to the glass, the fingers on the other side appeared to get closer to each other, like God and Adam in the Michelangelo painting. The mirror recognized that these digits were one and the same. Mathis withdrew his hand, and the hand in the mirror went in the opposite direction. He feared that touching the glass would allow the reflection to emerge from its world.

He *feared*.

He looked at the other mirror to the side, the medicine cabinet (sans medicine). There was the face again. And he looked behind him at the glass of the sliding door. Another face. He did not feel alone; he felt *followed*. Like he was being watched. And it terrified him.

"I am me... I am me..." He felt his face with both hands. "Have I always been this ugly?"

He took out his wallet and looked at his ID card. There was a permanent fingerprint. Mathis could get caught if he was not too careful from here on out. He cried out of paranoia.

Why does it feel so good to cry? Am I...feeding on myself?

To be multiplied was to be divided.

Mathis ran down the stairs and out of the mansion. He got into his car, wanting to drive off somewhere. He was not sure where, but he craved escape. But then he saw Mathias' face in the side view mirror, which read "OBJECTS IN MIRROR ARE CLOSER THAN THEY APPEAR." To drive away would be too dangerous.

He ran back into his home, mind flying fragmented. His mind. All over the place. Hardly focused. Full of thoughts. Such disorganized thoughts. Files filling a screen. Chaos. Not the kind he could control. Loose chaos. Tainting his drive. His internal drive. Divided in two. A tug of war. Extremities at odds. Uneven. Imbalanced. Unstable. No stable. No horses. Except for a mare. A *night* mare. Galloping. Growing a horn. Piercing his psyche. Psych. Double-psych. Nonsensical. The madness of Mathis.

He looked at his facial hair in the mirror and used his fingers to comb through the hair on his scalp. Hair could fall. He could be identified. He needed to be free from it.

He took a long walk to the store to buy some razors and clippers. His hair had stayed at a consistent length throughout the years, so he never had to trim it before. But now he needed to look substantially different from his source. So when he returned home, he shaved it all off of his face, making some accidental cuts along the way. The hair was a mess all over the sink.

He could smell the aftershave he had rubbed onto his face. With the burdening hairs gone, he slid his fingers from his earlobes to the smooth skin of his cheeks, and then down to the sides of his neck. He imagined that it would feel nicer if it involved the touch of another person.

No! I don't NEED companionship!

Mathis did not want this desire to fill his mind. He wanted to be separate from everyone else. To be different. And as he continued, he definitely looked different from before, bald on the scalp and clean-shaven in the face. But he could still recognize the eyes and skin of Mathias. Pressing his hands against his (facial) cheeks, he wanted to scream, and was so close to bringing Edvard Munch's vision to life.

In anger, he ran the razor down his right cheek, wanting Mathias to feel the pain. But it was Mathis feeling the pain, his blood not disappearing. Identifiable.

Mathis needed to change how he looked. He considered cutting off his face altogether, but quickly realized how much of a mess that would make. What he needed was a mask. But the prospect of purchases made him paranoid. Perhaps one might presume that the purchase of any mask at this time would automatically mean he was a serial killer. Halloween was too far away, and he needed something immediately, so that he could shed the image of Mathias.

Part Five
Aftertaste

Chapter 53
Taking the Shot

I t was April. Having traveled to a few fancy destinations, Candid was now settled in the Mexican city of Guanajuato. Low profile, which was what she needed at the moment. After all, Candid had to search for the rest.

Her luck had been in her favor. But after a recent attempt at gambling in a game of Loteria, she lost a bit of cash. Just a little bit. But it was enough to tip her off that her luck had run out. She did not know how or why. Whenever she had been gambling since taking the duck loan, though, she had been on a streak. But now that streak was broken, and she knew to be cautious.

Candid ate elotes, which were among her favorite snacks in Guanajuato. Corn on a cob, smothered with cheese, mayonnaise, and lime juice. She always asked for the corn kernels to come in a cup though. Eating them off of a stick made her feel uncomfortable. Corn on a cob brought Vlad the Impaler to mind, and the train of thought would lead to vampires and then to Mathis. She wanted to steer clear of such thoughts.

A statue of El Pípila watched over the city. He had a torch in his hand. Thankfully, it was made of stone, just like him. As the sun set, Candid set up her tripod and camera. The blue hour brought an exquisite sight of the city with its lights lit up. She had known about this spot for years, and now she was finally fulfilling her goal of photographing this city at just the right time. The photos came out looking incredible. She wished that she could share them online with the world.

Morbid thoughts were uninvited, and yet somehow they made their way into Candid's mind. One day, on a whim, she decided to check out a mummy museum. Once there, Candid felt like she was among her own people, though she was unsure whether her people were the dead or the exhibitors. She did not dare take pictures of the dead this time around. Candid found herself thankful that Mathis at least had the decency to keep his victims clothed. These mummies were naked, their chests sloping down into where their bellies should have been. Some faces looked like black cereal flake masks that could be peeled off. She was surprised by the lack of eye holes, which were covered by bone. The dark orifices of the mouths, however, remained open, yawning eternally. One mummy's arms resembled twig branches.

One mummy was on display in a glass box, its reflection visible on the side glass. It would have pleased to see a mummified Mathis Dillard in this display case, complete with a reflection proclaiming his defeat. That would have been a picture worth taking. Knowing that the fantasy could not harm her, she imagined a skeletal Mathis breaking out of the glass, walking toward her with the Tin Man steps he had taken before.

Other killers might have gone on the run, just as Candid was at the moment. It was unfortunate that some of them went uncaught. But Candid had the luxury of knowing that Mathis was quite content with his lair and had no intention of going anywhere. He was arrogant, but it seemed like a well-founded arrogance, given the fortunes of his unnatural state of existence. Stationary was his dwelling, and nobody wanted to hear the crunch of a crushed cockroach, so they stayed away.

Outside of the museum, she saw someone wearing a Grim Reaper costume, complete with a fake scythe and teeth like kernels of yellow corn. For a brief moment, she wondered whether it was Mathis in disguise. After the incident in London, it did not seem so farfetched to believe that he could pop up anywhere. To be sure, she took out her camera and snapped a photo.

The Reaper turned to Candid and approached her. Candid exhaled uncontrollably and backed up a bit. The Reaper stopped in front of her.

"Veinte pesos."

Candid looked at the screen, relieved to see that his image was visible. She took out her wallet and paid him.

"Gracias," the man said.

One day, there was a thunderstorm. Candid brought her tripod and camera outside and waited. She unclipped the tripod legs to extend them, and then she clipped them again. Waiting with much patience, she was eventually able to capture the lightning. There it was, visible on the screen. Her most coveted catch. But she could not share the lightning with anyone. She feared that a post online, no matter how anonymous, would somehow get the attention of Mathis. Candid was not sure how observant he was, but she had this idea that he could deduce the identity of a photographer based on the composition. Or maybe he could just hack into the web and track her location, and then hack and slash her to bits, leaving pieces of her to adorn some spider webs he could use to decorate his mansion.

Candid did not doubt that there was so much evil in the universe, and that perhaps it would never go away for good. But there was an evil that she felt might be in her power to prevent from poisoning the planet even further. She heard the calling. Not a calling from Mathis himself, but rather a calling to complete the killing of Mathis.

I should just kill him, she thought.

She remembered Randy, and his desire to end both Mathis and himself. She wondered whether it would be wise to try killing Mathis Dillard by teaming up with Randy Morales.

Nah. Fuck that guy.

She expected that Randy would probably mess things up. She had to make sure that this was done right. That Mathis' death would not be prolonged. In her eyes, she had earned this, and Randy was merely a drama queen.

Though a bit malformed, even through the shitstorm, corn does not get broken down.

She booked a flight. When the day came, the plane flew through the thunderstorm. She made it to the next airport, where an empty hallway was lit up by orange lights above a shiny floor. Orange stripes. A flame-filled floor. Fire on water that could not put it out. She felt like a fool flying back into the fire. It was raining outside, but the rain would not stop the storm within.

This time, Candid arrived with pliers *and* a sledgehammer. Her backpack was another bit of extra weight, but perhaps she could use it as a weapon as well if all else were to fail. She used the pliers on the barbed wire at the front of the mansion. She did not care so much about stealth. If Mathis knew that she was coming, then she wanted to face him head-on. She just wanted all this to end one way or another. Once it was safer, she climbed over the gate and went up to the window by the door. Candid put the pliers in her backpack, wanting to wield the sledgehammer with both hands. Then she broke the glass with the sledgehammer. She hoped that this weapon would be sufficient enough to hit Mathis in the head and make him dead. Maybe she would miss. Maybe she would swing so hard that the hammer would come full circle and put her out of her misery. Maybe a part of her was okay with just failing and dying.

She walked up the stairs, its steps still black from the scorch marks. Either Mathis was too lazy to redecorate, or he just loved this aesthetic. Candid would bet on the latter. When she got to the next floor, she found the door to his bedroom, and swung it open.

There she saw him lying on the floor, wearing a green face mask and lime-lensed glasses resembling the eyes of a mantis. He rolled his head to look at her. Through the lenses, she could see his watery eyes.

Candid bawled out laughing, dropping the sledgehammer to the floor.

"Oh my gosh! Look at you!"

"I have. I can look at me. I shouldn't be able to but I can. I want to be alone, and I don't. I see myself alone, and I see myself watched. How the fuck do you normies live with these contradictions?!"

"Where'd you get the...eyewear?"

"Stolen from a yard sale. Talk about a *Toy Story 2* situation."

"Did you kill anyone for them?"

"I wanted to. But I didn't wanna get caught."

He's paranoid? she thought.

Seeing Mathis like this made Candid feel significantly more confident.

"They look good on you."

"I have these memories. I remember seeing you in London, but it wasn't me. It was some guy named August. You threw him off the bridge, but I kept him alive. He fought me and defeated me. Well, not me, exactly."

He still lives, she thought.

Candid had not killed after all. If she were to kill Mathis, he would be her first. But now the question was whether to *let* this be her first. She pretty much had a clean slate, debts paid off and hands bereft of blood.

Candid got her camera out of her backpack. She took a picture of him. And there he was, on the screen, visible and vulnerable. Not quite the monster whom she had met before. He had lost some gravitas.

"What are you doing?" he asked.

She stored the camera in her backpack again.

"I only came to bid you goodbye."

"That's a lie."

"Making a rhyme, now?"

"No! I'm not him. You came to try to kill me, didn't you?"

"Thought about it. But I think you're well on your way to your own demolishment. You don't need my help."

"Why don't you *fight* me?"

"Nah. I'm good. Nacho shlick now, are you?"

Mathis sat up.

"What did you say?"

"I...you'll fuck up, be what I mean."

Mathis smiled.

"Say my name."

"Mathy."

"You can't even *shay* it, can you, *Candice*. Your *shlip* shows who you are now."

He started to cackle.

"Shut up," she said.

"All *thish* time I thought it *wash jusht shome hipshter* bullshit, but you *jusht* can't *pronounsh shome shoundsh*. Ahaha!"

Candid was infuriated. In her mind's eye, she saw herself running at Mathis and cutting off his head. But what would happen then? What if she were to leave a mark that would incriminate her? She returned to the sight of Mathis lying on the floor. Though he smiled, she knew he was in pain. And she felt something.

Is this pity? she wondered.

For a split second, she imagined Mathis in a fetal position, alone in a cave with nothing but his tears. Just withering away, a helpless—

Psshhh. As if. I've seen this fuckin' monster's murders!

Candid inhaled, exhaled, and responded.

"I'm not taking the bait. That be all you are. *Bait*. A worm on a hook, needed by nobody. No greater than the bug you wanna be. You'll be devoured by the fish, and the fish by a thing greater."

Mathis' smile went away.

"You don't care what happens to Randy Morales?"

"Do you?"

Mathis did not answer.

"Whatever," Candid said. "Not my problem. My work be done. All paid. Goodbye, Benny."

"You're just gonna make like a corn and flake? You can't leave me, Candy! You're not out of this!"

But she was. She could leave the story freely. Now, the storm was outside, not inside. And she could live with that. As she exited the mansion, she looked at the picture she had taken. And there, in the snapshot, was Mathis Dillard, seen at last. The sad expression did tempt her to turn back, only because it was a familiar expression she had seen on others, and that she herself had sported. But Candid repented, pressing onward into a more peaceful existence. She felt certain that Mathis Dillard would die sooner rather than later. But she had no desire to be a spectator at the hour of his demise. Candid Du Clips, with her problems eclipsed, would let Mathis and Randy have their little play date.

Boys will be boys. Toys kill the noise.

465

Chapter 54
Spring Cleaning

There was much controversy regarding Copper Petal University. After all the deaths, some suggested that the school be shut down. But with the danger gone, and after much investigation, it was decided that the vice chancellor would become the chancellor, and that those who struggled with finals could retake their exams. Some seniors did well enough to remain on track to graduate. Others did so terribly that having to remain for another year seemed highly likely. Especially since the events that took place would affect their study habits during spring quarter. Some speculated that all of this was luck resulting from the feedback of the ducks and geese disappearing into the Plo-Tunium Hole.

Though the Nap Kin were fewer than before, they still boothed for Goose Chase, attracting the attention of high school seniors visiting the campus to get a good look at all the campus orgs that were available. The email list gained more names than in previous years. It seemed that the Nap Kin had become very popular as a result of the catastrophic events they had experienced. With the Plo-Tunium within Mathias no longer affecting the campus, it was not so easy to contain such a secret. All the same, Goose Chase as a whole felt like it was missing some magic since there were no geese at all.

Randy did not attend Goose Chase. He was not sure where he stood now when it came to most of the Nap Kin. Gertrude had seemed very firm on her stance, and he was afraid to ask everyone else individually. But there was one whom he really wanted to talk to about where he stood: Naomi. And he just so happened to bump into her on his way out of class one day.

"Hey," Randy said walking over to her.

"Hey," she said, stopping for a moment.

"How's everyone else doing?"

"Adjusting." She shrugged.

"They say I'm on track to graduate at the end of this quarter."

"Congrats. Me, Gin, Seashell, Yo-Gert, and even Eight-Ball have to stay another year. Guess that means we'll have enough officers after all."

"How is...she?"

He knew that he did not have to say Gertrude's name for Naomi to know how to respond.

"I still don't think she wants to talk to you. I wouldn't push your luck."

"Are *you* and *I* able to talk?"

"I don't know. I can't predict when. Maybe sooner, maybe later. I can't guarantee what I—or any of us—will feel, though."

The vagueness of this answer concerned him.

"Generally," he said, "I'd like to see you sooner rather than later. But if I'm gonna see you for the last time, I'd rather it be later. So what is it now?"

"I can't answer that right now. You're gonna have to wait and see."

"Waiting can be such a drag. Especially without any tips."

Under other circumstances, Naomi might have laughed at that. But things were different now. And the lack of laughter hurt Randy in a way he never expected.

"I have to get to my next class," Naomi said. "Bye."

As she walked away, Randy waved goodbye halfheartedly, even though Naomi was no longer looking at him. He did not doubt that she had a class to attend, but he could tell that she did not wish to speak with him any further at the moment. It felt like the door was closed, and that he would never be invited again.

Randy went to Petal Lock Park. The trees that had been burned were gone, but the ones that had been untouched by the flames remained. From afar, he saw Pamela and Peyton listening to music on their ear buds and dancing around together. Like two pearls in a pod. It was too perfect for him to spoil.

Randy heard footsteps coming up from behind him

"They've found each other," Frederick said.

"Good for them." Randy sighed. "My friendships seem to be broken."

"It happens," Frederick said. "I kept myself from making friends, from making up my own notions of whom I thought they were. By shutting them out, I thought I'd keep myself from getting hurt."

"And did you, Frederick?"

"Maybe to an extent." Frederick shrugged. "Doesn't matter much now. I'm gonna graduate once this quarter ends. Maybe my philosophy degree will get me somewhere, but I've come to realize that Deep Dive Orchestra probably won't help me much."

Randy wondered how different things would have been had he spent more time with Frederick during freshman year.

"I'm sorry we didn't hang out much. But if you want, I can come to your town if I'm ever able."

"Don't feel obligated," Frederick said. "When we graduate, we'll each go back to our homes. And whenever you're in my neck of the woods, you won't feel as compelled to hit me up. And it won't hurt me as much because I'll expect this to be true."

"Come on, Frederick. I promise I'll visit soon. This summer."

"Promise will become less and less frequent. Might've been nice if we all had the option of staying here forever. People tend to stick with whoever is in the area. Too bad everyone in my neighborhood sucks."

Randy considered the artificiality of people. Sometimes people seemed so perfect that one did not want to hear about their faults. And then those artificial people got idolized. And the idea of having bonds with them got romanticized.

"Why?" Randy asked. "Why *can't* we all just live here forever?"

"Because everyone gets evicted from paradise sooner or later. Even if that paradise has bits of hell in it. Pay attention to what's around you every now and then. You'd see it's not all perfect. There was a time when you and I were the same. But I accepted my place and moved on. I've had my fill, and I know when to walk away."

"You didn't seem to know while you were fucking things up."

Frederick was stoic for a long moment. But then Randy noticed a slight glistening in his eyes, listening to the harsh words he had inflicted, the tears evicted from his eyes.

"A lapse in judgment," Frederick Filler finally answered. "There's no justification for what I did. Through imbalance and a fall into nothingness, I lost myself. And in doing so, I lost others who didn't mean much to me until I saw that they were gone. The missing trees are a reminder of that. I wouldn't even *want* to remain here."

"I'm sorry," Randy said.

"So am I."

Randy wanted to ask Frederick how it felt to kill someone. But it seemed like a sensitive subject. So he asked a different question instead.

"Is there balance, or is there nothing?"

"I can't answer for you. I'm just Frederick Filler, not fully realized. Frederick Filler, freefalling through fire in my own way. Goodbye, Randy Morales."

Chapter 55
Reception

As a side effect of the Plo-Tunium, those related to the students involved in the skirmish at room 315 knew what had happened there, thanks to visions that came to them. Friends and family of former occupants of that room became aware as well, and they mourned the losses of those whom they had long forgotten.

Anton's family had a funeral for him. His friends at Tree Culler Hotel were still devastated by his absence. Healing from the loss would not be easy after all the fun times they had spent with him. But life had to go on, and they knew that they had to push forward and keep on celebrating life.

In May, August's friends threw an early birthday party for him, complete with a cake baked by Fritz himself, based on a recipe that Anton had taught him.

By the end of spring term, August knew he would have to stay another year at CPU, based on his grades which had suffered as he had. August had improved toward the end of the term, but it was not enough. He did, however, have comfort in knowing that some of his friends back home would keep him company as they stayed another year. He and Reginald discussed living arrangements.

Cassie would have to repeat a year at her own school as well. Understandably she was a little frustrated, but she was thankful that she was free to see her friends and family back home.

Randy, however, would graduate. August had been told what happened to Gertrude's brother. He did not doubt that Randy did not mean for it to happen. He wanted to reach out to Randy, but he was not sure what he could say to make things better.

One day, August, Cassie, and Jade went to Crust Desserts. This time, the lemon meringue pie was very enjoyable. Eventually, their conversations led to August's unloading of the dilemma back home.

"I get why Gertrude's angry," August said. "Losing family is horrible. Sometimes I ask myself whether I'd forgive Randy if he'd left Grady right before he got attacked by those werewolves. And I feel awful just thinking about that hypothetical."

"You shouldn't beat yourself up too much," Jade said. "I'm not sure how *I* would feel if I came face to face with whoever—if anyone—took my brother away."

"It's easy to carry a grudge," Cassie said with a hint of regret. "But I think you should still at least say *something* to Randy. Even if he's done wrong, he didn't mean to do it. And people need to be reminded that they're not alone."

"Maybe you're right," Jade said. "Maybe Gertrude will never forgive Randy. That's a given. And it might be pointless trying to fix that. But you can still keep him company if you want."

"I can," August replied, taking out his cell phone. "It's been forever since I've talked to him."

"Not forever," Cassie said. "It's only forever if you continue the silence."

August nodded and typed out a few letters. But then he deleted them.

"No," he said. "It needs to be face to face. I'll call him when we're back at the hotel."

* * *

During dusk at Copper Petal, Randy was lying on his bed with the lights off when his phone rang and lit up with a notification. August was video calling him. A surprise. Not sure how to react, Randy hesitated to pick up. As it kept ringing, he struggled to figure out what he would say. Despite not having any words ready, he decided to answer. And then August's face appeared on the screen. He was in his hotel room.

"Hey, Randy," August said.

"Hey."

"How are you feeling?"

Randy could have lied, claiming to be fine, as was the norm. But truth spilled out of his mouth like vomit, but without the disgusting taste.

"I feel defeated. I don't think my friends over here wanna talk to me anymore. Gertrude's never gonna stop hating me. And I can't rewind to make things better. I feel like shit. And I know other people have had it worse. Even you." Randy wiped his eyes, not wanting to look like too much of a mess. "How are *you* feeling? It's easy to forget to ask back."

"Well, I'm feeling...safer. I don't feel completely better, the losses considered. But I'm trying to get on."

"I'm sorry about Grady. He was a good guy. I wish I could've gotten to know him better."

Randy really meant it. He knew how pathetic it was to be envious of the rapport that Grady had with the other Nap Kin. With Grady gone, Randy felt horrible about what he had felt.

"Yeah," August replied, taking a long blink of the eyes. "I miss him. I feel bad that I couldn't make it to his funeral over there."

"He wouldn't hold it against you. He'd understand."

"I know. But I wish I could've been there with the family."

There was a long moment of silence before Randy spoke again.

"I don't know what to say anymore. How to carry this conversation."

"Are you gonna be okay, Randy?"

"We'll see. I'm not gonna do anything crazy, if that's what you're worried about. I'm just gonna finish school and then accept what comes next."

"You can talk to me if you ever need to."

"I'll keep that in mind. Anyway, I'm really tired. So, I should go."

"All right. Take good care of yourself, Randy."

"I'll try."

Randy hung up. In truth, he did not intend to call or message August again about his troubles. He knew that August had been through much worse than he had. Randy did not want to burden anyone.

* * *

August believed Randy. But he still worried and hoped that he would be okay.

Later that month, August and his friends attended Tate and Georgia's wedding. The couple had it in London, and then everyone went to the hotel afterward. The hotel friends shared a table in the dining area.

"I can't believe the hotel let them have the reception here," Bessie said.

"You say that as if we didn't already know that was going on," Fritz replied.

"You seem to be doing much better," Jade told August.

"Yeah. There's still some pain deep down, but it has receded into the recycling bin. Things are a bit more comforting when your parents remember you again."

"I bet."

"It's pretty crazy to think about, though. There's an element out there called Plo-Tunium. Can someone going after that along with any other powerful stones we might not even know about? And combine them into some sort of weapon?"

"Sounds like a terrible idea," Verner said. "Whoever gets a bunch of such stones would probably get themselves killed. I don't think that type of shit is a big deal. Let someone else worry about deep shit like that."

"August," Jade said. "There's something I need to tell you..."

"Yeah?"

"You see, *I* am one of those stones."

August's jaw dropped.

"Wait, what?"

"I am one of those stones. Made sentient and turned into flesh and blood. Jade. There are six of us stones at war with each other. I was sent here to prevent Plo-Tunium from destroying Earth. I thought that it might be disguised as one of the standing stones at Stonehenge, but that wasn't the case. And it was here in the hotel, this whole time. There cannot be peace between all of us magical stones. If one of each of these types of stones gets put together, it will only be chaos."

Eyes wide, August was astonished. Perhaps jade was a more powerful stone than he had ever considered. And if it was true that stone could become flesh, then what else was possible? What other stones were there in the universe that could affect people? The possibilities seemed infinite.

But then Jade started laughing, and August felt stupid.

"You're messing with me!" August realized.

"I'm sorry!" Jade said. "I just couldn't resist. You should've seen the look on your face!"

"Hah!" Verner said. "Jade got you good! I wasn't convinced for a second."

"Sure you weren't," Jade said.

"So none of that is true then?" August asked.

"Nope," Jade said. "I promise I won't do that again. Wouldn't want anyone thinking I'm crying wolf in the future."

Tate started clinked his glass of wine with a spoon.

"I would like to make a toast," Tate said. "To good friends and everlasting love! Though some might stay together for a while, others may be apart for a really long time. But that shouldn't mean that the bonds are severed. I, for one, am glad to have met and known all of you here. And, thankfully, we have the interwebs to remain in touch. And I hope we will, even if I've been a bit of a butt at times."

"Just a bit," Verner interrupted, causing people to laugh.

"So, to friends, family, and everything in between!"

Everyone raised their glasses and clinked them with one another.

June came around, and it was time for goodbyes. At the airport, August said goodbye to his friends one by one, giving each of them a hug as he spoke to them.

"Cassie, I know we didn't spend as much time as we'd hoped, but I'm glad we at least had *some* time to hang out."

"Thanks for never giving up, August," Cassie said. "And remember, we can still be pen pals."

"Of course. And Bessie, try not to get into any other fights."

"I can't make any promises, but I'll try to be safe."

"Heh. And if you do get in a fight, I know you can hold your own. And Verner, I haven't forgotten all the laughs we've had with the drinks. And I'll keep on remembering them."

"Be sure to remind me of the jokes every now and then," Verner said. "Some of it never gets old. Especially if they stem from good times."

"Definitely. Tate, I'm glad we were able to get along after all."

"So am I. And thank you for everything. I know I was kinda full of it in the beginning, but I'm glad things worked out."

"Right. But just in case, Georgia, please make sure he stays out of trouble."

"Of course. I'll keep an eye on him. Thanks again for helping me remember what I love about him."

"Heh. And Fritz, I'm gonna miss those meals you shared with us."

"I'll be sure to keep sharing recipes. Good thing they make good conversation topics."

"I'm sure we'll find others as well. And Jade, thanks for talking some sense into me when I was losing it."

"We've been through some strange times. But try not to be a stranger."

"We'll keep in touch. I'll keep in touch with all of you. I promise."

After the heartfelt goodbyes, August headed to the airport. Though he took the plane without familiar company, he did not feel alone, knowing that he shared friendships with those whom he had met during this whole study abroad experience.

When the flight was over, he arrived back to the States, where his parents were there to greet him at the airport. Hit with the feeling of familiarity, he got in a group hug with them.

"So good to be back," August said. "So glad you remember."

"Geez, don't remind me," his dad said. "I still can't believe I said those things to you. How could I forget my own son?"

"Don't stress, Dad. It was an evil force, but it's gone now."

The group hug ended, and then they were ready to head home.

"So," his mom said. "August back in June? Summer must be ending soon!"

August let out a laugh that turned into a yawn.

"Feeling tired?" his dad asked.

"Yes. And it really *is* jet lag, thankfully. I think I'm home now."

Chapter 56
Car Parkage

Mathis did not feel so safe in his mansion anymore. Every day, he grew more and more paranoid, believing that evidence of his crimes might come to light and that the police would come after him. He considered setting the mansion on fire, but he did not want to draw attention to himself. He needed a new place. Somewhere close enough to CPU for him to keep tabs on those whom Randy held so dear.

Browsing online, he found a listing posted by a student named Preston Ward, who was searching for a subtenant to take his spot at an apartment for the summer. Mathis made an appointment with him. And on that appointment date, Mathis arrived at Preston's place. He knocked, and the student opened the door.

"Name?" Preston asked.

"Benjamin Fitz," Mathis lied.

"Ah okay. I wasn't one hundred percent on you being real. Pardon the pun, but it's a pet peeve of mine when people use pictures of their dog as a profile pic. You wouldn't be bringing a dog here, would you?"

"No. I gave it to a friend."

"Good. Also, don't get me started on profile pics with multiple people in them. It's like, who the hell are you, even? But I digress."

Preston gave him a tour of the apartment. On the first floor were a living room, a lavatory, and a kitchen. On the second floor were three bedrooms and another lavatory.

"So yeah!" Preston said once the tour was done. "This is it. How much did you wanna pay per month?"

"You said you and each of your roommates pay eight hundred a month?"

"Each, yeah."

"Tell you what? I can do two thousand a month if I get the whole place to myself."

"Wow, really? That's in your budget?"

"No more than that. I have really bad experiences with roommates. Real slobs, leaving their stuff everywhere. I just need a place all to myself for the summer, until I get back on my feet. I expect to get a promotion by the end of it. Really rising through the ranks."

"What's your job again?"

"Software development."

"Interesting. Some of my friends are into that, but it just makes me feel stupid. My parents wanted me to major in that, but I switched for my own health. Funny enough, I study health, now."

"Interesting," Mathis lied.

"Anyway, I'd have to check with my other roommates, but I'm sure they'd be cool with it. You'd also be getting a parking permit. And, just as a reminder, please keep in mind that this is off the books. So you can't let the office know that you're here. In fact, it'd be a lot safer if you didn't have anything mailed to you at this address."

"Understood. It's in all our best interest if nobody knows I'm here."

Within a day, Mathis heard back from Preston. His roommates ended up being fine with Mathis being the sole resident. They were desperate to find a subtenant as soon as possible.

On Randy's graduation day, Mathis sat in his car in a parking space near Randy's apartment. In his rear-view mirror, Mathis saw a car pulling up to the apartment. Randy got out of the apartment and into the car. Mathis inferred that this was Randy's family, and he took note of the license plate.

He followed them to the parking lot near the auditorium where the ceremony was scheduled to take place. Once Randy, his little sister, and his parents were a safe distance away, Mathis got out of his car. He looked around at the full parking lot. Several people were walking through, but none looked at him as he walked over to the car that Randy's family had parked. In Mathis' pocket was a GPS tracking device he had bought. When he was certain that nobody was watching, Mathis crouched down and attached the device to the bottom of the car, hidden out of plain sight.

* * *

The graduation ceremony arrived. Clad in grad cap and gown, Randy walked the walk and smiled the smile, a mask for his family to behold. When he stepped onto the stage to shake some hands, he found himself in front of an audience he did not want. It felt like walking through airport security and trying not to do anything wrong. There was very little eye contact and recognition.

This definitely did not feel the same as being onstage with Artie Docent. He was in the spotlight very briefly, with very few people in the audience knowing who he was. None of the people whom he had considered his friends were there.

* * *

That night, Mathis watched the Morales house from his car. They were having spaghetti for dinner. He thought about what it would be like to barge in through the door and flip the table, tomato sauce and blood spilling everywhere. Beheading Randy and his parents. Sticking their heads on pikes and setting them up in the front yard. Scarring the little sister for life.

He ran his finger across the eyelid scar. It used to not mean anything to him, but being able to see it in the mirror made him self-conscious.

The house lights were turned off.

Time for the lights to go out.

Mathis got out of his car and popped open the trunk. It contained his scythes and Candid's sledgehammer. He grabbed the scythes, closed the trunk, and walked up to the porch. He wanted to kick down the door.

But he did not, and he wondered why. Was it paranoia? Was it this portrait of the family?

No, he thought. *Fuck family.*

Still, he could not bring himself to kick down the door. He walked back to his car and remained there, staring at the house all night long, the rising sun bringing tears to his hardly blinking eyes.

Later, he saw the parents drive away. He followed. They went to a diner called Diner Things. It seemed to be date night for them. Mathis parked the car a safe distance from the establishment. He sat for a little while, applying the green face mask. After putting on the green glasses, he got out and popped open the trunk.

He really wanted to use the scythes. His trademark. But that was the problem. Anyone who caught onto his crimes could uncover a modus operandi. For a change, he would use the sledgehammer, and teach Candid a lesson about leaving her stuff lying around. Maybe a murder by hammer would lure her back, and he would finish the job. After picking up the hammer, he closed the trunk and walked over to the diner.

Randy's mother and father were still sitting in a booth by the window, though their meal seemed almost finished. He could tell from their smiles and laughter that they were having a good time. A loving couple. Together. Not alone. Lucky to have the children they had wanted.

Mathis shook the thought way.

I can take from them.

When Mathis saw them getting up from their table, he walked over to their car and retrieved the GPS tracking device. Then he crouched beside their vehicle and waited.

When they finally arrived, Mathis attacked. He swung the hammer at Mr. Morales' back. Feeling the vibration of metal against flesh was partially satisfying but also partially frightening as his victim reacted with a scream. Then he hit Mrs. Morales' knees. She screamed as well, and Mathis wanted it to stop.

This isn't right, he thought. *No. This is right. It's just the screaming that isn't right. I need to silence them. But why aren't I enjoying this?*

He summoned the desire to bash their heads fatally. Wanting to jump from a high height, he got on top of their car, his body positioned like a mantis.

But the alarm went off, and he was afraid of getting caught. Mathis could not finish the job. He had to run. So he did.

* * *

For Randy, being back home after graduation, so far away from all the people whom he had met in college, was a very isolating experience. He felt that he could not contact any of them. It was as if all his friends were gone, and it was just him, all alone.

Opening the closet in his room, Randy crouched down, looking at the monkey next to the red lamp. He picked up the monkey and stared into its eyes once again, wondering whether Aster was still there.

His cell phone rang, and he answered, putting the monkey back down. He got the call from the hospital about his parents' injuries. Apparently, they had been attacked in the parking lot. And though he did not know the exact circumstances, he was bombarded by the feeling that he had something to do with it. Shivering, he wanted to pull all his hair out.

It's all my fault. It's all my fault. It's all my fault...

He was not sure how long he stood there before taking action. Needing a ride, he downloaded an app onto his phone and then alert a driver about his location. As he waited impatiently, he wondered how Kayleigh would feel. He went over to the door to her room and knocked. She opened it up.

"Come with me," Randy said.

"What happened?" she asked.

"Mom and Dad are in the hospital."

"What?!"

"Come on."

Within half an hour, they were dropped off at the hospital. Randy led Kayleigh to the elevator and then to the third floor, where they found the room in which their parents were being kept. There, he saw his mom and dad in beds, side by side. They both smiled at the sight of their children. A doctor stood by with a clipboard.

"What's gonna happen to them?" Kayleigh asked, struggling to hold back her tears.

"They'll be fine," she answered. "They just need time to heal. Your dad will need a cane."

"And Mom?"

"She'll walk again, eventually."

Randy did not know how to act, whether to cry or act calm and collected so as not to worry Kayleigh, who, with her sorrowful face, seemed to have a better grasp of how to express what she felt.

"Someone hurt you?" Kayleigh asked them.

"Yes," their mom said. "But we're fine now."

"What did he look like?"

"He was wearing one of those green facial masks," her dad said. "And some bug-eye glasses. We told the police what he looked like."

"Will the police get him?"

"I hope so."

"But they *have* to catch him, right?"

"Sweetie," their mom said. "They're gonna do everything they can to catch him."

"And they *will*, right?"

Their parents exchanged looks with each other as if speaking telepathically. Then they looked back at their daughter.

"We don't wanna lie to you," their dad said. "We're not sure if he'll get caught. Or why he did it. Sometimes people do bad things and they don't get caught. But we're safe now."

"But for how long?" The volume of Kayleigh's voice was rising. "What if he finds you again? What if he hurts someone else?"

Randy's phone started ringing. He looked at the screen, and his heart sank when he saw the name attached to the number: Mathis Dillard.

Mouth wide open, he looked up at his parents.

"Randy?" their mom said, looking concerned.

"I'm sorry. I really need to take this call. I'll be right back."

Randy got out into the hallway and ran to the elevator. Once inside, he answered.

"Hello?" he said.

"Our appointment still stands...unlike your mom."

The familiar voice of Mathis Dillard.

He lives.

"Is this Joe?" Randy asked.

"Joe who?"

"Sloppy Joe. You were pretty sloppy. What changed? I heard Candid even got away. Is that what this is about? The one that got away?"

"You should be *thankful* that I didn't kill Mommy and Daddy."

"It's hard to be thankful when pieces of shit like you come back to life and come after people who don't deserve to get hurt."

The elevator door opened, and Randy started passing through the lobby.

"I never died," Mathis explained.

"Yes you did. I saw you on that bridge."

"That was *not* me! That vampire created me as an improvement over who he was, but I am *not* him!"

Randy was struggling to make sense of this, but he could tell that Mathis was being truthful.

"Stay the fuck away from my family."

"I wasn't sure you'd mind. From what I've gathered, you seem to prefer life with your friends than with your family."

Randy could have denied this. But for some reason he could not fathom, he felt like opening up.

"Sometimes it's easy to forget that it's all one life."

"Just one. No more."

"Is that a promise?"

"Sorry. I was talking to myself. *Just* myself, though."

"Someone's really done a number on you."

"Just *one*. Not two."

Randy could hear the anger burning through the phone.

"Only one of us will be standing," Randy said.

"Then we have an *under*standing," Mathis said. "What's past is prologue."

"If that's true, then that was a long-ass prologue."

"Let me finish! What's past is prologue. What's future is prolonged. But not anymore."

"Quoting Shakespeare doesn't make you deep. You just sound like a copycat."

"I am *not* a pastiche! I am the future!"

484

"No you're not," Randy said. "You know why? Because I will fuckin' kill you, you pretentious fuck. Just tell me where."

"I can keep watch on your friends. More blood to spill there. I've seen where they live. Convenient that most of them are roommates."

Now Randy knew exactly where to meet Mathis: Gertrude's house. And if accommodations remained consistent, Naomi and Chelsea would be there as well.

"More people to kill?" Randy asked. "Trying to overcompensate, I see."

He got outside, in front of the hospital.

"You haven't seen a thing, yet," Mathis replied. "I will turn *you* into a thing."

"Let me ask you something, Mathis. Would it be so hard for you to just stop?"

"And what? Sit on the couch day after day, feeling inactive? Are *you* comfortable with that life? At some point, one tells oneself, 'I should just end.' And it ends up being their own life, or that of another, that's ended. I stay on the move, kicking and screaming in this new life. Isn't that what babies do when they're born?"

"You don't sound reborn. Trying to relive glory days won't save you."

"I don't *need* to be saved. *You* need to be rescued, and nobody will come for you."

"Whoop-dee-fucking-doo. I'll see you in three months, you pismire."

Randy hung up before he could hear any more of Mathis' blather. The monster was out there somewhere, and Randy had no clue where. For the first time in a while, he feared the night, because he knew what awaited within it.

He went back inside and returned to his family.

"Something wrong?" his mom asked.

He was ready to lie. To say things were fine, and that he was just talking to a friend. But what came out was truer.

"I don't know what to do about all this."

"There's nothing you could have done," his mom said. "We'll stay strong. United as a family. Can you do that for us?"

Randy nodded.

"Yes. I can be strong."

* * *

Mathis walked away from the payphone and got back in his car. He had been too scared to use his own cell phone. And Randy had said his name during the call.

Can I be traced?

He tried to shake away the thoughts. Mathis tried convincing himself to not worry, but his heart kept racing.

The next day was a boring day at Preston's apartment. To keep himself busy and not too occupied with paranoid thoughts, Mathis bought some supplies. Cash only, of course. Not wanting to see his reflection, he taped paper over the mirrors of the lavatories in the apartment. Mathis pressed his hands on every strip. He knew that he would have to rely on his hands feeling his face and scalp on the subsequent times that he would shave.

He also kept the blinds closed over the windows and the glass sliding door during the day. But when the night came, he pulled the blinds of the sliding door aside so he could see the night. It was dark. Mathis should have enjoyed the dark. But he could not fully enjoy it with even so much as a hint of his reflection on the glass. Standing for a long moment, he was tempted to punch the glass.

But he repented, choosing instead to lie down on the carpeted floor. His reflection no longer visible from this angle, Mathis looked up at the night sky, with its glowing stars. He knew that they were fire, but he did not imagine the hellish flames. Instead, he found himself enchanted by the light. Even the light of the moon was somehow charming.

Night after night, he laid himself on the floor like this, watching the changing moon get fuller and fuller. The moonlight illuminating him. Mathis staring at the satellite until he fell asleep. It was not until the first of July that it was completely full. But then the light faded little by little. He knew that the moon would be full of light again.

But it would also go dark.

Chapter 57

Ghost Host

Though it took weeks, Randy's parents healed from their injuries. During all that time, guilt had been eating Randy up like a chimp chomping on fruit. Whenever he was not helping his parents around the house, he tried making time to build muscle by lifting dumbbells he had bought, with very little results. Sometimes he wanted to go jogging to continue his training, but he worried that Mathis would strike once he was out of the house.

For all I know, that fucker's still in town.

One night, Randy held up the monkey in front of his face, making eye contact.

"Aster? Can you hear me?" There was no answer. "Why did you *leave* me all alone?"

Randy looked into the eyes of the monkey. Once he sensed a presence, he tossed the stuffed animal to the ground. But then its eyes glowed green and gave him a distorted vision. He saw green reptilian scales, and they made him dizzy for a moment. He fell to the floor.

"What did you do to me?"

Still no answer. The eyes stopped glowing. Aster was there, but now she was gone.

He pulled himself up and got onto his bed. As he started lying down, he visited the studio in his mind once again, to see a friend who *had* remained...

"Hello, everybody!" Artie said, stepping onto the stage. "It is with a heavy heart that I announce this to be my last show."

"Awww..." the audience said collectively.

"Oh shut up!"

Collective laughter.

"I really am gonna miss all of you. We've had many great celebrities throughout my run. But for my last episode, I've invited my favorite guest. Yeah, that's right. I don't care if those other people I've interviewed hear. What are they gonna do? Not come on my show anymore? Hah! That's something for the next host to worry about. Who knows? Maybe they'll like the new guy. Anyway, you know him, and I know him. Give it up for the one, the only, Randy Morales!"

Randy sauntered onto the stage. The hands were clapping, but they were muted. Randy sat down in the guest chair.

"Hey Artie. Man. Whoever replaces you is gonna pale in comparison."

"Oh, you flatter me Randy." Artie held up a box of matches. "So, word is that you're scheduled for a match with Mathis Dillard. Is that correct? Because I've been hearing conflicting reports of it getting canceled, but I want to hear it from the horse's mouth."

"It's true. The match is on. There is a flame."

Silence.

"Tough crowd tonight," Artie said. "Come on, everybody! Stop making this such a bummer!"

Artie dropped the box of matches on the floor and then stood on top of his desk, conducting with his baton fingers. But the audience made no noise.

"I won't let them," Randy said. "Nobody's gonna cheer me on. When I die, Artie, you'll die too. But you won't be there when I'm fighting. Because you're not real. You're not really talking to me, just like none of those talk show hosts on TV were ever talking to me. It'll just be me, all alone. I don't deserve to keep on living. I want to be on their minds, and I want my mind to overwhelm everyone. Just one last act will fix everything."

Artie got down from the desk and faced Randy.

"When the show ends," Artie began, "do you think the characters go on? When we cut to commercial, we still move, don't we? And when we cut to end credits, we just go to sleep, don't we?"

"When I get cut," Randy explained, "I'm gonna get everlasting sleep." Randy looked at the window with the violet sky over the cityscape. This time, it looked two-dimensional. "That is not a window. There's not even a reflection on it. If it's too clear, then there is no glass. Hell, it's not even nighttime; I daydream all this shit, and you know it!"

"Really?" Artie responded. "What else is wrong with this picture?"

"There are no shadows around here. Because when I imagine a place, I imagine the objects and the people. But not their shadows. I've refused to see people's shadows, but I see them now. I have always been in your shadow. You can do everything, but I can't. We want everything to be bright, but we all have our shadows, don't we? It's not life without them. I shift the shadows."

Shadows appeared beneath every person and object within this fantasy. To break the awkward silence, Artie tried to segue into a new segment.

"Let's welcome the new host!" Artie said.

Surely enough, the ghost host appeared. He was dressed the same as Artie Docent—suit and all—but his face resembled Randy's, and he was a white-ish, ghastly being.

"I am Artie Crescent."

"Yep," Randy said. "That's the voice."

"Boo!" the audience said.

"Yes, that is what ghosts like me say!" Crescent said. "If you merge me with the shadow, you get the whole moon. There is no imagination, only amalgamation. But isn't that how it was in the beginning, when all worlds were just one?"

Randy looked at Artie Docent.

"I'll be Brandy, distilled wine, purified as I'm vaporized. When I die, that'll be the end of you. But I'll be sure to imagine—"

"Amalgamate," Crescent said.

"Sure. You'll meet someone you'll amalgamate with to have a family you deserve. It's the least I can do for you. And the only good thing I can do for anyone. Sucks that I can only do a good thing for someone not real. I see now. Those voices were me. I am the host. And I am the parasite. It's all the same. My mind is a black hole that draws in everything, distorting rather than uniting."

In this fantasy, Randy closed his eyes and clenched his fists, unleashing a power bursting through the exit doors in the form of blood flooding the emotionless audience, drowning them to death. An intense white light beamed down upon him, and it slowly turned lime green. Randy looked down at the box of matches. He picked it up, took one out. He scratched the match against the box, lighting it. He threw the fiery match into the blood, which then turned into lava burning the whole place down. Randy spoke to the dying audience.

"This is my wrath. I am the host. I am the parasite. Lunar loaner looms like rain, and things will never be the same. Lemons loom like rain, and only lime can ease the pain."

Chapter 58
The Last Lemonade Stand

Randy carried the red cafe lamp over to a dumpster and dropped it inside. He thought he heard the glass of the bulb break. No shadows would surround its glow anymore. And then he threw the monkey in there as well. Sure, he could have tossed it into the fire himself. But he wanted to believe that he was better than that. If he understood dumps correctly, then perhaps the stuffed animal would have to face the incinerator.

"Talk about a *Toy Story 3* situation," he said to himself.

In any case, Randy was sure that Aster would continue to live. The stuffed animals were not her, but rather her forms of communication. And it was clear that she no longer wanted to talk to him.

Randy told his parents that he needed to take care of some matters regarding the end of his lease at the apartment where he had been staying in Copper Petal throughout senior year. His parents were under the impression that he had gotten subtenants, but it was just him paying the rent. He bought a bus ticket for the afternoon of Saturday, September 26. Before leaving, he hugged his parents goodbye, and then he spoke with his sister in her room.

"Where are you going?" she asked.

"I need to take care of something at my apartment."

"How soon will you be back?"

"I can't say."

"Because of people like the one who hurt Mom and Dad?"

"Huh?"

"We can't know if we'll be back if there are people like him."

Feeling sorry that Kayleigh had seen the result of his feud, Randy gave her a hug.

"I promise that he will never hurt you."

Randy took a local bus to a bus station. From there, he took another bus to Copper Petal. A normal drive there was around six hours, and he knew that this journey would take a bit longer due to the stops, as well as the transfer he would have to make. Though there were other passengers on each of these buses, Randy felt alone. Toward the latter part of the journey, night on the freeway was a lonely experience for him. He could see no stars at the moment. He could not see the past. Just himself, the present reflected in the window glass, unaccompanied and without luggage.

When he arrived at the apartment and got inside, he took a tour of his own. He had already emptied his room back in June. Evan and Ted had cleaned out their rooms as well. And Vic's room, of course, had been emptied as well when his parents came by for his possessions months earlier. Feeling guilty, Randy had been sure not to be at the apartment when they came over. The lavatories had all been emptied. The kitchen cabinets had nothing within them, and the refrigerator had nothing for eating or drinking. The dining table was gone. There was no couch for comfort. And there was no TV for controllable noise. The apartment truly was empty.

"Same," Randy thought aloud.

He texted his parents to let them know that he had arrived. He could not bear to speak goodbyes again.

Through the walls, he could hear muffled voices of neighbors in the apartments that were each next door. But he felt far away from everyone, trapped in the space between. With no bedding, he simply slept on the carpeted floor, curled up with nothing to cover him.

The next day, he walked over to Petal Lock Park. He was relieved to see that neither Pamela nor Peyton were there. It would have been difficult for him to see Pamela again. He did the running routine as he remembered it. Though he was not sure how well this would prepare him for the coming night, he hoped it could help at least a bit.

All the exercise of the day worked up a thirst. So he went to the supermarket and bought a bottle of Silver Silencer. When he returned to the apartment, he sat it on the counter. No glass mug. He just wanted to drink it all from the bottle. Removing the cap, he was ready to flood his system.

He hesitated.

Then he pushed the bottle just enough to have it slide across the counter like an ice-skater in a rink. It fell off the edge and onto the kitchen floor, breaking into shards of glass, glaciers on the surface of a silver sea. Randy wanted to die sober rather than silver. And he would not need to worry about relieving himself of the burden of urine.

As he walked across the tile floor of the kitchen, he slipped on the silver, injuring his leg. Grabbing onto the refrigerator handle, he pulled himself up.

On the wall, he saw a few ants crawling.

"It's all yours now," he told them. "And my rotting corpse will be all yours, too."

He took a knife out of the drawer. Limping out of the apartment, Randy looked up at the moon. It was as orange as a jack-o'-lantern, unsettling smile and all. The redder it turned, the more it resembled a blood drop in the snow. Or was it a cotton ball pushed up against the bleeding heavens? A cotton ball would certainly not be as easy to chew on as snow. He thought about cotton candy, and then about a cheese wheel in the sky. Then he shook the thoughts away so that he would not desire anything else to consume in his final moments.

"Where's the lime?" Randy whispered.

He imagined that he was glowing lime green. Still limping, he stepped onward.

"I am their guardian angel. I am their guardian angel."

As much as he repeated this, he had trouble imagining himself with angel wings. They were simply invisible to his mind's eye.

"Where are the wings?"

No feathers sprouted from his back. He felt an emptiness following him as he kept walking. No weight was being carried, and that made him feel uneasy. Part of him wished that he had Candid to help him.

No, he thought. *There's no partnership. I have to do this alone.*

* * *

The death of Shelley had, unfortunately, left more room in the apartment occupied by Chelsea, Gertrude, and Naomi. But they did not mind having Pamela and Peyton move in with them. This night, they were having a little kickback. They had some cans of Spike's Charred Lemonade on the table. Pamela, being underage and not so curious about the beverage, did not partake. Judging from her friends' reactions, it seemed to burn a little bit. She got some amusement watching them intoxicated. Especially her sister, who was the most laid back that Pamela had ever seen her in a while.

At the moment, it was the five roommates plus Reginald, relaxing and listening to music.

But they were about to have another guest.

* * *

Wearing the glasses and the face mask, Mathis parked his car in the lot beside the apartment where Randy's friends resided. He had spied upon them over the last couple of months, using Candid's photos as frames of reference for their faces. Getting his equipment out of the trunk, he tucked the scythes into his sleeves, put the blowtorch in his jacket pocket, and tried carrying the sledgehammer. It was difficult carrying everything, but he wanted to be prepared.

Mathis got onto the sidewalk, which was lit up by light poles. One of them was in front of the lawn of his destination, and he stopped to examine it. A black pole holding up a white sphere the size of a volleyball. A light raised by darkness. Mathis, on the other hand, had not been raised by anyone, and his whole life had been darkness. For a moment, he heard memories of childhood laughter and crying. No doubt they belonged to many people whom The Landlord had possessed over the years.

Setting these sounds aside, he walked up to the porch. The blinds on the window were closed, and he could see his reflection on the glass. He had the urge to rush at the reflection and break it apart to enter the home.

And yet, he could not summon *any* motivation to barged into the building. Deep down, he felt as if he needed permission.

But why? he wondered. *I should feel free to just break in*!

He walked to the front door and, with his hand forming a fist, he expected himself to break down the door.

Instead, he knocked.

The music inside stopped. Quickly, Mathis hid his arms behind his back. The door swung open, answered by Gertrude, who was struggling to stand straight.

"May I come in?" Mathis asked.

"Who the hell are you?"

She laughed, smelling like alcohol.

This might be easier than I thought.

"Exterminator," Mathis answered.

"Huh. Those goggles for gas?"

"Yes."

"And what about the guac on your face?"

Pamela and Peyton walked over to the door. Peyton's smile faded.

"That voice..." Peyton said. "Oh my god." She backed away. "No. Moseley, you're dead. Everyone saw you die!"

"Please. Just let me in."

"Are you Mathias Moseley?" Peyton asked.

Too angry about the question, he did not answer right away. He tried to swallow his rage for the moment.

"Are you Mathias Moseley?" Peyton repeated.

"No."

"Who are you?" Gertrude asked.

"I'll tell you if you let me in."

"Are you his copy?" Pamela asked.

"Don't *call* me that!"

"Why are you here?" Peyton asked.

"Let me in and I'll tell you."

"Don't let him in!" Pamela ordered. "It's Mathis."

"This is too weird," Gertrude said. "Can't let you in."

She closed the door on him.

Feeling weakened, Mathis turned around and walked toward the light pole. Again, he heard the laughter. And the crying. All multiplying. The sphere, spinning in his mind's eye. A moon staring right at him.

Using the sledgehammer, Mathis made the moon go dark, letting the shards fall onto the sidewalk. He heard Randy's friends screaming inside the apartment. *These* were the sounds that Mathis craved.

Quickly, he strode to the other side of the building. Avoiding the sight of his reflection, he used the sledgehammer to smash the glass of the sliding door, letting it drop to the kitchen floor. The six friends looked at him in fear. Just what he wanted. But he also wanted to get in.

Even when enough broken glass had fallen to make space for him to get through, he just stood still in front of that door. Rather than move forward, he twitched and stuttered.

"L-let me in. Lemme in. Lem'in."

* * *

August, carrying a bottle of wine in one hand and a corkscrew in the other, approached the house from the sliding door side, where he saw a bald man standing outside the back entrance. The man turned around. Though he had a green face mask and bug-eye glasses, there was something familiar about him. An unsettling kind of familiar. They locked eyes and recognized each other.

August dropped the bottle, glass and wine forming a mess on the ground.

"You'll have to do," Mathis said.

"No!" Reginald yelled from inside. "Get away from him!"

Drunk, Reginald slipped and fell to the kitchen floor. Pamela looked shocked, and everyone else seemed too intoxicated to react.

The scythes came out of the bald man's sleeves, confirming that it was whom August thought it was: Mathis, the man in the mirror. But once the murderer got close to him, August shoved the corkscrew into Mathis' left hand. August's next impulse was to raise his foot to the monster's chin. This threw Mathis backward. While the killer was down, August tried pulling a scythe out of one of the sleeves. Mathis regained his momentum and shoved it into August's face, leaving a scar along a cheek. With a stern expression and his teeth grinding, August looked at Mathis' face.

"You killed all those people. Where's the heart? You have no respect for anyone!"

Mathis stepped forward.

"You know me very well, then. It'll be nice to hear you scream in person rather than in memory."

"You're gonna be all alone."

Smiling, Mathis picked August up by the armpits, which felt painfully uncomfortable.

"Good."

* * *

Randy limped closer and closer to the apartment, from the backside. He had a feeling that Mathis would attack from that side. And surely enough, there he was, holding August above the ground.

"No," Randy said.

Mathis picked up a scythe, which Randy was sure he would aim at the throat. Despite the pain in his leg, Randy ran. Mathis turned to see him, and then Randy tackled him to the ground. August fell as a result. Randy reached for a scythe, swung it upward, and let it fall on Mathis' shoulder.

"Ow!" Mathis cried.

Randy looked at August.

"Get inside. This is *my* fight. Go!"

August hesitated for a moment, but then he ran inside.

As Mathis got up, Randy took the knife out of his pocket and shoved it into Mathis' right thigh. Mathis removed the blade from his thigh, which seemed to be pissing blood. Since he had no toilet in which to aim, it was akin to the paw-work of a dog that gave no shits. Horrified, Mathis looked at the blood leaking out of him.

"My thigh is bleeding!"

"That's right!" Randy taunted. "Mathias bleeding!"

"No! I'm not him!"

He punched Randy in the face, knocking him down. Dizzy, Randy could see Mathis' face multiplied by two, looking down at him.

MAGNIFY!

Randy got kicked in the face by Mathis' boot. Randy pulled up a pant leg and bit Mathis in the ankle, pulling a bit of skin off. Mathis kept kicking. Randy rolled over and got up.

"Admit it!" Mathis said. "You *want* to die."

"Not as much as I want *you* to die!"

"Why do you try?"

Randy formed fists.

"Because I see myself in you!"

Randy ran up to Mathis and swung his knuckles at his face, inflicting pain successfully. He swung again, his knuckles cracking the glass of the lenses. As Mathis removed the glasses, Randy remembered the stab in the thigh, and gave Mathis a kick in that spot, causing him to scream. And then it disturbed Randy to hear the scream. He had never heard the ants scream. But he had to view Mathis as something less helpless than an ant. Something willing to hurt just for the hell of it rather than for survival.

Mathis used the bug-eye glasses to swat Randy across the face. Then he swung his right fist, hitting Randy in the jaw. Making his eyes visible, Mathis removed the glasses and threw them to the ground. Quickly, Randy grasped Mathis by the wrist and sank his teeth into the back of his hand, trying to be as fierce as a wolf. Mathis punched him away with his other fist. Randy had no skin on his teeth, but he saw the bite marks on Mathis' hand, with a bit of blood coming out, like red ants rushing out of an anthill.

* * *

As August got inside, everyone else was trying to pull Reginald.

"August," he said. "You're back from the store."

"What's going on out there?" Chelsea asked.

"Randy's here," August explained.

"Randy?" Reginald said.

"What the hell's he doing here?" Gertrude asked.

"Fighting the copy."

"Mathis," Pamela said. "The last remnant of Mathias."

"No," Naomi said. "This can't keep happening."

"We have to help Randy," Pamela said.

"Pam," Peyton ran her hand across her sister's arm. "Pam. Please. Be careful. You're my—"

"I will. August, call 9-1-1. We're gonna need cops *and* medics."

Pamela looked at the sledgehammer on the floor. She picked it up and ran outside, where Mathis was holding Randy up above his head. As Mathis threw him, Pamela ran behind him and hit his back with a sledgehammer, making him fall.

* * *

Randy was thrown onto the grass blades. He could feel his glow going from lime green to lawn green, a slightly darker shade on the grass blades.

"Sublime," he said, looking up at the sky.

The moon up above again. It was bleeding, becoming a pale face. Had it ever been alive? Now that its blood was gone, it was glowing, like an angelic specter. Randy imagined a divine lens, panning upward from him and judging his life: WASTED.

But it was not quite done.

Randy looked over at Pamela hitting Mathis in the shoulders with a sledgehammer.

"Go for the head!" he called out.

"No more killing!" Pamela yelled. "Look at him! He's vulnerable and can be locked up easily now!"

Mathis rolled away from Pamela. He took out a blowtorch and set fire to the grass between him and her, forcing Pamela to retreat into the apartment.

"Please," Randy said. "Leave them alone. I've already lost so much."

* * *

Mathis turned to Randy. He pounced on his prey and pinned him to the ground.

"Have mercy," Randy pleaded.

Mathis looked into Randy's eyes, each of which had his reflection. Two Mathias Moseleys.

"No. I'm a nihilist. Cry me a river and make it NILE!"

In a state of fury, Mathis gouged Randy's eyes, extinguishing the eye pair's sight. Letting the plague pour out of the sockets. He heard the boy scream.

No. Not a boy. This is a grown-ass adult I'm hurting.

"There is no you," Mathis said. "There is only *me*, and me alone!"

He blew fire into the eye sockets. Once Mathis stopped, Randy reached for the fire on his sockets and facepalmed the flames away with both hands.

How have I not killed you? Mathis wondered.

But then he remembered Mathias' warning.

The Plo-Tunium goes away if I die. Your victims would survive no matter how hard you try.

A taunting rhyme, echoing through Mathis' mind. If the source was dead, then Mathis would not be able to kill anyone, no matter how hard he tried. A curse that affected Mathis and kept his victims alive, regardless of science.

* * *

502

Randy was not sure whether his shadow was gone or whether it dominated his senses. There was darkness. He still felt blood below his eye sockets. To Mathis, it was red blood. To Randy's undying, hyperventilating imagination, it was blue paint. And pretty soon, he could feel water droplets. At first, he was unsure whether they came from sprinklers or whether they were cascading from the cottonesque firmaments floating in the sky above. The sky that transcended, not touching the ground yet somehow conquering it. Once his hearing got clearer, he could tell that it was the sprinkler system, hopefully putting out the fire. Randy imagined that blood was raining down from the moon, turning the cotton candy in the sky a bubble gum pink.

"Rain check..." Randy uttered.

Mathis breathed in and out. The water was probably making his face more visible, the green dripping onto the green. He sounded like he was regaining his strength and aggression. But then his voice was the most calm that Randy had ever heard it.

"Do you think it's raining anywhere else?"

Taken aback by the question, Randy did not know what to say right away. But after thinking for a few seconds, it felt right to answer how he did.

"Of course it is. People are suffering. Everywhere."

"Why? Why so many?"

"I don't know why. And there are those who go out and play in the rain. Nothing to do but *feel* something. Every rain drop is a person passing through. We feel them, and then they're gone. But it is so wonderful to feel them, before they're gone from our lives forever."

* * *

"So many..." Mathis said, letting the sprinkler system's rain wash over him. "I've taken so many."

A montage of murders ran through Mathis' mind. Not just the ones that were his own doing, but also the ones that had been committed by vampire over more years than he could count. Mathis felt like a blood-soaked child, wanting the pain to bleed out of him, wanting the water to wash it off of him so that a glowing light could appear in a doorway behind him. But he knew where he did not belong. The memories of the pain were still there, and he wanted the weight to be lifted.

* * *

Randy was not sure whether he imagined it or whether he was hearing it, but there were three sneezes in the air—from nature itself, it seemed—and then an operatic voice singing sorrow without words. Abstract, but discernible. And then there were the drum beats of fear, spaced apart, followed by an orchestral sounding set of synthesizer sounds in a crescendo that seemed to rescue the voice from its cries through a cosmic love that transcended definable boundaries. Randy imagined that Frederick Filler was present, playing one of the instruments. Or perhaps even all of them. Right here in the sea formed by the sprinklers.

And there was an invisible conductor had batons for fingers, pressing the air with hardened hands in a sweep of victory. Randy knew that Artie Docent was still with him, still wearing the same comforting crimson nose. Artie looked old, nearing the end of his happy life, yet still vibrant with energy. And he was having his swan song. Not a duck. Not a goose. A swan.

"If you could look into the mirror," Mathis asked Randy, "who would you want to see?"

"At this point...anyone."

"Doesn't it unsettle you to see someone living and breathing back at you, and not being able to have them talk to you?"

"If it's me, then yeah. Because I haunt myself. I chose to be this walking ghost, with nobody else in my heart other than myself."

"The heart... It hurts. So fucking much. You wanted to let everyone in. But the paths *bleed* together. Does it kill one to let people in?"

"It depends on the intentions. I kept everyone out and looked from afar. Now I don't know where they are. The windows are gone. No glass. Sand gone from my eyes."

"They can see *me* now." Mathis sounded frightened. "If I walk through a hall of mirrors, all will see me. There is no escape. And I don't mean for them. *I* have nowhere to hide. My image would be everywhere. Too much of me... We really are full of ourselves, aren't we?"

"Yeah," Randy answered. "Those who are full of themselves make fools of themselves. We're all just water, freefalling through fire. Hoping to put it out."

Mathis' next words sounded like a lugubrious struggle to escape his windpipe.

"I don't know how you do it. *Live* with yourself."

There was silence. Then a wet, choking sound. Randy figured out what was going on: Mathis Dillard had looked upward toward the sky and opened his mouth. Whether it be water or blood, he was choking on something. Randy's money was on the sprinkler water. There was more and more coughing, and Randy felt certain that Mathis was crying tearfully. When the body thudded on the ground, Randy knew that Mathis was dead. He was gone, like cookie dough in a crayon, colors consumed by light and dark.

Hearing the siren of an ambulance, Randy expected to survive. He decided to lie on the grass, waiting for the paramedics. He thought he could feel an ant crawling on his arm, or perhaps a phantom of a life he had obliterated long ago, back to haunt him. He did not flick the feeling away, and there was no bite.

Soon afterward, he felt himself being carried, and then being put on a gurney in the back of the ambulance. Everything moved around him because he could not. Some sort of bandage was wrapped around where his eyes used to be.

Time became difficult to track. Eventually, he found himself in a hospital bed, waiting. There was no comforting stuffed animal for him to hold. He wondered what Candid would think about how things played out. Whether she would feel sorry for him, or whether she would feel indifferent, or whether she would think he deserved it.

I lost my eyes, Candy.

Would she have laughed at that?

His parents, once notified, would take six hours to arrive at this hospital. He did not doubt that they would bring Kayleigh with them on the drive. He would see her again after all. Well, not *see* see. It would be different. He was unsure about how he would explain what had happened. And he did not really feel like putting his mind through all the effort of coming up with an elaborate story right away. He thought back to the fight, and how weak he had felt mentally.

Did Aster do something to me?

Maybe he would never get an answer from the entity whom he used to perceive as his friend.

He heard footsteps, not knowing who possessed them until he heard the voices.

"Hello, Randy," Pamela said.

"It's Pam and August," the latter said.

"I'm glad to hear you're fine," Randy said. "Did Mathis cut you, August?"

"I've gotten it looked at," August answered. "I'm fine."

"Good. How do I look?" There was an awkward silence. Before either could answer, Randy spoke again. "Where are Naomi, Gertrude, and the others? How are they?"

"They're fine," Pamela said. "They're waiting in the lobby."

"You're not just saying that to make me feel better, are you?"

"No," Pamela said. "They only allow two visitors at a time."

"I doubt anyone else really wants visit me after what happened."

"What *did* happen, Randy?" August asked. "You showed up looking pretty ready with a knife."

"And you weren't invited," Pamela added. "You led him to us, didn't you?"

"I didn't mean to. He was only gonna come after me, and then it just became a mess."

"Why?" August asked. "Why was he after you?"

The truth was a lot for Randy to say, so he was very selective with his words.

"I took a loan from him. We saw Mathias die, and I thought that was the end of it. But that wasn't him."

"It was his copy," Pamela said. "Mathias made him through a ritual. He called himself Mathis."

"That's him."

"There's more you aren't telling us," August said.

Randy tried keeping his lips sewn shut, but the words escaped.

"I wanted to die. I knew we'd all drift apart after graduation. Now it looks like I'll just have to live with that. Do Gertrude, Naomi, and the others really care about me now?"

"They care enough to see that you're okay," Pamela answered.

"I don't want them to see me like this. I can already feel you two judging me. Even though it's for a good reason, I just don't want to feel this. I'm sorry for all that I did. I'm glad that all of you are fine. But don't ask me whether I'm all right."

Ten silent seconds, and then he heard the footsteps leaving the room. He was left alone with his thoughts, knowing he was the problem.

Sometimes, legacy overshadowed happiness. For in the pursuit of legacy, the search for a definition of self was the most dangerous obsession. He had played the game and gambled away, a risk without rules. Without restraint, he lost sight of who everyone else was, and now he could only see himself.

But there was still someone whom he wanted by his side. Not someone in his imagination; someone real. A thought occurred to him. No, more powerful than just a mere thought. A *feeling*. A montage of the good times that had been experienced between two people, one of whom had not fully understood the nature of their relationship and what they had wanted from each other. It felt wrong to invite this familiar feeling that used to dwell within him. And yet it somehow felt authentic to who he was.

Even after all that had happened, he could not help it. After all the bridges had been burned. After all the ties had been severed. After all the pain that had been inflicted upon both parties. After all that, he still surrendered to the memories of what had been, wishing they were still reality. He longed for what once was, what he used to feel about this person. He opened the wound, regardless of how much the acidic desire stung his tongue. As unhealthy as it seemed, he breathed life to the confession.

"I miss her."

Acknowledgments

You have seen many names in this book, but I would be remiss if I did not include the following names of people who contributed to this strange journey. I owe some of my writing and editing experience to Cristian Munguia, who gave me the chance to contribute to *Dystopian Vol. 1.* And I owe further novel editing experience to Phil Maynard, who let me read *Marksman Unlimited* and was open to my edits.

Fiverr service providers Biancalice, Istvanszaboifj, and Obaniobodo proved to be very helpful with feedback, formatting, and cover art, respectively. Each of them worked in a timely fashion. I would also like to thank Cu Fleshman, Karen Parker, Nathaniel W.E. Intolubbe, and Rachelle Reiff for their valuable critiques of the story. Those early reactions really kept me confident that I had something even though there was more work to be done. A shout-out also goes to to Andy Mis, who, in a group chat, typed "looms like rain" instead of "looks like rain." Your typo provided the working title, and I worked from there. And thanks to my dog Olias for keeping me company as I typed away. He is the chillest chihuahua I know.

I am also very grateful for the various writing courses that I took at both University of California, Irvine and University of Sussex. They definitely shaped me as a writer. And I am certain that *Lemons Loom Like Rain* would not even have existed if I had attended neither of these schools. Much gratitude to the members of Anteater's Guide to the Galaxy, Creative Writers Guild at UC Irvine, English Majors' Association at UCI, and Sussex Short Fiction Society who let me read excerpts aloud during meetings. And thanks to Nja Onê for letting me read and act out various sentences out of order and without context for Improv at the Gallery.

As far as the online stuff goes, I am grateful that my dad Dan Shinder helped me navigate through this whole process. My brother Alex Shinder also took a really good photo for me to use on the Facebook page and the website. Speaking of which, thanks to Thomas Stark of One Stone Web for designing and hosting the website.

And, of course, thanks to my mom Maria Duran for supporting me as I took this path. You maintained your belief that I would make something of it.

And if I forgot anyone, I blame it on Plo-Tunium.